Seventy-five Below Zero

He piled dry spruce on top of the snow. The flame he got by touching a match to a small shred of birch bark; birch bark burned better than paper.

While the dog looked on, the man fed the young flames with twigs, working carefully and slowly, keenly aware of his danger. He knew there must be no failure. When it is seventy-five below zero, and a man's feet are wet, he must not fail in his first attempt to build a fire.

There are no second chances in the arctic.

TO BUILD A FIRE AND OTHER STORIES

Jack London

TOR®

A TOM DOHERTY ASSOCIATES BOOK
NEW YORK

TO BUILD A FIRE AND OTHER STORIES

All new material in this edition copyright © 1999 by Tom Doherty Associates, Inc.

A Tor Book
Published by Tom Doherty Associates, Inc.
175 Fifth Avenue
New York, NY 10010

Tor Books on the World Wide Web:
http://www.tor.com

Tor® is a registered trademark of Tom Doherty Associates, Inc.

ISBN: 0-812-56516-9

First Tor edition: May 1999

Printed in the United States of America

0 9 8 7 6 5 4 3 2 1

Contents

Introduction

It was Jack London who taught every voracious young reader the temperature at which saliva will freeze in mid-air. This is, without question, cool knowledge. To many people, he is simply remembered as that guy who wrote the book about the sled dog or the short stories about gold miners. Anyone who comes to London at this surface level will be richly rewarded with that most wonderful of simple pleasures: a good read. But the author does much more than merely spin a ripping yarn. Jack was no hack. True, he turned out a thousand words a day and often wrote for no other reason than to pay the bills. But he had a gift. Just as some men cannot move in an ungraceful way, some men would be hard-pressed to write shallow prose. The stereotypical adventure story is seen as a stage for wooden actors—all plot, no depth. Not so with London.

His characters, even his dogs, while larger than life, are well drawn. Though he might at times accomplish this characterization with a paragraph of description, he could also paint a whole life in a sentence. Consider this line near the opening of "To Build a Fire": "It was a steep bank, and he paused for breath at the top, excusing this act by looking at his watch." Wow. Many of us would pull this charade while in public view. This unnamed character even needs to perform the deception for himself. One sentence and we know him well. One story and we know him forever.

There are other surprises. Anyone coming cold to this author will have to leave some misconceptions along the trail. Though mostly self-taught, London was well educated and well-read. He writes with a broad vocabulary that would seem artificial in the hands of a less-skilled wordsmith. He was also well traveled. His stories go beyond the Yukon to Mexico, the South Pacific, the heart of the city, and the soul of the working man.

At times, the words fall on the ear with the ring of poetry. Read, for example, the opening line of "An Odyssey to the North." Here is prose far more lyrical than the best-known efforts of Robert Service, whose verse is also often set in the Klondike.

This richness of craft and depth of experience work especially well in short stories. Here, the writer can explore a subject with a degree of detail that would become mind-numbing in a longer work. Readers who have no interest at all in boxing will be absorbed by the elaborate strategies attempted by the aging fighter in "A Piece of Steak." Even the most ardent cat lover will, for the duration of some of the Klondike—ahem—*tails*, devour the intimate details of sled dog behavior.

The stories themselves are not all cut of the same cloth. There is a pleasing range in London's work, giving the reader great variety in theme, voice, viewpoint, style, and ending. Some tales end with an ironic twist of the sort identified with O. Henry and Saki. Others have the quiet feel of the kind of character study mostly identified with small literary magazines. Some characters fight against nature, others against inner demons. London even, toward the end of his career, explored the genre of science fiction.

Much more could be said, but it would be a crime to keep you lingering here, safe and warm, when adventure lurks in the pages ahead. Enjoy the trip.

—David Lubar

TO BUILD A FIRE
AND OTHER STORIES

To Build a Fire

Day had broken cold and gray, exceedingly cold and gray, when the man turned aside from the main Yukon trail and climbed the high earth-bank, where a dim and little-travelled trail led eastward through the fat spruce timberland. It was a steep bank, and he paused for breath at the top, excusing the act to himself by looking at his watch. It was nine o'clock. There was no sun nor hint of sun, though there was not a cloud in the sky. It was a clear day, and yet there seemed an intangible pall over the face of things, a subtle gloom that made the day dark, and that was due to the absence of sun. This fact did not worry the man. He was used to the lack of sun. It had been days since he had seen the sun, and he knew that a few more days must pass before that cheerful orb, due south, would just peep above the sky-line and dip immediately from view.

The man flung a look back along the way he had come. The Yukon lay a mile wide and hidden under three feet of ice. On top of this ice were as many feet of snow. It was all pure white, rolling in gentle undulations where the ice-jams of the freeze-up had formed. North and south, as far as his eye could see, it was unbroken white, save for a dark hair-line that curved and twisted from around the spruce-covered island to the south, and that curved and twisted away to the north, where it disappeared behind another spruce-covered island. This dark hair-line was the trail—the main trail—that led south five hundred miles to the Chilcoot Pass, Dyea, and salt water; and that led north seventy miles to Dawson, and still on to the north a thousand miles to Nulato, and finally to St. Michael on Bering Sea, a thousand miles and half a thousand more.

But all this—the mysterious, far-reaching hair-line trail, the absence of sun from the sky, the tremendous cold, and the strangeness and weirdness of it all—made no impression on the man. It was not because he was long used to it. He was a newcomer in the land, a *chechaquo*, and this was his first winter. The trouble with him was that he was without imagination. He was quick and alert in the things of life, but only in the things, and not in the significances. Fifty degrees below zero meant eighty-odd degrees of frost. Such fact impressed him as being cold and uncomfortable, and that was all. It did not lead him to meditate upon his frailty as a creature of temperature, and upon man's frailty in general, able only to live within certain narrow limits of heat and cold; and from there on it did not lead him to the conjectural field of immortality and man's place in the universe. Fifty degrees below zero stood for a bite of frost that hurt and that must be guarded against by the use of mittens, ear-flaps, warm moccasins, and thick socks. Fifty degrees below zero was to him just precisely fifty degrees below zero. That there should be anything more to it than that was a thought that never entered his head.

As he turned to go on, he spat speculatively. There was a sharp, explosive crackle that startled him. He spat again. And again, in the air, before it could fall to the snow, the spittle crackled. He knew that at fifty below spittle crackled on the snow, but this spittle had crackled in the air. Undoubtedly it was colder than fifty below—how much colder he did not know. But the temperature did not matter. He was bound for the old claim on the left fork of Henderson Creek, where the boys were already. They had come over across the divide from the Indian Creek country, while he had come the roundabout way to take a look at the possibilities of getting out logs in the spring from the islands in the Yukon. He would be in to camp by six o'clock; a bit after dark, it was true, but the boys would be there, a fire would be going, and a hot supper would be ready. As for lunch, he pressed his hand against the protruding bundle under his jacket. It was also under his shirt, wrapped up in a handkerchief and lying against the naked skin. It was the only way to keep the biscuits from freezing. He smiled agreeably to himself as he thought of those biscuits, each cut open and sopped in bacon grease, and each enclosing a generous slice of fried bacon.

He plunged in among the big spruce trees. The trail was faint. A foot of snow had fallen since the last sled had passed over, and he was glad he was without a sled, travelling light. In fact, he carried nothing but the lunch wrapped in the handkerchief. He was surprised, however, at the cold. It certainly was cold, he concluded, as he rubbed his numb nose and cheek-bones with his mittened hand. He was a warm-whiskered man, but the hair on his face did not protect the high cheek-bones and the eager nose that thrust itself aggressively into the frosty air.

At the man's heels trotted a dog, a bit native husky, the proper wolf-dog, gray-coated and without any visible or temperamental difference from its brother, the wild wolf. The animal was depressed by the tremendous cold. It knew that it was no time for travelling. Its instinct told it a truer tale than was told to the man by the man's judgment. In reality, it was not merely colder than fifty below zero; it was colder than sixty below, than seventy below. It was seventy-five below zero. Since the freezing-point is thirty-two above zero, it meant that one hundred and seven degrees of frost obtained. The dog did not know anything about thermometers. Possibly in its brain there was no sharp consciousness of a condition of very cold such as was in the man's brain. But the brute had its instinct. It experienced a vague but menacing apprehension that subdued it and made it slink along at the man's heels, and that made it question eagerly every unwonted movement of the man as if expecting him to go into camp or to seek shelter somewhere and build a fire. The dog had learned fire, and it wanted fire, or else to burrow under the snow and cuddle its warmth away from the air.

The frozen moisture of its breathing had settled on its fur in a fine powder of frost, and especially were its jowls, muzzle, and eyelashes whitened by its crystallized breath. The man's red beard and mustache were likewise frosted, but more solidly, the deposit taking the form of ice and increasing with every warm, moist breath he exhaled. Also, the man was chewing tobacco, and the muzzle of ice held his lips so rigidly that he was unable to clear his chin when he expelled the juice. The result was that a crystal beard of the color and solidity of amber was increasing its length on his chin. If he fell down it would shatter itself, like glass, into brittle fragments. But he did not mind the appendage. It was the penalty all tobacco-chewers paid in that country, and he had been out before in two cold snaps. They had not been so cold as this, he knew, but by the spirit thermometer at Sixty Mile he knew they had been registered at fifty below and at fifty-five.

He held on through the level stretch of woods for several miles, crossed a wide flat of niggerheads, and dropped down a bank to the frozen bed of a small stream. This was Henderson Creek, and he knew he was ten miles from the forks. He looked at his watch. It was ten o'clock. He was making four miles an hour, and he calculated that he would arrive at the forks at half-past twelve. He decided to celebrate that event by eating his lunch there.

The dog dropped in again at his heels, with a tail drooping discouragement, as the man swung along the creek-bed. The furrow of the old sled-trail was plainly visible, but a dozen inches of snow covered the marks of the last runners. In a month no man had come up or down that silent creek. The man held steadily on. He was not much given to thinking, and just then particularly he had nothing to think about save that he would eat lunch at the forks and that at six o'clock he would be in camp with the boys. There was nobody to talk to; and, had there been, speech would have been impossible because of the ice-muzzle on his mouth. So he continued monotonously to chew tobacco and to increase the length of his amber beard.

Once in a while the thought reiterated itself that it was very cold and that he had never experienced such cold. As he walked along he rubbed his cheek-bones and nose with the back of his mittened hand. He did this automatically, now and again changing hands. But rub as he would, the instant he stopped his cheek-bones went numb, and the following instant the end of his nose went numb. He was sure to frost his cheeks; he knew that, and experienced a pang of regret that he had not devised a nose-strap of the sort Bud wore in cold snaps. Such a strap passed across the cheeks, as well, and saved them. But it didn't matter much, after all. What were frosted cheeks? A bit painful, that was all; they were never serious.

Empty as the man's mind was of thoughts, he was keenly observant, and he noticed the changes in the creek, the curves and bends and timber-jams, and always he sharply noted where he placed his feet. Once, coming around a bend, he shied abruptly, like a startled horse, curved away from the place where he had been walking, and retreated several paces back along the trail. The creek he knew was frozen clear to the bottom,—no creek could contain water in that arctic winter,—but he knew also that there were springs that bubbled out from the hillsides and ran along under the snow and on top of the ice of the creek. He knew that the coldest snaps never froze these springs, and he knew likewise their danger. They were traps. They hid pools of water under the snow that might be three inches deep, or three feet. Sometimes a skin of ice half an inch thick covered them, and in turn was covered by the snow. Sometimes there were alternate layers of water and ice-skin, so that when one broke through he kept on breaking through for a while, sometimes wetting himself to the waist.

That was why he had shied in such panic. He had felt the give under his feet and heard the crackle of a snow-hidden ice-skin. And to get his feet wet in such a temperature meant trouble and danger. At the very least it meant delay, for he would be forced to stop and build a fire, and under its protection to bare his feet while he dried his socks and moccasins. He stood and studied the creek-bed and its banks, and decided that the flow of water came from the right. He reflected awhile, rubbing his nose and cheeks, then skirted to the left, stepping gingerly and testing the footing for each step. Once clear of the danger, he took a fresh chew of tobacco and swung along at his four-mile gait.

In the course of the next two hours he came upon several similar traps. Usually the snow above the hidden pools had a sunken, candied appearance that advertised the danger. Once again, however, he had a close call; and once, suspecting danger, he compelled the dog to go on in front. The dog did not want to go. It hung back until the man shoved it forward, and then it went quickly across the white, unbroken surface. Suddenly it broke through, floundered to one side, and got away to firmer footing. It had wet its forefeet and legs, and almost immediately the water that clung to it turned to ice. It made quick efforts to lick the ice off its legs, then dropped down in the snow and began to bite out the ice that had formed between the toes. This was a matter of instinct. To permit the ice to remain would mean sore feet. It did not know this. It merely obeyed the mysterious prompting that arose from the deep crypts of its being. But the man knew, having achieved a judgment on the subject, and he removed the mitten from his right hand and helped tear out the ice-particles. He did not expose his fingers more than a minute, and was astonished at the swift numbness that smote them. It certainly was cold. He pulled on the mitten hastily, and beat the hand savagely across his chest.

At twelve o'clock the day was at its brightest. Yet the sun was too far south on its winter journey to clear the horizon. The bulge of the earth intervened between it and Henderson Creek, where the man walked under a clear sky at noon and cast no shadow. At half-past twelve, to the minute, he arrived at the forks of the creek. He was pleased at the speed he had made. If he kept it up, he would certainly be with the boys by six. He unbuttoned his jacket and shirt and drew forth his lunch. The action consumed no more than a quarter of a minute, yet in that brief moment the numbness laid hold of the exposed fingers. He did not put the mitten on, but, instead, struck the fingers a dozen sharp smashes against his leg. Then he sat down on a snow-covered log to eat. The sting that followed upon the striking of his fingers against his leg ceased so quickly that he was startled. He had had no chance to take a bite of biscuit. He struck the fingers repeatedly and returned them to the mitten, baring the other hand for the purpose of eating. He tried to take a mouthful, but the ice-muzzle prevented. He had forgotten to build a fire and thaw out. He chuckled at his foolishness, and as he chuckled he noted the numbness creeping into the exposed fingers. Also, he noted that the stinging which had first come to his toes when he sat down was already passing away. He wondered whether the toes were warm or numb. He moved them inside the moccasins and decided that they were numb.

He pulled the mitten on hurriedly and stood up. He was a bit frightened. He stamped up and down until the stinging returned into the feet. It certainly was cold, was his thought. That man from Sulphur Creek had spoken the truth when telling how cold it sometimes got in the country. And he had laughed at him at the time! That showed one must not be too sure of things. There was no mistake about it, it *was* cold. He strode up and down, stamping his feet and threshing his arms, until reassured by the returning warmth. Then he got out matches and proceeded to make a fire. From the undergrowth, where high water of the previous spring had lodged a supply of seasoned twigs, he got his fire-wood. Working carefully from a small beginning, he soon had a roaring fire, over which he thawed the ice from his face and in the protection of which he ate his biscuits. For the moment the cold of space was outwitted. The dog took satisfaction in the fire, stretching out close enough for warmth and far enough away to escape being singed.

When the man had finished, he filled his pipe and took his comfortable time over a smoke. Then he pulled on his mittens, settled the ear-flaps of his cap firmly about his ears, and took the creek trail up the left fork. The dog was disappointed and yearned back toward the fire. This man did not know cold. Possibly all the generations of his ancestry had been ignorant of cold, of real cold, of cold one hundred and seven degrees below freezing-point. But the dog knew; all its ancestry knew, and it had inherited the knowledge. And it knew that it was not good to walk abroad in such fearful cold. It was the time to lie snug in a hole in the snow and wait for a curtain of cloud to be drawn across the face of outer space whence this cold came. On the other hand, there was no keen intimacy between the dog and the man. The one was the toil-slave of the other, and the only caresses it had ever received were the caresses of the whip-lash and of harsh and menacing throat-sounds that threatened the whip-lash. So the dog made no effort to communicate its apprehension to the man. It was not concerned in the welfare of the man; it was for its own sake that it yearned back toward the fire. But the man whistled, and spoke to it with the sound of whiplashes, and the dog swung in at the man's heels and followed after.

The man took a chew of tobacco and proceeded to start a new amber beard. Also, his moist breath quickly powdered with white his mustache, eyebrows, and lashes. There did not seem to be so many springs on the left fork of the Henderson, and for half an hour the man saw no signs of any. And then it happened. At a place where there were no signs, where the soft, unbroken snow seemed to advertise solidity beneath, the man broke through. It was not deep. He wet himself halfway to the knees before he floundered out to the firm crust.

He was angry, and cursed his luck aloud. He had hoped to get into camp with the boys at six o'clock, and this would delay him an hour, for he would have to build a fire and dry out his foot-gear. This was imperative at that low temperature—he knew that much; and he turned aside to the bank, which he climbed. On top, tangled in the under-brush about the trunks of several small spruce trees, was a high-water deposit of dry fire-wood—sticks and twigs, principally, but also larger portions of seasoned branches and fine, dry, last-year's grasses. He threw down several large pieces on top of the snow. This served for a foundation and prevented the young flame from drowning itself in the snow it otherwise would melt. The flame he got by touching a match to a small shred of birch-bark that he took from his pocket. This burned even more readily than paper. Placing it on the foundation, he fed the young flame with wisps of dry grass and with the tiniest dry twigs.

He worked slowly and carefully, keenly aware of his danger. Gradually, as the flame grew stronger, he increased the size of the twigs with which he fed it. He squatted in the snow, pulling the twigs out from their entanglement in the brush and feeding directly to the flame. He knew there must be no failure. When it is seventy-five below zero, a man must not fail in his first attempt to build a fire—that is, if his feet are wet. If his feet are dry, and he fails, he can run along the trail for half a mile and restore his circulation. But the circulation of wet and freezing feet cannot be restored by running when it is seventy-five below. No matter how fast he runs, the wet feet will freeze the harder.

All this the man knew. The old-timer on Sulphur Creek had told him about it the previous fall, and now he was appreciating the advice. Already all sensation had gone out of his feet. To build the fire he had been forced to remove his mittens, and the fingers had quickly gone numb. His pace of four miles an hour had kept his heart pumping blood to the surface of his body and to all the extremities. But the instant he stopped, the action of the pump eased down. The cold of space smote the unprotected tip of the planet, and he, being on that unprotected tip, received the full force of the blow. The blood of his body recoiled before it. The blood was alive, like the dog, and like the dog it wanted to hide away and cover itself up from the fearful cold. So long as he walked four miles an hour, he pumped that blood, willy-nilly, to the surface; but now it ebbed away and sank down into the recesses of his body. The extremities were the first to feel its absence. His wet feet froze the faster, and his exposed fingers numbed the faster, though they had not yet begun to freeze. Nose and cheeks were already freezing, while the skin of all his body chilled as it lost its blood.

But he was safe. Toes and nose and cheeks would be only touched by the frost, for the fire was beginning to burn with strength. He was feeding it with twigs the size of his finger. In another minute he would be able to feed it with branches the size of his wrist, and then he could remove his wet foot-gear, and, while it dried, he could keep his naked feet warm by the fire, rubbing them at first, of course, with snow. The fire was a success. He was safe. He remembered the advice of the old-timer on Sulphur Creek, and smiled. The old-timer had been very serious in laying down the law that no man must travel alone in the Klondike after fifty below. Well, here he was; he had had the accident; he was alone; and he had saved himself. Those old-timers were rather womanish, some of them, he thought. All a man had to do was to keep his head, and he was all right. Any man who was a man could travel alone. But it was surprising, the rapidity with which his cheeks and nose were freezing. And he had not thought his fingers could go lifeless in so short a time. Lifeless they were, for he could scarcely make them move together to grip a twig, and they seemed remote from his body and from him. When he touched a twig, he had to look and see whether or not he had hold of it. The wires were pretty well down between him and his finger-ends.

All of which counted for little. There was the fire, snapping and crackling and promising life with every dancing flame. He started to untie his moccasins. They were coated with ice; the thick German socks were like sheaths of iron halfway to the knees; and the moccasin strings were like rods of steel all twisted and knotted as by some conflagration. For a moment he tugged with his numb fingers, then, realizing the folly of it, he drew his sheath-knife.

But before he could cut the strings, it happened. It was his own fault or, rather, his mistake. He should not have built the fire under the spruce tree. He should have built it in the open. But it had been easier to pull the twigs from the brush and drop them directly on the fire. Now the tree under which he had done this carried a weight of snow on its boughs. No wind had blown for weeks, and each bough was fully freighted. Each time he had pulled a twig he had communicated a slight agitation to the tree—an imperceptible agitation, so far as he was concerned, but an agitation sufficient to bring about the disaster. High up in the tree one bough capsized its load of snow. This fell on the boughs beneath, capsizing them. This process continued, spreading out and involving the whole tree. It grew like an avalanche, and it descended without warning upon the man and the fire, and the fire was blotted out! Where it had burned was a mantle of fresh and disordered snow.

The man was shocked. It was as though he had just heard his own sentence of death. For a moment he sat and stared at the spot where the fire had been. Then he grew very calm. Perhaps the old-timer on Sulphur Creek was right. If he had only had a trail-mate he would have been in no danger now. The trail-mate could have built the fire.

Well, it was up to him to build the fire over again, and this second time there must be no failure. Even if he succeeded, he would most likely lose some toes. His feet must be badly frozen by now, and there would be some time before the second fire was ready.

Such were his thoughts, but he did not sit and think them. He was busy all the time they were passing through his mind. He made a new foundation for a fire, this time in the open, where no treacherous tree could blot it out. Next, he gathered dry grasses and tiny twigs from the high-water flotsam. He could not bring his fingers together to pull them out, but he was able to gather them by the handful. In this way he got many rotten twigs and bits of green moss that were undesirable, but it was the best he could do. He worked methodically, even collecting an armful of the larger branches to be used later when the fire gathered strength. And all the while the dog sat and watched him, a certain yearning wistfulness in its eyes, for it looked upon him as the fire-provider, and the fire was slow in coming.

When all was ready, the man reached in his pocket for a second piece of birch-bark. He knew the bark was there, and, though he could not feel it with his fingers, he could hear its crisp rustling as he fumbled for it. Try as he would, he could not clutch hold of it. And all the time, in his consciousness, was the knowledge that each instant his feet were freezing. This thought tended to put him in a panic, but he fought against it and kept calm. He pulled on his mittens with his teeth, and threshed his arms back and forth, beating his hands with all his might against his sides. He did this sitting down, and he stood up to do it; and all the while the dog sat in the snow, its wolf-brush of a tail curled around warmly over its forefeet, its sharp wolf-ears pricked forward intently as it watched the man. And the man, as he beat and threshed with his arms and hands, felt a great surge of envy as he regarded the creature that was warm and secure in its natural covering.

After a time he was aware of the first faraway signals of

sensation in his beaten fingers. The faint tingling grew stronger till it evolved into a stinging ache that was excruciating, but which the man hailed with satisfaction. He stripped the mitten from his right hand and fetched forth the birch-bark. The exposed fingers were quickly going numb again. Next he brought out his bunch of sulphur matches. But the tremendous cold had already driven the life out of his fingers. In his effort to separate one match from the others, the whole bunch fell in the snow. He tried to pick it out of the snow, but failed. The dead fingers could neither touch nor clutch. He was very careful. He drove the thought of his freezing feet, and nose, and cheeks, out of his mind, devoting his whole soul to the matches. He watched, using the sense of vision in place of that of touch, and when he saw his fingers on each side the bunch, he closed them—that is, he willed to close them, for the wires were down, and the fingers did not obey. He pulled the mitten on the right hand, and beat it fiercely against his knee. Then, with both mittened hands, he scooped the bunch of matches, along with much snow, into his lap. Yet he was no better off.

After some manipulation he managed to get the bunch between the heels of his mittened hands. In this fashion he carried it to his mouth. The ice crackled and snapped when by a violent effort he opened his mouth. He drew the lower jaw in, curled the upper lip out of the way, and scraped the bunch with his upper teeth in order to separate a match. He succeeded in getting one, which he dropped on his lap. He was no better off. He could not pick it up. Then he devised a way. He picked it up in his teeth and scratched it on his leg. Twenty times he scratched before he succeeded in lighting it. As it flamed he held it with his teeth to the birch-bark. But the burning brimstone went up his nostrils and into his lungs, causing him to cough spasmodically. The match fell into the snow and went out.

The old-timer on Sulphur Creek was right, he thought in the moment of controlled despair that ensued: after fifty below, a man should travel with a partner. He beat his hands, but failed in exciting any sensation. Suddenly he bared both hands, removing the mittens with his teeth. He caught the whole bunch between the heels of his hands. His arm-muscles not being frozen enabled him to press the hand-heels tightly against the matches. Then he scratched the bunch along his leg. It flared into flame, seventy sulphur matches at once! There was no wind to blow them out. He kept his head to one side to escape the strangling fumes, and held the blazing bunch to the birch-bark. As he so held it, he became aware of sensation in his hand. His flesh was burning. He could smell it. Deep down below the surface he could feel it. The sensation developed into pain that grew acute. And still he endured it, holding the flame of the matches clumsily to the bark that would not light readily because his own burning hands were in the way, absorbing most of the flame.

At last, when he could endure no more, he jerked his hands apart. The blazing matches fell sizzling into the snow, but the birch-bark was alight. He began laying dry grasses and the tiniest twigs on the flame. He could not pick and choose, for he had to lift the fuel between the heels of his hands. Small pieces of rotten wood and green moss clung to the twigs, and he bit them off as well as he could with his teeth. He cherished the flame carefully and awkwardly. It meant life, and it must not perish. The withdrawal of blood from the surface of his body now made him begin to shiver, and he grew more awkward. A large piece of green moss fell squarely on the little fire. He tried to poke it out with his fingers, but his shivering frame made him poke too far, and he disrupted the nucleus of the little fire, the burning grasses and tiny twigs separating and scattering. He tried to poke them together again, but in spite of the tenseness of the effort, his shivering got away with him, and the twigs were hopelessly scattered. Each twig gushed a puff of smoke and went out. The fire-provider had failed. As he looked apathetically about him, his eyes chanced on the dog, sitting across the ruins of the fire from him, in the snow, making restless, hunching movements, slightly lifting one forefoot and then the other, shifting its weight back and forth on them with wistful eagerness.

The sight of the dog put a wild idea into his head. He remembered the tale of the man, caught in a blizzard, who killed a steer and crawled inside the carcass, and so was saved. He would kill the dog and bury his hands in the warm body until the numbness went out of them. Then he could build another fire. He spoke to the dog, calling it to him; but in his voice was a strange note of fear that frightened the animal, who had never known the man to speak in such way before. Something was the matter, and its suspicious nature sensed danger—it knew not what danger, but somewhere, somehow, in its brain arose an apprehension of the man. It flattened its ears down at the sound of the man's voice, and its restless, hunching movements and the liftings and shiftings of its forefeet became more pronounced; but it would not come to the man. He got on his hands and knees and crawled toward the dog. This unusual posture again excited suspicion, and the animal sidled mincingly away.

The man sat up in the snow for a moment and struggled for calmness. Then he pulled on his mittens, by means of his teeth, and got upon his feet. He glanced down at first in order to assure himself that he was really standing up, for the absence of sensation in his feet left him unrelated to the earth. His erect position in itself started to drive the webs of suspicion from the dog's mind; and when he spoke peremptorily, with the sound of whip–lashes in his voice, the dog rendered its customary allegiance and came to him. As it came within reaching distance, the man lost his control. His arms flashed out to the dog, and he experienced genuine surprise when he discovered that his hands could not clutch, that there was neither bend nor feeling in the fingers. He had forgotten for the moment that they were frozen and that they were freezing more and more. All this happened quickly, and before the animal could get away, he encircled its body with his arms. He sat down in the snow, and in this fashion held the dog, while it snarled and whined and struggled.

But it was all he could do, hold its body encircled in his arms and sit there. He realized that he could not kill the dog. There was no way to do it. With his helpless hands he could neither draw nor hold his sheath-knife nor throttle the animal. He released it, and it plunged wildly away, with tail between its legs, and still snarling. It halted forty feet away and surveyed him curiously, with ears sharply pricked forward. The man looked down at his hands in order to locate them, and found them hanging on the ends of his arms. It struck him as curious that one should have to use his eyes in order to find out where his hands were. He began threshing his arms back and forth, beating the mittened hands against his sides. He did this for five minutes, violently, and his heart pumped enough blood up to the surface to put a stop to his shivering. But no sensation was aroused in the hands. He had an impression that they hung like weights on the ends of his arms, but when he tried to run the impression down, he could not find it.

A certain fear of death, dull and oppressive, came to him. This fear quickly became poignant as he realized that it was no longer a mere matter of freezing his fingers and toes, or of losing his hands and feet, but that it was a matter of life and death with the chances against him. This threw him into a panic, and he turned and ran up the creek-bed along the old, dim trail. The dog joined in behind and kept up with him. He ran blindly, without intention, in fear such as he had never known in his life. Slowly, as he ploughed and floundered through the snow, he began to see things again,—the banks of the creek, the old timber-jams, the leafless aspens, and the sky. The running made him feel better. He did not shiver. Maybe, if he ran on, his feet would thaw out; and, anyway, if he ran far enough, he would reach camp and the boys. Without doubt he would lose some fingers and toes and some of his face; but the boys would take care of him, and save the rest of him when he got there. And at the same time there was another thought in his mind that said he would never get to the camp and the boys; that it was too many miles away, that the freezing had too great a start on him, and that he would soon be stiff and dead. This thought he kept in the background and refused to consider. Sometimes it pushed itself forward and demanded to be heard, but he thrust it back and strove to think of other things.

It struck him as curious that he could run at all on feet so frozen that he could not feel them when they struck the earth and took the weight of his body. He seemed to himself to skim along above the surface, and to have no connection with the earth. Somewhere he had once seen a winged Mercury, and he wondered if Mercury felt as he felt when skimming over the earth.

His theory of running until he reached camp and the boys had one flaw in it: he lacked the endurance. Several times he stumbled, and finally he tottered, crumpled up, and fell. When he tried to rise, he failed. He must sit and rest, he decided, and next time he would merely walk and keep on going. As he sat and regained his breath, he noted that he was feeling quite warm and comfortable. He was not shivering, and it even seemed that a warm glow had come to his chest and trunk. And yet, when he touched his nose or cheeks, there was no sensation. Running would not thaw them out. Nor would it thaw out his hands and feet. Then the thought came to him that the frozen portions of his body must be extending. He tried to keep this thought down, to forget it, to think of something else; he was aware of the panicky feeling that it caused, and he was afraid of the panic. But the thought asserted itself, and persisted, until it produced a vision of his body totally frozen. This was too much, and he made another wild run along the trail. Once he slowed down to a walk, but the thought of the freezing extending itself made him run again.

And all the time the dog ran with him, at his heels. When he fell down a second time, it curled its tail over its forefeet and sat in front of him, facing him, curiously eager and intent. The warmth and security of the animal angered him, and he cursed it till it flattened down its ears appeasingly. This time the shivering came more quickly upon the man. He was losing in his battle with the frost. It was creeping into his body from all sides. The thought of it drove him on, but he ran no more than a hundred feet, when he staggered and pitched headlong. It was his last panic. When he had recovered his breath and control, he sat up and entertained in his mind the conception of meeting death with dignity. However, the conception did not come to him in such terms. His idea of it was that he had been making a fool of himself, running around like a chicken with its head cut off—such was the simile that occurred to him. Well, he was bound to freeze anyway, and he might as well take it decently. With this new-found peace of mind came the first glimmerings of drowsiness. A good idea, he thought, to sleep off to death. It was like taking an anæsthetic. Freezing was not so bad as people thought. There were lots worse ways to die.

He pictured the boys finding his body next day. Suddenly he found himself with them, coming along the trail and looking for himself. And, still with them, he came around a turn in the trail and found himself lying in the snow. He did not belong with himself any more, for even then he was out of himself, standing with the boys and looking at himself in the snow. It certainly was cold, was his thought. When he got back to the States he could tell the folks what real cold was. He drifted on from this to a vision of the old-timer on Sulphur Creek. He could see him quite clearly, warm and comfortable, and smoking a pipe.

"You were right, old hoss; you were right," the man mumbled to the old-timer of Sulphur Creek.

Then the man drowsed off into what seemed to him the most comfortable and satisfying sleep he had ever known. The dog sat facing him and waiting. The brief day drew to a close in a long, slow twilight. There were no signs of a fire to be made, and besides, never in the dog's experience had it known a man to sit like that in the snow and make no fire. As the twilight drew on, its eager yearning for the fire mastered it, and with a great lifting and shifting of forefeet, it whined softly, then flattened its ears down in anticipation of being chidden by the man. But the man remained silent. Later, the dog whined loudly. And still later it crept close to the man and caught the scent of death. This made the animal bristle and back away. A little longer it delayed, howling under the stars that leaped and danced and shone brightly in the cold sky. Then it turned and trotted up the trail in the direction of the camp it knew, where were the other food-providers and fire-providers.

Love of Life

"This out of all will remain—
  They have lived and have tossed;
So much of the game will be gain,
  Though the gold of the dice has been lost."

They limped painfully down the bank, and once the foremost of the two men staggered among the rough-strewn rocks. They were tired and weak, and their faces had the drawn expression of patience which comes of hardship long endured. They were heavily burdened with blanket packs which were strapped to their shoulders. Head-straps, passing across the forehead, helped support these packs. Each man carried a rifle. They walked in a stooped posture, the shoulders well forward, the head still farther forward, the eyes bent upon the ground.

"I wish we had just about two of them cartridges that's layin' in that cache of ourn," said the second man.

His voice was utterly and drearily expressionless. He spoke without enthusiasm; and the first man, limping into the milky stream that foamed over the rocks, vouchsafed no reply.

The other man followed at his heels. They did not remove their foot-gear, though the water was icy cold—so cold that their ankles ached and their feet went numb. In places the water dashed against their knees, and both men staggered for footing.

The man who followed slipped on a smooth boulder, nearly fell, but recovered himself with a violent effort, at the same time uttering a sharp exclamation of pain. He seemed faint and dizzy and put out his free hand while he reeled, as though seeking support against the air. When he had steadied himself he stepped forward, but reeled again and nearly fell. Then he stood still and looked at the other man, who had never turned his head.

The man stood still for fully a minute, as though debating with himself. Then he called out:

"I say, Bill, I've sprained my ankle."

Bill staggered on through the milky water. He did not look around. The man watched him go, and though his face was expressionless as ever, his eyes were like the eyes of a wounded deer.

The other man limped up the farther bank and continued straight on without looking back. The man in the stream watched him. His lips trembled a little, so that the rough thatch of brown hair which covered them was visibly agitated. His tongue even strayed out to moisten them.

"Bill!" he cried out.

It was the pleading cry of a strong man in distress, but Bill's head did not turn. The man watched him go, limping grotesquely and lurching forward with stammering gait up the slow slope toward the soft sky-line of the low-lying hill. He watched him go till he passed over the crest and disappeared. Then he turned his gaze and slowly took in the circle of the world that remained to him now that Bill was gone.

Near the horizon the sun was smouldering dimly, almost obscured by formless mists and vapors, which gave an impression of mass and density without outline or tangibility. The man pulled out his watch, the while resting his weight on one leg. It was four o'clock, and as the season was near the last of July or first of August,—he did not know the precise date within a week or two,—he knew that the sun roughly marked the northwest. He looked to the south and knew that somewhere beyond those bleak hills lay the Great Bear Lake; also, he knew that in that direction the Arctic Circle cut its forbidding way across the Canadian Barrens. This stream in which he stood was a feeder to the Coppermine River, which in turn flowed north and emptied into Coronation Gulf and the Arctic Ocean. He had never been there, but he had seen it, once, on a Hudson Bay Company chart.

Again his gaze completed the circle of the world about him. It was not a heartening spectacle. Everywhere was soft sky-line. The hills were all low-lying. There were no trees, no shrubs, no grasses—naught but a tremendous and terrible desolation that sent fear swiftly dawning into his eyes.

"Bill!" he whispered, once and twice; "Bill!"

He cowered in the midst of the milky water, as though the vastness were pressing in upon him with overwhelming force, brutally crushing him with its complacent awfulness. He began to shake as with an ague-fit, till the gun fell from his hand with a splash. This served to rouse him. He fought with his fear and pulled himself together, groping in the water and recovering the weapon. He hitched his pack farther over on his left shoulder, so as to take a portion of its weight from off the injured ankle. Then he proceeded, slowly and carefully, wincing with pain, to the bank.

He did not stop. With a desperation that was madness, unmindful of the pain, he hurried up the slope to the crest of the hill over which his comrade had disappeared—more grotesque and comical by far than that limping, jerking comrade. But at the crest he saw a shallow valley, empty of life. He fought with his fear again, overcame it, hitched the pack still farther over on his left shoulder, and lurched on down the slope.

The bottom of the valley was soggy with water, which the thick moss held, spongelike, close to the surface. This water squirted out from under his feet at every step, and each time he lifted a foot the action culminated in a sucking sound as the wet moss reluctantly released its grip. He picked his way from muskeg to muskeg, and followed the other man's footsteps along and across the rocky ledges which thrust like islets through the sea of moss.

Though alone, he was not lost. Farther on he knew he would come to where dead spruce and fir, very small and weazened, bordered the shore of a little lake, the *titchin-nichilie*, in the tongue of the country, the "land of little sticks." And into that lake flowed a small stream, the water of which was not milky. There was rush-grass on that stream—this he remembered well—but no timber, and he would follow it till its first trickle ceased at a divide. He would cross this divide to the first trickle of another stream, flowing to the west, which he would follow until it emptied into the river Dease, and here he would find a cache under an upturned canoe and piled over with many rocks. And in this cache would be ammunition for his empty gun, fish-hooks and lines, a small net—all the utilities for the killing and snaring of food. Also, he would find flour,—not much,—a piece of bacon, and some beans.

Bill would be waiting for him there, and they would paddle away south down the Dease to the Great Bear Lake. And south across the lake they would go, ever south, till they gained the Mackenzie. And south, still south, they would go, while the winter raced vainly after them, and the ice formed in the eddies, and the days grew chill and crisp, south to some warm Hudson Bay Company post, where timber grew tall and generous and there was grub without end.

These were the thoughts of the man as he strove onward. But hard as he strove with his body, he strove equally hard with his mind, trying to think that Bill had not deserted him, that Bill would surely wait for him at the cache. He was compelled to think this thought, or else there would not be any use to strive, and he would have lain down and died. And as the dim ball of the sun sank slowly into the northwest he covered every inch—and many times—of his and Bill's flight south before the downcoming winter. And he conned the grub of the cache and the grub of the Hudson Bay Company post over and over again. He had not eaten for two days; for a far longer time he had not had all he wanted to eat. Often he stooped and picked pale muskeg berries, put them into his mouth, and chewed and swallowed them. A muskeg berry is a bit of seed enclosed in a bit of water. In the mouth the water melts away and the seed chews sharp and bitter. The man knew there was no nourishment in the berries, but he chewed them patiently with a hope greater than knowledge and defying experience.

At nine o'clock he stubbed his toe on a rocky ledge, and from sheer weariness and weakness staggered and fell. He lay for some time, without movement, on his side. Then he slipped out of the pack-straps and clumsily dragged himself into a sitting posture. It was not yet dark, and in the lingering twilight he groped about among the rocks for shreds of dry moss. When he had gathered a heap he built a fire,—a smouldering, smudgy fire,—and put a tin pot of water on to boil.

He unwrapped his pack and the first thing he did was to count his matches. There were sixty-seven. He counted them three times to make sure. He divided them into several portions, wrapping them in oil paper, disposing of one bunch in his empty tobacco pouch, of another bunch in the inside bank of his battered hat, of a third bunch under his shirt on the chest. This accomplished, a panic came upon him, and he unwrapped them all and counted them again. There were still sixty-seven.

He dried his wet foot-gear by the fire. The moccasins were in soggy shreds. The blanket socks were worn through in places, and his feet were raw and bleeding. His ankle was throbbing, and he gave it an examination. It had swollen to the size of his knee. He tore a long strip from one of his two blankets and bound the ankle tightly. He tore other strips and bound them about his feet to serve for both moccasins and socks. Then he drank the pot of water, steaming hot, wound his watch, and crawled between his blankets.

He slept like a dead man. The brief darkness around midnight came and went. The sun arose in the northeast—at least the day dawned in that quarter, for the sun was hidden by gray clouds.

At six o'clock he awoke, quietly lying on his back. He gazed straight up into the gray sky and knew that he was hungry. As he rolled over on his elbow he was startled by a loud snort, and saw a bull caribou regarding him with alert curiosity. The animal was not more than fifty feet away, and instantly into the man's mind leaped the vision and the savor of a caribou steak sizzling and frying over a fire. Mechanically he reached for the empty gun, drew a bead, and pulled the trigger. The bull snorted and leaped away, his hoofs rattling and clattering as he fled across the ledges.

The man cursed and flung the empty gun from him. He groaned aloud as he started to drag himself to his feet. It was a slow and arduous task. His joints were like rusty hinges. They worked harshly in their sockets, with much friction, and each bending or unbending was accomplished only through a sheer exertion of will. When he finally gained his feet, another minute or so was consumed in straightening up, so that he could stand erect as a man should stand.

He crawled up a small knoll and surveyed the prospect. There were no trees, no bushes, nothing but a gray sea of moss scarcely diversified by gray rocks, gray lakelets, and gray streamlets. The sky was gray. There was no sun nor hint of sun. He had no idea of north, and he had forgotten the way he had come to this spot the night before. But he was not lost. He knew that. Soon he would come to the land of the little sticks. He felt that it lay off to the left somewhere, not far—possibly just over the next low hill.

He went back to put his pack into shape for travelling. He assured himself of the existence of his three separate parcels of matches, though he did not stop to count them. But he did linger, debating, over a squat moose-hide sack. It was not large. He could hide it under his two hands. He knew that it weighed fifteen pounds,—as much as all the rest of the pack,—and it worried him. He finally set it to one side and proceeded to roll the pack. He paused to gaze at the squat moose-hide sack. He picked it up hastily with a defiant glance about him, as though the desolation were trying to rob him of it; and when he rose to his feet to stagger on into the day, it was included in the pack on his back.

He bore away to the left, stopping now and again to eat muskeg berries. His ankle had stiffened, his limp was more pronounced, but the pain of it was as nothing compared with the pain of his stomach. The hunger pangs were sharp. They gnawed and gnawed until he could not keep his mind steady on the course he must pursue to gain the land of little sticks. The muskeg berries did not allay this gnawing, while they made his tongue and the roof of his mouth sore with their irritating bite.

He came upon a valley where rock ptarmigan rose on whirring wings from the ledges and muskegs. Ker—ker—ker was the cry they made. He threw stones at them, but could not hit them. He placed his pack on the ground and stalked them as a cat stalks a sparrow. The sharp rocks cut through his pants' legs till his knees left a trail of blood; but the hurt was lost in the hurt of his hunger. He squirmed over the wet moss, saturating his clothes and chilling his body; but he was not aware of it, so great was his fever for food. And always the ptarmigan rose, whirring, before him, till their ker—ker—ker became a mock to him, and he cursed them and cried aloud at them with their own cry.

Once he crawled upon one that must have been asleep.

He did not see it till it shot up in his face from its rocky nook. He made a clutch as startled as was the rise of the ptarmigan, and there remained in his hand three tail-feathers. As he watched its flight he hated it, as though it had done him some terrible wrong. Then he returned and shouldered his pack.

As the day wore along he came into valleys or swales where game was more plentiful. A bank of caribou passed by, twenty and odd animals, tantalizingly within rifle range. He felt a wild desire to run after them, a certitude that he could run them down. A black fox came toward him, carrying a ptarmigan in his mouth. the man shouted. It was a fearful cry, but the fox, leaping away in fright, did not drop the ptarmigan.

Late in the afternoon he followed a stream, milky with lime, which ran through sparse patches of rush-grass. Grasping these rushes firmly near the root, he pulled up what resembled a young onion-sprout no larger than a shingle-nail. It was tender, and his teeth sank into it with a crunch that promised deliciously of food. But its fibers were tough. It was composed of stringy filaments saturated with water, like the berries, and devoid of nourishment. He threw off his pack and went into the rush-grass on hands and knees, crunching and munching, like some bovine creature.

He was very weary and often wished to rest—to lie down and sleep; but he was continually driven on—not so much by his desire to gain the land of little sticks as by his hunger. He searched little ponds for frogs and dug up the earth with his nails for worms, though he knew in spite that neither frogs nor worms existed so far north.

He looked into every pool of water vainly, until, as the long twilight came on, he discovered a solitary fish, the size of a minnow, in such a pool. He plunged his arm in up to the shoulder, but it eluded him. He reached for it with both hands and stirred up the milky mud at the bottom. In his excitement he fell in, wetting himself to the waist. Then the water was too muddy to admit of his seeing the fish, and he was compelled to wait until the sediment had settled.

The pursuit was renewed, till the water was again muddied. But he could not wait. He unstrapped the tin bucket and began to bale the pool. He baled wildly at first, splashing himself and flinging the water so short a distance that it ran back into the pool. He worked more carefully, striving to be cool, though his heart was pounding against his chest and his hands were trembling At the end of half an hour the pool was nearly dry. Not a cupful of water remained. And there was no fish. He found a hidden crevice among the stones through which it had escaped to the adjoining and larger pool—a pool which he could not empty in a night and a day. Had he known of the crevice, he could have closed it with a rock at the beginning and the fish would have been his.

Thus he thought, and crumpled up and sank down upon the wet earth. At first he cried softly to himself, then he cried loudly to the pitiless desolation that ringed him around; and for a long time after he was shaken by great dry sobs.

He built a fire and warmed himself by drinking quarts of hot water, and made camp on a rocky ledge in the same fashion he had the night before. The last thing he did was to see that his matches were dry and to wind his watch. The blankets were wet and clammy. His ankle pulsed with pain. But he knew only that he was hungry, and through his restless sleep he dreamed of feasts and banquets and of food served and spread in all imaginable ways.

He awoke chilled and sick. There was no sun. The gray of earth and sky had become deeper, more profound. A raw wind was blowing, and the first flurries of snow were whitening the hilltops. The air about him thickened and grew white while he made a fire and boiled more water. It was wet snow, half rain, and the flakes were large and soggy. At first they melted as soon as they came in contact with the earth, but ever more fell, covering the ground, putting out the fire, spoiling his supply of moss-fuel.

This was a signal for him to strap on his pack and stumble onward, he knew not where. He was not concerned with the land of little sticks, nor with Bill and the cache under the upturned canoe by the river Dease. He was mastered by the verb "to eat." He was hunger-mad. He took no heed of the course he pursued, so long as that course led him through the swale bottoms. He felt his way through the wet snow to the watery muskeg berries, and went by feel as he pulled up the rush-grass by the roots. But it was tasteless stuff and did not satisfy. He found a weed that tasted sour and he ate all he could find of it, which was not much, for it was a creeping growth, easily hidden under the several inches of snow.

He had no fire that night, nor hot water, and crawled under his blanket to sleep the broken hunger-sleep. The snow turned into a cold rain. He awakened many times to feel it falling on his upturned face. Day came—a gray day and no sun. It had ceased raining. The keenness of his hunger had departed. Sensibility, as far as concerned the yearning for food, had been exhausted. There was a dull, heavy ache in his stomach, but it did not bother him so much. He was more rational, and once more he was chiefly interested in the land of little sticks and the cache by the river Dease.

He ripped the remnant of one of his blankets into strips and bound his bleeding feet. Also, he recinched the injured ankle and prepared himself for a day of travel. When he came to his pack, he paused long over the squat moose-hide sack, but in the end it went with him.

The snow had melted under the rain, and only the hill-tops showed white. The sun came out, and he succeeded in locating the points of the compass, though he knew now that he was lost. Perhaps, in his previous days' wanderings, he had edged away too far to the left. He now bore off to the right to counteract the possible deviation from his true course.

Though the hunger pangs were no longer so exquisite, he realized that he was weak. He was compelled to pause for frequent rests, when he attacked the muskeg berries and rush-grass patches. His tongue felt dry and large, as though covered with a fine hairy growth, and it tasted bitter in his mouth. His heart gave him a great deal of trouble. When he had travelled a few minutes it would begin a remorseless thump, thump, thump, and then leap up and away in a painful flutter of beats that choked him and made him go faint and dizzy.

In the middle of the day he found two minnows in a large pool. It was impossible to bale it, but he was calmer now and managed to catch them in his tin bucket. They were no longer than his little finger, but he was not particularly hungry. The dull ache in his stomach had been growing duller and fainter. It seemed almost that his stomach was dozing. He ate the fish raw, masticating with painstaking care, for the eating was an act of pure reason. While he had no desire to eat, he knew that he must eat to live.

In the evening he caught three more minnows, eating two and saving the third for breakfast. The sun had dried stray shreds of moss, and he was able to warm himself with hot water. He had not covered more than ten miles that day; and the next day, travelling whenever his heart permitted him, he covered no more than five miles. But his stomach did not give him the slightest uneasiness. It had gone to sleep. He was in a strange country, too, and the caribou were growing more plentiful, also the wolves. Often their yelps drifted across the desolation, and once he saw three of them slinking away before his path.

Another night; and in the morning, being more rational, he untied the leather string that fastened the squat moosehide sack. From its open mouth poured a yellow stream of coarse gold-dust and nuggets. He roughly divided the gold in halves, caching one half on a prominent ledge, wrapped in a piece of blanket, and returning the other half to the sack. He also began to use strips of the one remaining blanket for his feet. He still clung to his gun, for there were cartridges in that cache by the river Dease.

This was a day of fog, and this day hunger awoke in him again. He was very weak and was afflicted with a giddiness which at times blinded him. It was no uncommon thing now for him to stumble and fall; and stumbling once, he fell squarely into a ptarmigan nest. There were four newly hatched chicks, a day old—little specks of pulsating life no more than a mouthful; and he ate them ravenously, thrusting them alive into his mouth and crunching them like egg-shells between his teeth. The mother ptarmigan beat about him with great outcry. He used his gun as a club with which to knock her over, but she dodged out of reach. He threw stones at her and with one chance shot broke a wing. Then she fluttered away, running, trailing the broken wing, with him in pursuit.

The little chicks had no more than whetted his appetite. He hopped and bobbed clumsily along on his injured ankle, throwing stones and screaming hoarsely at times; at other times hopping and bobbing silently along, picking himself up grimly and patiently when he fell, or rubbing his eyes with his hand when the giddiness threatened to overpower him.

The chase led him across swampy ground in the bottom of the valley, and he came upon footprints in the soggy moss. They were not his own—he could see that. They must be Bill's. But he could not stop, for the mother ptarmigan was running on. He would catch her first, then he would return and investigate.

He exhausted the other ptarmigan; but he exhausted himself. She lay panting on her side. He lay panting on his side, a dozen feet away, unable to crawl to her. And as he recovered she recovered, fluttering out of reach as his hungry hand went out to her. The chase was resumed. Night settled down and she escaped. He stumbled from weakness and pitched head foremost on his face, cutting his cheek, his pack upon his back. He did not move for a long while; then he rolled over on his side, wound his watch, and lay there until morning.

Another day of fog. Half of his last blanket had gone

into foot-wrappings. He failed to pick up Bill's trail. It did not matter. His hunger was driving him too compellingly—only—only he wondered if Bill, too, were lost. By midday the irk of his pack became too oppressive. Again he divided the gold, this time merely spilling half of it on the ground. In the afternoon he threw the rest of it away, there remaining to him only the half-blanket, the tin bucket, and the rifle.

An hallucination began to trouble him. He felt confident that one cartridge remained to him. It was in the chamber of the rifle and he had overlooked it. On the other hand, he knew all the time that the chamber was empty. But the hallucination persisted. He fought it off for hours, then threw his rifle open and was confronted with emptiness. The disappointment was as bitter as though he had really expected to find the cartridge.

He plodded on for half an hour, when the hallucination arose again. Again he fought it, and still it persisted, till for very relief he opened his rifle to unconvince himself. At times his mind wandered farther afield, and he plodded on, a mere automaton, strange conceits and whimsicalities gnawing at his brain like worms. But these excursions out of the real were of brief duration, for ever the pangs of the hunger-bite called him back. He was jerked back abruptly once from such an excursion by a sight that caused him nearly to faint. He reeled and swayed, doddering like a drunken man to keep from falling. Before him stood a horse. A horse! He could not believe his eyes. A thick mist was in them, intershot with sparkling points of light. He rubbed his eyes savagely to clear his vision, and beheld, not a horse, but a great brown bear. The animal was studying him with bellicose curiosity.

The man had brought his gun halfway to his shoulder before he realized. He lowered it and drew his hunting-knife from its beaded sheath at his hip. Before him was meat and life. He ran his thumb alone the edge of his knife. It was sharp. The point was sharp. He would fling himself upon the bear and kill it. But his heart began its warning thump, thump, thump. Then followed the wild up-ward leap and tattoo of flutters, the pressing as of an iron band about his forehead, the creeping of the dizziness into his brain.

His desperate courage was evicted by a great surge of fear. In his weakness, what if the animal attacked him? He drew himself up to his most imposing stature, gripping the knife and staring hard at the bear. The bear advanced clumsily a couple of steps, reared up, and gave vent to a tentative growl. If the man ran, he would run after him; but the man did not run. He was animated now with the courage of fear. He, too, growled, savagely, terribly, voic-ing the fear that is to life germane and that lies twisted about life's deepest roots.

The bear edged away to one side, growling menacingly, himself appalled by this mysterious creature that appeared upright and unafraid. But the man did not move. He stood like a statue till the danger was past, when he yielded to a fit of trembling and sank down into the wet moss.

He pulled himself together and went on, afraid now in a new way. It was not the fear that he should die passively from lack of food, but that he should be destroyed vio-lently before starvation had exhausted the last particle of the endeavor in him that made toward surviving. There were the wolves. Back and forth across the desolation drifted their howls, wearing the very air into a fabric of menace that was so tangible that he found himself, arms in the air, pressing it back from him as it might be the walls of a wind-blown tent.

Now and again the wolves, in packs of two and three, crossed his path. But they sheered clear of him. They were not in sufficient numbers, and besides they were hunting the caribou, which did not battle, while this strange crea-ture that walked erect might scratch and bite.

In the late afternoon he came upon scattered bones where the wolves had made a kill. The débris had been a caribou calf an hour before, squawking and running and very much alive. He contemplated the bones, clean-picked and polished, pink with the cell-life in them which had not yet died. Could it possible by that he might be that ere the day was done! Such was life, eh? A vain and fleeting thing. It was only life that pained. There was no hurt in death. To die was to sleep. It meant cessation, rest. Then why was he not content to die?

But he did not moralize long. He was squatting in the moss, a bone in his mouth, sucking at the shreds of life that still dyed it faintly pink. The sweet meaty taste, thin and elusive almost as a memory, maddened him. He closed his jaws on the bones and crunched. Sometimes it was the bone that broke, sometimes his teeth. Then he crushed the bones between rocks, pounded them to a pulp, and swallowed them. He pounded his fingers, too, in his haste, and yet found a moment in which to feel surprise at the fact that his fingers did not hurt much when caught under the descending rock.

Came frightful days of snow and rain. He did not know when he made camp, when he broke camp. He travelled in the night as much as in the day. He rested wherever he fell, crawled on whenever the dying life in him flickered up and burned less dimly. He, as a man, no longer strove. It was the life in him, unwilling to die, that drove him on. He did not suffer. His nerves had become blunted, numb while his mind was filled with weird visions and delicious dreams.

But ever he sucked and chewed on the crushed bones of the caribou calf, the least remnants of which he had gathered up and carried with him. He crossed no more hills or divides, but automatically followed a large stream which flowed through a wide and shallow valley. He did not see this stream nor this valley. He saw nothing save visions. Soul and body walked or crawled side by side, yet apart, so slender was the thread that bound them.

He awoke in his right mind, lying on his back on a rocky ledge. The sun was shining bright and warm. Afar off he heard the squawking of caribou calves. He was aware of vague memories of rain and wind and snow, but whether he had been beaten by the storm for two days or two weeks he did not know.

For some time he lay without movement, the genial sunshine pouring upon him and saturating his miserable body with its warmth. A fine day, he thought. Perhaps he could manage to locate himself. By a painful effort he rolled over on his side. Below him flowed a wide and sluggish river. Its unfamiliarity puzzled him. Slowly he followed it with his eyes, winding in wide sweeps among the bleak, bare hills, bleaker and barer and lower-lying than any hills he had yet encountered. Slowly, deliberately, without excitement or more than the most casual interest, he followed the course of the strange stream toward the sky-line and saw it emptying into a bright and shining sea. He was still unexcited. Most unusual, he thought, a vision or a mirage—more likely a vision, a trick of his disordered mind. He was confirmed in this by sight of a ship lying at anchor in the midst of the shining sea. He closed his eyes for a while, then opened them. Strange how the vision persisted! Yet not strange. He knew there were no seas or ships in the heart of the barren lands, just as he had known there was no cartridge in the empty rifle.

He heard a snuffle behind him—a half-choking gasp or cough. Very slowly, because of his exceeding weakness and stiffness, he rolled over on his other side. He could see nothing near at hand, but he waited patiently. Again came the snuffle and cough, and outlined between two jagged rocks not a score of feet away he made out the gray head of a wolf. The sharp ears were not pricked so sharply as he had seen them on other wolves; the eyes were bleared and bloodshot, the head seemed to droop limply and forlornly. The animal blinked continually in the sunshine. It seemed sick. As he looked it snuffled and coughed again.

This, at least, was real, he thought, and turned on the other side so that he might see the reality of the world which had been veiled from him before by the vision. But the sea still shone in the distance and the ship was plainly discernible. Was it reality, after all? He closed his eyes for a long while and thought, and then it came to him. He had been making north by east, away from the Dease Divide and into the Coppermine Valley. This wide and sluggish river was the Coppermine. That shining sea was the Arctic Ocean. That ship was a whaler, strayed east, far east, from the mouth of the Mackenzie, and it was lying at anchor in Coronation Gulf. He remembered the Hudson Bay Company chart he had seen long ago, and it was all clear and reasonable to him.

He sat up and turned his attention to immediate affairs. He had worn through the blanket-wrappings, and his feet were shapeless lumps of raw meat. His last blanket was gone. Rifle and knife were both missing. He had lost his hat somewhere, with the bunch of matches in the band, but the matches against his chest were safe and dry inside the tobacco pouch and oil paper. He looked at his watch. It marked eleven o'clock and was still running. Evidently he had kept it wound.

He was calm and collected. Though extremely weak, he had no sensation of pain. He was not hungry. The thought of food was not even pleasant to him, and whatever he did was done by his reason alone. He ripped off his pants' legs to the knees and bound them about his feet. Somehow he had succeeded in retaining the tin bucket. He would have some hot water before he began what he foresaw was to be a terrible journey to the ship.

His movements were slow. He shook as with a palsy. When he started to collect dry moss, he found he could not rise to his feet. He tried again and again, then contented himself with crawling about on hands and knees. Once he crawled near to the sick wolf. The animal dragged itself reluctantly out of his way, licking its chops with a tongue which seemed hardly to have the strength to curl. The man noticed that the tongue was not the customary healthy red. It was a yellowish brown and seemed coated with a rough and half-dry mucus.

After he had drunk a quart of hot water the man found

he was able to stand, and even to walk as well as a dying man might be supposed to walk. Every minute or so he was compelled to rest. His steps were feeble and uncertain, just as the wolf's that trailed him were feeble and uncertain; and that night, when the shining sea was blotted out by blackness, he knew he was nearer to it by no more than four miles.

Throughout the night he heard the cough of the sick wolf, and now and then the squawking of the caribou calves. There was life all around him, but it was strong life, very much alive and well, and he knew the sick wolf clung to the sick man's trail in the hope that the man would die first. In the morning, on opening his eyes, he beheld it regarding him with a wistful and hungry stare. It stood crouched, with tail between its legs, like a miserable and woe-begone dog. It shivered in the chill morning wind, and grinned dispiritedly when the man spoke to it in a voice that achieved no more than a hoarse whisper.

The sun rose brightly, and all morning the man tottered and fell toward the ship on the shining sea. The weather was perfect. It was the brief Indian Summer of the high latitudes. It might last a week. To-morrow or next day it might be gone.

In the afternoon the man came upon a trail. It was of another man, who did not walk, but who dragged himself on all fours. The man thought it might be Bill, but he thought in a dull, uninterested way. He had no curiosity. In fact, sensation and emotion had left him. He was no longer susceptible to pain. Stomach and nerves had gone to sleep. Yet the life that was in him drove him on. He was very weary, but it refused to die. It was because it refused to die that he still ate muskeg berries and minnows, drank his hot water, and kept a wary eye on the sick wolf.

He followed the trail of the other man who dragged himself along, and soon came to the end of it—a few fresh-picked bones where the soggy moss was marked by the foot-pads of many wolves. He saw a squat moose-hide sack, mate to his own, which had been torn by sharp teeth.

He picked it up, though its weight was almost too much for his feeble fingers. Bill had carried it to the last. Ha! ha! He would have the laugh on Bill. He would survive and carry it to the ship in the shining sea. His mirth was hoarse and ghastly, like a raven's croak, and the sick wolf joined him, howling lugubriously. The man ceased suddenly. How could he have the laugh on Bill if that were Bill; if those bones, so pinky-white and clean, were Bill?

He turned away. Well, Bill had deserted him; but he would not take the gold, nor would he suck Bill's bones. Bill would have, though, had it been the other way around, he mused as he staggered on.

He came to a pool of water. Stooping over in quest of minnows, he jerked his head back as though he had been stung. He had caught sight of his reflected face. So horrible was it that sensibility awoke long enough to be shocked. There were three minnows in the pool, which was too large to drain; and after several ineffectual attempts to catch them in the tin bucket he forbore. He was afraid, because of his great weakness, that he might fall in and drown. It was for this reason that he did not trust himself to the river astride one of the many drift-logs which lines its sand-spits.

That day he decreased the distance between him and the ship by three miles; the next day by two—for he was crawling now as Bill had crawled; and the end of the fifth day found the ship still seven miles away and him unable to make even a mile a day. Still the Indian Summer held on, and he continued to crawl and faint, turn and turn about; and ever the sick wolf coughed and wheezed at his heels. His knees had become raw meat like his feet, and though he padded them with the shirt from his back it was a red track he left behind him on the moss and stones. Once, glancing back, he saw the wolf licking hungrily his bleeding trial, and he saw sharply what his own end might be—unless—unless he could get the wolf. Then began as grim a tragedy of existence as was ever played—a sick man that crawled, a sick wolf that limped, two creatures dragging their dying carcasses across the desolation and hunting each other's lives.

Had it been a well wolf, it would not have mattered so much to the man; but the thought of going to feed the maw of that loathsome and all but dead thing was repugnant to him. He was finicky. His mind had begun to wander again, and to be perplexed by hallucinations, while his lucid intervals grew rarer and shorter.

He was awakened once from a faint by a wheeze close in his ear. The wolf leaped lamely back, losing its footing and falling in its weakness. It was ludicrous, but he was not amused. Nor was he even afraid. He was too far gone for that. But his mind was for the moment clear, and he lay and considered. The ship was no more than four miles away. He could see it quite distinctly when he rubbed the mists out of his eyes, and he could see the white sail of a small boat cutting the water of the shining sea. But he could never crawl those four miles. He knew that, and was very calm in the knowledge. He knew that he could not crawl half a mile. And yet he wanted to live. It was unreasonable that he should die after all he had undergone. Fate asked too much of him. And, dying, he declined to die. It was stark madness, perhaps, but in the very grip of Death he defied Death and refused to die.

He closed his eyes and composed himself with infinite precaution. He steeled himself to keep above the suffocating languor that lapped like a rising tide through all the wells of his being. It was very like a sea, this deadly languor, that rose and rose and drowned his consciousness bit by bit. Sometimes he was all but submerged, swimming through oblivion with a faltering stroke; and again, by some strange alchemy of soul, he would find another shred of will and strike out more strongly.

Without movement he lay on his back, and he could hear, slowly drawing near and nearer, the wheezing intake and output of the sick wolf's breath. It drew closer, ever closer, through an infinitude of time, and he did not move. It was at his ear. The harsh dry tongue grated like sandpaper against his cheek. His hands shot out—or at least he willed them to shoot out. The fingers were curved like talons, but they closed on empty air. Swiftness and certitude require strength, and the man had not this strength.

The patience of the wolf was terrible. The man's patience was no less terrible. For half a day he lay motionless, fighting off unconsciousness and waiting for the thing that was to feed upon him and upon which he wished to feed. Sometimes the languid sea rose over him and he dreamed long dreams; but ever through it all, waking and dreaming, he waited for the wheezing breath and the harsh caress of the tongue.

He did not hear the breath, and he slipped slowly from some dream to the feel of the tongue along his hand. He waited. The fangs pressed softly; the pressure increased; the wolf was exerting its last strength in an effort to sink teeth in the food for which it had waited so long. But the man had waited long, and the lacerated hand closed on the jaw. Slowly, while the wolf struggled feebly and the hand clutched feebly, the other hand crept across to a grip. Five minutes later the whole weight of the man's body was on top of the wolf. The hands had not sufficient strength to choke the wolf, but the face of the man was pressed close to the throat of the wolf and the mouth of the man was full of hair. At the end of half an hour the man was aware of a warm trickle in his throat. It was not pleasant. It was like molten lead being forced into his stomach, and it was forced by his will alone. Later the man rolled over on his back and slept.

There were some members of a scientific expedition on the whale-ship *Bedford*. From the deck they remarked a strange object on the shore. It was moving down the beach toward the water. They were unable to classify it, and, being scientific men, they climbed into the whaleboat alongside and went ashore to see. And they saw something that was alive but which could hardly be called a man. It was blind, unconscious. It squirmed along the ground like some monstrous worm. Most of its efforts were ineffectual, but it was persistent, and it writhed and twisted and went ahead perhaps a score of feet an hour.

Three weeks afterward the man lay in a bunk on the whale-ship *Bedford*, and with tears streaming down his wasted cheeks told who he was and what he had undergone. He also babbled incoherently of his mother, of sunny Southern California, and a home among the orange groves and flowers.

The days were not many after that when he sat at table with the scientific men and ship's officers. He gloated over the spectacle of so much food, watching it anxiously as it went into the mouths of others. With the disappearance of each mouthful an expression of deep regret came into his eyes. He was quite sane, yet he hated those men at mealtime. He was haunted by a fear that the food would not last. He inquired of the cook, the cabin-boy, the captain, concerning the food stores. They reassured him countless times; but he could not believe them, and pried cunningly about the lazarette to see with his own eyes.

It was noticed that the man was getting fat. He grew stouter with each day. The scientific men shook their heads and theorized. They limited the man at his meals, but still his girth increased and he swelled prodigiously under his shirt.

The sailors grinned. they knew. And when the scientific men set a watch on the man, they knew too. They saw him slouch for'ard after breakfast, and, like a mendicant, with outstretched palm, accost a sailor. The sailor grinned and passed him a fragment of sea biscuit. He clutched it avariciously, looked at it as a miser looks at gold, and thrust it into his shirt bosom. Similar were the donations from other grinning sailors.

The scientific men were discreet. They let him alone. But they privily examined his bunk. It was lined with hardtack; the mattress was stuffed with hardtack; every nook and cranny was filled with hardtack. Yet he was sane. He was taking precautions against another possible famine—that was all. He would recover from it, the scientific men said; and he did, ere the *Bedford's* anchor rumbled down in San Francisco Bay.

The Chinago

"The coral waxes, the palm grows, but man departs."
—Tahitian proverb

Ah Cho did not understand French. He sat in the crowded court room, very weary and bored, listening to the unceasing, explosive French that now one official and now another uttered. It was just so much gabble to Ah Cho, and he marvelled at the stupidity of the Frenchmen who took so long to find out the murderer of Chung Ga, and who did not find him at all. The five hundred coolies on the plantation knew that Ah San had done the killing, and here was Ah San not even arrested. It was true that all the coolies had agreed secretly not to testify against one another; but then, it was so simple, the Frenchmen should have been able to discover that Ah San was the man. They were very stupid, these Frenchmen.

Ah Cho had done nothing of which to be afraid. He had had no hand in the killing. It was true he had been present at it, and Schemmer, the overseer of the plantation, had rushed into the barracks immediately afterward and caught him there, along with four or five others; but what of that? Chung Ga had been stabbed only twice. It stood to reason that five or six men could not inflict two stab wounds. At the most, if a man had struck but once, only two men could have done it.

So it was that Ah Cho reasoned, when he, along with his four companions, had lied and blocked and obfuscated in their statements to the court concerning what had taken place. They had heard the sounds of the killing, and, like Schemmer, they had run to the spot. They had got there before Schemmer—that was all. True, Schemmer had testified that, attracted by the sound of quarrelling as he chanced to pass by, he had stood for at least five minutes outside; that then, when he entered, he found the prisoners already inside; and that they had not entered just before, because he had been standing by the one door to the barracks. But what of that? Ah Cho and his four fellow-prisoners had testified that Schemmer was mistaken. In the end they would be let go. They were all confident of that. Five men could not have their heads cut off for two stab wounds. Besides, no foreign devil had seen the killing. But these Frenchmen were so stupid. In China, as Ah Cho well knew, the magistrate would order all of them to the torture and learn the truth. The truth was very easy to learn under torture. But these Frenchmen did not torture—bigger fools they! Therefore they would never find out who killed Chung Ga.

But Ah Cho did not understand everything. The English Company that owned the plantation had imported into Tahiti, at great expense, the five hundred coolies. The stockholders were clamoring for dividends, and the Company had not yet paid any; wherefore the Company did not want its costly contract laborers to start the practice of killing one another. Also, there were the French, eager and willing to impose upon the Chinagos the virtues and excellences of French law. There was nothing like setting an example once in a while; and, besides, of what use was New

Caledonia except to send men to live out their days in misery and pain in payment of the penalty for being frail and human?

Ah Cho did not understand all this. He sat in the court room and waited for the baffled judgment that would set him and his comrades free to go back to the plantation and work out the terms of their contracts. This judgment would soon be rendered. Proceedings were drawing to a close. He could see that. There was no more testifying, no more gabble of tongues. The French devils were tired, too, and evidently waiting for the judgment. And as he waited he remembered back in his life to the time when he had signed the contract and set sail in the ship for Tahiti. Times had been hard in his seacoast village, and when he indentured himself to labor for five years in the South Seas at fifty cents Mexican a day, he had thought himself fortunate. There were men in his village who toiled a whole year for ten dollars Mexican, and there were women who made nets all the year round for five dollars, while in the houses of shopkeepers there were maid-servants who received four dollars for a year of service. And here he was to receive fifty cents a day; for one day, only one day, he was to receive that princely sum! What if the work were hard? At the end of the five years he would return home—that was in the contract—and he would never have to work again. He would be a rich man for life, with a house of his own, a wife, and children growing up to venerate him. Yes, and back of the house he would have a small garden, a place of meditation and repose, with goldfish in a tiny lakelet, and wind bells tinkling in the several trees, and there would be a high wall all around so that his meditation and repose should be undisturbed.

Well, he had worked out three of those five years. He was already a wealthy man (in his own country), through his earnings, and only two years more intervened between the cotton plantation on Tahiti and the meditation and repose that awaited him. But just now he was losing money because of the unfortunate accident of being present at the killing of Chung Ga. He had lain three weeks in prison, and for each day of those three weeks he had lost fifty cents. But now judgment would soon be given, and he would go back to work.

Ah Cho was twenty-two years old. He was happy and good-natured, and it was easy for him to smile. While his body was slim in the Asiatic way, his face was rotund. It was round, like the moon, and it irradiated a gentle complacence and a sweet kindliness of spirit that was unusual among his countrymen. Nor did his looks belie him. He never caused trouble, never took part in wrangling. He did not gamble. His soul was not harsh enough for the soul that must belong to a gambler. He was content with little things and simple pleasures. The hush of the quiet in the cool of the day after the blazing toil in the cotton field was to him an infinite satisfaction. He could sit for hours gazing at a solitary flower and philosophizing about the mysteries and riddles of being. A blue heron on a tiny crescent of sandy beach, a silvery splatter of flying fish, or a sunset of pearl and rose across the lagoon, could entrance him to all forgetfulness of the procession of wearisome days and of the heavy lash of Schemmer.

Schemmer, Karl Schemmer, was a brute, a brutish brute. But he earned his salary. He got the last particle of strength out of the five hundred slaves; for slaves they were until their term of years was up. Schemmer worked hard to extract the strength from those five hundred sweating bodies and to transmute it into bales of fluffy cotton ready for export. His dominant, iron-clad, primeval brutishness was what enabled him to effect the transmutation. Also, he was assisted by a thick leather belt, three inches wide and a yard in length, with which he always rode and which, on occasion, could come down on the naked back of a stooping coolie with a report like a pistol-shot. These reports were frequent when Schemmer rode down the furrowed field.

Once, at the beginning of the first year of contract labor, he had killed a coolie with a single blow of his fist. He had not exactly crushed the man's head like an egg-shell, but the blow had been sufficient to addle what was inside, and, after being sick for a week, the man had died. But the Chinese had not complained to the French devils that ruled over Tahiti. It was their own lookout. Schemmer was their problem. They must avoid his wrath as they avoided the venom of the centipedes that lurked in the grass or crept into the sleeping quarters on rainy nights. The Chinagos— such they were called by the indolent, brown-skinned is-land folk—saw to it that they did not displease Schemmer too greatly. This was equivalent to rendering up to him a full measure of efficient toil. That blow of Schemmer's fist had been worth thousands of dollars to the Company, and no trouble ever came of it to Schemmer.

The French, with no instinct for colonization, futile in their childish playgame of developing the resources of the island, were only too glad to see the English Company succeed. What matter of Schemmer and his redoubtable fist? The Chinago that died? Well, he was only a Chinago. Besides, he died of sunstroke, as the doctor's certificate at-tested. True, in all the history of Tahiti no one had ever died of sunstroke. But it was that, precisely that, which made the death of this Chinago unique. The doctor said as much in his report. He was very candid. Dividends must be paid, or else one more failure would be added to the long history of failure in Tahiti.

There was no understanding these white devils. Ah Cho pondered their inscrutableness as he sat in the court room waiting the judgment. There was no telling what went on at the back of their minds. He had seen a few of the white devils. They were all alike—the officers and sailors on the ship, the French officials, the several white men on the plantation, including Schemmer. Their minds all moved in mysterious ways there was no getting at. They grew angry without apparent cause, and their anger was always dan-gerous. They were like wild beasts at such times. They worried about little things, and on occasion could out-toil even a Chinago. They were not temperate as Chinagos were temperate; they were gluttons, eating prodigiously and drinking more prodigiously. A Chinago never knew when an act would please them or arouse a storm of wrath. A Chinago could never tell. What pleased one time, the very next time might provoke an outburst of anger. There was a curtain behind the eyes of the white devils that screened the backs of their minds from the Chinago's gaze. And then, on top of it all, was that terrible efficiency of the white devils, that ability to do things, to make things go, to work results, to bend to their wills all creeping, crawling things, and the powers of the very elements themselves. Yes, the white men were strange and wonderful, and they were devils. Look at Schemmer.

Ah Cho wondered why the judgment was so long in forming. Not a man on trial had laid hand on Chung Ga. Ah San alone had killed him. Ah San had done it, bending Chung Ga's head back with one hand by a grip of his queue, and with the other hand, from behind, reaching over and driving the knife into his body. Twice had he driven it in. There in the court room, with closed eyes, Ah Cho saw the killing acted over again—the squabble, the vile words bandied back and forth, the filth and insult flung upon venerable ancestors, the curses laid upon unbegotten generations, the leap of Ah San, the grip on the queue of Chung Ga, the knife that sank twice into his flesh, the bursting open of the door, the irruption of Schemmer, the dash for the door, the escape of Ah San, the flying belt of Schemmer that drove the rest into the corner, and the firing of the revolver as a signal that brought help to Schemmer. Ah Cho shivered as he lived it over. One blow of the belt had bruised his cheek, taking off some of the skin. Schemmer had pointed to the bruises when, on the witness-stand, he had identified Ah Cho. It was only just now that the marks had become no longer visible. That had been a blow. Half an inch nearer the centre and it would have taken out his eye. Then Ah Cho forgot the whole happening in a vision he caught of the garden of meditation and repose that would be his when he returned to his own land.

He sat with impassive face, while the magistrate rendered the judgment. Likewise were the faces of his four companions impassive. And they remained impassive when the interpreter explained that the five of them had been found guilty of the murder of Chung Ga, and that Ah Chow should have his head cut off, Ah Cho serve twenty years in prison in New Caledonia, Wong Li twelve years, and Ah Tong ten years. There was no use in getting excited about it. Even Ah Chow remained expressionless as a mummy, though it was his head that was to be cut off. The magistrate added a few words, and the interpreter explained that Ah Chow's face having been most severely bruised by Schemmer's strap had made his identification so positive that, since one man must die, he might as well be that man. Also, the fact that Ah Cho's face likewise had been severely bruised, conclusively proving his presence at the murder and his undoubted participation, had merited him the twenty years of penal servitude. And down to the ten years of Ah Tong, the proportioned reason for each sentence was explained. Let the Chinagos take the lesson to heart, the Court said finally, for they must learn that the law would be fulfilled in Tahiti though the heavens fell.

The five Chinagos were taken back to jail. They were not shocked nor grieved. The sentences being unexpected was quite what they were accustomed to in their dealings with the white devils. From them a Chinago rarely expected more than the unexpected. The heavy punishment for a crime they had not committed was no stranger than the countless strange things that white devils did. In the weeks that followed, Ah Cho often contemplated Ah Chow with mild curiosity. His head was to be cut off by the guillotine that was being erected on the plantation. For him there would be no declining years, no gardens of tranquillity. Ah Cho philosophized and speculated about life and death. As for himself, he was not perturbed. Twenty years were merely twenty years. By that much was his garden removed from him—that was all. He was young, and the patience of Asia was in his bones. he could wait those twenty years, and by that time the heats of his blood would be assuaged and he would be better fitted for that garden of calm delight. He thought of a name for it; he would call it The Garden of the Morning Calm. He was made happy all day by the thought, and he was inspired to devise a moral maxim on the virtue of patience, which maxim proved a great comfort, especially to Wong Li and Ah Tong. Ah Chow, however, did not care for the maxim. His head was to be separated from his body in so short a time that he had no need for patience to wait for that event. He smoked well, ate well, slept well, and did not worry about the slow passage of time.

Cruchot was a gendarme. He had seen twenty years of service in the colonies, from Nigeria and Senegal to the South Seas, and those twenty years had not perceptibly brightened his dull mind. He was as slow-witted and stupid as in his peasant days in the south of France. He knew discipline and fear of authority, and from God down to the sergeant of gendarmes the only difference to him was the measure of slavish obedience which he rendered. In point of fact, the sergeant bulked bigger in his mind than God, except on Sundays when God's mouthpieces had their say. God was usually very remote, while the sergeant was ordinarily very close at hand.

Cruchot it was who received the order from the Chief Justice to the jailer commanding that functionary to deliver over to Cruchot the person of Ah Chow. Now, it happened that the Chief Justice had given a dinner the night before to the captain and officers of the French man-of-war. His hand was shaking when he wrote out the order, and his eyes were aching so dreadfully that he did not read over the order. It was only a Chinago's life he was signing away, anyway. So he did not notice that he had omitted the final letter in Ah Chow's name. The order read "Ah Cho," and, when Cruchot presented the order, the jailer turned over to him the person of Ah Cho. Cruchot took that person beside him on the seat of a wagon, behind two mules, and drove away.

Ah Cho was glad to be out in the sunshine. He sat beside the gendarme and beamed. He beamed more ardently than ever when he noted the mules headed south toward Atimaono. Undoubtedly Schemmer had sent for him to be brought back. Schemmer wanted him to work. Very well, he would work well. Schemmer would never have cause to complain. It was a hot day. There had been a stoppage of the trades. The mules sweated, Cruchot sweated, and Ah Cho sweated. But it was Ah Cho that bore the heat with the least concern. He had toiled three years under that sun on the plantation. He beamed and beamed with such genial good nature that even Cruchot's heavy mind was stirred to wonderment.

"You are very funny," he said at last.

Ah Cho nodded and beamed more ardently. Unlike the magistrate, Cruchot spoke to him in the Kanaka tongue, and this, like all Chinagos and all foreign devils, Ah Cho understood.

"You laugh too much," Cruchot chided. "One's heart should be full of tears on a day like this."

"I am glad to get out of the jail."

"Is that all?" The gendarme shrugged his shoulders.

"Is it not enough?" was the retort.

"Then you are not glad to have your head cut off?"

Ah Cho looked at him in abrupt perplexity and said:—

"Why, I am going back to Atimaono to work on the plantation for Schemmer. Are you not taking me to Atimaono?"

Cruchot stroked his long mustaches reflectively. "Well well," he said finally, with a flick of the whip at the off mule, "so you don't know?"

"Know what?" Ah Cho was beginning to feel a vague alarm. "Won't Schemmer let me work for him any more?"

"Not after to-day." Cruchot laughed heartily. It was a good joke. "You see, you won't be able to work after to-day. A man with his head off can't work, eh?" He, poked the Chinago in the ribs, and chuckled.

Ah Cho maintained silence while the mules trotted a hot mile. Then he spoke: "Is Schemmer going to cut off my head?"

Cruchot grinned as he nodded.

"It is a mistake," said Ah Cho, gravely. "I am not the Chinago that is to have his head cut off. I am Ah Cho. The honorable judge has determined that I am to stop twenty years in New Caledonia."

The gendarme laughed. It was a good joke, this funny Chinago trying to cheat the guillotine. The mules trotted through a cocoanut grove and for a half mile beside the sparkling sea before Ah Cho spoke again.

"I tell you I am not Ah Chow. The honorable judge did not say that my head was to go off."

"Don't be afraid," said Cruchot, with the philanthropic intention of making it easier for his prisoner. "It is not difficult to die that way." He snapped his fingers. "It is quick—like that. It is not like hanging on the end of a rope and kicking and making faces for five minutes. It is like killing a chicken with a hatchet. You cut its head off, that is all. And it is the same with a man. Pouf!—it is over. It doesn't hurt. You don't even think it hurts. You don't think. Your head is gone, so you cannot think. It is very good. That is the way I want to die—quick, ah, quick. You are lucky to die that way. You might get the leprosy and fall to pieces slowly, a finger at a time, and now and again a thumb, also the toes. I knew a man who was burned by hot water. It took him two days to die. You could hear him yelling a kilometer away. But you? Ah! so easy! Chck!—the knife cuts your neck like that. It is finished. The knife may even tickle. Who can say? Nobody who died that way ever came back to say."

He considered this last an excruciating joke, and permitted himself to be convulsed with laughter for half a minute. Part of his mirth was assumed, but he considered it his humane duty to cheer up the Chinago.

"But I tell you I am Ah Cho," the other persisted. "I don't want my head cut off."

Cruchot scowled. The Chinago was carrying the foolishness too far.

"I am not Ah Chow——" Ah Cho began.

"That will do," the gendarme interrupted. He puffed up his cheeks and strove to appear fierce.

"I tell you I am not——" Ah Cho began again.

"Shut up!" bawled Cruchot.

After that they rode along in silence. It was twenty miles from Papeete to Atimaono, and over half the distance was covered by the time the Chinago again ventured into speech.

"I saw you in the court room, when the honorable judge sought after our guilt," he began. "Very good. And do you remember that Ah Chow, whose head is to be cut off——do you remember that he——Ah Chow——was a tall man? Look at me."

He stood up suddenly, and Cruchot saw that he was a short man. And just as suddenly Cruchot caught a glimpse of a memory picture of Ah Chow, and in that picture Ah Chow was tall. To the gendarme all Chinagos looked alike. One face was like another. But between tallness and shortness he could differentiate, and he knew that he had the wrong man beside him on the seat. He pulled up the mules abruptly, so that the pole shot ahead of them, elevating their collars.

"You see, it was a mistake," said Ah Cho, smiling pleasantly.

But Cruchot was thinking. Already he regretted that he had stopped the wagon. He was unaware of the error of the Chief Justice, and he had no way of working it out; but he did know that he had been given this Chinago to take to Atimaono and that it was his duty to take him to Atimaono. What if he was the wrong man and they cut his head off? It was only a Chinago when all was said, and what was a Chinago, anyway? Besides, it might not be a mistake. He did not know what went on in the minds of his superiors. They knew their business best. Who was he to do their thinking for them? Once, in the long ago, he had attempted to think for them, and the sergeant had said: "Cruchot, you are a fool! The quicker you know that, the better you will get on. You are not to think; you are to obey and leave thinking to your betters." He smarted under the recollection. Also, if he turned back to Papeete, he would delay the execution at Atimaono, and if he were wrong in turning back, he would get a reprimand from the sergeant who was waiting for the prisoner. And, furthermore, he would get a reprimand from Papeete as well.

He touched the mules with the whip and drove on. He looked at his watch. He would be half an hour late as it was, and the sergeant was bound to be angry. He put the mules into a faster trot. The more Ah Cho persisted in explaining the mistake, the more stubborn Cruchot became. The knowledge that he had the wrong man did not make his temper better. The knowledge that it was through no mistake of his confirmed him in the belief that the wrong he was doing was the right. And, rather than incur the displeasure of the sergeant, he would willingly have assisted a dozen wrong Chinagos to their doom.

As for Ah Cho, after the gendarme had struck him over the head with the butt of the whip and commanded him in a loud voice to shut up, there remained nothing for him to do but to shut up. The long ride continued in silence. Ah Cho pondered the strange ways of the foreign devils. There was no explaining them. What they were doing with him was of a piece with everything they did. First they found guilty five innocent men, and next they cut off the head of the man that even they, in their benighted ignorance, had deemed meritorious of no more than twenty years' imprisonment. And there was nothing he could do. He could only sit idly and take what these lords of life measured out to him. Once, he got in a panic, and the sweat upon his body turned cold; but he fought his way out of it. He endeavored to resign himself to his fate by remembering and repeating certain passages from the "Yin Chih Wen" ("The Tract of the Quiet Way"); but, instead, he kept seeing his dream-garden of meditation and repose. This bothered him, until he abandoned himself to the dream and sat in his garden listening to the tinkling of the wind-bells in the several trees. And lo! sitting thus, in the dream, he was able to remember and repeat the passages from "The Tract of the Quiet Way."

So the time passed nicely until Atimaono was reached and the mules trotted up to the foot of the scaffold, in the shade of which stood the impatient sergeant. Ah Cho was hurried up the ladder of the scaffold. Beneath him on one side he saw assembled all the coolies of the plantation. Schemmer had decided that the event would be a good object-lesson, and so had called in the coolies from the fields and compelled them to be present. As they caught sight of Ah Cho they babbled among themselves in low voices. They saw the mistake; but they kept it to themselves. The inexplicable white devils had doubtlessly changed their minds. Instead of taking the life of one innocent man, they were taking the life of another innocent man. Ah Chow or Ah Cho—what did it matter which? They could never understand the white dogs any more than could the white dogs understand them. Ah Cho was going to have his head cut off, but they, when their two remaining years of servitude were up, were going back to China.

Schemmer had made the guillotine himself. He was a handy man, and though he had never seen a guillotine, the French officials had explained the principle to him. It was on his suggestion that they had ordered the execution to take place at Atimaono instead of at Papeete. The scene of the crime, Schemmer had argued, was the best possible place for the punishment, and, in addition, it would have a salutary influence upon the half-thousand Chinagos on the plantation. Schemmer had also volunteered to act as executioner, and in that capacity he was now on the scaffold, experimenting with the instrument he had made. A banana tree, of the size and consistency of a man's neck, lay under the guillotine. Ah Cho watched with fascinated eyes. The German, turning a small crank, hoisted the blade to the top of the little derrick he had rigged. A jerk on a stout piece of cord loosed the blade and it dropped with a flash, neatly severing the banana trunk.

"How does it work?" The sergeant, coming out on top the scaffold, had asked the question.

"Beautifully," was Schemmer's exultant answer. "Let me show you."

Again he turned the crank that hoisted the blade, jerked the cord, and sent the blade crashing down on the soft tree. But this time it went no more than two-thirds of the way through.

The sergeant scowled. "That will not serve," he said.

Schemmer wiped the sweat from his forehead. "What it needs is more weight," he announced. Walking up to the edge of the scaffold, he called his orders to the blacksmith for a twenty-five-pound piece of iron. As he stooped over to attach the iron to the broad top of the blade, Ah Cho glanced at the sergeant and saw his opportunity.

"The honorable judge said that Ah Chow was to have his head cut off," he began.

The sergeant nodded impatiently. He was thinking of the fifteen-mile ride before him that afternoon, to the windward side of the island, and of Berthe, the pretty half-caste daughter of Lafière, the pearl-trader, who was waiting for him at the end of it.

"Well, I am not Ah Chow. I am Ah Cho. The honorable jailer has made a mistake. Ah Chow is a tall man, and you see I am short."

The sergeant looked at him hastily and saw the mistake. "Schemmer!" he called, imperatively. "Come here."

The German grunted, but remained bent over his task till the chunk of iron was lashed to his satisfaction. "Is your Chinago ready?" he demanded.

"Look at him," was the answer. "Is he the Chinago?"

Schemmer was surprised. He swore tersely for a few seconds, and looked regretfully across at the thing he had made with his own hands and which he was eager to see work. "Look here," he said finally, "we can't postpone this affair. I've lost three hours' work already out of those five hundred Chinagos. I can't afford to lose it all over again for the right man. Let's put the performance through just the same. It is only a Chinago."

The sergeant remembered the long ride before him, and the pearl-trader's daughter, and debated with himself.

"They will blame it on Cruchot—if it is discovered," the German urged. "But there's little chance of its being discovered. Ah Chow won't give it away, at any rate."

"The blame won't lie with Cruchot, anyway," the sergeant said. "It must have been the jailer's mistake."

"Then let's go on with it. They can't blame us. Who can tell one Chinago from another? We can say that we merely carried out the instructions with the Chinago that was turned over to us. Besides, I really can't take all those coolies a second time away from their labor."

They spoke in French, and Ah Cho, who did not understand a word of it, nevertheless knew that they were determining his destiny. He knew, also, that the decision rested with the sergeant, and he hung upon the official's lips.

"All right," announced the sergeant. "Go ahead with it. He is only a Chinago."

"I'm going to try it once more, just to make sure." Schemmer moved the banana trunk forward under the knife, which he had hoisted to the top of the derrick.

Ah Cho tried to remember maxims from "The Tract of the Quiet Way." "Live in concord," came to him; but it was not applicable. He was not going to live. He was about to die. No, that would not do. "Forgive malice"— yes, but there was no malice to forgive. Schemmer and the rest were doing this thing without malice. It was to them merely a piece of work that had to be done, just as clearing the jungle, ditching the water, and planting cotton were pieces of work that had to be done. Schemmer jerked the cord, and Ah Cho forgot "The Tract of the Quiet Way." The knife shot down with a thud, making a clean slice of the tree.

"Beautiful!" exclaimed the sergeant, pausing in the act of lighting a cigarette. "Beautiful, my friend."

Schemmer was pleased at the praise.

"Come on, Ah Chow," he said, in the Tahitian tongue.

"But I am not Ah Chow—" Ah Cho began.

"Shut up!" was the answer. "If you open your mouth again, I'll break your head."

The overseer threatened him with a clenched fist, and he remained silent. What was the good of protesting? Those foreign devils always had their way. He allowed himself to be lashed to the vertical board that was the size of his body. Schemmer drew the buckles tight—so tight that the straps cut into his flesh and hurt. But he did not complain. The hurt would not last long. He felt the board tilting over in the air toward the horizontal, and closed his eyes. And in that moment he caught a last glimpse of his garden of meditation and repose. It seemed to him that he sat in the garden. A cool wind was blowing, and the bells in the several trees were tinkling softly. Also, birds were making sleepy noises, and from beyond the high wall came the subdued sound of village life.

Then he was aware that the board had come to rest, and from muscular pressures and tensions he knew that he was lying on his back. He opened his eyes. Straight above him he saw the suspended knife blazing in the sunshine. He saw the weight which had been added, and noted that one of Schemmer's knots had slipped. Then he heard the sergeant's voice in sharp command. Ah Cho closed his eyes hastily. He did not want to see the knife descend. But he felt it—for one great fleeting instant. And in that instant he remembered Cruchot and what Cruchot had said. But Cruchot was wrong. The knife did not tickle. That much he knew before he ceased to know.

Told in the Drooling Ward

Me? I'm not a drooler. I'm the assistant. I don't know what Miss Jones or Miss Kelsey could do without me. There are fifty-five low-grade droolers in this ward, and how could they ever all be fed if I wasn't around? I like to feed droolers. They don't make trouble. They can't. Something's wrong with most of their legs and arms, and they can't talk. They're very low grade. I can walk, and talk, and do things. You must be careful with the droolers and not feed them too fast. Then they choke. Miss Jones says I'm an expert. When a new nurse comes I show her how to do it. It's funny watching a new nurse try to feed them. She goes at it so slow and careful that supper time would be around before she finished shoving down their breakfast. Then I show her, because I'm an expert. Dr. Dalrymple says I am, and he ought to know. A drooler can eat twice as fast if you know how to make him.

My name's Tom. I'm twenty-eight years old. Everybody knows me in the institution. This is an institution, you know. It belongs to the State of California and is run by politics. I know. I've been here a long time. Everybody trusts me. I run errands all over the place, when I'm not busy with the droolers. I like droolers. It makes me think how lucky I am that I ain't a drooler.

I like it here in the Home. I don't like the outside. I know. I've been around a bit, and run away, and adopted. Me for the Home, and for the drooling ward best of all. I don't look like a drooler, do I? You can tell the difference soon as you look at me. I'm an assistant, expert assistant. That's going some for a feeb. Feeb? Oh, that feeble-minded. I thought you knew. We're all feebs in here.

But I'm a high-grade feeb. Dr. Dalrymple says I'm too smart to be in the Home, but I never let on. It's a pretty good place. And I don't throw fits like lots of the feebs. You see that house up there through the trees. The high-grade epilecs all live in it by themselves. They're stuck up because they ain't just ordinary feebs. They call it the club house, and they say they're just as good as anybody outside, only they're sick. I don't like them much. They laugh at me, when they ain't busy throwing fits. But I don't care. I never have to be scared about falling down and busting my head. Sometimes they run around in circles trying to find a place to sit down quick, only they don't. Low-grade epilecs are disgusting, and high-grade epilecs put on airs. I'm glad I ain't an epilec. There ain't anything to them. They just talk big, that's all.

Miss Kelsey says I talk too much. But I talk sense, and that's more than the other feebs do. Dr. Dalrymple says I have the gift of language. I know it. You ought to hear me talk when I'm by myself, or when I've got a drooler to listen. Sometimes I think I'd like to be a politician, only it's too much trouble. They're all great talkers; that's how they hold their jobs.

Nobody's crazy in this institution. They're just feeble in their minds. Let me tell you something funny. There's about a dozen high-grade girls that set the tables in the big dining room. Sometimes when they're done ahead of time, they all sit down in chairs in a circle and talk. I sneak up to the door and listen, and I nearly die to keep from laughing. Do you want to know what they talk? It's like this. They don't say a word for a long time. And then one says, "Thank God I'm not feeble-minded." And all the rest nod their heads and look pleased. And then nobody says anything for a time. After which the next girl in the circle says, "Thank God I'm not feeble-minded," and they nod their heads all over again. And it goes on around the circle, and they never say anything else. Now they're real feebs, ain't they? I leave it to you. I'm not that kind of a feeb, thank God.

Sometimes I don't think I'm a feeb at all. I play in the band and read music. We're all supposed to be feebs in the band except the leader. He's crazy. We know it, but we never talk about it except amongst ourselves. His job is politics, too, and we don't want him to lose it. I play the drum. They can't get along without me in this institution. I was sick once, so I know. It's a wonder the drooler ward didn't break down while I was in hospital.

I could get out of here if I wanted to. I'm not so feeble as some might think. But I don't let on. I have too good a time. Besides, everything would run down if I went away. I'm afraid some time they'll find out I'm not a feeb and send me out into the world to earn my own living. I know the world, and I don't like it. The Home is fine enough for me.

You see how I grin sometimes. I can't help that. But I can put it on a lot. I'm not bad, though. I look at myself in the glass. My mouth is funny, I know that, and it lops down, and my teeth are bad. You can tell a feeb anywhere by looking at his mouth and teeth. But that doesn't prove I'm a feeb. It's just because I'm lucky that I look like one.

I know a lot. If I told you all I know, you'd be surprised. But when I don't want to know, or when they want me to do something I don't want to do, I just let my mouth lop down and laugh and make foolish noises. I watch the foolish noises made by the low-grades, and I can fool anybody. And I know a lot of foolish noises. Miss Kelsey called me a fool the other day. She was very angry, and that was where I fooled her.

Miss Kelsey asked me once why I don't write a book about feebs. I was telling her what was the matter with little Albert. He's a drooler, you know, and I can always tell the way he twists his left eye what's the matter with him. So I was explaining it to Miss Kelsey, and, because she didn't know, it made her mad. But some day, mebbe, I'll write that book. Only it's so much trouble. Besides, I'd sooner talk.

Do you know what a micro is? It's the kind with the little heads no bigger than your fist. They're usually droolers, and they live a long time. The hydros don't drool. They have the big heads, and they're smarter. But they never grow up. They always die. I never look at one without thinking he's going to die. Sometimes, when I'm feeling lazy, or the nurse is mad at me, I wish I was a drooler with nothing to do and somebody to feed me. But I guess I'd sooner talk and be what I am.

Only yesterday Doctor Dalrymple said to me, "Tom," he said, "I just don't know what I'd do without you." And he ought to know, seeing as he's had the bossing of a thousand feebs for going on two years. Dr. Whatcomb was before him. They get appointed, you know. It's politics. I've seen a whole lot of doctors here in my time. I was here before any of them. I've been in this institution twenty-five years. No, I've got no complaints. The institution couldn't be run better.

It's a snap to be a high-grade feeb. Just look at Doctor Dalrymple. He has troubles. He holds his job by politics. You bet we high-graders talk politics. We know all about it, and it's bad. An institution like this oughtn't to be run on politics. Look at Doctor Dalrymple. He's been here two years and learned a lot. Then politics will come along and throw him out and send a new doctor who don't know anything about feebs.

I've been acquainted with just thousands of nurses in my time. Some of them are nice. But they come and go.

Most of the women get married. Sometimes I think I'd
like to get married. I spoke to Dr. Whatcomb about it
once, but he told me he was very sorry, because feebs ain't
allowed to get married. I've been in love. She was a nurse.
I won't tell you her name. She had blue eyes, and yellow
hair, and a kind voice, and she liked me. She told me so.
And she always told me to be a good boy. And I was, too,
until afterward, and then I ran away. You see, she went off
and got married, and she didn't tell me about it.

I guess being married ain't what it's cracked up to be.
Dr. Anglin and his wife used to fight. I've seen them. And
once I heard her call him a feeb. Now nobody has a right
to call anybody a feeb that ain't. Dr. Anglin got awful mad
when she called him that. But he didn't last long. Politics
drove him out, and Doctor Mandeville came. He didn't
have a wife. I heard him talking one time with the engineer. The engineer and his wife fought like cats and dogs,
and that day Doctor Mandeville told him he was damn
glad he wasn't tied to no petticoats. A petticoat is a skirt.
I knew what he meant, if I was a feeb. But I never let on.
You hear lots when you don't let on.

I've seen a lot in my time. Once I was adopted, and
went away on the railroad over forty miles to live with a
man named Peter Bopp and his wife. They had a ranch.
Doctor Anglin said I was strong and bright, and I said I
was, too. That was because I wanted to be adopted. And
Peter Bopp said he'd give me a good home, and the law-
yers fixed up the papers.

But I soon made up my mind that a ranch was no place
for me. Mrs. Bopp was scared to death of me and wouldn't
let me sleep in the house. They fixed up the woodshed and
made me sleep there. I had to get up at four o'clock and
feed the horses, and milk cows, and carry the milk to the
neighbours. They called it chores, but it kept me going all
day. I chopped wood, and cleaned chicken houses, and
weeded vegetables, and did most everything on the place.
I never had any fun. I hadn't no time.

Let me tell you one thing. I'd sooner feed mush and

milk to feebs than milk cows with the frost on the ground. Mrs. Bopp was scared to let me play with her children. And I was scared, too. They used to make faces at me when nobody was looking, and call me "Looney." Everybody called me Looney Tom. And the other boys in the neighbourhood threw rocks at me. You never see anything like that in the Home here. The feebs are better behaved.

Mrs. Bopp used to pinch me and pull my hair when she thought I was too slow, and I only made foolish noises and went slower. She said I'd be the death of her some day. I left the boards off the old well in the pasture, and the pretty new calf fell in and got drowned. Then Peter Bopp said he was going to give me a licking. He did, too. He took a strap halter and went at me. It was awful. I'd never had a licking in my life. They don't do such things in the Home, which is why I say the Home is the place for me.

I know the law, and I knew he had no right to lick me with a strap halter. That was being cruel. I didn't say anything. I just waited, which shows you what kind of feeb I am. I waited a long time, and got slower, and made more foolish noises; but he wouldn't send me back to the Home, which was what I wanted. But one day, it was the first of the month, Mrs. Brown gave me three dollars, which was for her milk bill with Peter Bopp. That was in the morning. When I brought the milk in the evening I was to bring back the receipt. But I didn't. I just walked down to the station, bought a ticket like any one, and rode on the train back to the Home. That's the kind of feeb I am.

Doctor Anglin was gone then, and Doctor Mandeville had his place. I walked right into his office. He didn't know me. "Hello," he said, "this ain't visiting day." "I ain't a visitor," I said. "I'm Tom. I belong here." Then he whistled and showed he was surprised. I told him all about it, and showed him the marks of the strap halter, and he got madder and madder all the time and said he'd attend to Mr. Peter Bopp's case.

And mebbe you think some of them little droolers weren't glad to see me.

I walked right into the ward. There was a new nurse feeding little Albert. "Hold on," I said. "That ain't the way. Don't you see how he's twisting that left eye? Let me show you." Mebbe she thought I was a new doctor, for she just gave me the spoon, and I guess I filled little Albert up with the most comfortable meal he'd had since I went away. Droolers ain't bad when you understand them. I heard Miss Jones tell Miss Kelsey once that I had an amazing gift in handling droolers.

Some day, mebbe, I'm going to talk with Doctor Dalrymple and get him to give me a declaration that I ain't a feeb. Then I'll get him to make me a real assistant in the drooling ward, with forty dollars a month and my board. And then I'll marry Miss Jones and live right on here. And if she won't have me, I'll marry Miss Kelsey or some other nurse. There's lots of them that want to get married. And I won't care if my wife gets mad and calls me a feeb. What's the good? And I guess when one's learned to put up with droolers a wife won't be much worse.

I didn't tell you about when I ran away. I hadn't no idea of such a thing, and it was Charley and Joe who put me up to it. They're high-grade epilecs, you know. I'd been up to Doctor Wilson's office with a message, and was going back to the drooling ward, when I saw Charley and Joe hiding around the corner of the gymnasium and making motions to me. I went over to them.

"Hello," Joe said. "How's droolers?"

"Fine," I said. "Had any fits lately?"

That made them mad, and I was going on, when Joe said, "We're running away. Come on."

"What for?" I said.

"We're going up over the top of the mountain," Joe said.

"And find a gold mine," said Charley. "We don't have fits any more. We're cured."

"All right," I said. And we sneaked around back of the gymnasium and in among the trees. Mebbe we walked along about ten minutes, when I stopped.

"What's the matter?" said Joe.

"Wait," I said. "I got to go back."

"What for?" said Joe.

And I said, "To get little Albert."

And they said I couldn't, and got mad. But I didn't care. I knew they'd wait. You see, I've been here twenty-five years, and I know the back trails that lead up the mountain, and Charley and Joe didn't know those trails. That's why they wanted me to come.

.So I went back and got little Albert. He can't walk, or talk, or do anything except drool, and I had to carry him in my arms. We went on past the last hayfield, which was as far as I'd ever gone. Then the woods and brush got so thick, and me not finding any more trail, we followed the cow-path down to a big creek and crawled through the fence which showed where the Home land stopped.

We climbed up the big hill on the other side of the creek. It was all big trees, and no brush, but it was so steep and slippery with dead leaves we could hardly walk. By and by we came to a real bad place. It was forty feet across, and if you slipped you'd fall a thousand feet, or mebbe a hundred. Anyway, you wouldn't fall—just slide. I went across first, carrying little Albert. Joe came next. But Charley got scared right in the middle and sat down.

"I'm going to have a fit," he said.

"No, you're not," said Joe. "Because if you was you wouldn't 'a' sat down. You take all your fits standing."

"This is a different kind of a fit," said Charley, beginning to cry.

He shook and shook, but just because he wanted to he couldn't scare up the least kind of a fit.

Joe got mad and used awful language. But that didn't help none. So I talked soft and kind to Charley. That's the way to handle feebs. If you get mad, they get worse. I know. I'm that way myself. That's why I was almost the death of Mrs. Bopp. She got mad.

It was getting along in the afternoon, and I knew we had to be on our way, so I said to Joe:

"Here, stop your cussing and hold Albert. I'll go back and get him."

And I did, too; but he was so scared and dizzy he crawled along on hands and knees while I helped him. When I got him across and took Albert back in my arms, I heard somebody laugh and looked down. And there was a man and woman on horseback looking up at us. He had a gun on his saddle, and it was her who was laughing.

"Who in hell's that?" said Joe, getting scared. "Somebody to catch us?"

"Shut up your cussing," I said to him. "That is the man who owns this ranch and writes books."

"How do you do, Mr. Endicott," I said down to him.

"Hello," he said. "What are you doing here?"

"We're running away," I said.

And he said, "Good luck. But be sure and get back before dark."

"But this is a real running away," I said.

And then both he and his wife laughed.

"All right," he said. "Good luck just the same. But watch out the bears and mountain lions don't get you when it gets dark."

Then they rode away laughing, pleasant like; but I wished he hadn't said that about the bears and mountain lions.

After we got around the hill, I found a trail, and we went much faster. Charley didn't have any more signs of fits, and began laughing and talking about gold mines. The trouble was with little Albert. He was almost as big as me. You see, all the time I'd been calling him little Albert, he'd been growing up. He was so heavy I couldn't keep up with Joe and Charley. I was all out of breath. So I told them they'd have to take turns in carrying him, which they said they wouldn't. Then I said I'd leave them and they'd get lost, and the mountain lions and bears would eat them. Charley looked like he was going to have a fit right there, and Joe said, "Give him to me." And after that we carried him in turn.

We kept right on up that mountain. I don't think there was any gold mine, but we might 'a' got to the top and found it, if we hadn't lost the trail, and if it hadn't got dark, and if little Albert hadn't tired us all out carrying him. Lots of feebs are scared of the dark, and Joe said he was going to have a fit right there. Only he didn't. I never saw such an unlucky boy. He never could throw a fit when he wanted to. Some of the feebs can throw fits as quick as a wink.

By and by it got real black, and we were hungry, and we didn't have no fire. You see, they don't let feebs carry matches, and all we could do was just shiver. And we'd never thought about being hungry. You see, feebs always have their food ready for them, and that's why it's better to be a feeb than earning your living in the world.

And worse than everything was the quiet. There was only one thing worse, and it was the noises. There was all kinds of noises every once in a while, with quiet spells in between. I reckon they were rabbits, but they made noises in the brush like wild animals—you know, rustle rustle, thump, bump, crackle crackle, just like that. First Charley got a fit, a real one, and Joe threw a terrible one. I don't mind fits in the Home with everybody around. But out in the woods on a dark night is different. You listen to me, and never go hunting gold mines with epilecs, even if they are high-grade.

I never had such an awful night. When Joe and Charley weren't throwing fits they were making believe, and in the darkness the shivers from the cold which I couldn't see seemed like fits, too. And I shivered so hard I thought I was getting fits myself. And little Albert, with nothing to eat, just drooled and drooled. I never seen him as bad as that before. Why, he twisted that left eye of his until it ought to have dropped out. I couldn't see it, but I could tell from the movements he made. And Joe just lay and cussed and cussed, and Charley cried and wished he was back in the Home.

We didn't die, and next morning we went right back the way we'd come. And little Albert got awful heavy. Doctor Wilson was mad as could be, and said I was the worst feeb in the institution, along with Joe and Charley. But Miss Striker, who was a nurse in the drooling ward then, just put her arms around me and cried, she was that happy I'd got back. I thought right there that mebbe I'd marry her. But only a month afterward she got married to the plumber that came up from the city to fix the gutter-pipes of the new hospital. And little Albert never twisted his eye for two days, it was that tired.

Next time I run away I'm going right over that mountain. But I ain't going to take epilecs along. They ain't never cured, and when they get scared or excited they throw fits to beat the band. But I'll take little Albert. Somehow I can't get along without him. And anyway, I ain't going to run away. The drooling ward's a better snap than gold mines, and I hear there's a new nurse coming. Beside, little Albert's bigger than I am now, and I could never carry him over a mountain. And he's growing bigger every day. It's astonishing.

The Mexican

Nobody knew his history—they of the Junta least of all. He was their "little mystery," their "big patriot," and in his way he worked as hard for the coming Mexican Revolution as did they. They were tardy in recognizing this, for not one of the Junta liked him. The day he first drifted into their crowded, busy rooms, they all suspected him of being a spy—one of the bought tools of the Diaz secret service. Too many of the comrades were in civil and military prisons scattered over the United States, and others of them, in irons, were even then being taken across the border to be lined up against adobe walls and shot.

At the first sight the boy did not impress them favorably. Boy he was, not more than eighteen and not over large for his years. He announced that he was Felipe Rivera, and that it was his wish to work for the Revolution. That was all—not a wasted word, no further explanation. He stood waiting. There was no smile on his lips, no geniality in his eyes. Big dashing Paulino Vera felt an inward shudder. Here was something forbidding, terrible, inscrutable. There was something venomous and snakelike in the boy's black eyes. They burned like cold fire, as with a vast, concentrated bitterness. He flashed them from the faces of the conspirators to the typewriter which little Mrs. Sethby was industriously operating. His eyes rested on hers but an instant—she had chanced to look up—and she, too, sensed the nameless something that made her pause. She was compelled to read back in order to regain the swing of the letter she was writing.

Paulino Vera looked questioningly at Arrellano and Ramos, and questioningly they looked back and to each other. The indecision of doubt brooded in their eyes. This slender boy was the Unknown, vested with all the menace of the Unknown. He was unrecognizable, something quite beyond the ken of honest, ordinary revolutionists whose fiercest hatred for Diaz and his tyranny after all was only that of honest and ordinary patriots. Here was something else, they knew not what. But Vera, always the most impulsive, the quickest to act, stepped into the breach.

"Very well," he said coldly. "You say you want to work for the Revolution. Take off your coat. Hang it over there. I will show you—come—where are the buckets and cloths. The floor is dirty. You will begin by scrubbing it, and by scrubbing the floors of the other rooms. The spittoons need to be cleaned. Then there are the windows."

"Is it for the Revolution?" the boy asked.

"It is for the Revolution," Vera answered.

Rivera looked cold suspicion at all of them, then proceeded to take off his coat.

"It is well," he said.

And nothing more. Day after day he came to his work—sweeping, scrubbing, cleaning. He emptied the ashes from the stoves, brought up the coal and kindling, and lighted the fires before the most energetic one of them was at his desk.

"Can I sleep here?" he asked once.

Ah, ha! So that was it—the hand of Diaz showing through! To sleep in the rooms of the Junta meant access to their secrets, to the lists of names, to the addresses of comrades down on Mexican soil. The request was denied, and Rivera never spoke of it again. He slept they knew not where, and ate they knew not where nor how. Once, Arrellano offered him a couple of dollars. Rivera declined the money with a shake of the head. When Vera joined in and tried to press it upon him, he said:

"I am working for the Revolution."

It takes money to raise a modern revolution, and always the Junta was pressed. The members starved and toiled, and the longest day was none too long, and yet there were times when it appeared as if the Revolution stood or fell on no more than the matter of a few dollars. Once, the first time, when the rent of the house was two months behind and the landlord was threatening dispossession, it was Felipe Rivera, the scrub-boy in the poor, cheap clothes, worn and threadbare, who laid sixty dollars in gold on May Sethby's desk. There were other times. Three hundred letters, clicked out on the busy typewriters (appeals for assistance, for sanctions from the organized labor groups, requests for square news deals to the editors of newspapers, protests against the high-handed treatment of revolutionists by the United States courts), lay unmailed, awaiting postage. Vera's watch had disappeared—the old-fashioned gold repeater that had been his father's. Like-wise had gone the plain gold band from May Sethby's third finger. Things were desperate. Ramos and Arrellano pulled their long mustaches in despair. The letters must go off, and the Post Office allowed no credit to purchasers of stamps. Then it was that Rivera put on his hat and went out. When he came back he laid a thousand two-cent stamps on May Sethby's desk.

"I wonder if it is the cursed gold of Diaz?" said Vera to the comrades.

They elevated their brows and could not decide. And Felipe Rivera, the scrubber for the Revolution, continued, as occasion arose, to lay down gold and silver for the Junta's use.

And still they could not bring themselves to like him. They did not know him. His ways were not theirs. He gave no confidences. He repelled all probing. Youth that he was, they could never nerve themselves to dare to question him.

"A great and lonely spirit, perhaps, I do not know. I do not know," Arrellano said helplessly.

"He is not human," said Ramos.

"His soul has been seared," said May Sethby. "Light and laughter have been burned out of him. He is like one dead, and yet he is fearfully alive."

"He has been through hell," said Vera. "No man could look like that who has not been through hell—and he is only a boy."

Yet they could not like him. He never talked, never inquired, never suggested. He would stand listening, expressionless, a thing dead, save for his eyes, coldly burning, while their talk of the Revolution ran high and warm. From face to face and speaker to speaker his eyes would turn, boring like gimlets of incandescent ice, disconcerting and perturbing.

"He is no spy," Vera confided to May Sethby. "He is a patriot—mark me, the greatest patriot of us all. I know it, I feel it, here in my heart and head I feel it. But him I know not at all."

"He has a bad temper," said May Sethby.

"I know," said Vera, with a shudder. "He has looked at me with those eyes of his. They do not love; they threaten; they are savage as a wild tiger's. I know, if I should prove unfaithful to the Cause, that he would kill me. He has no heart. He is pitiless as steel, keen and cold as frost. He is like moonshine in a winter night when a man freezes to death on some lonely mountain top. I am not afraid of Diaz and all his killers; but this boy, of him am I afraid. I tell you true. I am afraid. He is the breath of death."

Yet Vera it was who persuaded the others to give the first trust to Rivera. The line of communication between Los Angeles and Lower California had broken down.

Three of the comrades had dug their own graves and been shot into them. Two more were United States prisoners in Los Angeles. Juan Alvarado, the Federal commander, was a monster. All their plans did he checkmate. They could no longer gain access to the active revolutionists, and the incipient ones, in Lower California.

Young Rivera was given his instructions and dispatched south. When he returned, the line of communication was reëstablished, and Juan Alvarado was dead. He had been found in bed, a knife hilt-deep in his breast. This had exceeded Rivera's instructions, but they of the Junta knew the times of his movements. They did not ask him. He said nothing. But they looked at one another and conjectured.

"I have told you," said Vera. "Diaz has more to fear from this youth than from any man. He is implacable. He is the hand of God."

The bad temper, mentioned by May Sethby, and sensed by them all, was evidenced by physical proofs. Now he appeared with a cut lip, a blackened cheek, or a swollen ear. It was patent that he brawled, somewhere in that outside world where he ate and slept, gained money, and moved in ways unknown to them. As the time passed, he had come to set type for the little revolutionary sheet they published weekly. There were occasions when he was unable to set type, when his knuckles were bruised and battered, when his thumbs were injured and helpless, when one arm or the other hung wearily at his side while his face was drawn with unspoken pain.

"A wastrel," said Arrellano.

"A frequenter of low places," said Ramos.

"But where does he get the money?" Vera demanded. "Only to-day, just now, have I learned that he paid the bill for white paper—one hundred and forty dollars."

"There are his absences," said May Sethby. "He never explains them."

"We should set a spy upon him," Ramos propounded.

"I should not care to be that spy," said Vera. "I fear you would never see me again, save to bury me. He has a terrible passion. Not even God would he permit to stand between him and the way of his passion."

"I feel like a child before him," Ramos confessed.

"To me he is power—he is the primitive, the wild wolf,—the striking rattlesnake, the stinging centipede," said Arrellano.

"He is the Revolution incarnate," said Vera. "He is the flame and the spirit of it, the insatiable cry for vengeance that makes no cry but that slays noiselessly. He is a destroying angel moving through the still watches of the night."

"I could weep over him," said May Sethby. "He knows nobody. He hates all people. Us he tolerates, for we are the way of his desire. He is alone . . . lonely." Her voice broke in a half sob and there was dimness in her eyes.

Rivera's ways and times were truly mysterious. There were periods when they did not see him for a week at a time. Once, he was away a month. These occasions were always capped by his return, when, without advertisement or speech, he laid gold coins on May Sethby's desk. Again, for days and weeks, he spent all his time with the Junta. And yet again, for irregular periods, he would disappear through the heart of each day, from early morning until late afternoon. At such times he came early and remained late. Arrellano had found him at midnight, setting type with fresh swollen knuckles, or mayhap it was his lip, new-split, that still bled.

II

The time of the crisis approached. Whether or not the Revolution would be depended upon the Junta, and the Junta was hard-pressed. The need for money was greater than ever before, while money was harder to get. Patriots had given their last cent and now could give no more. Section gang laborers—fugitive peons from Mexico—were contributing half their scanty wages. But more than that was needed. The heart-breaking, conspiring, undermining toil of years approached fruition. The time was ripe. The Revolution hung on the balance. One shove more, one last heroic effort, and it would tremble across the scales to victory. They knew their Mexico. Once started, the Revolution would take care of itself. The whole Diaz machine would go down like a house of cards. The border was ready to rise. One Yankee, with a hundred I. W. W. men, waited the word to cross over the border and begin the conquest of Lower California. But he needed guns. And clear across to the Atlantic, the Junta in touch with them all and all of them needing guns, mere adventurers, soldiers of fortune, bandits, disgruntled American union men, socialists, anarchists, rough-necks, Mexican exiles, peons escaped from bondage, whipped miners from the bull-pens of Cœur d'Alene and Colorado who desired only the more vindictively to fight—all the flotsam and jetsam of wild spirits from the madly complicated modern world. And it was guns and ammunition, ammunition and guns—the unceasing and eternal cry.

Fling this heterogeneous, bankrupt, vindictive mass across the border, and the Revolution was on. The custom house, the northern ports of entry, would be captured. Diaz could not resist. He dared not throw the weight of his armies against them, for he must hold the south. And through the south the flame would spread despite. The people would rise. The defenses of city after city would crumple up. State after state would totter down. And at last, from every side, the victorious armies of the Revolution would close in on the City of Mexico itself, Diaz's last stronghold.

But the money. They had the men, impatient and urgent, who would use the guns. They knew the traders who would sell and deliver the guns. But to culture the Revolution thus far had exhausted the Junta. The last dollar had been spent, the last resource and the last starving patriot milked dry, and the great adventure still trembled on the scales. Guns and ammunition! The ragged battalions must be armed. But how? Ramos lamented his confiscated estates. Arrellano wailed the spendthriftness of his youth. May Sethby wondered if it would have been different had they of the Junta been more economical in the past.

"To think that the freedom of Mexico should stand or fall on a few paltry thousands of dollars," said Paulino Vera.

Despair was in all their faces. José Amarillo, their last hope, a recent convert, who had promised money, had been apprehended at his hacienda in Chihuahua and shot against his own stable wall. The news had just come through.

Rivera, on his knees, scrubbing, looked up, with suspended brush, his bare arms flecked with soapy, dirty water.

"Will five thousand do it?" he asked.

They looked their amazement. Vera nodded and swallowed. He could not speak, but he was on the instant invested with a vast faith.

"Order the guns," Rivera said, and thereupon was guilty of the longest flow of words they had ever heard him utter. "The time is short. In three weeks I shall bring you the five thousand. It is well. The weather will be warmer for those who fight. Also, it is the best I can do."

Vera fought his faith. It was incredible. Too many fond hopes had been shattered since he had begun to play the revolution game. He believed this threadbare scrubber of the Revolution, and yet he dared not believe.

"You are crazy," he said.

"In three weeks," said Rivera. "Order the guns."

He got up, rolled down his sleeves, and put on his coat.

"Order the guns," he said. "I am going now."

III

After hurrying and scurrying, much telephoning and bad language, a night session was held in Kelly's office. Kelly was rushed with business; also, he was unlucky. He had brought Danny Ward out from New York, arranged the fight for him with Billy Carthey, the date was three weeks away, and for two days now, carefully concealed from the sporting writers, Carthey had been lying up, badly injured. There was no one to take his place. Kelly had been burning the wires East to every eligible lightweight, but they were tied up with dates and contracts. And how hope had revived, though faintly.

"You've got a hell of a nerve," Kelly addressed Rivera, after one look, as soon as they got together.

Hate that was malignant was in Rivera's eyes, but his face remained impassive.

"I can lick Ward," was all he said.

"How do you know? Ever see him fight?"

Rivera shook his head.

"He can beat you up with one hand and both eyes closed."

Rivera shrugged his shoulders.

"Haven't you got anything to say?" the fight promoter snarled.

"I can lick him."

"Who'd you ever fight, anyway?" Michael Kelly demanded. Michael was the promoter's brother, and ran the Yellowstone poolrooms where he made goodly sums on the fight game.

Rivera favored him with a bitter, unanswering stare.

The promoter's secretary, a distinctively sporty young man, sneered audibly.

"Well, you know Roberts," Kelly broke the hostile silence. "He ought to be here. I've sent for him. Sit down and wait, though from the looks of you, you haven't got a chance. I can't throw the public down with a bum fight.

Ringside seats are selling at fifteen dollars, you know that."

When Roberts arrived, it was patent that he was mildly drunk. He was a tall, lean, slack-jointed individual, and his walk, like his talk, was a smooth and languid drawl.

Kelly went straight to the point.

"Look here, Roberts, you've been braggin' you discovered this little Mexican. You know Carthey's broke his arm. Well, this little yellow streak has the gall to blow in to-day and say he'll take Carthey's place. What about it?"

"It's all right, Kelly," came the slow response. "He can put up a fight."

"I suppose you'll be sayin' next that he can lick Ward," Kelly snapped.

Roberts considered judicially.

"No, I won't say that. Ward's a top-notcher and a ring general. But he can't hashhouse Rivera in short order. I know Rivera. Nobody can get his goat. He ain't got a goat that I could ever discover. And he's a two-handed fighter. He can throw in the sleep-makers from any position."

"Never mind that. What kind of a show can he put up? You've been conditioning and training fighters all your life. I take off my hat to your judgment. Can he give the public a run for its money?"

"He sure can, and he'll worry Ward a might heap on top of it. You don't know that boy. I do. I discovered him. He ain't got a goat. He's a devil. He's a wizzy-wooz if anybody should ask you. He'll make Ward sit up with a show of local talent that'll make the rest of you sit up. I won't say he'll lick Ward, but he'll put up such a show that you'll all know he's a comer."

"All right." Kelly turned to his secretary. "Ring up Ward. I warned him to show up if I thought it worth while. He's right across at the Yellowstone, throwin' chests and doing the popular." Kelly turned back to the conditioner. "Have a drink?"

Roberts sipped his highball and unburdened himself.

"Never told you how I discovered the little cuss. It was

a couple of years ago he showed up out at the quarters. I was getting Prayne ready for his fight with Delaney. Prayne's wicked. He ain't got a tickle of mercy in his make-up. He'd chopped up his pardner's something cruel, and I couldn't find a willing boy that'd work with him. I'd noticed this little starved Mexican kid hanging around, and I was desperate. So I grabbed him, slammed on the gloves, and put him in. He was tougher'n rawhide, but weak. And he didn't know the first letter in the alphabet of boxing. Prayne chopped him to ribbons. But he hung on for two sickening rounds, when he fainted. Starvation, that was all. Battered? You couldn't have recognized him. I gave him half a dollar and a square meal. You oughta seen him wolf it down. He hadn't had a bite for a couple of days. That's the end of him, thinks I. But next day he showed up, stiff an' sore, ready for another half and a square meal. And he done better as time went by. Just a born fighter, and tough beyond belief. He hasn't a heart. He's a piece of ice. And he never talked eleven words in a string since I known him. He saws wood and does his work."

"I've seen 'm," the secretary said. "He's worked a lot for you."

"All the big little fellows has tried out on him," Roberts answered. "And he's learned from 'em. I've seen some of them he could lick. But his heart wasn't in it. I reckoned he never liked the game. He seemed to act that way."

"He's been fighting some before the little clubs the last few months," Kelly said.

"Sure. But I don't know what struck'm. All of a sudden his heart got into it. He just went out like a streak and cleaned up all the little local fellows. Seemed to want the money, and he's won a bit, though his clothes don't look it. He's peculiar. Nobody knows his business. Nobody knows how he spends his time. Even when he's on the job, he plumb up and disappears most of each day soon as his work is done. Sometimes he just blows away for weeks at a time. But he don't take advice. There's a fortune in it for the fellow that gets the job of managin' him, only he won't consider it. And you watch him hold out for the cash money when you get down to terms."

It was at this stage that Danny Ward arrived. Quite a party it was. His manager and trainer were with him, and he breezed in like a gusty draught of geniality, good-nature, and all-conqueringness. Greetings flew about, a joke here, a retort there, a smile or a laugh for everybody. Yet it was his way, and only partly sincere. He was a good actor, and he had found geniality a most valuable asset in the game of getting on in the world. But down underneath he was the deliberate, cold-blooded fighter and business man. The rest was a mask. Those who knew him or trafficked with him said that when it came to brass tacks he was Danny-on-the-Spot. He was invariably present at all business discussions, and it was urged by some that his manager was a blind whose only function was to serve as Danny's mouth-piece.

Rivera's way was different. Indian blood, as well as Spanish, was in his veins, and he sat back in a corner, silent, immobile, only his black eyes passing from face to face and noting everything.

"So that's the guy," Danny said, running an appraising eye over his proposed antagonist. "How de do, old chap."

Rivera's eyes burned venomously, but he made no sign of acknowledgment. He disliked all Gringos, but this Gringo he hated with an immediacy that was unusual even in him.

"Gawd!" Danny protested facetiously to the promoter. "You ain't expectin' me to fight a deef mute." When the laughter subsided, he made another hit. "Los Angeles must be on the dink when this is the best you can scare up. What kindergarten did you get 'm from?"

"He's a good little boy, Danny, take it from me," Roberts defended. "Not as easy as he looks."

"And half the house is sold already," Kelly pleaded. "You'll have to take 'm on, Danny. It's the best we can do."

Danny ran another careless and unflattering glance over Rivera and sighed.

"I gotta be easy with 'm, I guess. If only he don't blow up."

Roberts snorted.

"You gotta be careful," Danny's manager warned. "No taking chances with a dub that's likely to sneak a lucky one across."

"Oh, I'll be careful all right, all right," Danny smiled. "I'll get 'm at the start an' nurse 'm along for the dear public's sake. What d' ye say to fifteen rounds, Kelly— An' then the hay for him?"

"That'll do," was the answer. "As long as you make it realistic."

"Then let's get down to biz." Danny paused and calculated. "Of course, sixty-five per cent; of gate receipts, same as with Carthey. But the split'll be different. Eighty will just about suit me." And to his manager, "That right?"

The manager nodded.

"Here, you, did you get that?" Kelly asked Rivera.

Rivera shook his head.

"Well it's this way," Kelly exposited. "The purse'll be sixty-five per cent. of the gate receipts. You're a dub, and an unknown. You and Danny split, twenty per cent. goin' to you, an' eighty to Danny. That's fair, isn't it, Roberts?"

"Very fair, Rivera," Roberts agreed. "You see, you ain't got a reputation yet."

"What will sixty-five per cent. of the gate receipts be?" Rivera demanded.

"Oh, maybe five thousand, maybe as high as eight thousand," Danny broke in to explain. "Something like that. Your share'll come to something like a thousand or sixteen hundred. Pretty good for takin' a licking from a guy with my reputation. What d'ye say?"

Then Rivera took their breaths away.

"Winner takes all," he said with finality.

A dead silence prevailed.

"It's like candy from a baby," Danny's manager proclaimed.

Danny shook his head.

"I've been in the game too long," he explained. "I'm not casting reflections on the referee, or the present company. I'm not sayin' nothing about book-makers an' frame-ups that sometimes happen. But what I do say is that it's poor business for a fighter like me. I play safe. There's no tellin'. Mebbe I break my arm, eh? Or some guy slips me a bunch of dope?" He shook his head solemnly. "Win or lose, eighty is my split. What d'ye say, Mexican?"

Rivera shook his head.

Danny exploded. He was getting down to brass tacks now.

"Why, you dirty little greaser! I've a mind to knock your block off right now."

Roberts drawled his body to interposition between hostilities.

"Winner takes all," Rivera repeated sullenly.

"Why do you stand out that way?" Danny asked.

"I can lick you," was the straight answer.

Danny half started to take off his coat. But, as his manager knew, it was a grand stand play. The coat did not come off, and Danny allowed himself to be placated by the group. Everybody sympathized with him. Rivera stood alone.

"Look here, you little fool," Kelly took up the argument. "You're nobody. We know what you've been doing the last few months—putting away little local fighters. But Danny is class. His next fight after this will be for the championship. And you're unknown. Nobody ever heard of you out of Los Angeles."

"They will," Rivera answered with a shrug, "after this fight."

"You think for a second you can lick me?" Danny blurted in.

Rivera nodded.

"Oh, come; listen to reason," Kelly pleaded. "Think of the advertising."

"I want the money," was Rivera's answer.

"You couldn't win from me in a thousand years," Danny assured him.

"Then what are you holding out for?" Rivera countered. "If the money's that easy, why don't you go after it?"

"I will, so help me!" Danny cried with abrupt conviction. "I'll beat you to death in the ring, my boy—you monkeyin' with me this way. Make out the articles, Kelly. Winner take all. Play it up in the sportin' columns. Tell 'em it's a grudge fight. I'll show this fresh kid a few."

Kelly's secretary had begun to write, when Danny interrupted.

"Hold on!" He turned to Rivera. "Weights?"

"Ringside," came the answer.

"Not on your life, Fresh Kid. If winner takes all, we weigh in at ten A.M."

"And winner takes all?" Rivera queried.

Danny nodded. That settled it. He would enter the ring in full ripeness of strength.

"Weigh in at ten," Rivera said.

The secretary's pen went on scratching.

"It means five pounds," Roberts complained to Rivera. "You've given too much away. You've thrown the fight right there. Danny'll be as strong as a bull. You're a fool. He'll lick you sure. You ain't got the chance of a dewdrop in hell."

Rivera's answer was a calculated look of hatred. Even this Gringo he despised, and him had he found the whitest Gringo of them all.

IV

Barely noticed was Rivera as he entered the ring. Only a very slight and very scattering ripple of half-hearted hand-clapping greeted him. The house did not believe in him. He was the lamb led to slaughter at the hands of the great Danny. Besides, the house was disappointed. It had expected a rushing battle between Danny Ward and Billy Carthey, and here it must put up with this poor little tyro. Still further, it had manifested its disapproval of the change by betting two, and even three, to one on Danny. And where a betting audience's money is, there is its heart.

The Mexican boy sat down in his corner and waited. The slow minutes lagged by. Danny was making him wait. It was an old trick, but ever it worked on the young, new fighters. They grew frightened, sitting thus and facing their own apprehensions and a callous, tobacco-smoking audience. But for once the trick failed. Roberts was right. Rivera had no goat. He, who was more delicately coördinated, more finely nerved and strung than any of them, had no nerves of this sort. The atmosphere of foredoomed defeat in his own corner had no effect on him. His handlers were Gringos and strangers. Also they were scrubs—the dirty driftage of the fight game, without honor, without efficiency. And they were chilled, as well, with certitude that theirs was the losing corner.

"Now you gotta be careful," Spider Hagerty warned him. Spider was his chief second. "Make it last as long as you can—them's my instructions from Kelly. If you don't, the papers'll call it another bum fight and give the game a bigger black eye in Los Angeles."

All of which was not encouraging. But Rivera took no notice. He despised prize fighting. It was the hated game of the hated Gringo. He had taken up with it, as a chopping block for others in the training quarters, solely because he was starving. The fact that he was marvelously made for it, had meant nothing. He hated it. Not until he had come in to the Junta, had he fought for money, and he had found the money easy. Not first among the sons of men had he been to find himself successful at a despised vocation.

He did not analyze. He merely knew that he must win

this fight. There could be not other outcome. For behind him, nerving him to this belief, were profounder forces than any the crowded house dreamed. Danny Ward fought for money, and for the easy ways of life that money would bring. But the things Rivera fought for burned in his brain—blazing and terrible visions, that, with eyes wide open, sitting lonely in the corner of the ring and waiting for his tricky antagonist, he saw as clearly as he had lived them.

He saw the white-walled, water-power factories of Rio Blanco. He saw the six thousand workers, starved and wan, and the little children, seven and eight years of age, who toiled long shifts for ten cents a day. He saw the perambulating corpses, the ghastly death's heads of men who labored in the dye-rooms. He remembered that he had heard his father call the dye-rooms the "suicide-holes," where a year was death. He saw the little patio, and his mother cooking and moiling at crude housekeeping and finding time to caress and love him. And his father he saw, large, big-moustached and deep-chested, kindly above all men, who loved all men and whose heart was so large that there was love to overflowing still left for the mother and the little muchacho playing in the corner of the patio. In those days his name had not been Felipe Rivera. It had been Fernandez, his father's and mother's name. Him had they called Juan. Later, he had changed it himself, for he had found the name of Fernandez hated by prefects of police, *jefes politicos*, and *rurales*.

Big, hearty Joaquin Fernandez! A large place he occupied in Rivera's visions. He had not understood at the time, but looking back he could understand. He could see him setting type in the little printery, or scribbling endless hasty, nervous lines on the much-cluttered desk. And he could see the strange evenings, when workmen, coming secretly in the dark like men who did ill deeds, met with his father and talked long hours where he, the muchacho, lay not always asleep in the corner.

As from a remote distance he could hear Spider Hagerty saying to him: "No layin' down at the start. Them's instructions. Take a beatin' an' earn your dough."

Ten minutes had passed, and he still sat in his corner. There were no signs of Danny, who was evidently playing the trick to the limit.

But more visions burned before the eye of Rivera's memory. The strike, or, rather, the lockout, because the workers of Rio Blanco had helped their striking brothers of Puebla. The hunger, the expeditions in the hills for berries, the roots and herbs that all ate and that twisted and pained the stomachs of all of them. And then, the nightmare; the waste of ground before the company's store; the thousands of starving workers; General Rosalio Martinez and the soldiers of Porfirio Diaz; and the death-spitting rifles that seemed never to cease spitting, while the workers' wrongs were washed and washed again in their own blood. And that night! He saw the flat cars, piled high with the bodies of the slain, consigned to Vera Cruz, food for the sharks of the bay. Again he crawled over the grisly heaps, seeking and finding, stripped and mangled, his father and mother. His mother he especially remembered—only her face projecting, her body burdened by the weight of dozens of bodies. Again the rifles of the soldiers of Porfirio Diaz cracked, and again he dropped to the ground and slunk away like some hunted coyote of the hills.

To his ears came a great roar, as of the sea, and he saw Danny Ward, leading his retinue of trainers and seconds, coming down the center aisle. The house was in wild uproar for the popular hero who was bound to win. Everybody proclaimed him. Everybody was for him. Even Rivera's own seconds warmed to something akin to cheerfulness when Danny ducked jauntily through the ropes and entered the ring. His face continually spread to an unending succession of smiles, and when Danny smiled he smiled in every feature, even to the laughter-wrinkles of the corners of the eyes and into the depths of the eyes themselves. Never was there so genial a fighter. His face was a running advertisement of good feeling, of good fellowship. He knew everybody. He joked, and laughed, and greeted his friends through the ropes. Those farther away, unable to suppress their admiration, cried loudly: "Oh, you Danny!" It was a joyous ovation of affection that lasted a full five minutes.

Rivera was disregarded. For all that the audience noticed, he did not exist. Spider Hagerty's bloated face bent down close to his.

"No gettin' scared," the Spider warned. "An' remember instructions. You gotta last. No layin' down. If you lay down, we got instructions to beat you up in the dressing rooms. Savve? You just gotta fight."

The house began to applaud. Danny was crossing the ring to him. Danny bent over, caught Rivera's right hand in both his own and shook it with impulsive heartiness. Danny's smile-wreathed face was close to his. The audience yelled its appreciation of Danny's display of sporting spirit. He was greeting his opponent with the fondness of a brother. Danny's lips moved, and the audience, interpreting the unheard words to be those of a kindly-natured sport, yelled again. Only Rivera heard the low words.

"You little Mexican rat," hissed from between Danny's gaily smiling lips, "I'll fetch the yellow outa you."

Rivera made no move. He did not rise. He merely hated with his eyes.

"Get up, you dog!" some man yelled through the ropes from behind.

The crowd began to hiss and boo him for his unsportsmanlike conduct, but he sat unmoved. Another great outburst of applause was Danny's as he walked back across the ring.

When Danny stripped, there was ohs! and ahs! of delight. His body was perfect, alive with easy suppleness and health and strength. The skin was white as a woman's, and as smooth. All grace, and resilience, and power resided therein. He had proved it in scores of battles. His photographs were in all the physical culture magazines.

A groan went up as Spider Hagerty peeled Rivera's sweater over his head. His body seemed leaner, because of the swarthiness of the skin. He had muscles, but they made no display like his opponent's. What the audience neglected to see was the deep chest. Nor could it guess the toughness of the fiber of the flesh, the instantaneousness of the cell explosions of the muscles, the fineness of the nerves that wired every part of him into a splendid fighting mechanism. All the audience saw was a brown-skinned boy of eighteen with what seemed the body of a boy. With Danny it was different. Danny was a man of twenty-four, and his body was a man's body. The contrast was still more striking as they stood together in the center of the ring receiving the referee's last instructions.

Rivera noticed Roberts sitting directly behind the newspaper men. He was drunker than usual, and his speech was correspondingly slower.

"Take it easy, Rivera," Roberts drawled. "He can't kill you, remember that. He'll rush you at the go-off, but don't get rattled. You just cover up, and stall, and clinch. He can't hurt you much. Just make believe to yourself that he's choppin' out on you at the trainin' quarters."

Rivera made no sign that he had heard.

"Sullen little devil," Roberts muttered to the man next to him. "He always was that way."

But Rivera forgot to look his usual hatred. A vision of countless rifles blinded his eyes. Every face in the audience, far as he could see, to the high dollar-seats, was transformed into a rifle. And he saw the long Mexican border arid and sun-washed and aching, and along it he saw the ragged bands that delayed only for the guns.

Back in his corner he waited, standing up. His seconds had crawled out through the ropes, taking the canvas stool with them. Diagonally across the squared ring, Danny faced him. The gong struck, and the battle was on. The audience howled its delight. Never had it seen a battle open more convincingly. The papers were right. It was a grudge fight. Three-quarters of the distance Danny covered in the rush to get together, his intention to eat up the Mexican lad plainly advertised. He assailed with not one blow, nor two, nor a dozen. He was a gyroscope of blows, a whirlwind of destruction. Rivera was nowhere. He was overwhelmed, buried beneath avalanches of punches delivered from every angle and position by a past master in the art. He was overborne, swept back against the ropes, separated by the referee, and swept back against the ropes again.

It was not a fight. It was a slaughter, a massacre. Any audience, save a prize fighting one, would have exhausted its emotions in that first minute. Danny was certainly showing what he could do—a splendid exhibition. Such was the certainty of the audience, as well as its excitement and favoritism, that it failed to take notice that the Mexican still stayed on his feet. It forgot Rivera. It rarely saw him, so closely was he enveloped in Danny's man-eating attack. A minute of this went by, and two minutes. Then, in a separation, it caught a clear glimpse of the Mexican. His lip was cut, his nose was bleeding. As he turned and staggered into a clinch, the welts of oozing blood, from his contacts with the ropes, showed in red bars across his back. But what the audience did not notice was that his chest was not heaving and that his eyes were coldly burning as ever. Too many aspiring champions, in the cruel welter of the training camps, had practiced this man-eating attack on him. He had learned to live through for a compensation of from half a dollar a go up to fifteen dollars a week—a hard school, and he was schooled hard.

Then happened the amazing thing. The whirling, blurring mix-up ceased suddenly. Rivera stood alone. Danny, the redoubtable Danny, lay on his back. His body quivered as consciousness strove to return to it. He had not staggered and sunk down, nor had he gone over in a long slumping fall. The right hook of Rivera had dropped him in midair with the abruptness of death. The referee shoved Rivera back with one hand, and stood over the fallen gladiator counting the seconds. It is the custom of prizefighting audiences to cheer a clean knock-down blow. But this audience did not cheer. The thing had been too unexpected. It watched the toll of the seconds in tense silence, and through this silence the voice of Roberts rose exultantly:

"I told you he was a two-handed fighter!"

By the fifth second, Danny was rolling over on his face, and when seven was counted, he rested on one knee, ready to rise after the count of nine and before the count of ten. If his knee still touched the floor at "ten," he was considered "down," and also "out." The instant his knee left the floor, he was considered "up," and in that instant it was Rivera's right to try to put him down again. Rivera took no chances. The moment that knee left the floor he would strike again. He circled around, but the referee circled in between, and Rivera knew that the seconds he counted were very slow. All Gringos were against him, even the referee.

At "nine" the referee gave Rivera a sharp thrust back. It was unfair, but it enabled Danny to rise, the smile back on his lips. Doubled partly over, with arms wrapped about face and abdomen, he cleverly stumbled into a clinch. By all the rules of the game the referee should have broken it, but he did not, and Danny clung on like a surf-battered barnacle and moment by moment recuperated. The last minute of the round was going fast. If he could live to the end, he would have a full minute in his corner to revive. And live to the end he did, smiling through all desperateness and extremity.

"The smile that won't come off!" somebody yelled, and the audience laughed loudly in its relief.

"The kick that Greaser's got is something God-awful," Danny gasped in his corner to his adviser while his handlers worked frantically over him.

The second and third rounds were tame. Danny, a tricky

and consummate ring general, stalled and blocked and held
on, devoting himself to recovering from that dazing first-
round blow. In the fourth round he was himself again.
Jarred and shaken, nevertheless his good condition had enabled him to regain his vigor. But he tried no man-eating
tactics. The Mexican had proved a tartar. Instead, he
brought to bear his best fighting powers. In tricks and skill
and experience he was the master, and though he could
land nothing vital, he proceeded scientifically to chop and
wear down his opponent. He landed three blows to
Rivera's one, but they were punishing blows only, and not
deadly. It was the sum of many of them that constituted
deadliness. He was respectful of this two-handed dub with
the amazing short-arm kicks in both his fists.

In defense, Rivera developed a disconcerting straight-
left. Again and again, attack after attack he straight-lefted
away from him with accumulated damage to Danny's
mouth and nose. But Danny was protean. That was why he
was the coming champion. He could change from style to
style of fighting at will. He now devoted himself to
infighting. In this he was particularly wicked, and it enabled him to avoid the other's straight-left. Here he set the
house wild repeatedly, capping it with a marvelous lock-
break and lift of an inside upper-cut that raised the Mexican in the air and dropped him to the mat. Rivera rested
on one knee, making the most of the count, and in the soul
of him he knew the referee was counting short seconds on
him.

Again, in the seventh, Danny achieved the diabolical inside uppercut. He succeeding only in staggering Rivera,
but, in the ensuing moment of defenseless helplessness, he
smashed him with another blow through the ropes.
Rivera's body bounced on the heads of the newspaper men
below, and they boosted him back to the edge of the platform outside the ropes. Here he rested on one knee, while
the referee raced off the seconds. Inside the ropes, through
which he must duck to enter the ring, Danny waited for

him. Nor did the referee intervene or thrust Danny back.

The house was beside itself with delight.

"Kill 'm, Danny, kill 'm!" was the cry.

Scores of voices took it up until it was like a war-chant of wolves.

Danny did his best, but Rivera, at the count of eight, instead of nine, came unexpectedly through the ropes and safely into a clinch. Now the referee worked, tearing him away so that he could be hit, giving Danny every advantage that an unfair referee can give.

But Rivera lived, and the daze cleared from his brain. It was all of a piece. They were the hated Gringos and they were all unfair. And in the worst of it visions continued to flash and sparkle in his brain—long lines of railroad track that simmered across the desert; *rurales* and American constables; prisons and calabooses; tramps at water tanks—all the squalid and painful panorama of his odyssey after Rio Blanca and the strike. And, resplendent and glorious, he saw the great, red Revolution sweeping across his land. The guns were there before him. Every hated face was a gun. It was for the guns he fought. He was the guns. He was the Revolution. He fought for all Mexico.

The audience began to grow incensed with Rivera. Why didn't he take the licking that was appointed him? Of course he was going to be licked, but why should he be so obstinate abut it? Very few were interested in him, and they were the certain, definite percentage of a gambling crowd that plays long shots. Believing Danny to be the winner, nevertheless they had put their money on the Mexican at four to ten and one to three. More than a trifle was up on the point of how many rounds Rivera could last. Wild money had appeared at the ringside proclaiming that he could not last seven rounds, or even six. The winners of this, now that their cash risk was happily settled, had joined in cheering on the favorite.

Rivera refused to be licked. Through the eighth round his opponent strove vainly to repeat the uppercut. In the ninth, Rivera stunned the house again. In the midst of a clinch he broke the lock with a quick, lithe movement, and in the narrow space between their bodies his right lifted from the waist. Danny went to the floor and took the safety of the count. The crowd was appalled. He was being bested at his own game. His famous right-uppercut had been worked back on him. Rivera made no attempt to catch him as he arose at "nine." The referee was openly blocking that play, though he stood clear when the situation was reversed and it was Rivera who desired to rise.

Twice in the tenth, Rivera put through the right-uppercut, lifted from waist to opponent's chin. Danny grew desperate. The smile never left his face, but he went back to his man-eating rushes. Whirlwind as he would, he could not damage Rivera, while Rivera, through the blur and whirl, dropped him to the mat three times in succession. Danny did not recuperate so quickly now, and by the eleventh round he was in a serious way. But from then till the fourteenth he put up the gamest exhibition of his career. He stalled and blocked, fought parsimoniously, and strove to gather strength. Also, he fought as foully as a successful fighter knows how. Every trick and device he employed, butting in the clinches with the seeming of accident, pinioning Rivera's glove between arm and body, heeling his glove on Rivera's mouth to clog his breathing. Often, in the clinches, through his cut and smiling lips he snarled insults unspeakable and vile in Rivera's ear. Everybody, from the referee to the house, was with Danny and was helping Danny. And they knew what he had in mind. Bested by this surprise-box of an unknown, he was pinning all on a single punch. He offered himself for punishment, fished, and feinted, and drew, for that one opening that would enable him to whip a blow through with all his strength and turn the tide. As another and greater fighter had done before him, he might do—a right and left, to solar plexus and across the jaw. He could do it, for he was noted for the strength of punch that remained in his arms as long as he could keep his feet.

Rivera's seconds were not half-caring for him in the intervals between rounds. Their towels made a showing, but drove little air into his panting lungs. Spider Hagerty talked advice to him, but Rivera knew it was wrong advice. Everybody was against him. He was surrounded by treachery. In the fourteenth round he put Danny down again, and himself stood resting, hands dropped at side, while the referee counted. In the other corner Rivera had been noting suspicious whisperings. He saw Michael Kelly make his way to Roberts and bend and whisper. Rivera's ears were a cat's, desert-trained, and he caught snatches of what was said. He wanted to hear more, and when his opponent arose he maneuvered the fight into a clinch over against the ropes.

"Got to," he could hear Michael, while Roberts nodded. "Danny's got to win—I stand to lose a mint—I've got a ton of money covered—my own—If he lasts the fifteenth I'm bust—The boy'll mind you. Put something across."

And thereafter Rivera saw no more visions. They were trying to job him. Once again he dropped Danny and stood resting, his hands at his side. Roberts stood up.

"That settled him," he said. "Go to your corner."

He spoke with authority, as he had often spoken to Rivera at the training quarters. But Rivera looked hatred at him and waited for Danny to rise. Back in his corner in the minute interval, Kelly, the promoter, came and talked to Rivera.

"Throw it, damn you," he rasped in a harsh low voice. "You gotta lay down, Rivera. Stick with me and I'll make your future. I'll let you lick Danny next time. But here's where you lay down."

Rivera showed with his eyes that he heard, but he made neither sign of assent nor dissent.

"Why don't you speak?" Kelly demanded angrily.

"You lose, anyway," Spider Hagerty supplemented. "The referee'll take it away from you. Listen to Kelly, and lay down."

"Lay down, kid," Kelly pleaded, "and I'll help you to the championship."

Rivera did not answer.

"I will, so help me, kid."

At the strike of the gong Rivera sensed something impending. The house did not. Whatever it was it was there inside the ring with him and very close. Danny's earlier surety seemed returned to him. The confidence of his advance frightened Rivera. Some trick was about to be worked. Danny rushed, but Rivera refused the encounter. He side-stepped away into safety. What the other wanted was a clinch. It was in some way necessary to the trick. Rivera backed and circled away, yet he knew, sooner or later, the clinch and the trick would come. Desperately he resolved to draw it. He made as if to effect the clinch with Danny's next rush. Instead, at the last instant, just as their bodies should have come together, Rivera darted nimbly back. And in the same instant Danny's corner raised a cry of foul. Rivera had fooled them. The referee paused irresolutely. The decision that trembled on his lips was never uttered, for a shrill, boy's voice from the gallery piped, "Raw work!"

Danny cursed Rivera openly, and forced him, while Rivera danced away. Also, Rivera made up his mind to strike no more blows at the body. In this he threw away half his chance of winning, but he knew if he was to win at all it was with the outfighting that remained to him. Given the least opportunity, they would lie a foul on him. Danny threw all caution to the winds. For two rounds he tore after and into the boy who dared not meet him at close quarters. Rivera was struck again and again; he took blows by the dozens to avoid the perilous clinch. During this supreme final rally of Danny's the audience rose to its feet and went mad. It did not understand. All it could see was that its favorite was winning after all.

"Why don't you fight?" it demanded wrathfully of Rivera. "You're yellow! You're yellow!" "Open up, you cur! Open up!" "Kill 'm, Danny! Kill 'm!" "You sure got 'm! Kill 'm!"

In all the house, bar none, Rivera was the only cold man. By temperament and blood he was the hottest-passioned there; but he had gone through such vastly greater heats that this collective passion of ten thousand throats, rising surge on surge, was to his brain no more than the velvet cool of a summer twilight.

Into the seventeenth round Danny carried his rally. Rivera, under a heavy blow, dropped and sagged. His hands dropped helplessly as he reeled backward. Danny thought it was his chance. The boy was at his mercy. Thus Rivera, feigning, caught him off his guard, lashing out a clean drive to the mouth. Danny went down. When he arose, Rivera felled him with a down-chop of the right on neck and jaw. Three times he repeated this. It was impossible for any referee to call these blows foul.

"Oh, Bill! Bill!" Kelly pleaded to the referee.

"I can't," that official lamented back. "He won't give me a chance."

Danny, battered and heroic, still kept coming up. Kelly and others near to the ring began to cry out to the police to stop it, though Danny's corner refused to throw in the towel. Rivera saw the fat police captain starting awkwardly to climb through the ropes, and was not sure what it meant. There were so many ways of cheating in this game of the Gringos. Danny, on his feet, tottered groggily and helplessly before him. The referee and the captain were both reaching for Rivera when he struck the last blow. There was no need to stop the fight, for Danny did not rise.

"Count!" Rivera cried hoarsely to the referee.

And when the count was finished, Danny's seconds gathered him up and carried him to his corner.

"Who wins?" Rivera demanded.

Reluctantly, the referee caught his gloved hand and held it aloft.

There were no congratulations for Rivera. He walked to

his corner unattended, where his seconds had not yet placed his stool. He leaned backward on the ropes and looked his hatred at them, swept it on and about him till the whole ten thousand Gringos were included. His knees trembled under him, and he was sobbing from exhaustion. Before his eyes the hated faces swayed back and forth in the giddiness of nausea. Then he remembered they were the guns. The guns were his. The Revolution could go on.

War

He was a young man, not more than twenty-four or five, and he might have sat his horse with the careless grace of his youth had he not been so catlike and tense. His black eyes roved everywhere, catching the movements of twigs and branches where small birds hopped, questing ever onward through the changing vistas of trees and brush, and returning always to the clumps of undergrowth on either side. And as he watched, so did he listen, though he rode on in silence, save for the boom of heavy guns from far to the west. This had been sounding monotonously in his ears for hours, and only its cessation would have aroused his notice. For he had business closer to hand. Across his saddle-bow was balanced a carbine.

So tensely was he strung, that a bunch of quail, exploding into flight from under his horse's nose, startled him to such an extent that automatically, instantly, he had reined in and fetched the carbine halfway to his shoulder. He grinned sheepishly, recovered himself, and rode on. So tense was he, so bent upon the work he had to do, that the sweat stung his eyes unwiped, and unheeded rolled down his nose and spattered his saddle pommel. The band of his cavalryman's hat was fresh-stained with sweat. The roan horse under him was likewise wet. It was high noon of a breathless day of heat. Even the birds and squirrels did not dare the sun, but sheltered in shady hiding places among the trees.

Man and horse were littered with leaves and dusted with yellow pollen, for the open was ventured no more than was compulsory. They kept to the brush and trees, and invariably the man halted and peered out before crossing a dry glade or naked stretch of upland pasturage. He worked always to the north, though his way was devious, and it was from the north that he seemed most to apprehend that for which he was looking. He was no coward, but his courage was only that of the average civilized man, and he was looking to live, not die.

Up a small hillside he followed a cowpath through such dense scrub that he was forced to dismount and lead his horse. But when the path swung around to the west, he abandoned it and headed to the north again along the oak-covered top of the ridge.

The ridge ended in a steep descent—so steep that he zigzagged back and forth across the face of the slope, sliding and stumbling among the dead leaves and matted vines and keeping a watchful eye on the horse above that threatened to fall down upon him. The sweat ran from him, and the pollen-dust, settling pungently in mouth and nostrils, increased his thirst. Try as he would, nevertheless the descent was noisy, and frequently he stopped, panting in the dry heat and listening for any warning from beneath.

At the bottom he came out on a flat, so densely forested that he could not make out its extent. Here the character of the woods changed, and he was able to remount. Instead of the twisted hillside oaks, tall straight trees, big-trunked and prosperous, rose from the damp fat soil. Only here and there were thickets, easily avoided, while he encountered winding, park-like glades where the cattle had pastured in the days before war had run them off.

His progress was more rapid now, as he came down into the valley, and at the end of half an hour he halted at an ancient rail fence on the edge of a clearing. He did not like the openness of it, yet his path lay across to the fringe of trees that marked the banks of the stream. It was a mere quarter of a mile across that open, but the thought of venturing out in it was repugnant. A rifle, a score of them, a thousand, might lurk in that fringe by the stream.

Twice he essayed to start, and twice he paused. He was appalled by his own loneliness. The pulse of war that beat from the West suggested the companionship of battling thousands; here was naught but silence, and himself, and possible death-dealing bullets from a myriad ambushes. And yet his task was to find what he feared to find. He must go on, and on, till somewhere, some time, he encountered another man, or other men, from the other side, scouting, as he was scouting, to make report, as he must make report, of having come in touch.

Changing his mind, he skirted inside the woods for a distance, and again peeped forth. This time, in the middle of the clearing, he saw a small farmhouse. There were no signs of life. No smoke curled from the chimney, not a barnyard fowl clucked and strutted. The kitchen door stood open, and he gazed so long and hard into the black aperture that it seemed almost that a farmer's wife must emerge at any moment.

He licked the pollen and dust from his dry lips, stiffened himself, mind and body, and rode out into the blazing sunshine. Nothing stirred. He went on past the house, and approached the wall of trees and bushes by the river's bank. One thought persisted maddeningly. It was of the crash into his body of a high-velocity bullet. It made him feel very fragile and defenseless, and he crouched lower in the saddle.

Tethering his horse in the edge of the wood, he continued a hundred yards on foot till he came to the stream.

Twenty feet wide it was, without perceptible current, cool and inviting, and he was very thirsty. But he waited inside his screen of leafage, his eyes fixed on the screen on the opposite side. To make the wait endurable, he sat down, his carbine resting on his knees. The minutes passed, and slowly his tenseness relaxed. At last the decided there was no danger; but just as he prepared to part the bushes and bend down to the water, a movement along the opposite bushes caught his eye.

It might be a bird. But he waited. Again there was an agitation of the bushes, and then, so suddenly that it almost startled a cry from him, the bushes parted and a face peered out. It was a face covered with several weeks' growth of ginger-colored beard. The eyes were blue and wide apart, with laughter-wrinkles in the corners that showed despite the tired and anxious expression of the whole face.

All this he could see with microscopic clearness, for the distance was no more than twenty feet. And all this he saw in such brief time, that he saw it as he lifted his carbine to his shoulder. He glanced along the sights, and knew that he was gazing upon a man who was as good as dead. It was impossible to miss at such point blank range.

But he did not shoot. Slowly he lowered the carbine and watched. A hand, clutching a water-bottle, became visible and the ginger beard bent downward to fill the bottle. He could hear the gurgle of the water. Then arm and bottle and ginger beard disappeared behind the closing bushes. A long time he waited, when, with thirst unslaked, he crept back to his horse, rode slowly across the sun-washed clearing, and passed into the shelter of the woods beyond.

II

Another day, hot and breathless. A deserted farmhouse, large, with many outbuildings and an orchard, standing in a clearing. From the woods, on a roan horse, carbine across pommel, rode the young man with the quick black eyes. He breathed with relief as he gained the house. That a fight had taken place here earlier in the season was evident. Clips and empty cartridges, tarnished with verdigris, lay on the ground, which, while wet, had been torn up by the hoofs of horses. Hard by the kitchen garden were graves, tagged and numbered. From the oak tree by the kitchen door, in tattered, weather-beaten garments, hung the bodies of two men. The faces, shriveled and defaced, bore no likeness to the faces of men. The roan horse snorted beneath them, and the rider caressed and soothed it and tied it farther away.

Entering the house, he found the interior a wreck. He trod on empty cartridges as he walked from room to room to reconnoiter from the windows. Men had camped and slept everywhere, and on the floor of one room he came upon stains unmistakable where the wounded had been laid down.

Again outside, he led the horse around behind the barn and invaded the orchard. A dozen trees were burdened with ripe apples. He filled his pockets, eating while he picked. Then a thought came to him, and he glanced at the sun, calculating the time of his return to camp. He pulled off his shirt, tying the sleeves and making a bag. This he proceeded to fill with apples.

As he was about to mount his horse, the animal suddenly pricked up its ears. The man, too, listened, and heard, faintly, the thud of hoofs on soft earth. He crept to the corner of the barn and peered out. A dozen mounted men, strung out loosely, approaching from the opposite side of the clearing, were only a matter of a hundred yards or so away. They rode on to the house. Some dismounted, while others remained in the saddle as an earnest that their stay would be short. They seemed to be holding a council, for he could hear them talking excitedly in the detested tongue of the alien invader. The time passed, but they seemed unable to reach a decision. He put the carbine away in its boot, mounted, and waited impatiently, balancing the shirt of apples on the pommel.

He heard footsteps approaching, and drove his spurs so fiercely into the roan as to force a surprised groan from the animal as it leaped forward. At the corner of the barn he saw the intruder, a mere boy of nineteen or twenty for all of his uniform, jump back to escape being run down. At the same moment the roan swerved, and its rider caught a glimpse of the aroused men by the house. Some were springing from their horses, and he could see the rifles going to their shoulders. He passed the kitchen door and the dried corpses swinging in the shade, compelling his foes to run around the front of the house. A rifle cracked, and a second, but he was going fast, leaning forward, low in the saddle, one hand clutching the shirt of apples, the other guiding the horse.

The top bar of the fence was four feet high, but he knew his roan and leaped it at full career to the accompaniment of several scattered shots. Eight hundred yards straight away were the woods, and the roan was covering the distance with mighty strides. Every man was now firing. They were pumping their guns so rapidly that he no longer heard individual shots. A bullet went through his hat, but he was unaware, though he did know when another tore through the apples on the pommel. And he winced and ducked even lower when a third bullet, fired low, struck a stone between the horse's legs and ricochetted off through the air, buzzing and humming like some incredible insect.

The shots died down as the magazines were emptied, until, quickly, there was no more shooting. The young man was elated. Through that astonishing fusillade he had come unscathed. He glanced back. Yes, they had emptied their magazines. He could see several reloading. Others were running back behind the house for their horses. As he looked, two already mounted, came back into view around the corner, riding hard. And at the same moment, he saw the man with the unmistakable ginger beard kneel down on the ground, level his gun, and coolly take his time for the long shot.

The young man threw his spurs into the horse, crouched very low, and swerved in his flight in order to distract the other's aim. And still the shot did not come. With each jump of the horse, the woods sprang nearer. They were only two hundred yards away, and still the shot was delayed.

And then he heard it, the last thing he was to hear, for he was dead ere he hit the ground in the long crashing fall from his saddle. And they, watching at the house, saw him fall, saw his body bounce when it struck the earth, and saw the burst of red-cheeked apples that rolled about him. They laughed at the unexpected eruption of apples, and clapped their hands in applause of the long shot by the man with the ginger beard.

South of the Slot

Old San Francisco, which is the San Francisco of only the other day, the day before the Earthquake, was divided midway by the Slot. The Slot was an iron crack that ran along the center of Market street, and from the Slot arose the burr of the ceaseless, endless cable that was hitched at will to the cars it dragged up and down. In truth, there were two slots, but in the quick grammar of the West time was saved by calling them, and much more that they stood for, "The Slot." North of the Slot were the theaters, hotels, and shopping district, the banks and the staid, respectable business houses. South of the Slot were the factories, slums, laundries, machine-shops, boiler works, and the abodes of the working class.

The Slot was the metaphor that expressed the class cleavage of Society, and no man crossed this metaphor, back and forth, more successfully than Freddie Drummond. He made a practice of living in both worlds, and in both worlds he lived signally well. Freddie Drummond was a professor in the Sociology Department of the University of California, and it was as a professor of sociology that the first crossed over the Slot, lived for six months in the great labor-ghetto, and wrote "The Unskilled Laborer"—a book that was hailed everywhere as an able contribution to the literature of progress, and as a splendid reply to the literature of discontent. Politically and economically it was nothing if not orthodox. Presidents of great railway systems bought whole editions of it to give to their employees. The Manufacturers' Association alone distributed fifty thousand copies of it. In a way, it was almost as immoral as the far-famed and notorious "Message to Garcia," while in its pernicious preachment of thrift and content it ran "Mrs. Wiggs of the Cabbage Patch" a close second.

At first, Freddie Drummond found it monstrously difficult to get along among the working people. He was not used to their ways, and they certainly were not used to his. They were suspicious. He had no antecedents. He could talk of no previous jobs. His hands were soft. His extraordinary politeness was ominous. His first idea of the rôle he would play was that of a free and independent American who chose to work with his hands and no explanations given. But it wouldn't do, as he quickly discovered. At the beginning they accepted him, very provisionally, as a freak. A little later, as he began to know his way about better, he insensibly drifted into the rôle that would work—namely, he was a man who had seen better days, very much better days, but who was down in his luck, though, to be sure, only temporarily.

He learned many things, and generalized much and often erroneously, all of which can be found in the pages of "The Unskilled Laborer." He saved himself, however, after the sane and conservative manner of his kind, by labeling his generalizations as "tentative." One of his first experiences was in the great Wilmax Cannery, where he was put on piece-work making small packing cases. A box factory supplied the parts, and all Freddie Drummond had to do was to fit the parts into a form and drive in the wire nails with a light hammer.

It was not skilled labor, but it was piece-work. The ordinary laborers in the cannery got a dollar and a half per day. Freddie Drummond found the other men on the same job with him jogging along and earning a dollar and seventy-five cents a day. By the third day he was able to earn the same. But he was ambitious. He did not care to jog along and, being unusually able and fit, on the fourth day earned two dollars. The next day, having keyed himself up to an exhausting high-tension, he earned two dollars and a half. His fellow workers favored him with scowls and black looks, and made remarks, slangily witty and which he did not understand, about sucking up to the boss and pace-making and holding her down when the rains set in. He was astonished at their malingering on piece-work, generalized about the inherent laziness of the unskilled laborer, and proceeded next day to hammer out three dollars' worth of boxes.

And that night, coming out of the cannery, he was interviewed by his fellow workmen, who were very angry and incoherently slangy. He failed to comprehend the motive behind their action. The action itself was strenuous. When he refused to ease down his pace and bleated about freedom of contract, independent Americanism, and the dignity of toil, they proceeded to spoil his pace-making ability. It was a fierce battle, for Drummond was a large man and an athlete, but the crowd finally jumped on his ribs, walked on his face, and stamped on his fingers, so that it was only after lying in bed for a week that he was able to get up and look for another job. All of which is duly narrated in that first book of his, in the chapter entitled "The Tyranny of Labor."

A little later, in another department of the Wilmax Cannery, lumping as a fruit-distributor among the women, he essayed to carry two boxes of fruit at a time, and was promptly reproached by the other fruit-lumpers. It was palpable malingering; but he was there, he decided, not to change conditions, but to observe. So he lumped one box thereafter, and so well did he study the art of shirking that he wrote a special chapter on it, with the last several paragraphs devoted to tentative generalizations.

In those six months he worked at many jobs and developed into a very good imitation of a genuine worker. He was a natural linguist, and he kept notebooks, making a scientific study of the workers' slang or argot, until he could talk quite intelligibly. This language also enabled him more intimately to follow their mental processes, and thereby to gather much data for a projected chapter in some future book which he planned to entitle "Synthesis of Working-Class Psychology."

Before he arose to the surface from that first plunge into the underworld he discovered that he was a good actor and demonstrated the plasticity of his nature. He was himself astonished at his own fluidity. Once having mastered the language and conquered numerous fastidious qualms, he found that he could flow into any nook of working-class life and fit it so snugly as to feel comfortably at home. As he said, in the preface to his second book, "The Toiler," he endeavored really to know the working people, and the only possible way to achieve this was to work beside them, eat their food, sleep in their beds, be amused with their amusements, think their thoughts, and feel their feelings.

He was not a deep thinker. He had no faith in new theories. All his norms and criteria were conventional. His Thesis, on the French Revolution, was noteworthy in college annals, not merely for its painstaking and voluminous accuracy, but for the fact that it was the dryest, deadest, most formal, and most orthodox screed ever written on the subject. He was a very reserved man, and his natural inhibition was large in quantity and steel-like in quality. He had but few friends. He was too undemonstrative, too frigid. He had no vices, nor had anyone ever discovered any temptations. Tobacco he detested, beer he abhorred, and he was never known to drink anything stronger than an occasional light wine at dinner.

When a freshman he had been baptized "Ice-Box" by his warmer-blooded fellows. As a member of the faculty he was known as "Cold-Storage." He had but one grief, and that was "Freddie." He had earned it when he played full-back on the 'Varsity eleven, and his formal soul had never succeeded in living it down. "Freddie" he would ever be, except officially, and through nightmare vistas he looked into a future when his world would speak of him as "Old Freddie."

For he was very young to be a Doctor of Sociology, only twenty-seven, and he looked younger. In appearance and atmosphere he was a strapping big college man, smooth-faced and easy-mannered, clean and simple and wholesome, with a known record of being a splendid athlete and an implied vast possession of cold culture of the inhibited sort. He never talked shop out of class and committee rooms, except later on, when his books showered him with distasteful public notice and he yielded to the extent of reading occasional papers before certain literary and economic societies.

He did everything right—too right; and in dress and comportment was inevitably correct. Not that the was a dandy. Far from it. He was a college man, in dress and carriage as like as a pea to the type that of late years is being so generously turned out of our institutions of higher learning. His handshake was satisfyingly strong and stiff. His blue eyes were coldly blue and convincingly sincere. His voice, firm and masculine, clean and crisp of enunciation, was pleasant to the ear. The one drawback to Freddie Drummond was his inhibition. He never unbent. In his football days, the higher the tension of the game, the cooler he grew. He was noted as a boxer, but he was regarded as an automaton, with the inhuman precision of a machine judging distance and timing blows, guarding, blocking, and stalling. He was rarely punished himself, while he rarely punished an opponent. He was too clever and too controlled to permit himself to put a pound more weight into a punch than he intended. With him it was a matter of exercise. It kept him fit.

As time went by, Freddie Drummond found himself more frequently crossing the Slot and losing himself in South of Market. His summer and winter holidays were spent there, and, whether it was a week or a week-end, he found the time spent there to be valuable and enjoyable. And there was so much material to be gathered. His third book, "Mass and Master," became a text-book in the American universities; and almost before he knew it, he was at work on a fourth one, "The Fallacy of the Inefficient."

Somewhere in his make-up there was a strange twist or quirk. Perhaps it was a recoil from his environment and training, or from the tempered seed of his ancestors, who had been bookmen generation preceding generation; but at any rate, he found enjoyment in being down in the working-class world. In his own world he was "Cold-Storage," but down below he was "Big" Bill Totts, who could drink and smoke, and slang and fight, and be an all-around favorite. Everybody liked BIll, and more than one working girl made love to him. At first he had been merely a good actor, but as time went on, simulation became second nature. He no longer played a part, and he loved sausages, sausages and bacon, than which, in his own proper sphere, there was nothing more loathsome in the way of food.

From doing the thing for the need's sake, he came to doing the thing for the thing's sake. He found himself regretting as the time drew near for him to go back to his lecture-room and his inhibition. And he often found himself waiting with anticipation for the dreamy time to pass when he could cross the Slot and cut loose and play the devil. He was not wicked, but as "Big" Bill Totts he did a myriad things that Freddie Drummond would never have been permitted to do. Moreover, Freddie Drummond never would have wanted to do them. That was the strangest part of his discovery. Freddie Drummond and Bill Totts were two totally different creatures. The desires and tastes and impulses of each ran counter to the other's. Bill Totts could shirk at a job with clear conscience, while Freddie Drummond condemned shirking as vicious, criminal, and un-American, and devoted whole chapters to condemnation of the vice. Freddie Drummond did not care for dancing, but Bill Totts never missed the nights at the various dancing clubs, such as the Magnolia, The Western Star, and The Elite; while he won a massive silver cup, standing thirty inches high, for being the best-sustained character at the Butchers and Meat Workers' annual grand masked ball. And Bill Totts liked the girls and the girls liked him, while Freddie Drummond enjoyed playing the ascetic in this particular, was open in his opposition to equal suffrage, and cynically bitter in his secret condemnation of coeducation.

Freddie Drummond changed his manners with his dress, and without effort. When he entered the obscure little room used for his transformation scenes, he carried himself just a bit too stiffly. He was too erect, his shoulders were an inch too far back, while his face was grave, almost harsh, and practically expressionless. But when he emerged in Bill Tott's clothes he was another creature. Bill Totts did not slouch, but somehow his whole form limbered up and became graceful. The very sound of the voice was changed, and the laugh was loud and hearty, while loose speech and an occasional oath were as a matter of course on his lips. Also, Bill Totts was a trifle inclined to later hours, and at times, in saloons, to be good-naturedly bellicose with other workmen. Then, too, at Sunday picnics or when coming home form the show, either arm betrayed a practiced familiarity in stealing around girls' waists, while he displayed a wit keen and delightful in the flirtatious badinage that was expected of a good fellow in his class.

So thoroughly was Bill Totts himself, so thoroughly a workman, a genuine denizen of South of the Slot, that he was as class-conscious as the average of his kind, and his hatred for a scab even exceeded that of the average loyal union man. During the Water Front Strike, Freddie Drummond was somehow able to stand apart from the unique combination, and, coldly critical, watch Bill Totts hilariously slug scab longshoremen. For Bill Totts was a dues-paying member of the Longshoremen Union and had a right to be indignant with the usurpers of his job. "Big" Bill Totts was so very big, and so very able, that it was "Big" Bill to the front when trouble was brewing. From acting outraged feelings, Freddie Drummond, in the rôle of his other self, came to experience genuine outrage, and it was only when he returned to the classic atmosphere of the university that he was able, sanely and conservatively, to generalize upon his underworld experiences and put them down on paper as a trained sociologist should. That Bill Totts lacked the perspective to raise him above class-consciousness, Freddie Drummond clearly saw. But Bill Totts could not see it. When he saw a scab taking his job away, he saw red at the same time, and little else did he see. It was Freddie Drummond, irreproachably clothed and comported, seated at his study desk or facing his class in "Sociology I," who saw Bill Totts, and all around Bill Totts, and all around the whole scab and union-labor problem and its relation to the economic welfare of the United States in the struggle for the world market. Bill Totts really wasn't able to see beyond the next meal and the prize-fight the following night at the Gaiety Athletic-Club.

It was while gathering material for "Women and Work" that Freddie received his first warning of the danger he was in. He was too successful at living in both worlds. This strange dualism he had developed was after all very unstable, and, as he sat in his study and mediated, he saw that it could not endure. It was really a transition stage, and if he persisted he saw that he would inevitably have to drop one world or the other. He could not continue in both. And as he looked at the row of volumes that graced the upper shelf of his revolving book-case, his volumes, beginning with his Thesis and ending with "Women and Work," he decided that that was the world he would hold to and stick by. Bill Totts had served his purpose, but he had become a too dangerous accomplice. Bill Totts would have to cease.

Freddie Drummond's fright was due to Mary Condon, President of the International Glove Workers' Union No. 947. He had seen her, first, from the spectators' gallery, at the annual convention of the Northwest Federation of Labor, and he had seen her through Bill Totts' eyes, and that individual had been most favorably impressed by her. She was not Freddie Drummond's sort at all. What if she were a royal-bodied woman, graceful and sinewy as a panther, with amazing black eyes that could fill with fire or laughter-love, as the mood might dictate? He detested women with a too exuberant vitality and a lack of . . . well, of inhibition. Freddie Drummond accepted the doctrine of evolution because it was quite universally accepted by college men, and he flatly believed that man had climbed up the ladder of life out of the weltering muck and mess of lower and monstrous organic things. But he was a trifle ashamed of this genealogy, and preferred not to think of it. Wherefore, probably, he practiced his iron inhibition and preached it to others, and preferred women of his own type, who could shake free of the bestial and regrettable ancestral line and by discipline and control emphasize the wideness of the gulf that separated them from what their dim forbears had been.

Bill Totts had none of these considerations. He had liked Mary Condon from the moment his eyes first rested on her in the convention hall, and he had made it a point, then and there, to find out who she was. The next time he met her, and quite by accident, was when he was driving an express wagon for Pat Morrissey. It was in a lodging house in Mission Street, where he had been called to take a trunk into storage. The landlady's daughter had called him and led him to the little bedroom, the occupant of which, a glove-maker, had just been removed to hospital.

But Bill did not know this. He stooped, up-ended the trunk, which was a large one, got it on his shoulder, and struggled to his feet with his back toward the open door. At that moment he heard a woman's voice.

"Belong to the union?" was the question asked.

"Aw, what's it to you?" he retorted. "Run along now, an' git outa my way. I wanta turn round."

The next he knew, big as he was, he was whirled half around and sent reeling backward, the trunk overbalancing him, till he fetched up with a crash against the wall. He started to swear, but the same instant found himself looking into Mary Condon's flashing, angry eyes.

"Of course I b'long to the union," he said. "I was only kiddin' you."

"Where's your card?" she demanded in business-like tones.

"In my pocket. But I can't git it out now. This trunk's too damn heavy. Come on down to the wagon an' I'll show it to you."

"Put that trunk down," was the command.

"What for? I got a card, I'm tellin' you."

"Put it down, that's all. No scab's going to handle that trunk. You ought to be ashamed of yourself, you big coward, scabbing on honest men. Why don't you join the union and be a man?"

Mary Condon's color had left her face, and it was apparent that she was in a rage.

"To think of a big man like you turning traitor to his class. I suppose you're aching to join the militia for a chance to shoot down union drivers the next strike. You may belong to the militia already, for that matter. You're the sort——"

"Hold on, now, that's too much!" Bill dropped the trunk to the floor with a bang, straightened up, and thrust his hand into his inside coat pocket. "I told you I was only kiddin'. There, look at that."

It was a union card properly enough.

"All right, take it along," Mary Condon said. "And the next time don't kid."

Her face relaxed as she noticed the ease with which he got the big trunk to his shoulder, and her eyes glowed as they glanced over the graceful massiveness of the man. But Bill did not see that. He was too busy with the trunk.

The next time he saw Mary Condon was during the Laundry Strike. The Laundry Workers, but recently organized, were green at the business, and had petitioned Mary Condon to engineer the strike. Freddie Drummond had had an inkling of what was coming, and had sent Bill Totts to join the union and investigate. Bill's job was in the washroom, and the men had been called out first, that morning, in order to stiffen the courage of the girls; and Bill chanced to be near the door to the mangle-room when Mary Condon started to enter. The superintendent, who was both large and stout, barred her way. He wasn't going to have his girls called out, and he'd teach her a lesson to mind her own business. And as Mary tried to squeeze past him he thrust her back with a fat hand on her shoulder. She glanced around and saw Bill.

"Here you, Mr. Totts," she called. "Lend a hand. I want to get in."

Bill experienced a startle of warm surprise. She had remembered his name from his union card. The next moment the superintendent had been plucked from the doorway raving about rights under the law, and the girls were deserting their machines. During the rest of that short and successful strike, Bill constituted himself Mary Condon's henchman and messenger, and when it was over returned to the University to be Freddie Drummond and to wonder what Bill Totts could see in such a woman.

Freddie Drummond was entirely safe, but Bill had fallen in love. There was no getting away from the fact of it, and it was this fact that had given Freddie Drummond his warning. Well, he had done his work, and his adventures could cease. There was no need for him to cross the Slot again. All but the last three chapters of his latest, "Labor Tactics and Strategy," was finished, and he had sufficient material on hand adequately to supply those chapters.

Another conclusion he arrived at, was that in order to sheet-anchor himself as Freddie Drummond, closer ties and relations in his own social nook were necessary. It was time that he was married, anyway, and he was fully aware that if Freddie Drummond didn't get married, Bill Totts assuredly would, and the complications were too awful to contemplate. And so, enters Catherine Van Vorst. She was a college woman herself, and her father, the one wealthy member of the faculty, was the head of the Philosophy Department as well. It would be a wise marriage from every standpoint, Freddie Drummond concluded when the engagement was consummated and announced. In appearance cold and reserved, aristocratic and wholesomely conservative, Catherine Van Vorst, though warm in her way, possessed an inhibition equal to Drummond's.

All seemed well with him, but Freddie Drummond could not quite shake off the call of the underworld, the lure of the free and open, of the unhampered, irresponsible life South of the Slot. As the time of his marriage approached, he felt that he had indeed sowed wild oats, and he felt, moreover, what a good thing it would be if he could have but one wild fling more, play the good fellow and the wastrel one last time, ere he settled down to gray lecture-rooms and sober matrimony. And, further to tempt him, the very last chapter of "Labor Tactics and Strategy" remained unwritten for lack of a trifle more of essential data which he had neglected to gather.

So Freddie Drummond went down for the last time as Bill Totts, got his data, and, unfortunately, encountered Mary Condon. Once more installed in his study, it was not a pleasant thing to look back upon. It made his warning doubly imperative. Bill Totts had behaved abominably. Not only had he met Mary Condon at the Central Labor Council, but he had stopped in at a chop-house with her, on the way home, and treated her to oysters. And before they parted at her door, his arms had been about her, and he kissed her on the lips and kissed her repeatedly. And her last words in his ear, words uttered softly with a catchy sob in the throat that was nothing more nor less than a love cry, were "Bill ... dear, dear Bill."

Freddie Drummond shuddered at the recollection. He saw the pit yawning for him. He was not by nature a polygamist, and he was appalled at the possibilities of the situation. It would have to be put an end to, and it would end in one only of two ways: either he must become wholly Bill Totts and be married to Mary Condon, or he must remain wholly Freddie Drummond and be married to Catherine Van Vorst. Otherwise, his conduct would be beneath contempt and horrible.

In the several months that followed, San Francisco was torn with labor strife. The unions and the employers' associations had locked horns with determination that looked as if they intended to settle the matter, one way or the other, for all time. But Freddie Drummond corrected proofs, lectured classes, and did not budge. He devoted himself to Catherine Van Vorst, and day by day found more to respect and admire in her—nay, even to love in her. The Street Car Strike tempted him, but not so severely as he would have expected; and the great Meat Strike came on and left him cold. The ghost of Bill Totts had been successfully laid, and Freddie Drummond with rejuvenescent zeal tackled a brochure, long-planned, on the topic of "diminishing returns."

The wedding was two weeks off, when, one afternoon, in San Francisco, Catherine Van Vorst picked him up and whisked him away to see a Boys' Club, recently instituted by the settlement workers with whom she was interested. It was her brother's machine, but they were alone with the exception of the chauffeur. At the junction with Kearny Street, Market and Geary Streets intersect like the sides of a sharp-angled letter "V." They, in the auto, were coming

down Market with the intention of negotiating the sharp
apex and going up Geary. But they did not know what was
coming down Geary, timed by fate to meet them at the
apex. While aware from the papers that the Meat Strike
was on and that it was an exceedingly bitter one, all
thought of it at that moment was farthest from Freddie
Drummond's mind. Was he not seated beside Catherine?
And, besides, he was carefully exposing to her his views
on settlement work—views that Bill Totts' adventures had
played a part in formulating.

Coming down Geary Street were six meat wagons. Beside each scab driver sat a policeman. Front and rear, and
along each side of this procession, marched a protecting
escort of one hundred police. Behind the police rear guard,
at a respectful distance, was an orderly but vociferous
mob, several blocks in length, that congested the street
from sidewalk to sidewalk. The Beef Trust was making an
effort to supply the hotels, and, incidentally, to begin the
breaking of the strike. The St. Francis had already been
supplied, at a cost of many broken windows and broken
heads, and the expedition was marching to the relief of the
Palace Hotel.

All unwitting, Drummond sat beside Catherine, talking
settlement work, as the auto, honking methodically and
dodging traffic, swung in a wide curve to get around the
apex. A big coal wagon, loaded with lump coal and drawn
by four huge horses, just debouching from Kearny Street
as though to turn down Market, blocked their way. The
driver of the wagon seemed undecided, and the chauffeur,
running slow but disregarding some shouted warning from
the crossing policemen, swerved the auto to the left, vio-
lating the traffic rules, in order to pass in front of the
wagon.

At that moment Freddie Drummond discontinued his
conversation. Nor did he resume it again, for the situation
was developing with the rapidity of a transformation
scene. He heard the roar of the mob at the rear, and caught

a glimpse of the helmeted police and the lurching meat
wagons. At the same moment, laying on his whip and
standing up to his task, the coal driver rushed horses and
wagon squarely in front of the advancing procession,
pulled the horses up sharply, and put on the big brake.
Then he made his lines fast to the brake-handle and sat
down with the air of one who had stopped to stay. The
auto had been brought to a stop, too, by his big panting
leaders which had jammed against it.

Before the chauffeur could back clear, an old Irishman,
driving a rickety express wagon and lashing his one horse
to a gallop, had locked wheels with the auto. Drummond
recognized both horse and wagon, for he had driven them
often himself. The Irishman was Pat Morrissey. On the
other side a brewery wagon was locking with the coal
wagon, and an east-bound Kearny-Street car, wildly
clanging its gong, the motorman shouting defiance at the
crossing policeman, was dashing forward to complete the
blockade. And wagon after wagon was locking and blocking and adding to the confusion. The meat wagons halted.
The police were trapped. The roar at the rear increased as
the mob came on to the attack, while the vanguard of the
police charged the obstructing wagons.

"We're in for it," Drummond remarked coolly to Catherine.

"Yes," she nodded, with equal coolness. "What savages
they are."

His admiration for her doubled on itself. She was indeed
his sort. He would have been satisfied with her even if she
had screamed and clung to him, but this—this was magnificent. She sat in that storm center as calmly as if it had
been no more than a block of carriages at the opera.

The police were struggling to clear a passage. The
driver of the coal wagon, a big man in shirt sleeves,
lighted a pipe and sat smoking. He glanced down complacently at a captain of police who was raving and cursing
at him, and his only acknowledgment was a shrug of the

shoulders. From the rear arose the rat-tat-tat of clubs on heads and a pandemonium of cursing, yelling, and shouting. A violent accession of noise proclaimed that the mob had broken through and was dragging a scab from a wagon. The police captain reinforced from his vanguard, and the mob at the rear was repelled. Meanwhile, window after window in the high office building on the right had been opened, and the class-conscious clerks were raining a shower of office furniture down on the heads of police and scabs. Waste-baskets, ink-bottles, paper-weights, type writers—anything and everything that came to hand was filling the air.

A policeman, under orders from his captain, clambered to the lofty seat of the coal wagon to arrest the driver. And the driver, rising leisurely and peacefully to meet him, suddenly crumpled him in his arms and threw him down on top of the captain. The driver was a young giant, and when he climbed on top his load and poised a lump of coal in both hands, a policeman, who was just scaling the wagon from the side, let go and dropped back to earth. The captain ordered half a dozen of his men to take the wagon. The teamster, scrambling over the load from side to side, beat them down with huge lumps of coal.

The crowd on the sidewalks and the teamsters on the locked wagons roared encouragement and their own delight. The motorman, smashing helmets with his controller bar, was beaten into insensibility and dragged from his platform. The captain of police, beside himself at the repulse of his men, led the next assault on the coal wagon. A score of police were swarming up the tall-sided fortress. But the teamster multiplied himself. At times there were six or eight policemen rolling on the pavement and under the wagon. Engaged in repulsing an attack on the rear end of his fortress, the teamster turned about to see the captain just in the act of stepping on to the seat from the front end. He was still in the air and in most unstable equilibrium, when the teamster hurled a thirty-pound lump of coal. It caught the captain fairly on the chest, and he went over backward, striking on a wheeler's back, tumbling on to the ground, and jamming against the rear wheel of the auto.

Catherine thought he was dead, but he picked himself up and charged back. She reached out her gloved hand and patted the flank of the snorting, quivering horse. But Drummond did not notice the action. He had eyes for nothing save the battle of the coal wagon, while somewhere in his complicated psychology, one Bill Totts was heaving and straining in an effort to come to life. Drummond believed in law and order and the maintenance of the established, but this riotous savage within him would have none of it. Then, if ever, did Freddie Drummond call upon his iron inhibition to save him. But it is written that the house divided against itself must fall. And Freddie Drummond found that he had divided all the will and force of him with Bill Totts, and between them the entity that constituted the pair of them was being wrenched in twain.

Freddie Drummond sat in the auto, quite composed, alongside Catherine Van Vorst; but looking out of Freddie Drummond's eyes was Bill Totts, and somewhere behind those eyes, battling for the control of their mutual body, were Freddie Drummond, the sane and conservative sociologist, and Bill Totts, the class-conscious and bellicose union workingman. It was Bill Totts, looking out of those eyes, who saw the inevitable end of the battle on the coal wagon. He saw a policeman gain the top of the load, a second, and a third. They lurched clumsily on the loose footing, but their long riot-clubs were out and swinging. One blow caught the teamster on the head. A second he dodged, receiving it on the shoulder. For him the game was plainly up. He dashed in suddenly, clutched two policemen in his arms, and hurled himself a prisoner to the pavement, his hold never relaxing on his two captors.

Catherine Van Vorst was sick and faint at the sight of the blood and brutal fighting. But her qualms were vanquished by the sensational and most unexpected happening that followed. The man beside her emitted an unearthly and uncultured yell and rose to his feet. She saw him spring over the front seat, leap to the broad rump of the wheeler, and from there gain the wagon. His onslaught was like a whirlwind. Before the bewildered officer on top the load could guess the errand of this conventionally clad but excited-seeming gentleman, he was the recipient of a punch that arched him back through the air to the pavement. A kick in the face led an ascending policeman to follow his example. A rush of three more gained the top and locked with Bill Totts in a gigantic clinch, during which his scalp was opened by a club, and coat, vest, and half his starched shirt were torn from him. But the three policemen were flung wide and far, and Bill Totts, raining down lumps of coal, held the fort.

The captain led gallantly to the attack, but was bowled over by a chunk of coal that burst on his head in black baptism. The need of the police was to break the blockade in front before the mob could break in at the rear, and Bill Totts' need was to hold the wagon till the mob did break through. So the battle of the coal went on.

The crowd had recognized its champion. "Big" Bill, as usual, had come to the front, and Catherine Van Vorst was bewildered by the cries of "Bill! O you Bill!" that arose on every hand. Pat Morrissey, on his wagon seat, was jumping and screaming in ecstasy, "Eat 'em, Bill! Eat 'em! Eat 'em alive!" From the sidewalk she heard a woman's voice cry out, "Look out, Bill—front end!" Bill took the warning and with well-directed coal cleaned the front end of the wagon of assailants. Catherine Van Vorst turned her head and saw on the curb of the sidewalk a woman with vivid coloring and flashing black eyes who was staring with all her soul at the man who had been Freddie Drummond a few minutes before.

The windows of the office building became vociferous with applause. Af fresh shower of office chairs and filing cabinets descended. The mob had broken through on one

side the line of wagons, and was advancing, each segre-
gated policeman the center of a fighting group. The scabs
were torn from their seats, the traces of the horses cut, and
the frightened animals put in flight. Many policemen
crawled under the coal wagon for safety, while the loose
horses, with here and there a policeman on their backs
or struggling at their heads to hold them, surged across
the sidewalk opposite the jam and broke into Market
Street.

Catherine Van Vorst heard the woman's voice calling
in warning. She was back on the curb again, and crying
out:

"Beat it, Bill! Now's your time! Beat it!"

The police for the moment had been swept away. Bill
Totts leaped to the pavement and made his way to the
woman on the sidewalk. Catherine Van Vorst saw her
throw her arms around him and kiss him on the lips; and
Catherine Van Vorst watched him curiously as he went on
down the sidewalk, one arm around the woman, both talking and laughing, and he with a volubility and abandon
she could never have dreamed possible.

The police were back again and clearing the jam while
waiting for reinforcements and new drivers and horses.
The mob had done its work and was scattering, and Catherine Van Vorst, still watching, could see the man she had
known as Freddie Drummond. He towered a head above
the crowd. His arm was still about the woman. And she in
the motorcar, watching, saw the pair cross Market Street,
cross the Slot, and disappear down Third Street into the labor ghetto.

In the years that followed no more lectures were given
in the University of California by one Freddie Drummond,
and no more books on economics and the labor question
appeared over the name of Frederick A. Drummond. On
the other hand there arose a new labor leader, William
Totts by name. He it was who married Mary Condon,

President of the International Glove Workers' Union No. 974; and he it was who called the notorious Cooks and Waiters' strike, which, before its successful termination, brought out with it scores of other unions, among which, of the more remotely allied, were the Chicken Pickers and the Undertakers.

The Water Baby

I lent a weary ear to old Kohokumu's interminable chant-ing of the deeds and adventures of Maui, the Prome-thean demigod of Polynesia who fished up dry land from ocean depths with hooks made fast to heaven, who lifted up the sky whereunder previously men had gone on all fours, not having space to stand erect, and who made the sun with its sixteen snared legs stand still and agree there-after to traverse the sky more slowly—the sun being evi-dently a trade-unionist and believing in the six-hour day, while Maui stood for the open shop and the twelve-hour day.

"Now this," said Kohokumu, "is from Queen Liliuo-kalani's own family mele:

" 'Maui became restless and fought the sun
with a noose that he laid.
And winter won the sun,
And summer was won by Maui. . . .' "

Born in the Islands myself, I know the Hawaiian myths better than this old fisherman, although I possessed not his memorization that enabled him to recite them endless hours.

"And you believe all this?" I demanded in the sweet Hawaiian tongue.

"It was a long time ago," he pondered. "I never saw Maui with my own eyes. But all our old men from all the way back tell us these things, as I, an old man, tell them to my sons and grandsons, who will tell them to their sons and grandsons all the way ahead to come."

"You believe," I persisted, "that whopper of Maui roping the sun like a wild steer, and that other whopper of heaving up the sky from off the earth?"

"I am of little worth, and am not wise, O Lakana," my fisherman made answer. "Yet have I read the Hawaiian bible the missionaries translated to us, and there have I read that your Big Man of the Beginning made the earth and sky and sun and moon and stars, and all manner of animals from horses to cockroaches and from centipedes and mosquitoes to sea lice and jellyfish, and man and woman and everything, and all in six days. Why, Maui didn't do anything like that much. He didn't *make* anything. He just put things in order, that was all, and it took him a long, long time to make the improvements. And anyway, it is much easier and more reasonable to believe the little whopper than the big whopper."

And what could I reply? He had me on the matter of reasonableness. Besides, my head ached. And the funny thing, as I admitted to myself, was that evolution teaches in no uncertain voice that man did run on all fours ere he came to walk upright, that astronomy states flatly that the speed of the revolution of the earth on its axis has diminished steadily, thus increasing the length of day, and that the seismologists accept that all the islands of Hawaii were elevated from the ocean floor by volcanic action.

Fortunately, I saw a bamboo pole, floating on the surface several hundred feet away, suddenly up-end and start a very devil's dance. This was a diversion from the profitless discussion, and Kohokumu and I dipped our paddles and raced the little outrigger canoe to the dancing pole. Kohokumu caught the line that was fast to the butt of the pole and underhanded it in until a two-foot *ukikiki*, battling fiercely to the end, flashed its wet silver in the sun and began beating a tattoo on the inside bottom of the canoe. Kohokumu picked up a squirming, slimy squid, with his teeth bit a chunk of live bait out of it, attached the bait to the hook, and dropped line and sinker overside. The stick floated flat on the surface of the water, and the canoe drifted slowly away. With a survey of the crescent composed of a score of such sticks all lying flat, Kohokumu wiped his hands on his naked sides and lifted the wearisome and centuries-old chant of Kuali:

" 'Oh, the great fishhook of Maui!
Manai-i-ka-lani—"made fast to the heavens"!
An earth-twisted cord ties the hook,
Engulfed from lofty Kauiki!
Its bait the red-billed Alae,
The bird to Hina sacred!
It sinks far down to Hawaii,
Struggling and in pain dying!
Caught is the land beneath the water,
Floated up, up to the surface,
But Hina hid a wing of the bird
And broke the land beneath the water!
Below was the bait snatched away
And eaten at once by the fishes,
The Ulua of the deep muddy places!' "

His aged voice was hoarse and scratchy from the drinking of too much swipes at a funeral the night before, nothing of which contributed to make me less irritable. My head ached. The sun glare on the water made my eyes ache, while I was suffering more than half a touch of mal de mer from the antic conduct of the outrigger on the blobby sea. The air was stagnant. In the lee of Waihee, between the white beach and the reef, no whisper of breeze eased the still sultriness. I really think I was too miserable to summon the resolution to give up the fishing and go in to shore.

Lying back with closed eyes, I lost count of time. I even forgot that Kohokumu was chanting till reminded of it by his ceasing. An exclamation made me bare my eyes to the stab of the sun. He was gazing down through the water glass.

"It's a big one," he said, passing me the device and slipping overside feetfirst into the water.

He went under without splash and ripple, turned over, and swam down. I followed his progress through the water glass, which is merely an oblong box a couple of feet long, open at the top, the bottom sealed water-tight with a sheet of ordinary glass.

Now Kohokumu was a bore, and I was squeamishly out of sorts with him for his volubleness, but I could not help admiring him as I watched him go down. Past seventy years of age, lean as a spear, and shriveled like a mummy, he was doing what few young athletes of my race would do or could do. It was forty feet to bottom. There, partly exposed but mostly hidden under the bulge of a coral lump, I could discern his objective. His keen eyes had caught the projecting tentacle of a squid. Even as he swam, the tentacle was lazily withdrawn, so that there was no sign of the creature. But the brief exposure of the portion of one tentacle had advertised its owner as a squid of size.

The pressure at a depth of forty feet is no joke for a young man, yet it did not seem to inconvenience this oldster. I am certain it never crossed his mind to be inconvenienced. Unarmed, bare of body save for a brief *malo* or loin cloth, he was undeterred by the formidable creature that constituted his prey. I saw him steady himself with his right hand on the coral lump, and thrust his left arm into the hole to the shoulder. Half a minute elapsed, during which time he seemed to be groping and rooting around with his left hand. Then tentacle after tentacle, myriad-suckered and wildly waving, emerged. Laying hold of his arm, they writhed and coiled about his flesh like so many snakes. With a heave and a jerk appeared the entire squid, a proper devilfish or octopus.

But the old man was in no hurry for his natural element, the air above the water. There, forty feet beneath, wrapped about by an octopus that measured nine feet across from tentacle tip to tentacle tip and that could well drown the stoutest swimmer, he cooly and casually did the one thing that gave to him his empery over the monster. He shoved his lean, hawklike face into the very center of the slimy, squirming mass, and with his several ancient fangs bit into the heart and the life of the matter. This accomplished, he came upward slowly, as a swimmer should who is changing atmospheres from the depths. Alongside the canoe, still in the water and peeling off the grisly clinging thing, the incorrigible old sinner burst into the *pule* of triumph which had been chanted by countless squid-catching generations before him:

" 'O Kanaloa of the taboo nights!
Stand upright on the solid floor!
Stand upon the floor where lies the squid!
Stand up to take the squid of the deep sea!
Rise up, O Kanaloa!
Stir up! Stir up! Let the squid awake!
Let the squid that lies flat awake!
Let the squid that lies spread out. . . .' "

I closed my eyes and ears, not offering to lend him a hand, secure in the knowledge that he could climb back unaided into the unstable craft without the slightest risk of upsetting it.

"A very fine squid," he crooned. "It is a wahine squid. I shall now sing to you the song of the cowrie shell, the red cowrie shell that we used as a bait for the squid—"

"You were disgraceful last night at the funeral," I headed him off. "I heard all about it. You made much noise. You sang till everybody was deaf. You insulted the son of the widow. You drank swipes like a pig. Swipes are not good for your extreme age. Some day you will wake up dead. You ought to be a wreck to-day—"

"Ha!" he chuckled. "And you, who drank no swipes, who was a babe unborn when I was already an old man, who went to bed last night with the sun and the chickens—this day you are a wreck. Explain me that. My ears are as thirsty to listen as was my throat thirsty last night. And here to-day, behold, I am, as that Englishman who came here in his yacht used to say, I am in fine form, in devilish fine form."

"I give you up," I retorted, shrugging my shoulders. "Only one thing is clear, and that is that the devil doesn't want you. Report of your singing has gone before you."

"No," he pondered the idea carefully. "It is not that. The devil will be glad for my coming, for I have some very fine songs for him, and scandals and old gossips of the high aliis that will make him scratch his sides. So let me explain to you the secret of my birth. The Sea is my mother. I was born in a double canoe, during a Kona gale, in the channel of Kahoolawe. From her, the Sea, my mother, I received my strength. Whenever I return to her arms, as for a breast clasp, as I have returned this day, I grow strong again and immediately. She, to me, is the milk giver, the life source—"

"Shades of Antæus!" thought I.

"Some day," old Kohokumu rambled on, "when I am really old, I shall be reported of men as drowned in the sea. This will be an idle thought of men. In truth, I shall have returned into the arms of my mother, there to rest under the heart of her breast until the second birth of me, when I shall emerge into the sun a flashing youth of splendor like Maui himself when he was golden young."

"A queer religion," I commented.

"When I was younger I muddled my poor head over

queerer religions," old Kohokumu retorted. "But listen, O Young Wise One, to my elderly wisdom. This I know: as I grow old I seek less for the truth from without me, and find more of the truth from within me. Why have I thought this thought of my return to my mother and of my rebirth from my mother into the sun? You do not know. I do not know, save that, without whisper of man's voice or printed word, without prompting from otherwhere, this thought has arisen from within me, from the deeps of me that are as deep as the sea. I am not a god. I do not make things. Therefore I have not made this thought. I do not know its father or its mother. It is of old time before me, and therefore it is true. Man does not make truth. Man, if he be not blind, only recognizes truth when he sees it. Is this thought that I have thought a dream?"

"Perhaps it is you that are a dream," I laughed. "And that I and sky and sea and the iron-hard land are dreams, all dreams."

"I have often thought that," he assured me soberly. "It may well be so. Last night I dreamed I was a lark bird, a beautiful singing lark of the sky like the larks on the upland pastures of Haleakala. And I flew up, up toward the sun, singing, singing, as old Kohokumu never sang. I tell you now that I dreamed I was a lark bird singing in the sky. But may not I, the real I, be the lark bird? And may not the telling of it be the dream that I, the lark bird, am dreaming now? Who are you to tell me aye or no? Dare you tell me I am not a lark bird asleep and dreaming that I am old Kohokumu?"

I shrugged my shoulders, and he continued triumphantly.

"And how do you know but what you are old Maui himself asleep and dreaming that you are John Lakana talking with me in a canoe? And may you not awake, old Maui yourself, and scratch your sides and say that you had a funny dream in which you dreamed you were a haole?"

"I don't know," I admitted. "Besides, you wouldn't believe me."

"There is much more in dreams than we know," he assured me with great solemnity. "Dreams go deep, all the way down, maybe to before the beginning. May not old Maui have only dreamed he pulled Hawaii up from the bottom of the sea? The would this Hawaii land be a dream, and you and I and the squid there only parts of Maui's dream? And the lark bird, too?"

He sighed and let his head sink on his breast.

"And I worry my old head about the secrets undiscoverable," he resumed, "until I grow tired and want to forget, and so I drink swipes, and go fishing, and sing old songs, and dream I am a lark bird singing in the sky. I like that best of all, and often I dream it when I have drunk much swipes—"

In great dejection of mood he peered down into the lagoon through the water glass.

"There will be no more bites for a while," he announced. "The fish sharks are prowling around, and we shall have to wait until they are gone. And so that the time shall not be heavy, I will sing you the canoe-hauling song to Lono. You remember:

" 'Give to me the trunk of the tree, O Lono!
Give me the tree's main root, O Lono!
Give me the ear of the tree, O Lono!—' "

"For the love of mercy, don't sing!" I cut him short. "I've got a headache, and your singing hurts. You may be in devilish fine form to-day, but your throat is rotten. I'd rather you talked about dreams, or told me whoppers."

"It is too bad that you are sick, and you so young," he conceded cheerily. "And I shall not sing any more. I shall tell you something you do not know and have never heard; something that is no dream and no whopper, but is what I know to have happened. Not very long ago there lived here, on the beach beside this very lagoon, a young boy whose name was Keikiwai, which, as you know, means Water Baby. He was truly a water baby. His gods were the sea and fish gods, and he was born with knowledge of the language of fishes, which the fishes did not know until the sharks found it out one day when they heard him talk it.

"It happened this way. The word had been brought, and the commands, by swift runners, that the king was making a progress around the island, and that on the next day a luau was to be served him by the dwellers here of Waihee. It was always a hardship, when the king made a progress, for the few dwellers in small places to fill his many stomachs with food. For he came always with his wife and her women, with his priests and sorcerers, his dancers and flute players and hula singers, and fighting men and servants, and his high chiefs with their wives, and sorcerers and fighting men and servants.

"Sometimes, in small places like Waihee, the path of his journey was marked afterward by leanness and famine. But a king must be fed, and it is not good to anger a king. So, like warning in advance of disaster, Waihee heard of his coming, and all food-getters of field and pond and mountain and sea were busied with getting food for the feast. And behold, everything was got, from the choicest of royal taro to sugar-cane joints for the roasting, from opihis to limu, from fowl to wild pig and poi-fed puppies—everything save one thing. The fishermen failed to get lobsters.

"Now be it known that the king's favorite food was lobster. He esteemed it above all *kao-kao* (food), and his runners had made special mention of it. And there were no lobsters, and it is not good to anger a king in the belly of him. Too many sharks had come inside the reef. That was the trouble. A young girl and an old man had been eaten by them. And of the young men who dared dive for lobsters, one was eaten, and one lost an arm, and another lost one hand and one foot.

"But there was Keikiwai, the Water Baby, only eleven years old, but half fish himself and talking the language of fishes. To his father the head men came, begging him to send the Water Baby to get lobsters to fill the king's belly and divert his anger.

"Now this, what happened, was known and observed. For the fishermen and their women, and the taro growers and the bird catchers, and the head men, and all Waihee, came down and stood back from the edge of the rock where the Water Baby stood and looked down at the lobsters far beneath on the bottom.

"And a shark, looking up with its cat's eyes, observed him, and sent out the shark call of 'fresh meat' to assemble all the sharks in the lagoon. For the sharks work thus together, which is why they are strong. And the sharks answered the call till there were forty of them, long ones and short ones and lean ones and round ones, forty of them by count; and they talked to one another, saying: 'Look at that tidbit of a child, that morsel delicious of human-flesh sweetness without the salt of the sea in it, of which salt we have too much, savory and good to eat, melting to delight under our hearts as our bellies embrace it and extract from it its sweet.'"

"Much more they said, saying: 'He has come for the lobsters. When he dives in he is for one of us. Not like the old man we ate yesterday, tough to dryness with age, nor like the young men whose members were too hard-muscled, but tender, so tender that he will melt in our gullets ere our bellies receive him. When he dives in, we will all rush for him, and the lucky one of us will get him, and, gulp, he will be gone, one bite and one swallow, into the belly of the luckiest one of us.'

"And Keikiwai, the Water Baby, heard the conspiracy, knowing the shark language; and he addressed a prayer, in the shark language, to the shark god Moku-halii, and the sharks heard and waved their tails to one another and winked their cat's eyes in token that they understood his talk. And then he said: 'I shall now dive for a lobster for the king. And no hurt shall befall me, because the shark with the shortest tail is my friend and will protect me.'

"And, so saying, he picked up a chunk of lava rock and

tossed it into the water, with a big splash, twenty feet to one side. The forty sharks rushed for the splash, while he dived, and by the time they discovered they had missed him, he had gone to the bottom and come back and climbed out, within his hand a fat lobster, a wahine lobster, full of eggs, for the king.

" 'Ha!' said the sharks, very angry. 'There is among us a traitor. The titbit of a child, the morsel of sweetness, has spoken, and has exposed the one among us who has saved him. Let us now measure the length of our tails!'

"Which they did, in a long row, side by side, the shorter-tailed ones cheating and stretching to gain length on themselves, the longer-tailed ones cheating and stretching in order not to be out-cheated and out-stretched. They were very angry with the one with the shortest tail, and him they rushed upon from every side and devoured till nothing was left of him.

"Again they listened while they waited for the Water Baby to dive in. And again the Water Baby made his prayer in the shark language to Moku-halii, and said: 'The shark with the shortest tail is my friend and will protect me.' And again the Water Baby tossed in a chunk of lava, this time twenty feet away off to the other side. The sharks rushed for the splash, and in their haste ran into one another, and splashed with their tails till the water was all foam and they could see nothing, each thinking some other was swallowing the titbit. And the Water Baby came up and climbed out with another fat lobster for the king.

"And the thirty-nine sharks measured tails, devouring the one with the shortest tail, so that there were only thirty-eight sharks. And the Water Baby continued to do what I have said, and the sharks to do what I have told you, while for each shark that was eaten by his brothers there was another fat lobster laid on the rock for the king. Of course, there was much quarreling and argument among the sharks when it came to measuring tails; but in the end it worked out in rightness and justice, for, when only two sharks were left, they were the two biggest of the original forty.

"And the Water Baby again claimed the shark with the shortest tail was his friend, fooled the two sharks with another lava chunk, and brought up another lobster. The two sharks each claimed the other had the shorter tail, and each fought to eat the other, and the one with the longer tail won—"

"Hold, O Kohokumu!" I interrupted. "Remember that that shark had already—"

"I know just what you are going to say," he snatched his recital back from me. "And you are right. It took him so long to eat the thirty-ninth shark, for inside the thirty-ninth shark were already the nineteen other sharks he had eaten, and inside the fortieth shark were already the nineteen other sharks he had eaten, and he did not have the appetite he had started with. But do not forget he was very big shark to begin with.

"It took him so long to eat the other shark, and the nineteen sharks inside the other shark, that he was still eating when darkness fell and the people of Waihee went away home with all the lobsters for the king. And didn't they find the last shark on the beach next morning dead and burst wide open with all he had eaten?"

Kohokumu fetched a full stop and held my eyes with his own shrewd ones.

"Hold, O Lakana!" he checked the speech that rushed to my tongue. "I know what next you would say. You would say that with my own eyes I did not see this, and therefore that I do not know what I have been telling you. But I do know, and I can prove it. My father's father knew the grandson of the Water Baby's father's uncle. Also, there, on the rocky point to which I point my finger now, is where the Water Baby stood and dived. I have dived for lobsters there myself. It is a great place for lobsters. Also, and often, have I seen sharks there. And there, on the bottom, as I should know, for I have seen and counted them, are the thirty-nine lava rocks thrown in by the Water Baby as I have described."

"But—" I began.

"Ha!" he baffled me. "Look! While we have talked the fish have begun again to bite."

He pointed to three of the bamboo poles erect and devil-dancing in token that fish were hooked and struggling on the lines beneath. As he bent to his paddle, he muttered, for my benefit:

"Of course I know. The thirty-nine lava rocks are still there. You can count them any day for yourself. Of course I know, and I know for a fact."

All Gold Canyon

It was the green heart of the canyon, where the walls swerved back from the rigid plan and relieved their harshness of line by making a little sheltered nook and filling it to the brim with sweetness and roundness and softness. Here all things rested. Even the narrow stream ceased its turbulent down-rush long enough to form a quiet pool. Knee-deep in the water, with drooping head and half-shut eyes, drowsed a red-coated, many-antlered buck.

On one side, beginning at the very lip of the pool, was a tiny meadow, a cool, resilient surface of green that extended to the base of the frowning wall. Beyond the pool a gentle slope of earth ran up and up to meet the opposing wall. Fine grass covered the slope—grass that was spangled with flowers, with here and there patches of color, orange and purple and golden. Below, the canyon was shut in. There was no view. The walls leaned together abruptly and the canyon ended in a chaos of rocks, moss-covered and hidden by a green screen of vines and creepers and boughs of trees. Up the canyon rose far hills and peaks, the big foot-hills, pine-covered and remote. And far beyond, like clouds upon the border of the sky, towered minarets of white, where the Sierra's eternal snows flashed austerely the blazes of the sun.

Thee was no dust in the canyon. The leaves and flowers were clean and virginal. The grass was young velvet. Over the pool three cottonwoods sent their snowy fluffs fluttering down the quiet air. On the slope the blossoms of the wine-wooded manzanita filled the air with springtime odors, while the leaves, wise with experience, were already beginning their vertical twist against the coming aridity of summer. In the open spaces on the slope, beyond the farthest shadow-reach of the manzanita, poised the mariposa lilies, like so many flights of jeweled moths suddenly arrested and on the verge of trembling into flight again. Here and there that woods harlequin, the madrone, permitting itself to be caught in the act of changing its pea-green trunk to madder-red, breathed its fragrance into the air from great clusters of waxen bells. Creamy white were these bells, shaped like lilies-of-the-valley, with the sweetness of perfume that is of the springtime.

There was not a sigh of wind. The air was drowsy with its weight of perfume. It was a sweetness that would have been cloying had the air been heavy and humid. But the air was sharp and thin. It was as starlight transmuted into atmosphere, shot through and warmed by sunshine, and flower-drenched with sweetness.

An occasional butterfly drifted in and out through the patches of light and shade. And from all about rose the low and sleepy hum of mountain bees—feasting Sybarites that jostled one another good-naturedly at the board, nor found time for rough discourtesy. So quietly did the little stream drip and ripple its way through the canyon that it spoke only in faint and occasional gurgles. The voice of the stream was as a drowsy whisper, ever interrupted by dozings and silences, ever lifted again in the awakenings.

The motion of all things was a drifting in the heart of the canyon. Sunshine and butterflies drifted in and out among the trees. The hum of the bees and the whisper of the stream were a drifting of sound. And the drifting sound and drifting color seemed to weave together in the making of a delicate and intangible fabric which was the spirit of the place. It was a spirit of peace that was not of death, but of smooth-pulsing life, of quietude that was not silence, of movement that was not action, of repose that was quick with existence without being violent with struggle and travail. The spirit of the place was the spirit of the peace of the living, somnolent with the easement and content of prosperity, and undisturbed by rumors of far wars.

The red-coated, many-antlered buck acknowledged the lordship of the spirit of the place and dozed knee-deep in the cool, shaded pool. There seemed no flies to vex him and he was languid with rest. Sometimes his ears moved when the stream awoke and whispered; but they moved lazily, with foreknowledge that it was merely the stream grown garrulous at discovery that it had slept.

But there came a time when the buck's ears lifted and tensed with swift eagerness for sound. His head was turned down the canyon. His sensitive, quivering nostrils scented the air. His eyes could not pierce the green screen through which the stream rippled away, but to his ears came the voice of a man. It was a steady, monotonous, singsong voice. Once the buck heard the harsh clash of metal upon rock. At the sound he snorted with a sudden start that jerked him through the air from water to meadow, and his feet sank into the young velvet, while he pricked his ears and again scented the air. Then he stole across the tiny meadow, pausing once and again to listen, and faded away out of the canyon like a wraith, soft-footed and without sound.

The clash of steel-shod soles against the rocks began to be heard, and the man's voice grew louder. It was raised in a sort of chant and became distinct with nearness, so that the words could be heard:

"Turn around an' tu'n yo' face
Untoe them sweet hills of grace
    (D' pow'rs of sin yo' am scornin'!).
Look about an' look aroun',
Fling yo' sin-pack on d' groun'
    (Yo' will meet wid d' Lord in d' mornin'!)."

A sound of scrambling accompanied the song, and the spirit of the place fled away on the heels of the red-coated buck. The green screen was burst asunder, and a man peered out at the meadow and the pool and the sloping side-hill. He was a deliberate sort of man. He took in the scene with one embracing glance, then ran his eyes over the details to verify the general impression. Then, and not until then, did he open his mouth in vivid and solemn approval:

"Smoke of life an' snakes of purgatory! Will you just look at that! Wood an' water an' grass an' a side-hill! A pocket-hunter's delight an' a cayuse's paradise! Cool green for tired eyes! Pink pills for pale people ain't in it. A secret pasture for prospectors and a resting-place for tired burros, by damn!"

He was a sandy-complexioned man in whose face geniality and humor seemed the salient characteristics. It was a mobile face, quick-changing to inward mood and thought. Thinking was in him a visible process. Ideas chased across his face like wind-flaws across the surface of a lake. His hair, sparse and unkempt of growth, was as indeterminate and colorless as his complexion. It would seem that all the color of his frame had gone into his eyes, for they were startlingly blue. Also, they were laughing and merry eyes; within them much of the naïveté and wonder of the child; and yet, in an unassertive way, they contained much of calm self-reliance and strength of purpose founded upon self-experience and experience of the world.

From out the screen of vines and creepers he flung ahead of him a miner's pick and shovel and gold-pan. Then he crawled out himself into the open. He was clad in

faded overalls and black cotton shirt, with hobnailed brogans on his feet, and on his head a hat whose shapeless-
ness and stains advertised the rough usage of wind and
rain and sun and camp-smoke. He stood erect, seeing
wide-eyed the secrecy of the scene and sensuously inhal-
ing the warm, sweet breath of the canyon-garden through
nostrils that dilated and quivered with delight. His eyes
narrowed to laughing slits of blue, his face wreathed itself
in joy, and his mouth curled in a smile as he cried aloud:

"Jumping dandelions and happy hollyhocks, but that
smells good to me! Talk about you attar o' roses an' co-
logne factories! They ain't in it!"

He had the habit of soliloquy. His quick-changing facial
expressions might tell every thought and mood, but the
tongue, perforce, ran hard after, repeating, like a second
Boswell.

The man lay down on the lip of the pool and drank long
and deep of its water. "Tastes good to me," he murmured,
lifting his head and gazing across the pool at the side-hill,
while he wiped his mouth with the back of his hand. The
side-hill attracted his attention. Still lying on his stomach,
he studied the hill formation long and carefully. It was a
practised eye that travelled up the slope to the crumbling
canyon-wall and back and down again to the edge of the
pool. He scrambled to his feet and favored the side-hill
with a second survey.

"Looks good to me," he concluded, picking up his pick
and shovel and gold-pan.

He crossed the stream below the pool, stepping agilely
from stone to stone. Where the side-hill touched the water
he dug up a shovelful of dirt and put it into the gold-pan.
He squatted down, holding the pan in his two hands, and
partly immersing it in the stream. Then he imparted to the
pan a deft circular motion that sent the water sluicing in
and out through the dirt and gravel. The larger and the
lighter particles worked to the surface, and these, by a
skilful dipping movement of the pan, he spilled out and
over the edge. Occasionally, to expedite matters, he rested

the pan and with his fingers raked out the large pebbles and pieces of rock.

The contents of the pan diminished rapidly until only fine dirt and the smallest bits of gravel remained. At this stage he began to work very deliberately and carefully. It was fine washing, and he washed fine and finer, with a keen scrutiny and delicate and fastidious touch. At last the pan seemed empty of everything but water; but with a quick semicircular flirt that sent the water flying over the shallow rim into the stream, he disclosed a layer of black sand on the bottom of the pan. So thin was this layer that it was like a streak of paint. He examined it closely. In the midst of it was a tiny golden speck. He dribbled a little water in over the depressed edge of the pan. With a quick flirt he sent the water sluicing across the bottom, turning the grains of black sand over and over. A second tiny golden speck rewarded his effort.

The washing had now become very fine—fine beyond all need of ordinary placer-mining. He worked the black sand, a small portion at a time, up the shallow rim of the pan. Each small portion he examined sharply, so that his eyes saw every grain of it before he allowed it to slide over the edge and away. Jealously, bit by bit, he let the black sand slip away. A golden speck, no larger than a pin-point, appeared on the rim, and by his manipulation of the water it returned to the bottom of the pan. And in such fashion another speck was disclosed, and another. Great was his care of them. Like a shepherd he herded his flock of golden specks so that not one should be lost. At last, of the pan of dirt nothing remained but his golden herd. He counted it, and then, after all his labor, sent it flying out of the pan with one final swirl of water.

But his blue eyes were shining with desire as he rose to his feet. "Seven," he muttered aloud, asserting the sum of the specks for which he had toiled so hard and which he had so wantonly thrown away. "Seven," he repeated, with the emphasis of one trying to impress a number on his memory.

He stood still a long while, surveying the hillside. In his eyes was a curiosity, new-aroused and burning. There was an exultance about his bearing and a keenness like that of a hunting animal catching the fresh scent of game.

He moved down the stream a few steps and took a second panful of dirt.

Again came the careful washing, the jealous herding of the golden specks, and the wantonness with which he sent them flying into the stream when he had counted their number.

"Five," he muttered, and repeated, "five."

He could not forbear another survey of the hill before filling the pan farther down the stream. His golden herds diminished. "Four, three, two, two, one," were his memory-tabulations as he moved down the stream. When but one speck of gold rewarded his washing, he stopped and built a fire of dry twigs. Into this he thrust the gold-pan and burned it till it was blue-black. He held up the pan and examined it critically. Then he nodded approbation. Against such a color-background he could defy the tiniest yellow speck to elude him.

Still moving down the stream, he panned again. A single speck was his reward. A third pan contained no gold at all. Not satisfied with this, he panned three times again, taking his shovels of dirt within a foot of one another. Each pan proved empty of gold, and the fact, instead of discouraging him, seemed to give him satisfaction. His elation increased with each barren washing, until he arose, exclaiming jubilantly:

"If it ain't the real thing, may God knock off my head with sour apples!"

Returning to where he had started operations, he began to pan up the stream. At first his golden herds increased—increased prodigiously. "Fourteen, eighteen, twenty-one, twenty-six," ran his memory tabulations. Just above the pool he struck his richest pan—thirty-five colors.

"Almost enough to save," he remarked regretfully as he allowed the water to sweep them away.

The sun climbed to the top of the sky. The man worked on. Pan by pan, he went up the stream, the tally of results steadily decreasing.

"It's just booful, the way it peters out," he exulted when a shovelful of dirt contained no more than a single speck of gold.

And when no specks at all were found in several pans, he straightened up and favored the hillside with a confident glance.

"Ah, ha! Mr. Pocket!" he cried out, as though to an auditor hidden somewhere above him beneath the surface of the slope. "Ah, ha! Mr. Pocket! I'm a-comin', I'm a-comin', an' I'm shorely gwine to get yer! You heah me, Mr. Pocket? I'm gwine to get yer as shore as punkins ain't cauliflowers!"

He turned and flung a measuring glance at the sun poised above him in the azure of the cloudless sky. Then he went down the canyon, following the line of shovel-holes he had made in filling the pans. He crossed the stream below the pool and disappeared through the green screen. There was little opportunity for the spirit of the place to return with its quietude and repose, for the man's voice, raised in ragtime song, still dominated the canyon with possession.

After a time, with a greater clashing of steel-shod feet on rock, he returned. The green screen was tremendously agitated. It surged back and forth in the throes of a struggle. There was a loud grating and clanging of metal. The man's voice leaped to a higher pitch and was sharp with imperativeness. A large body plunged and panted. There was a snapping and ripping and rending, and amid a shower of falling leaves a horse burst through the screen. On its back was a pack, and from this trailed broken vines and torn creepers. The animal gazed with astonished eyes at the scene into which it had been precipitated, then dropped its head to the grass and began contentedly to graze. A second horse scrambled into view, slipping once on the mossy rocks and regaining equilibrium when its hoofs sank into the yielding surface of the meadow. It was riderless, though on its back was a high-horned Mexican saddle, scarred and discolored by long usage.

The man brought up the rear. He threw off pack and saddle, with an eye to camp location, and gave the animals their freedom to graze. He unpacked his food and got out frying-pan and coffee-pot. He gathered an armful of dry wood, and with a few stones made a place for his fire.

"My!" he said, "but I've got an appetite. I could scoff iron-filings an' horseshoe nails an' thank you kindly, ma'am, for a second helpin'."

He straightened up, and while he reached for matches in the pocket of his overalls, his eyes travelled across the pool to the side-hill. His fingers had clutched the match-box, but they relaxed their hold and the hand came out empty. The man wavered perceptibly. He looked at his preparations for cooking and he looked at the hill.

"Guess I'll take another whack at her," he concluded, starting to cross the stream.

"They ain't no sense in it, I know," he mumbled apologetically. "But keepin' grub back an hour ain't goin' to hurt none, I reckon."

A few feet back from his first line of test-pans he started a second line. The sun dropped down the western sky, the shadows lengthened, but the man worked on. He began a third line of test-pans. He was cross-cutting the hillside, line by line, as he ascended. The centre of each line produced the richest pans, while the ends came where no colors showed in the pan. And as he ascended the hillside the lines grew perceptibly shorter. The regularity with which their length diminished served to indicate that somewhere up the slope the last line would be so short as to have scarcely length at all, and that beyond could come only a point. The design was growing into an inverted "V." The converging sides of this "V" marked the boundaries of the gold-bearing dirt.

The apex of the "V" was evidently the man's goal. Often he ran his eye along the converging sides and on up the hill, trying to divine the apex, the point where the gold-bearing dirt must cease. Here resided "Mr. Pocket"— for so the man familiarly addressed the imaginary point above him on the slope, crying out:

"Come down out o' that, Mr. Pocket! Be right smart an' agreeable, an' come down!"

"All right," he would add later, in a voice resigned to determination. "All right, Mr. Pocket. It's plain to me I got to come right up an' snatch you out bald-headed. An' I'll do it! I'll do it!" he would threaten still later.

Each pan he carried down to the water to wash, and as he went higher up the hill the pans grew richer, until he began to save the gold in an empty baking-powder can which he carried carelessly in his hip-pocket. So engrossed was he in his toil that he did not notice the long twilight of oncoming night. It was not until he tried vainly to see the gold colors in the bottom of the pan that he realized the passage of time. He straightened up abruptly. An expression of whimsical wonderment and awe overspread his face as he drawled:

"Gosh darn my buttons! if I didn't plumb forget dinner!"

He stumbled across the stream in the darkness and lighted his long-delayed fire. Flapjacks and bacon and warmed-over beans constituted his supper. Then he smoked a pipe by the smouldering coals, listening to the night noises and watching the moonlight stream through the canyon. After that he unrolled his bed, took off his heavy shoes, and pulled the blankets up to his chin. His face showed white in the moonlight, like the face of a corpse. but it was a corpse that knew its resurrection, for the man rose slightly on one elbow and gazed across at his hillside.

"Good night, Mr. Pocket," he called sleepily. "Good night."

He slept through the early gray of morning until the direct rays of the sun smote his closed eyelids, when he awoke with a start and looked about him until he had established the continuity of his existence and identified his present self with the days previously lived.

To dress, he had merely to buckle on his shoes. He glanced at his fireplace and at his hillside, wavered, but fought down the temptation and started the fire.

"Keep yer shirt on, Bill; keep yer shirt on," he admonished himself. "What's the good of rushin'? No use in gettin' all het up an' sweaty. Mr. Pocket'll wait for you. He ain't a-runnin' away before you can get yer breakfast. Now, what you want, Bill, is something fresh in yer bill o' fare. So it's up to you to go an' get it."

He cut a short pole at the water's edge and drew from one of his pockets a bit of line and a draggled fly that had once been a royal coachman.

"Mebbe they'll bite in the early morning," he muttered, as he made his first cast into the pool. And a moment later he was gleefully crying: "What 'd I tell you, eh? What 'd I tell you?"

He had no reel, nor any inclination to waste time, and by main strength, and swiftly, he drew out of the water a flashing ten-inch trout. Three more, caught in rapid succession, furnished his breakfast. When he came to the stepping-stones on his way to his hillside, he was struck by a sudden thought, and paused.

"I'd just better take a hike down-stream a ways," he said. "There's no tellin' what cuss may be snoopin' around."

But he crossed over on the stones, and with a "I really oughter take that hike," the need of the precaution passed out of his mind and he fell to work.

At nightfall he straightened up. The small of his back was stiff from stooping toil, and as he put his hand behind him to soothe the protesting muscles, he said:

"Now what d'ye think of that, by damn? I clean forgot my dinner again! If I don't watch out, I'll sure be degeneratin' into a two-meal-a-day crank."

"Pockets is the damnedest things I ever see for makin' a man absent-minded," he communed that night, as he crawled into his blankets. Nor did he forget to call up the hillside, "Good night, Mr. Pocket! Good night!"

Rising with the sun, and snatching a hasty breakfast, he was early at work. A fever seemed to be growing in him, nor did the increasing richness of the test-pans allay this fever. There was a flush in his cheek other than that made by the heat of the sun, and he was oblivious to fatigue and the passage of time. When he filled a pan with dirt, he ran down the hill to wash it; nor could he forbear running up the hill again, panting and stumbling profanely, to refill the pan.

He was now a hundred yards from the water, and the inverted "V" was assuming definite proportions. The width of the pay-dirt steadily decreased, and the man extended in his mind's eye the sides of the "V" to their meeting-place far up the hill. This was his goal, the apex of the "V," and he panned many times to locate it.

"Just about two yards above that manzanita bush an' a yard to the right," he finally concluded.

Then the temptation seized him. "As plain as the nose on your face," he said, as he abandoned his laborious cross-cutting and climbed to the indicated apex. He filled a pan and carried it down the hill to wash. It contained no trace of gold. He dug deep, and he dug shallow, filling and washing a dozen pans, and was unrewarded even by the tiniest golden speck. He was enraged at having yielded to the temptation, and cursed himself blasphemously and pridelessly. Then he went down the hill and took up the cross-cutting.

"Slow an' certain, Bill; slow an' certain," he crooned. "Short-cuts to fortune ain't in your line, an' it's about time you know it. Get wise, Bill; get wise. Slow an' certain's the only hand you can play; so go to it, an' keep to it, too."

As the cross-cuts decreased, showing that the sides of the "V" were converging, the depth of the "V" increased. The gold-trace was dipping into the hill. It was only at thirty inches beneath the surface that he could get colors in his pan. The dirt he found at twenty-five inches from the surface, and at thirty-five inches, yielded barren pans. At the base of the "V," by the water's edge, he had found the gold colors at the grass roots. The higher he went up the hill, the deeper the gold dipped. To dig a hole three feet deep in order to get one test-pan was a task of no mean magnitude; while between the man and the apex intervened an untold number of such holes to be dug. "An' there's no tellin' how much deeper it'll pitch," he sighed, in a moment's pause, while his fingers soothed his aching back.

Feverish with desire, with aching back and stiffening muscles, with pick and shovel gouging and mauling the soft brown earth, the man toiled up the hill. Before him was the smooth slope, spangled with flowers and made sweet with their breath. Behind him was devastation. It looked like some terrible eruption breaking out on the smooth skin of the hill. His slow progress was like that of a slug, befouling beauty with a monstrous trail.

Though the dipping gold-trace increased the man's work, he found consolation in the increasing richness of the pans. Twenty cents, thirty cents, fifty cents, sixty cents, were the values of the gold found in the pans, and at nightfall he washed his banner pan, which gave him a dollar's worth of gold-dust from a shovelful of dirt.

"I'll just bet it's my luck to have some inquisitive cuss come buttin' in here on my pasture," he mumbled sleepily that night as he pulled the blankets up to his chin.

Suddenly he sat upright. "Bill!" he called sharply. "Now, listen to me, Bill; d'ye hear! It's up to you, tomorrow mornin', to mosey round an' see what you can see. Understand? Tomorrow morning, an' don't you forget it!"

He yawned and glanced across at his side-hill. "Good night, Mr. Pocket," he called.

In the morning he stole a march on the sun, for he had finished breakfast when its first rays caught him, and he was climbing the wall of the canyon where it crumbled away and gave footing. From the outlook at the top he found himself in the midst of loneliness. As far as he could see, chain after chain of mountains heaved themselves into his vision. To the east his eyes, leaping the miles between range and range and between many ranges, brought up at last against the white-peaked Sierras—the main crest, where the backbone of the Western world reared itself against the sky. To the north and south he could see more distinctly the cross-systems that broke through the main trend of the sea of mountains. To the west the ranges fell away, one behind the other, diminishing and fading into the gentle foothills that, in turn, descended into the great valley which he could not see.

And in all that mighty sweep of earth he saw no sign of man nor of the handiwork of man—save only the torn bosom of the hillside at his feet. The man looked long and carefully. Once, far down his own canyon, he thought he saw in the air a faint hint of smoke. He looked again and decided that it was the purple haze of the hills made dark by a convolution of the canyon wall at its back.

"Hey, you, Mr. Pocket!" he called down into the canyon. "Stand out from under! I'm a-comin', Mr. Pocket! I'm a-comin'!"

The heavy brogans on the man's feet made him appear clumsy-footed, but he swung down from the giddy height as lightly and airily as a mountain goat. A rock, turning under his foot on the edge of the precipice, did not disconcert him. He seemed to know the precise time required for the turn to culminate in disaster, and in the meantime he utilized the false footing itself for the momentary earth-contact necessary to carry him on into safety. Where the earth sloped so steeply that it was impossible to stand for a second upright, the man did not hesitate. His foot pressed the impossible surface for but a fraction of the fatal second and gave him the bound that carried him onward. Again, where even the fraction of a second's footing was out of the question, he would swing his body past by a moment's hand-grip on a jutting knob of rock, a crevice, or a precariously rooted shrub. At last, with a wild leap and yell, he exchanged the face of the wall for an earth-slide and finished the descent in the midst of several tons of sliding earth and gravel.

His first pan of the morning washed out over two dollars in coarse gold. It was from the centre of the "V." To either side the diminution in the values of the pans was swift. His lines of cross-cutting holes were growing very short. The converging sides of the inverted "V" were only a few yards apart. Their meeting-point was only a few yards above him. But the pay-streak was dipping deeper and deeper into the earth. By early afternoon he was sinking the test-holes five feet before the pans could show the gold-trace.

For that matter, the gold-trace had become something more than a trace; it was a placer mine in itself, and the man resolved to come back after he had found the pocket and work over the ground. But the increasing richness of the pans began to worry him. By late afternoon the worth of the pans had grown to three and four dollars. The man scratched his head perplexedly and looked a few feet up the hill at the manzanita blush that marked approximately the apex of the "V." He nodded his head and said oracularly:

"It's one o'two things, Bill; one o' two things. Either Mr. Pocket's spilled himself all out an' down the hill, or else Mr. Pocket's that damned rich you maybe won't be able to carry him all away with you. And that 'd be hell, wouldn't it, now?" He chuckled at contemplation of so pleasant a dilemma.

Nightfall found him by the edge of the stream, his eyes wrestling with the gathering darkness over the washing of a five-dollar pan.

"Wisht I had an electric light to go on working," he said.

He found sleep difficult that night. Many times he composed himself and closed his eyes for slumber to overtake him; but his blood pounded with too strong desire, and as many times his eyes opened and he murmured wearily, "Wisht it was sun-up."

Sleep came to him in the end, but his eyes were open with the first paling of the stars, and the gray of dawn caught him with breakfast finished and climbing the hillside in the direction of the secret abiding-place of Mr. Pocket.

The first cross-cut the man made, there was space for only three holes, so narrow had become the pay-streak and so close was he to the fountainhead of the golden stream he had been following for four days.

"Be ca'm, Bill; be ca'm," he admonished himself, as he broke ground for the final hole where the sides of the "V" had at last come together in a point.

"I've got the almighty cinch on you, Mr. Pocket, an' you can't lose me," he said many times as he sank the hole deeper and deeper.

Four feet, five feet, six feet, he dug his way down into the earth. The digging grew harder. His pick grated on broken rock. He examined the rock.

"Rotten quartz," was his conclusion as, with the shovel, he cleared the bottom of the hole of loose dirt. He attacked the crumbling quartz with the pick, bursting the disintegrating rock asunder with every stroke.

He thrust his shovel into the loose mass. His eye caught a gleam of yellow. He dropped the shovel and squatted suddenly on his heels. As a farmer rubs the clinging earth from fresh-dug potatoes, so the man, a piece of rotten quartz held in both hands, rubbed the dirt away.

"Sufferin' Sardanopolis!" he cried, "Lumps an' chunks of it! Lumps an' chunks of it!"

It was only half rock he held in his hand. The other half was virgin gold. He dropped it into his pan and examined another piece. Little yellow was to be seen, but with his strong fingers he crumbled the rotten quartz away till both hands were filled with glowing yellow. He rubbed the dirt away from fragment after fragment, tossing them into the gold-pan. It was a treasure-hole. So much had the quartz rotted away that there was less of it than there was of gold. Now and again he found a piece to which no rock clung—a piece that was all gold. A chunk, where the pick had laid open the heart of the gold, glittered like a handful of yellow jewels, and he cocked his head at it and slowly turned it around and over to observe the rich play of the light upon it.

"Talk about yer Too Much Gold diggin's!" the man snorted contemptuously. "Why, this diggin' 'd make it look like thirty cents. This diggin' is All Gold. An' right here an' now I name this yere canyon 'All Gold Canyon,' b' gosh!"

Still squatting on his heels, he continued examining the fragments and tossing them into the pan. Suddenly there came to him a premonition of danger. It seemed a shadow had fallen upon him. But there was no shadow. His heart had given a great jump up into his throat and was choking him. Then his blood slowly chilled and he felt the sweat of his shirt cold against his flesh.

He did not spring up nor look around. He did not move. He was considering the nature of the premonition he had received, trying to locate the source of the mysterious force that had warned him, striving to sense the imperative presence of the unseen thing that threatened him. There is an aura of things hostile, made manifest by messengers too refined for the senses to know; and this aura he felt, but knew not how he felt it. His was the feeling as when a cloud passes over the sun. It seemed that between him and life had passed something dark and smothering and menacing; a gloom, as it were, that swallowed up life and made for death—his death.

Every force of his being impelled him to spring up and confront the unseen danger, but his soul dominated the panic, and he remained squatting on his heels, in his hands a chunk of gold. He did not dare to look around, but he knew by now that there was something behind him and above him. He made believe to be interested in the gold in his hand. He examined it critically, turned it over and over, and rubbed the dirt from it. And all the time he knew that something behind him was looking at the gold over his shoulder.

Still feigning interest in the chunk of gold in his hand, he listened intently and he heard the breathing of the thing behind him. His eyes searched the ground in front of him for a weapon, but they saw only the uprooted gold, worthless to him now in his extremity. There was his pick, a handy weapon on occasion; but this was not such an occasion. The man realized his predicament. He was in a narrow hole that was seven feet deep. His head did not come to the surface of the ground. He was in a trap.

He remained squatting on his heels. He was quite cool and collected; but his mind, considering every factor, showed him only his helplessness. He continued rubbing the dirt from the quartz fragments and throwing the gold into the pan. There was nothing else for him to do. Yet he knew that he would have to rise up, sooner or later, and face the danger that breathed at his back. The minutes passed, and with the passage of each minute he knew that by so much he was nearer the time when he must stand up, or else—and his wet shirt went cold against his flesh again at the thought—or else he might receive death as he stooped there over his treasure.

Still he squatted on his heels, rubbing dirt from gold and debating in just what manner he should rise up. He might rise up with a rush and claw his way out of the hole to meet whatever threatened on the even footing above ground. Or he might rise up slowly and carelessly, and feign casually to discover the thing that breathed at his back. His instinct and every fighting fibre of his body favored the mad, clawing rush to the surface. His intellect, and the craft thereof, favored the slow and cautious meeting with the thing that menaced and which he could not see. And while he debated, a loud, crashing noise burst on his ear. At the same instant he received a stunning blow on the left side of the back, and from the point of impact felt a rush of flame through his flesh. He sprang up in the air, but halfway to his feet collapsed. His body crumpled in like a leaf withered in sudden heat, and he came down, his chest across his pan of gold, his face in the dirt and rock, his legs tangled and twisted because of the restricted space at the bottom of the hole. His legs twitched convulsively several times. His body was shaken as with a mighty ague. There was a slow expansion of the lungs, accompanied by a deep sigh. Then the air was slowly, very slowly, exhaled, and his body as slowly flattened itself down into inertness.

Above, revolver in hand, a man was peering down over the edge of the hole. He peered for a long time at the prone and motionless body beneath him. After a while the stranger sat down on the edge of the hole so that he could see into it, and rested the revolver on his knee. Reaching his hand into a pocket, he drew out a wisp of brown paper. Into this he dropped a few crumbs of tobacco. The combination became a cigarette, brown and squat, with the ends turned in. Not once did he take his eyes from the body at the bottom of the hole. He lighted the cigarette and drew its smoke into his lungs with a caressing intake of the breath. He smoked slowly. Once the cigarette went out and he relighted it. And all the while he studied the body beneath him.

In the end he tossed the cigarette stub away and rose to his feet. He moved to the edge of the hole. Spanning it, a hand resting on each edge, and with the revolver still in the right hand, he muscled his body down into the hole. While his feet were yet a yard from the bottom he released his hands and dropped down.

At the instant his feet struck bottom he saw the pocket-miner's arm leap out, and his own legs knew a swift, jerking grip that overthrew him. In the nature of the jump his revolver-hand was above his head. Swiftly as the grip had flashed about his legs, just as swiftly he brought the revolver down. He was still in the air, his fall in process of completion, when he pulled the trigger. The explosion was deafening in the confined space. The smoke filled the hole so that he could see nothing. He struck the bottom on his back, and like a cat's the pocket-miner's body was on top of him. Even as the miner's body passed on top, the stranger crooked in his right arm to fire; and even in that instant the miner, with a quick thrust of elbow, struck his wrist. The muzzle was thrown up and the bullet thudded into the dirt of the side of the hole.

The next instant the stranger felt the miner's hand grip his wrist. The struggle was now for the revolver. Each man strove to turn it against the other's body. The smoke in the hole was clearing. The stranger, lying on his back, was beginning to see dimly. But suddenly he was blinded by a handful of dirt deliberately flung into his eyes by his antagonist. In that moment of shock his grip on the revolver was broken. In the next moment he felt a smashing darkness descend upon his brain, and in the midst of the darkness even the darkness ceased.

But the pocket-miner fired again and again, until the revolver was empty. Then he tossed it from him and, breathing heavily, sat down on the dead man's legs.

The miner was sobbing and struggling for breath. "Measly skunk!" he panted; "a-campin' on my trail an' lettin' me do the work, an' then shootin' me in the back!"

He was half crying from anger and exhaustion. He peered at the face of the dead man. It was sprinkled with loose dirt and gravel, and it was difficult to distinguish the features.

"Never laid eyes on him before," the miner concluded his scrutiny. "Just a common an' ordinary thief, damn him! An' he shot me in the back! He shot me in the back!"

He opened his shirt and felt himself, front and back, on his left side.

"Went clean through, and no harm done!" he cried jubilantly. "I'll bet he aimed all right all right; but he drew the gun over when he pulled the trigger—the cuss! But I fixed 'm! Oh, I fixed 'm!"

His fingers were investigating the bullet-hole in his side, and a shade of regret passed over his face. "It's goin' to be stiffer'n hell," he said. "An' it's up to me to get mended an' get out o' here."

He crawled out of the hole and went down the hill to his camp. Half an hour later he returned, leading his pack-horse. His open shirt disclosed the rude bandages with which he had dressed his wound. He was slow and awkward with his left-hand movements, but that did not prevent his using the arm.

The bight of the pack-rope under the dead man's shoulders enabled him to heave the body out of the hole. Then he set to work gathering up his gold. He worked steadily for several hours, pausing often to rest his stiffening shoulder and to exclaim:

"He shot me in the back, the measly skunk! He shot me in the back!"

When his treasure was quite cleaned up and wrapped securely into a number of blanket-covered parcels, he made an estimate of its value.

"Four hundred pounds, or I'm a Hottentot," he concluded. "Say two hundred in quartz an' dirt—that leaves two hundred pounds of gold. Bill! Wake up! Two hundred pounds of gold! Forty thousand dollars! An' it's yourn—all yourn!"

He scratched his head delightedly and his fingers blundered into an unfamiliar groove. They quested along it for several inches. It was a crease through his scalp where the second bullet had ploughed.

He walked angrily over to the dead man.

"You would, would you?" he bullied. "You would, eh? Well, I fixed you good an' plenty, an' I'll give you decent burial, too. That's more'n you'd have done for me."

He dragged the body to the edge of the hole and toppled it in. It struck the bottom with a dull crash, on its side, the face twisted up to the light. The miner peered down at it.

"An' you shot me in the back!" he said accusingly.

With pick and shovel he filled the hole. Then he loaded the gold on his horse. It was too great a load for the animal, and when he had gained his camp he transferred part of it to his saddle-horse. Even so, he was compelled to abandon a portion of his outfit—pick and shovel and gold-pan, extra food and cooking utensils, and divers odds and ends.

The sun was at the zenith when the man forced the horses at the screen of vines and creepers. To climb the huge boulders the animals were compelled to uprear and struggle blindly through the tangled mass of vegetation. Once the saddle-horse fell heavily and the man removed the pack to get the animal on its feet. After it started on its way again the man thrust his head out from among the leaves and peered up at the hillside.

"The measly skunk!" he said, and disappeared.

There was a ripping and tearing of vines and boughs. The trees surged back and forth, marking the passage of the animals through the midst of them. There was a clashing of steel-shod hoofs on stone, and now and again an oath or a sharp cry of command. Then the voice of the man was raised in song:—

"Tu'n around an' tu'n yo' face
Untoe them sweet hills of grace
        (D' pow'rs of sin yo' am scornin'!).
Look about an' look aroun',
Fling yo' sin-pack on d' groun'
    (Yo' will meet wid d' Lord in d' mornin'!)."

The song grew faint and fainter, and through the silence crept back the spirit of the place. The stream once more drowsed and whispered; the hum of the mountain bees rose sleepily. Down through the perfume-weighted air fluttered the snowy fluffs of the cottonwoods. The butterflies drifted in and out among the trees, and over all blazed the quiet sunshine. Only remained the hoof-marks in the meadow and the torn hillside to mark the boisterous trail of the life that had broken the peace of the place and passed on.

Koolau the Leper

Because we are sick they take away our liberty. We have obeyed the law. We have done nothing wrong. And yet they would put us in prison. Molokai is a prison. That you know. Niuli, there, his sister was sent to Molokai seven years ago. He has not seen her since. Nor will he ever see her. She must stay there until she dies. This is not her will. It is not Niuli's will. It is the will of the white men who rule the land. And who are these white men?

"We know. We have it from our fathers and our father's fathers. They came like lambs, speaking softly. Well might they speak softly for we are many and strong, and all the islands were ours. As I say, they spoke softly. They were of two kinds. The one kind asked our permission, our gracious permission, to preach to us the word of God. The other kind asked our permission, our gracious permission, to trade with us. That was the beginning. To-day all the islands are theirs, all the land, all the cattle—everything is theirs. They that preached the word of God and they that preached the word of Rum have foregathered and become great chiefs. They live like kings in houses of many rooms, with multitudes of servants to care for them. They who had nothing have everything, and if you, or I, or any Kanaka be hungry, they sneer and say, 'Well, why don't you work? There are the plantations.' "

Koolau paused. He raised one hand, and with gnarled and twisted fingers lifted up the blazing wreath of hibiscus that crowned his black hair. The moonlight bathed the scene in silver. It was a night of peace, though those who sat about him and listened had all the seeming of battle-wrecks. Their faces were leonine. Here a space yawned in a face where should have been a nose, and there an arm-stump showed where a hand had rotted off. They were men and women beyond the pale, the thirty of them, for upon them had been placed the mark of the beast.

They sat, flower-garlanded, in the perfumed, luminous night, and their lips made uncouth noises and their throats rasped approval of Koolau's speech. They were creatures who once had been men and women. But they were men and women no longer. They were monsters—in face and form grotesque caricatures of everything human. They were hideously maimed and distorted, and had the seeming of creatures that had been racked in millenniums of hell. Their hands, when they possessed them, were like harpy-claws. Their faces were the misfits and slips, crushed and bruised by some mad god at play in the machinery of life. Here and there were features which the mad god had smeared half away, and one woman wept scalding tears from twin pits of horror, where her eyes once had been. Some were in pain and groaned from their chests. Others coughed, making sounds like the tearing of tissue. Two were idiots, more like huge apes marred in the making, un-til even an ape were an angel. They mowed and gibbered in the moonlight, under crowns of drooping, golden blos-soms. One, whose bloated ear-lobe flapped like a fan upon his shoulder, caught up a gorgeous flower of orange and scarlet and with it decorated the monstrous ear that flip-flapped with his every movement.

And over these things Koolau was king. And this was his kingdom,—a flower-throttled gorge, with beetling cliffs and crags, from which floated the blattings of wild goats. On three sides the grim walls rose, festooned in fantastic draperies of tropic vegetation and pierced by cave-entrances—the rocky lairs of Koolau's subjects. On the fourth side the earth fell away into a tremendous abyss, and, far below, could be seen the summits of lesser peaks and crags, at whose based foamed and rumbled the Pacific surge. In fine weather a boat could land on the rocky beach that marked the entrance of Kalalau Valley, but the weather must be very fine. And a cool-headed mountaineer might climb from the beach to the head of Kalalau Valley, to this pocket among the peaks where Koolau ruled; but such a mountaineer must be very cool of head, and he must know the wild-goat trails as well. The marvel was that the mass of human wreckage that constituted Koolau's people should have been able to drag its helpless misery over the giddy goat-trails to this inaccessible spot.

"Brothers," Koolau began.

But one of the mowing, apelike travesties emitted a wild shriek of madness, and Koolau waited while the shrill cachinnation was tossed back and forth among the rocky walls and echoed distantly through the pulseless night.

"Brothers, is it not strange? Ours was the land, and behold, the land is not ours. What did these preachers of the word of God and the word of Rum give us for the land? Have you received one dollar, as much as one dollar, any one of you, for the land? Yet it is theirs, and in return they tell us we can go to work on the land, their land, and that what we produce by our toil shall be theirs. Yet in the old days we did not have to work. Also, when we are sick, they take away our freedom."

"Who brought the sickness, Koolau?" demanded Kilo-liana, a lean and wiry man with a face so like a laughing faun's that one might expect to see the cloven hoofs under him. They were cloven, it was true, but the cleavages were great ulcers and livid putrefactions. Yet this was Kiloliana, the most daring climber of them all, the man who knew every goat-trail and who had led Koolau and his wretched followers into the recesses of Kalalau.

"Ay, well questioned," Koolau answered. "Because we would not work the miles of sugar-cane where once our horses pastured, they brought the Chinese slaves from over seas. And with them came the Chinese sickness—that which we suffer from and because of which they would imprison us on Molokai. We were born on Kauai. We have been to the other islands, some here and some there, to Oahu, to Maui, to Hawaii, to Honolulu. Yet always did we come back to Kauai. Why did we come back? There must be a reason. Because we love Kauai. We were born here. Here we have lived. And here shall we die—unless—unless—there be weak hearts amongst us. Such we do not want. They are fit for Molokai. And if there be such, let them not remain. To-morrow the soldiers land on the shore. Let the weak hearts go down to them. They will be sent swiftly to Molokai. As for us, we shall stay and fight. But know that we will not die. We have rifles. You know the narrow trails where men must creep, one by one. I, alone, Koolau, who was once a cowboy on Niihau, can hold the trail against a thousand men. Here is Kapahei, who was once a judge over men and a man with honor, but who is now a hunted rat, like you and me. Hear him. He is wise."

Kapahei arose. Once he had been a judge. He had gone to college at Punahou. He had sat at meat with lords and chiefs and the high representatives of alien powers who protected the interests of traders and missionaries. Such had been Kapahei. But now, as Koolau had said, he was a hunted rat, a creature outside the law, sunk so deep in the mire of human horror that he was above the law as well as beneath it. His face was featureless, save for gaping orifices and for the lidless eyes that burned under hairless brows.

"Let us not make trouble," he began. "We ask to be left alone. But if they do not leave us alone, then is the trouble theirs, and the penalty. My fingers are gone, as you see." He held up his stumps of hands that all might see. "Yet have I the joint of one thumb left, and it can pull a trigger as firmly as did its lost neighbor in the old days. We love Kauai. Let us live here, or die here, but do not let us go to the prison of Molokai. The sickness is not ours. We have not sinned. The men who preached the word of God and the word of Rum brought the sickness with the coolie slaves who work the stolen land. I have been a judge. I know the law and the justice, and I say to you it is unjust to steal a man's land, to make that man sick with the Chinese sickness, and then to put that man in prison for life."

"Life is short, and the days are filled with pain," said Koolau. "Let us drink and dance and be happy as we can."

From one of the rocky lairs calabashes were produced and passed around. The calabashes were filled with the fierce distillation of the root of the *ti*-plant; and as the liquid fire coursed through them and mounted to their brains, they forgot that they had once been men and women, for they were men and women once more. The woman who wept scalding tears from open eye-pits was indeed a woman apulse with life as she plucked the strings of an *ukulele* and lifted her voice in a barbaric love-call such as might have come from the dark forest-depths of the primeval world. The air tingled with her cry, softly imperious and seductive. Upon a mat, timing his rhythm to the woman's song, Kiloliana danced. It was unmistakable. Love danced in all his movements, and, next, dancing with him on the mat, was a woman whose heavy hips and generous breast gave the lie to her disease-corroded face. It was a dance of the living dead, for in their disintegrating bodies life still loved and longed. Ever the woman whose sightless eyes ran scalding tears chanted her love-cry, ever the dancers danced of love in the warm night, and ever the calabashes went around till in all their brains were maggots crawling of memory and desire. And with the woman on the mat danced a slender maid whose face was beautiful and unmarred, but whose twisted arms that rose and fell marked the disease's ravage. And the two idiots, gibbering and mouthing strange noises, danced apart, grotesque, fantastic, travestying love as they themselves had been travestied by life.

But the woman's love-cry broke midway, the calabashes were lowered, and the dancers ceased, as all gazed into the abyss above the sea, where a rocket flared like a wan phantom through the moonlit air.

"It is the soldiers," said Koolau. "To-morrow there will be fighting. It is well to sleep and be prepared."

The lepers obeyed, crawling away to their lairs in the cliff, until only Koolau remained, sitting motionless in the moonlight, his rifle across his knees, as he gazed far down to the boats landing on the beach.

The far head of Kalalau Valley had been well chosen as a refuge. Except Kiloliana, who knew back-trails up the precipitous walls, no man could win to the gorge save by advancing across a knife-edged ridge. This passage was a hundred yards in length. At best, it was a scant twelve inches wide. On either side yawned the abyss. A slip, and to right or left the man would fall to his death. But once across he would find himself in an earthly paradise. A sea of vegetation laved the landscape, pouring its green billows from wall to wall, dripping from the cliff-lips in great vine-masses, and flinging a spray of ferns and air-plants into the multitudinous crevices. During the many months of Koolau's rule, he and his followers had fought with this vegetable sea. The choking jungle, with its riot of blossoms, had been driven back from the bananas, oranges, and mangoes that grew wild. In little clearings grew the wild arrowroot; on stone terraces, filled with soil scrapings, were the *taro* patches and the melons; and in every open space where the sunshine penetrated, were *papaia* trees burdened with their golden fruit.

Koolau had been driven to this refuge from the lower valley by the beach. And if he were driven from it in turn, he knew of gorges among the jumbled peaks of the inner fastnesses where he could lead his subjects and live. And now he lay with his rifle beside him, peering down through a tangled screen of foliage at the soldiers on the beach. He noted that they had large guns with them, from which the sunshine flashed as from mirrors. The knife-edged passage lay directly before him. Crawling upward along the trail that led to it he could see tiny specks of men. He knew they were not the soldiers, but the police. When they failed, then the soldiers would enter the game.

He affectionately rubbed a twisted hand along the rifle barrel and made sure that the sights were clean. He had learned to shoot as a wild-cattle hunter on Niihau, and on that island his skill as a marksman was unforgotten. As the toiling specks of men grew nearer and larger, he estimated the range, judged the deflection of the wind that swept at right angles across the line of fire, and calculated the chances of overshooting marks that were so far below his level. But he did not shoot. Not until they reached the beginning of the passage did he make his presence known. He did not disclose himself, but spoke from the thicket.

"What do you want?" he demanded.

"We want Koolau, the leper," answered the man who led the native police, himself a blue-eyed American.

"You must go back," Koolau said.

He knew the man, a deputy sheriff, for it was by him that he had been harried out of Niihau, across Kauai, to Kalalau Valley, and out of the valley to the gorge.

"Who are you?" the sheriff asked.

"I am Koolau, the leper," was the reply.

"Then come out. We want you. Dead or alive, there is a thousand dollars on your head. You cannot escape."

Koolau laughed aloud in the thicket.

"Come out!" the sheriff commanded, and was answered by silence.

He conferred with the police, and Koolau saw that they were preparing to rush him.

"Koolau," the sheriff called. "Koolau, I am coming across to get you."

"Then look first and well about you at the sun and sea and sky, for it will be the last time you behold them."

"That's all right, Koolau," the sheriff said soothingly. "I know you're a dead shot. But you won't shoot me. I have never done you any wrong."

Koolau grunted in the thicket.

"I say, you know, I've never done you any wrong, have I?" the sheriff persisted.

"You do me wrong when you try to put me in prison," was the reply. "And you do me wrong when you try for the thousand dollars on my head. If you will live, stay where you are."

"I've got to come across and get you. I'm sorry. But it is my duty."

"You will die before you get across."

The sheriff was no coward. Yet was he undecided. He gazed into the gulf on either side, and ran his eyes along the knife-edge he must travel. Then he made up his mind.

"Koolau," he called.

But the thicket remained silent.

"Koolau, don't shoot. I am coming."

The sheriff turned, gave some orders to the police, then started on his perilous way. He advanced slowly. It was like walking a tight rope. He had nothing to lean upon but the air. The lava rock crumbled under his feet, and on either side the dislodged fragments pitched downward through the depths. The sun blazed upon him, and his face was wet with sweat. Still he advanced, until the halfway point was reached.

"Stop!" Koolau commanded from the thicket. "One more step and I shoot."

The sheriff halted, swaying for balance as he stood poised above the void. His face was pale, but his eyes were determined. He licked his dry lips before he spoke.

"Koolau, you won't shoot me. I know you won't."

He started once more. The bullet whirled him half

about. On his face was an expression of querulous surprise as he reeled to the fall. He tried to save himself by throwing his body across the knife-edge; but at that moment he knew death. The next moment the knife-edge was vacant. Then came the rush, five policemen, in single file, with superb steadiness, running along the knife-edge. At the same instant the rest of the posse opened fire on the thicket. It was madness. Five times Koolau pulled the trigger, so rapidly that his shots constituted a rattle. Changing his position and crouching low under the bullets that were biting and singing through the bushes, he peered out. Four of the police had followed the sheriff. The fifth lay across the knife-edge, still alive. On the farther side, no longer firing, were the surviving police. On the naked rock there was no hope for them. Before they could clamber down Koolau could have picked off the last man. But he did not fire, and, after a conference, one of them took off a white undershirt and waved it as a flag. Followed by another, he advanced along the knife-edge to their wounded comrade. Koolau gave no sign, but watched them slowly withdraw and become specks as they descended into the lower valley.

Two hours later, from another thicket. Koolau watched a body of police trying to make the ascent from the opposite side of the valley. He saw the wild goats flee before them as they climbed higher and higher, until he doubted his judgment and sent for Kiloliana who crawled in beside him.

"No, there is no way," said Kiloliana.

"The goats?" Koolau questioned.

"They come over from the next valley, but they cannot pass to this. There is no way. Those men are not wiser than goats. They may fall to their deaths. Let us watch."

"They are brave men," said Koolau. "Let us watch."

Side by side they lay among the morning-glories, with the yellow blossoms of the *hau* dropping upon them from overhead, watching the motes of men toil upward, till the thing happened, and three of them, slipping, rolling, sliding; dashed over a cliff-lip and fell sheer half a thousand feet.

Kiloliana chuckled.

"We will be bothered no more," he said.

"They have war guns," Koolau made answer. "The soldiers have not yet spoken."

In the drowsy afternoon, most of the lepers lay in their rock dens asleep. Koolau, his rifle on his knees, fresh-cleaned and ready, dozed in the entrance to his own den. The maid with the twisted arm lay below in the thicket and kept watch on the knife-edge passage. Suddenly Koolau was startled wide awake by the sound of an explosion on the beach. The next instant the atmosphere was incredibly rent asunder. The terrible sound frightened him. It was as if all the gods had caught the envelope of the sky in their hands and were ripping it apart as a woman rips apart a sheet of cotton cloth. But it was such an immense ripping, growing swiftly nearer. Koolau glanced up apprehensively, as if expecting to see the thing. Then high up on the cliff overhead the shell burst in a fountain of black smoke. The rock was shattered, the fragments falling to the foot of the cliff.

Koolau passed his hand across his sweaty brow. He was terribly shaken. He had had no experience with shell-fire, and this was more dreadful than anything he had imagined.

"One," said Kapahei, suddenly bethinking himself to keep count.

A second and a third shell flew screaming over the top of the wall, bursting beyond view. Kapahei methodically kept the count. The lepers crowded into the open space before the caves. At first they were frightened, but as the shells continued their flight overhead the leper folk became reassured and began to admire the spectacle. The two idiots shrieked with delight, prancing wild antics as each air-tormenting shell went by. Koolau began to recover his confidence. No damage was being done. Evidently they could not aim such large missiles at such long range with the precision of a rifle.

But a change came over the situation. The shells began to fall short. One burst below in the thicket by the knife-edge. Koolau remembered the maid who lay there on watch, and ran down to see. The smoke was still rising from the bushes when he crawled in. He was astounded. The branches were splintered and broken. Where the girl had lain was a hole in the ground. The girl herself was in shattered fragments. The shell had burst right on her.

First peering out to make sure no soldiers were attempting the passage, Koolau started back on the run for the caves. All the time the shells were moaning, whining, screaming by, and the valley was rumbling and reverberating with the explosions. As he came in sight of the caves, he saw the two idiots cavorting about, clutching each other's hands with their stumps of fingers. Even as he ran, Koolau saw a spout of black smoke rise from the ground, near to the idiots. They were flung apart bodily by the explosion. One lay motionless, but the other was dragging himself by his hands toward the cave. His legs trailed out helplessly behind him, while the blood was pouring from his body. He seemed bathed in blood, and as he crawled he cried like a little dog. The rest of the lepers, with the exception of Kapahei, had fled into the caves.

"Seventeen," said Kapahei. "Eighteen," he added.

This last shell had fairly entered into one of the caves. The explosion caused all the caves to empty. But from the particular cave no one emerged. Koolau crept in through the pungent, acrid smoke. Four bodies, frightfully mangled, lay about. One of them was the sightless woman whose tears till now had never ceased.

Outside, Koolau found his people in a panic and already beginning to climb the goat trail that led out of the gorge and on among the jumbled heights and chasms. The wounded idiot, whining feebly and dragging himself along on the ground by his hands, was trying to follow. But at

the first pitch of the wall his helplessness overcame him
and he fell back.

"It would be better to kill him," said Koolau to Kapahei,
who still sat in the same place.

"Twenty-two," Kapahei answered. "Yes, it would be a
wise thing to kill him. Twenty-three—twenty-four."

The idiot whined sharply when he saw the rifle leveled
at him. Koolau hesitated, then lowered the gun.

"It is a hard thing to do," he said.

"You are a fool, twenty-six, twenty-seven," said Kapahei. "Let me show you."

He arose and, with a heavy fragment of rock in his
hand, approached the wounded thing. As he lifted his arm
to strike, a shell burst full upon him, relieving him of the
necessity of the act and at the same time putting an end to
his count.

Koolau was alone in the gorge. He watched the last of
his people drag their crippled bodies over the brow of the
height and disappear. Then he turned and went down to
the thicket where the maid had been killed. The shell-fire
still continued, but he remained; for far below he could see
the soldiers climbing up. A shell burst twenty feet away.
Flattening himself into the earth, he heard the rush of the
fragments above his body. A shower of *hau* blossoms
rained upon him. He lifted his head to peer down the trail,
and sighed. He was very much afraid. Bullets from rifles
would not have worried him, but this shell-fire was abominable. Each time a shell shrieked by he shivered and
crouched; but each time he lifted his head again to watch
the trail.

At last the shells ceased. This, he reasoned, was because
the soldiers were drawing near. They crept along the trail
in single file, and he tried to count them until he lost track.
At any rate, there were a hundred or so of them—all come
after Koolau the leper. He felt a fleeting prod of pride.
With war guns and rifles, police and soldiers, they came
for him, and he was only one man, a crippled wreck of a
man at that. They offered a thousand dollars for him, dead

or alive. In all his life he had never possessed that much money. The thought was a bitter one. Kapahei had been right. He, Koolau, had done no wrong. Because the *haoles* wanted labor with which to work the stolen land, they had brought in the Chinese coolies, and with them had come the sickness. And now, because he had caught the sickness, he was worth a thousand dollars—but not to himself. It was his worthless carcass, rotten with disease or dead from a bursting shell, that was worth all that money.

When the soldiers reached the knife-edged passage, he was prompted to warn them. But his gaze fell upon the body of the murdered maid, and he kept silent. When six had ventured on the knife-edge, he opened fire. Nor did he cease when the knife-edge was bare. He emptied his magazine, reloaded, and emptied it again. He kept on shooting. All his wrongs were blazing in his brain, and he was in a fury of vengeance. All down the goat trail the soldiers were firing, and though they lay flat and sought to shelter themselves in the shallow inequalities of the surface, they were exposed marks to him. Bullets whistled and thudded about him, and an occasional ricochet sang sharply through the air. One bullet ploughed a crease through his scalp, and a second burned across his shoulder-blade without breaking the skin.

It was a massacre, in which one man did the killing. The soldiers began to retreat, helping along their wounded. As Koolau picked them off he became aware of the smell of burnt meat. He glanced about him at first, and then discovered that it was his own hands. The heat of the rifle was doing it. The leprosy had destroyed most of the nerves in his hands. Though his flesh burned and he smelled it, there was no sensation.

He lay in the thicket, smiling, until he remembered the war guns. Without doubt they would open up on him again, and this time upon the very thicket from which he had inflicted the damage. Scarcely had he changed his position to a nook behind a small shoulder of the wall where he had noted that no shells fell, than the bombardment recommenced. He counted the shells. Sixty more were thrown into the gorge before the war-guns ceased. The tiny area was pitted with their explosion, until it seemed impossible that any creature could have survived. So the soldiers thought, for, under the burning afternoon sun, they climbed the goat trail again. And again the knife-edged passage was disputed, and again they fell back to the beach.

For two days longer Koolau held the passage, though the soldiers contented themselves with flinging shells into his retreat. Then Pahau, a leper boy, came to the top of the wall at the back of the gorge and shouted down to him that Kiloliana, hunting goats that they might eat, had been killed by a fall, and that the women were frightened and knew not what to do. Koolau called the boy down and left him with a spare gun with which to guard the passage. Koolau found his people disheartened. The majority of them were too helpless to forage food for themselves under such forbidding circumstances, and all were starving. He selected two women and a man who were not too far gone with the disease, and sent them back to the gorge to bring up food and mats. The rest he cheered and consoled until even the weakest took a hand in building rough shelters for themselves.

But those he had dispatched for food did not return, and he started back for the gorge. As he came out on the brow of the wall, half a dozen rifles cracked. A bullet tore through the fleshy part of his shoulder, and his cheek was cut by a sliver of rock where a second bullet smashed against the cliff. In the moment that this happened, and he leaped back, he saw that the gorge was alive with soldiers. His own people had betrayed him. The shell-fire had been too terrible, and they had preferred the prison of Molokai.

Koolau dropped back and unslung one of his heavy cartridge-belts. Lying among the rocks, he allowed the head and shoulders of the first soldier to rise clearly into view before pulling trigger. Twice this happened, and then, after some delay, in place of a head and shoulders a white flag was thrust above the edge of the wall.

"What do you want?" he demanded.

"I want you, if you are Koolau the leper," came the answer.

Koolau forgot where he was, forget everything, as he lay and marvelled at the strange persistence of these *haoles* who would have their will though the sky fell in. Aye, they would have their will over all men and all things, even though they died in getting it. He could not but admire them, too, what of that will in them that was stronger than life and that bent all things to their bidding. He was convinced of the hopelessness of his struggle. There was no gainsaying that terrible will of the *haoles*. Though he killed a thousand, yet would they rise like the sands of the sea and come upon him, ever more and more. They never knew when they were beaten. That was their fault and their virtue. It was where his own kind lacked. He could see, now, how the handful of the preachers of God and the preachers of Rum had conquered the land. It was because—

"Well, what have you got to say? Will you come with me?"

It was the voice of the invisible man under the white flag. There he was, like any *haole*, driving straight toward the end determined.

"Let us talk," said Koolau.

The man's head and shoulders arose, then his whole body. He was a smooth-faced, blue-eyed youngster of twenty-five, slender and natty in his captain's uniform. He advanced until halted, then seated himself a dozen feet away:—

"You are a brave man," said Koolau wonderingly. "I could kill you like a fly."

"No, you couldn't," was the answer.

"Why not?"

"Because you are a man, Koolau, though a bad one. I know your story. You kill fairly."

Koolau grunted, but was secretly pleased.

"What have you done with my people?" he demanded. "The boy, the two women, and the man?"

"They gave themselves up, as I have now come for you to do."

Koolau laughed incredulously.

"I am a free man," he announced. "I have done no wrong. All I ask is to be left alone. I have lived free, and I shall die free. I will never give myself up."

"Then your people are wiser than you," answered the young captain. "Look—they are coming now."

Koolau turned and watched the remnant of his band approach. Groaning and sighing, a ghastly procession, it dragged its wretchedness past. It was given to Koolau to taste a deeper bitterness, for they hurled imprecations and insults at him as they went by; and the panting hag who brought up the rear halted, and with skinny, harpy-claws extended, shaking her snarling death's head from side to side, she laid a curse upon him. One by one they dropped over the lip-edge and surrendered to the hiding soldiers.

"You can go now," said Koolau to the captain. "I will never give myself up. That is my last word. Good-by."

The captain slipped over the cliff to his soldiers. The next moment, and without a flag of truce, he hoisted his hat on his scabbard, and Koolau's bullet tore through it. That afternoon they shelled him out from the beach, and as he retreated into the high inaccessible pockets beyond, the soldiers followed him.

For six weeks they hunted him from pocket to pocket, over the volcanic peaks and along the goat trails. When he hid in the lantana jungle, they formed lines of beaters, and through lantana jungle and guava scrub they drove him like a rabbit. But ever he turned and doubled and eluded. There was no cornering him. When pressed too closely, his sure rifle held them back and they carried their wounded down the goat trails to the beach. There were times when they did the shooting as his brown body showed for a moment through the underbrush. Once, five of them caught him on an exposed goat trail between pockets. They emptied their rifles at him as he limped and climbed along his dizzy way. Afterward they found blood-stains and knew that he was wounded. At the end of six weeks they gave up. The soldiers and police returned to Honolulu, and Kalalau Valley was left to him for his own, though headhunters ventured after him from time to time and to their own undoing.

Two years later, and for the last time, Koolau crawled unto a thicket and lay down among the *ti*-leaves and wild ginger blossoms. Free he had lived, and free he was dying. A slight drizzle of rain began to fall, and he drew a ragged blanket about the distorted wreck of his limbs. His body was covered with an oilskin coat. Across his chest he laid his Mauser rifle, lingering affectionately for a moment to wipe the dampness from the barrel. The hand with which he wiped had no fingers left upon it with which to pull the trigger.

He closed his eyes, for, from the weakness in his body and the fuzzy turmoil in his brain, he knew that his end was near. Like a wild animal he had crept into hiding to die. Half-conscious, aimless and wandering, he lived back in his life to his early manhood on Niihau. As life faded and the drip of the rain grew dim in his ears, it seemed to him that he was once more in the thick of the horse-breaking, with raw colts rearing and bucking under him, his stirrups tied together beneath, or charging madly about the breaking corral and driving the helping cowboys over the rails. The next instant, and with seeming naturalness, he found himself pursuing the wild bulls of the upland pastures, roping them and leading them down to the valleys. Again the sweat and dust of the branding pen stung his eyes and bit his nostrils.

All his lusty, whole-bodied youth was his, until the sharp pangs of impending dissolution brought him back. He lifted his monstrous hands and gazed at them in wonder. But how? Why? Why should the wholeness of that wild youth of his change to this? Then he remembered, and once again, and for a moment, he was Koolau, the leper. His eyelids fluttered wearily down and the drip of the rain ceased in his ears. A prolonged trembling set up in his body. This, too, ceased. He half-lifted his head, but it fell back. Then his eyes opened, and did not close. His last thought was of his Mauser, and he pressed it against his chest with his folded, fingerless hands.

The Apostate

Now I wake me up to work;
I pray the Lord I may not shirk
If I should die before the night,
I pray the Lord my work's all right.
                                    Amen.

"If you don't git up, Johnny, I won't give you a bite to eat!"

The threat had no effect on the boy. He clung stubbornly to sleep, fighting for its oblivion as the dreamer fights for his dream. The boy's hands loosely clenched themselves; and he made feeble, spasmodic blows at the air. These blows were intended for his mother, but she betrayed practised familiarity in avoiding them as she shook him roughly by the shoulder.

"Lemme 'lone!"

It was a cry that began, muffled, in the deeps of sleep, that swiftly rushed upward, like a wail, into passionate belligerence, and that died away and sank down into an inarticulate whine. It was a bestial cry, as of a soul in torment, filled with infinite protest and pain.

But she did not mind. She was a sad-eyed, tired-faced women, and she had grown used to this task, which she repeated every day of her life. She got a grip on the bedclothes and tried to strip them down; but the boy; ceasing his punching, clung to them desperately. In a huddle, at the foot of the bed, he still remained covered. Then she tried dragging the bedding to the floor. The boy opposed her. She braced herself. Hers was the superior weight, and the boy and bedding gave, the former instinctively following the latter in order to shelter against the chill of the room that bit into his body.

As he toppled on the edge of the bed it seemed that he must fall head-first to the floor. But consciousness fluttered up in him. He righted himself and for a moment perilously balanced. Then he struck the floor on his feet. On the instant his mother seized him by the shoulders and shook him. Again his fists struck out, this time with more force and directness. At the same time his eyes opened. She released him. He was awake.

"All right," he mumbled.

She caught up the lamp and hurried out, leaving him in darkness.

"You'll be docked," she warned back at him.

He did not mind the darkness. When he had got into his clothes, he went out into the kitchen. His tread was very heavy for so thin and light a boy. His legs dragged with their own weight, which seemed unreasonable because they were such skinny legs. He drew a broken-bottomed chair to the table.

"Johnny!" his mother called sharply.

He arose as sharply from the chair, and, without a word, went to the sink. It was a greasy, filthy sink. A smell came up from the outlet. He took no notice of it. That a sink should smell was to him part of the natural order, just as it was a part of he natural order that the soap should be grimy with dish-water and hard to lather. Nor did he try very hard to make it lather. Several splashes of the cold water from the running faucet completed the function. He did not wash his teeth. For that matter he had never seen a tooth-brush, nor did he know that there existed beings in the world who were guilty of so great a foolishness as tooth washing.

"You might wash yourself wunst a day without bein' told," his mother complained.

She was holding a broken lid on the pot as she poured two cups of coffee. He made no remark, for this was a standing quarrel between them, and the one thing upon which his mother was hard as adamant. "Wunst" a day it was compulsory that he should wash his face. He dried himself on a greasy towel, damp and dirty and ragged, that left his face covered with shreds of lint.

"I wish we didn't live so far away," she said, as he sat down, "I try to do the best I can. You know that. But a dollar on the rent is such a savin', an' we've more room here. You know that."

He scarcely followed her. He had heard it all before, many times. The range of her thought was limited, and she was ever barking back to the hardship worked upon them by living so far from the mills.

"A dollar means more grub," he remarked sententiously. "I'd sooner do the walkin' an' git the grub."

He ate hurriedly, half chewing the bread and washing the unmasticated chunks down with coffee. The hot and muddy liquid went by the name of coffee. Johnny thought it was coffee—and excellent coffee. That was one of the few of life's illusions that remained to him. He had never drunk real coffee in his life.

In addition to the bread, there was a small piece of cold pork. His mother refilled his cup with coffee. As he was finishing the bread, he began to watch if more was forthcoming. She intercepted his questioning glance.

"Now, don't be hoggish, Johnny," was her comment. "You've had your share. Your brothers an' sisters are smaller'n you."

He did not answer the rebuke. He was not much of a talker. Also, he ceased his hungry glancing for more. He was uncomplaining, with a patience that was as terrible as the school in which it had been learned. He finished his coffee, wiped his mouth on the back of his hand, and started to rise.

"Wait a second," she said hastily. "I guess the loaf kin stand you another slice—a thin un."

There was legerdemain in her actions. With all the seeming of cutting a slice from the loaf for him, she put loaf and slice back in the bread box and conveyed to him one of her own two slices. She believed she had deceived him, but he had noted her sleight-of-hand. Nevertheless, he took the bread shamelessly. He had a philosophy that his mother, what of her chronic sickliness, was not much of an eater anyway.

She saw that he was chewing the bread dry, and reached over and emptied her coffee cup into his.

"Don't set good somehow on my stomach this morning," she explained.

A distant whistle, prolonged and shrieking, brought both of them to their feet. She glanced at the tin alarm-clock on the shelf. The hands stood at half-past five. The rest of the factory world was just arousing from sleep. She drew a shawl about her shoulders, and on her head put a dingy hat, shapeless and ancient.

"We've got to run," she said, turning the wick of the lamp and blowing down the chimney.

They groped their way out and down the stairs. It was clear and cold, and Johnny shivered at the first contact with the outside air. The stars had not yet begun to pale in the sky, and the city lay in blackness. Both Johnny and his mother shuffled their feet as they walked. There was no ambition in the leg muscles to swing the feet clear of the ground.

After fifteen silent minutes, his mother turned off to the right.

"Don't be late," was her final warning from out of the dark that was swallowing her up.

He made no response, steadily keeping on his way. In the factory quarter, doors were opening everywhere, and he was soon one of a multitude that pressed onward through the dark. As he entered the factory gate the whistle blew again. He glanced at the east. Across a ragged sky-line of housetops a pale light was beginning to creep. This much he saw of the day as he turned his back upon it and joined his work gang.

He took his place in one of many long rows of machines. Before him, above a bin filled with small bobbins, were large bobbins revolving rapidly. Upon these he wound the jute-twine of the small bobbins. The work was simple. All that was required was celerity. The small bobbins were emptied so rapidly, and there were so many large bobbins that did the emptying, that there were no idle moments.

He worked mechanically. When a small bobbin ran out, he used his left hand for a brake, stopping the large bobbin and at the same time, with thumb and forefinger, catching the flying end of twine. Also, at the same time, with his right hand, he caught up the loose twine-end of a small bobbin. These various acts with both hands were performed simultaneously and swiftly. Then there would come a flash of his hands as he looped the weaver's knot and released the bobbin. There was nothing difficult about weaver's knots. He once boasted he could tie them in his sleep. And for that matter, he sometimes did, toiling centuries long in a single night at tying an endless succession of weaver's knots.

Some of the boys shirked, wasting time and machinery by not replacing the small bobbins when they ran out. And there was an overseer to prevent this. He caught Johnny's neighbor at the trick, and boxed his ears.

"Look at Johnny there—why ain't you like him?" the overseer wrathfully demanded.

Johnny's bobbins were running full blast, but he did not

thrill at the indirect praise. There had been a time . . . but that was long ago, very long ago. His apathetic face was expressionless as he listened to himself being held up as a shining example. He was the perfect worker. He knew that. He had been told so, often. It was a commonplace, and besides it didn't seem to mean anything to him any more. From the perfect worker he had evolved into the perfect machine. When his work went wrong, it was with him as with the machine, due to faulty material. It would have been as possible for a perfect nail-die to cut imperfect nails as for him to make a mistake.

And small wonder. There had never been a time when he had not been in intimate relationship with machines. Machinery had almost been bred into him, and at any rate he had been brought up on it. Twelve years before, there had been a small flutter of excitement in the loom room of this very mill. Johnny's mother had fainted. They stretched her out on the floor in the midst of the shrieking machines. A couple of elderly women were called from their looms. The foreman assisted. And in a few minutes there was one more soul in the loom room than had entered by the doors. It was Johnny, born with the pounding, crashing roar of the looms in his ears, drawing with his first breath the warm, moist air that was thick with flying lint. He had coughed that first day in order to rid his lungs of the lint; and for the same reason he had coughed ever since.

The boy alongside of Johnny whimpered and sniffed. The boy's face was convulsed with hatred for the overseer who kept a threatening eye on him from a distance; but every bobbin was running full. The boy yelled terrible oaths into the whirling bobbins before him; but the sound did not carry half a dozen feet, the roaring of the room holding it in and containing it like a wall.

Of all this Johnny took no notice. He had a way of accepting things. Besides, things grow monotonous by repetition, and this particular happening he had witnessed many times. It seemed to him as useless to oppose the overseer as to defy the will of a machine. Machines were made to go in certain ways and to perform certain tasks. It was the same with the overseer.

But at eleven o'clock there was excitement in the room. In an apparently occult way the excitement instantly permeated everywhere. The one-legged boy who worked on the other side of Johnny bobbed swiftly across the floor to a bin truck that stood empty. Into this he dived out of sight, crutch and all. The superintendent of the mill was coming along, accompanied by a young man. He was well dressed and wore a starched shirt—a gentleman in Johnny's classification of men, and also, "the Inspector."

He looked sharply at the boys as he passed along. Sometimes he stopped and asked questions. When he did so, he was compelled to shout at the top of his lungs, at which moments his face was ludicrously contorted with the strain of making himself heard. His quick eye noted the empty machine alongside of Johnny's, but he said nothing. Johnny also caught his eye, and he stopped abruptly. He caught Johnny by the arm to draw him back a step from the machine: but with an exclamation of surprise he released the arm.

"Pretty skinny," the superintendent laughed anxiously.

"Pipe stems," was the answer. "Look at those legs. The boy's got the rickets—incipient, but he's got them. If epilepsy doesn't get him in the end, it will be because tuberculosis gets him first."

Johnny listened, but did not understand. Furthermore he was not interested in future ills. There was an immediate and more serious ill that threatened him in the form of the inspector.

"Now, my boy, I want you to tell me the truth," the inspector said, or shouted, bending close to the boy's ear to make him hear. "How old are you?"

"Fourteen," Johnny lied, and he lied with the full force of his lungs. So loudly did he lie that it started him off in a dry, hacking cough that lifted the lint which had been settling in his lungs all morning.

"Looks sixteen at least," said the superintendent.

"Or sixty," snapped the inspector.

"He's always looked that way."

"How long?" asked the inspector, quickly.

"For years. Never gets a bit older."

"Or younger, I dare say. I suppose he's worked here all those years?"

"Off and on—but that was before the new law was passed," the superintendent hastened to add.

"Machine idle?" the inspector asked, pointing at the unoccupied machine beside Johnny's, in which the part-filled bobbins were flying like mad.

"Looks that way." The superintendent motioned the overseer to him and shouted in his ear and pointed at the machine. "Machine's idle," he reported back to the inspector.

They passed on, and Johnny returned to his work, relieved in that the ill had been averted. But the one-legged boy was not so fortunate. The sharp-eyed inspector haled him out at arm's length from the bin truck. His lips were quivering, and his face had all the expression of one upon whom was fallen profound and irremediable disaster. The overseer looked astounded, as though for the first time he had laid eyes on the boy, while the superintendent's face expressed shock and displeasure.

"I know him," the inspector said. "He's twelve years old. I've had him discharged from three factories inside the year. This makes the fourth."

He turned to the one-legged boy. "You promised me, word and honor, that you'd go to school."

The one-legged boy burst into tears. "Please, Mr. Inspector, two babies died on us, and we're awful poor."

"What makes you cough that way?" the inspector demanded, as though charging him with crime.

And as in denial of guilt, the one-legged boy replied: "It ain't nothin'. I jes' caught a cold last week, Mr. Inspector, that's all."

In the end the one-legged boy went out of the room with the inspector, the latter accompanied by the anxious and protesting superintendent. After that monotony settled down again. The long morning and the longer afternoon wore away and the whistle blew for quitting time. Darkness had already fallen when Johnny passed out through the factory gate. In the interval the sun had made a golden ladder of the sky, flooded the world with its gracious warmth, and dropped down and disappeared in the west behind a ragged sky-line of housetops.

Supper was the family meal of the day—the one meal at which Johnny encountered his younger brothers and sisters. It partook of the nature of an encounter, to him, for he was very old, while they were distressingly young. He had no patience with their excessive and amazing juvenility. He did not understand it. His own childhood was too far behind him. He was like an old and irritable man, annoyed by the turbulence of their young spirits that was to him arrant silliness. He glowered silently over his food, finding compensation in the thought that they would soon have to go to work. That would take the edge off of them and make them sedate and dignified—like him. Thus it was, after the fashion of the human, that Johnny made of himself a yardstick with which to measure the universe.

During the meal, his mother explained in various ways and with infinite repetition that she was trying to do the best she could; so that it was with relief, the scant meal ended, that Johnny shoved back his chair and arose. He debated for a moment between bed and the front door, and finally went out the latter. He did not go far. He sat down on the stoop, his knees drawn up and his narrow shoulders drooping forward, his elbows on his knees and the palms of his hands supporting his chin.

As he sat there, he did no thinking. He was just resting. So far as his mind was concerned, it was asleep. His brothers and sisters came out, and with other children played noisily about him. An electric globe on the corner lighted their frolics. He was peevish and irritable, that they knew; but the spirit of adventure lured them into teasing him. They joined hands before him, and, keeping time with their bodies, chanted in his face weird and uncomplimentary doggerel. At first he snarled curses at them—curses he had learned from the lips of various foremen. Finding this futile, and remembering his dignity, he relapsed into dogged silence.

His brother Will, next to him in age, having just passed his tenth birthday, was the ring-leader. Johnny did not possess particularly kindly feelings toward him. His life had early been embittered by continual giving over and giving way to Will. He had a definite feeling that Will was greatly in his debt and was ungrateful about it. In his own playtime, far back in the dim past, he had ben robbed of a large part of that playtime, by being compelled to take care of Will. Will was a baby then, and then, as now, their mother had spent her days in the mills. To Johnny had fallen the part of little father and little mother as well.

Will seemed to show the benefit of the giving over and the giving way. He was well-built, fairly rugged, as tall as his elder brother and even heavier. It was as though the life-blood of the one had been diverted into the other's veins. And in spirits it was the same. Johnny was jaded, worn out, without resilience, while his younger brother seemed bursting and spilling over with exuberance.

The mocking chant rose louder. Will leaned closer as he danced, thrusting out his tongue. Johnny's left arm shot out and caught the other around the neck. At the same time he rapped his bony fist to the other's nose. It was a pathetically bony fist, but that it was sharp to hurt was evidenced by the squeal of pain it produced. The other children were uttering frightened cries, while Johnny's sister, Jennie, had dashed into the house.

He thrust Will from him, kicked him savagely on the shins, then reached for him and slammed him face downward in the dirt. Nor did he release him till the face had been rubbed into the dirt several times. Then the mother arrived, an anæmic whirlwind of solicitude and maternal wrath.

"Why can't he leave me along?" was Johnny's reply to her upbraiding. "Can't he see I'm tired?"

"I'm as big as you," Will raged in her arms, his face a mess of tears, dirt, and blood. "I'm as big as you now, an' I'm goin' to git bigger. Then I'll lick you—see if I don't."

"You ought to be to work, seein' how big you are," Johnny snarled. "That's what's the matter with you. You ought to be to work. An' it's up to your ma to put you to work."

"But he's too young," she protested. "He's only a little boy."

"I was younger'n him when I started to work."

Johnny's mouth was open, further to express the sense of unfairness that he felt, but the mouth closed with a snap. He turned gloomily on his heel and stalked into the house and to bed. The door of his room was open to let in warmth from the kitchen. As he undressed in the semi-darkness he could hear his mother talking with a neighbor woman who had dropped in. His mother was crying, and her speech was punctuated with spiritless sniffles.

"I can't make out what's gittin' into Johnny," he could hear her say. "He didn't used to be this way. He was a patient little angel."

"An' he *is* a good boy," she hastened to defend. "He's worked faithful, an' he did go to work too young. But it wasn't my fault. I do the best I can, I'm sure."

Prolonged sniffling from the kitchen, and Johnny murmured to himself as his eyelids closed down. "You betcher life I've worked faithful."

The next morning he was torn bodily by his mother from the grip of sleep. Then came the meagre breakfast, the tramp through the dark, and the pale glimpse of day across the housetops as he turned his back on it and went in through the factory gate. It was another day, of all the days, and all the days were alike.

And yet there had been variety in his life—at the times he changed from one job to another, or was taken sick. When he was six, he was little mother and father to Will and the other children still younger. At seven he went into the mills—winding bobbins. When he was eight, he got work in another mill. His new job was marvellously easy. All he had to do was to sit down with a little stick in his hand and guide a stream of cloth that flowed past him. This stream of cloth came out of the maw of a machine, passed over a hot roller, and went on its way elsewhere. But he sat always in the one place, beyond the reach of daylight, a gas-jet flaring over him, himself part of the mechanism.

He was very happy at that job, in spite of the moist heat, for he was still young and in possession of dreams and illusions. And wonderful dreams he dreamed as he watched the streaming cloth streaming endlessly by. But there was no exercise about the work, no call upon his mind, and he dreamed less and less, while his mind grew torpid and drowsy. Nevertheless, he earned two dollars a week, and two dollars represented the difference between acute starvation and chronic underfeeding.

But when he was nine, he lost his job. Measles was the cause of it. After he recovered, he got work in a glass factory. The pay was better, and the work demanded skill. It was piece-work, and the more skilful he was, the bigger wages he earned. Here was incentive. And under this incentive he developed into a remarkable worker.

It was simple work, the tying of glass stoppers into small bottles. At his waist he carried a bundle of twine. He held the bottles between his knees so that he might work with both hands. Thus, in a sitting position and bending over his own knees, his narrow shoulders grew humped and his chest was contracted for ten hours each day. This was not good for the lungs, but he tied three hundred dozen bottles a day.

The superintendent was very proud of him, and brought visitors to look at him. In ten hours three hundred dozen bottles passed through his hands. This meant that he had attained machine-like perfection. All waste movements were eliminated. Every motion of his thin arms, every movement of a muscle in the thin fingers, was swift and accurate. He worked at high tension, and the result was that he grew nervous. At night his muscles twitched in his sleep, and in the daytime he could not relax and rest. He remained keyed up and his muscles continued to twitch. Also he grew sallow and his lint-cough grew worse. Then pneumonia laid hold of the feeble lungs within the contracted chest, and he lost his job in the glass-works.

Now he had returned to the jute mills where he had first begun with winding bobbins. But promotion was waiting for him. He was a good worker. He would next go on the starcher, and later he would go into the loom room. There was nothing after that except increased efficiency.

The machinery ran faster than when he had first gone to work, and his mind ran slower. He no longer dreamed at all, though his earlier years had been full of dreaming. Once he had been in love. It was when he first began guiding the cloth over the hot roller, and it was with the daughter of the superintendent. She was much older than he, a young woman, and he had seen her at a distance only a paltry half-dozen times. But that made no difference. On the surface of the cloth stream that poured past him, he pictured radiant futures wherein he performed prodigies of toil, invented miraculous machines, won to the mastership of the mills, and in the end took her in his arms and kissed her soberly on the brow.

But that was all in the long ago, before he had grown too old and tired to love. Also, she had married and gone away, and his mind had gone to sleep. Yet it had been a wonderful experience, and he used often to look back upon it as other men and women look back upon the time they believed in fairies. He had never believed in fairies nor Santa Claus; but he had believed implicitly in the smiling future his imagination had wrought into the steaming cloth stream.

He had become a man very early in life. At seven, when he drew his first wages, began his adolescence. A certain feeling of independence crept up in him, and the relationship between him and his mother changed. Somehow, as an earner and breadwinner, doing his own work in the world, he was more like an equal with her. Manhood, full-blown manhood, had come when he was eleven, at which time he had gone to work on the night shift for six months. No child works on the night shift and remains a child.

There had been several great events in his life. One of these had been when his mother bought some California prunes. Two others had been the two times when she cooked custard. Those had been events. He remembered them kindly. And at that time his mother had told him of a blissful dish she would sometime make—"floating island," she had called it, "better than custard." For years he had looked forward to the day when he would sit down to the table with floating island before him, until at last he had relegated the idea of it to the limbo of unattainable ideals.

Once he found a silver quarter lying on the sidewalk. That, also, was a great event in his life, withal a tragic one. He knew his duty on the instant the silver flashed on his eyes, before even he had picked it up. At home, as usual, there was not enough to eat, and home he should have taken it as he did his wages every Saturday night. Right conduct in this case was obvious; but he never had any spending of his money, and he was suffering from candy hunger. He was ravenous for the sweets that only on red-letter days he had ever tasted in his life.

He did not attempt to deceive himself. He knew it was sin, and deliberately he sinned when he went on a fifteen-cent candy debauch. Ten cents he saved for a future orgy; but not being accustomed to the carrying of money, he lost the ten cents. This occurred at the time when he was suffering all the torments of conscience, and it was to him an act of divine retribution. He had a frightened sense of the closeness of an awful and wrathful God. God had seen, and God had been swift to punish, denying him even the full wages of sin.

In memory he always looked back upon that event as the one great criminal deed of his life, and at the recollection his conscience always awoke and gave him another twinge. It was the one skeleton in his closet. Also, being so made and circumstanced, he looked back upon the deed with regret. He was dissatisfied with the manner in which he had spent the quarter. He could have invested it better, and, out of his later knowledge of the quickness of God, he would have beaten God out by spending the whole quarter at one fell swoop. In retrospect he spent the quarter a thousand times, and each time to better advantage.

There was one other memory of the past, dim and faded, but stamped into his soul everlasting by the savage feet of his father. It was more like a nightmare than a remembered vision of a concrete thing—more like the race-memory of man that makes him fall in his sleep and that goes back to his arboreal ancestry.

This particular memory never came to Johnny in broad daylight when he was wide awake. It came at night, in bed, at the moment that his consciousness was sinking down and losing itself in sleep. It always aroused him to frightened wakefulness, and for the moment, in the first sickening start, it seemed to him that he lay crosswise on the foot of the bed. In the bed were the vague forms of his father and mother. He never saw what his father looked like. He had but one impression of his father, and that was that he had savage and pitiless feet.

His earlier memories lingered with him, but he had no late memories. All days were alike. Yesterday or last year were the same as a thousand years—or a minute. Nothing ever happened. There were no events to mark the march of time. Time did not march. It stood always still. It was only the whirling machines that moved, and they moved nowhere—in spite of the fact that they moved faster.

When he was fourteen, he went to work on the starcher. It was a colossal event. Something had at last happened that could be remembered beyond a night's sleep or a week's pay-day. It marked an era. It was a machine Olympiad, a thing to date from. "When I went to work on the starcher," or, "after," or "before I went to work on the starcher," were sentences often on his lips.

He celebrated his sixteenth birthday by going into the loom room and taking a loom. Here was an incentive again, for it was piece-work. And he excelled, because the clay of him had been moulded by the mills into the perfect machine. At the end of three months he was running two looms, and, later, three and four.

At the end of his second year at the looms he was turning out more yards than any other weaver, and more than twice as much as some of the less skilful ones. And at home things began to prosper as he approached the full stature of his earning power. Not, however, that his increased earnings were in excess of need. The children were growing up. They ate more. And they were going to school, and school-books cost money. And somehow, the faster he worked, the faster climbed the prices of things. Even the rent went up, though the house had fallen from bad to worse disrepair.

He had grown taller; but with his increased height he seemed leaner than ever. Also, he was more nervous. With the nervousness increased his peevishness and irritability. The children had learned by many bitter lessons to fight shy of him. His mother respected him for his earning power, but somehow her respect was tinctured with fear.

There was no joyousness in life for him. The procession of the days he never saw. The nights he slept away in twitching unconsciousness. The rest of the time he worked, and his consciousness was machine consciousness. Outside this his mind was a blank. He had no ideals, and but one illusion; namely, that he drank excellent coffee. He was a work-beast. He had no mental life whatever; yet deep down in the crypts of his mind, unknown to him, were being weighed and sifted every hour of his toil, every movement of his hands, every twitch of his muscles, and preparations were making for a future course of action that would amaze him and all his little world.

It was in the late spring that he came home from work one night aware of unusual tiredness. There was a keen expectancy in the air as he sat down to the table, but he did not notice. He went through the meal in moody silence, mechanically eating what was before him. The children um'd and ah'd and made smacking noises with their mouths. But he was deaf to them.

"D'ye know what you're eatin'?" his mother demanded at last, desperately.

He looked vacantly at the dish before him, and vacantly at her.

"Floatin' island," she announced triumphantly.

"Oh," he said.

"Floating island!" the children chorussed loudly.

"Oh," he said. And after two or three mouthfuls, he added, "I guess I ain't hungry to-night."

He dropped the spoon, shoved back his chair, and arose wearily from the table.

"An' I guess I'll go to bed."

His feet dragged more heavily than usual as he crossed the kitchen floor. Undressing was a Titan's task, a monstrous futility, and he wept weakly as he crawled into bed, one shoe still on. He was aware of a rising, swelling something inside his head that made his brain thick and fuzzy. His lean fingers felt as big as his wrist, while in the ends of them was a remoteness of sensation vague and fuzzy like his brain. The small of his back ached intolerably. All his bones ached. He ached everywhere. And in his head began the shrieking, pounding, crashing, roaring of a million looms. All space was filled with flying shuttles. They darted in and out, intricately, amongst the stars. He worked a thousand looms himself, and ever they speeded up, faster and faster, and his brain unwound, faster and faster, and became the thread that fed the thousand flying shuttles.

He did not go to work next morning. He was too busy weaving colossally on the thousand looms that ran inside his head. His mother went to work, but first she sent for the doctor. It was a severe attack of la grippe, he said. Jennie served as nurse and carried out his instructions.

It was a very severe attack, and it was a week before Johnny dressed and tottered feebly across the floor. Another week, the doctor said, and he would be fit to return to work. The foreman of the loom room visited him on Sunday afternoon, the first day of his convalescence. The est weaver in the room, the foreman told his mother. His job would be held for him. He could come back to work a week from Monday.

"Why don't you thank 'im, Johnny?" his mother asked anxiously.

"He's ben that sick he ain't himself yet," she explained apologetically to the visitor.

Johnny sat hunched up and gazing steadfastly at the floor. He sat in the same position long after the foreman had gone. It was warm outdoors, and he sat on the stoop in the afternoon. Sometimes his lips moved. He seemed lost in endless calculations.

Next morning, after the day grew warm, he took his seat on the stoop. He had pencil and paper this time with which to continue his calculations, and he calculated painfully and amazingly.

"What comes after millions?" he asked at noon, when Will came home from school. "An' how d'ye work 'em?"

That afternoon finished his task. Each day, but without paper and pencil, he returned to the stoop. He was greatly absorbed in the one tree that grew across the street. He studied it for hours at a time, and was unusually interested when the wind swayed its branches and fluttered its leaves. Throughout the week he seemed lost in a great communion with himself. On Sunday, sitting on the stoop, he laughed aloud, several times, to the perturbation of his mother, who had not heard him laugh in years.

Next morning, in the early darkness, she came to his bed to rouse him. He had had his fill of sleep all week, and awoke easily. He made no struggle, nor did he attempt to hold on to the bedding when she stripped it from him. He lay quietly, and spoke quietly.

"It ain't no use, ma."

"You'll be late," she said, under the impression that he was still stupid with sleep.

"I'm awake, ma, an' I tell you it ain't no use. You might as well lemme alone. I ain't goin' to git up."

"But you'll lose your job!" she cried.

"I ain't goin' to git up," he repeated in a strange, passionless voice.

She did not go to work herself that morning. This was sickness beyond any sickness she had ever known. Fever and delirium she could understand; but this was insanity. She pulled the bedding up over him and sent Jennie for the doctor.

When that person arrived, Johnny was sleeping gently, and gently he awoke and allowed his pulse to be taken.

"Nothing the matter with him," the doctor reported. "Badly debilitated, that's all. Not much meat on his bones."

"He's always been that way," his mother volunteered.

"No go 'way, ma, an' let me finish my snooze."

Johnny spoke sweetly and placidly, and sweetly and placidly he rolled over on his side and went to sleep.

At ten o'clock he awoke and dressed himself. He walked out into the kitchen, where he found his mother with a frightened expression on her face.

"I'm goin' away, ma," he announced, "an' I jes' want to say good-by."

She threw her apron over her head and sat down suddenly and wept. He waited patiently.

"I might a-known it," she was sobbing.

"Where?" she finally asked, removing the apron from her head and gazing up at him with a stricken face in which there was little curiosity.

"I don't know—anywhere."

As he spoke, the tree across the street appeared with dazzling brightness on his inner vision. It seemed to lurk just under his eyelids, and he could see it whenever he wished.

"An' your job?" she quavered.

"I ain't never goin' to work again.".

"My God, Johnny!" she wailed, "don't say that!"

What he had said was blasphemy to her. As a mother who hears her child deny God, was Johnny's mother shocked by his words.

"What's got into you, anyway?" she demanded, with a lame attempt at imperativeness.

"Figures," he answered. "Jes' figures. I've ben doin' a lot of figurin' this week, an' it's most surprisin'."

"I don't see what that's got to do with it," she sniffled.

Johnny smiled patiently, and his mother was aware of a distinct shock at the persistent absence of his peevishness and irritability.

"I'll show you," he said. "I'm plum' tired out. What makes me tired? Moves. I've been movin' ever since I was born. I'm tired of movin', an' I ain't goin' to move any more. Remember when I worked in the glass-house? I used to do three hundred dozen a day. Now I reckon I made about ten different moves to each bottle. That's thirty-six thousan' moves a day. Ten days, three hundred an' sixty thousan' moves a day. One month, one million an' eighty thousan' moves. Chuck out the eighty thousan'—" he spoke with the complacent beneficence of a philanthropist—"chuck out the eighty thousan', that leaves a million moves a month—twelve million moves a year.

"At the looms I'm movin' twic'st as much. That makes twenty-five million moves a year, an' it seems to me I've ben a movin' that way 'most a million years.

"Now this week I ain't moved at all. I ain't made one move in hours an' hours. I tell you it was swell, jes' settin' there, hours an' hours, an' doin' nothin'. I ain't never been happy before. I never had any time. I've ben movin' all the time. That ain't no way to be happy. An' I ain't goin' to do it any more. I'm jes' goin' to set, an' set, an' rest, an' rest, and then rest some more."

"But what's goin' to come of Will an' the children?" she asked despairingly.

"That's it, 'Will an' the children,' " he repeated.

But there was no bitterness in his voice. He had long known his mother's ambition for the younger boy, but the thought of it no longer rankled. Nothing mattered any more. Not even that.

"I know, ma, what you've ben plannin' for Will— keepin' him in school to make a bookkeeper out of him. But it ain't no use, I've quit. He's got to go to work."

"An' after I have brung you up the way I have," she wept, starting to cover her head with the apron and changing her mind.

"You never brung me up," he answered with sad kindliness. "I brung myself up, ma, an' I brung up Will. He's bigger'n me, an' heavier, an' taller. When I was a kid, I reckon I didn't git enough to eat. When he come along an' was a kid, I was workin' an' earnin' grub for him too. But that's done with. Will can go to work, same as me, or he can go to hell, I don't care which. I'm tired. I'm goin' now. Ain't you goin' to say good-by?"

She made no reply. The apron had gone over her head again, and she was crying. He paused a moment in the doorway.

"I'm sure I done the best I knew how," she was sobbing.

He passed out of the house and down the street. A wan delight came into his face at the sight of the lone tree. "Jes' ain't goin' to do nothin'," he said to himself, half aloud, in a crooning tone. He glanced wistfully up at the sky, but the bright sun dazzled and blinded him.

It was a long walk he took, and he did not walk fast. It took him past the jute-mill. The muffled roar of the loom room came to his ears, and he smiled. It was a gentle, placid smile. He hated no one, not even the pounding, shrieking machines. There was no bitterness in him, nothing but an inordinate hunger for rest.

The houses and factories thinned out and the open spaces increased as he approached the country. At last the city was behind him, and he was walking down a leafy lane beside the railroad track. He did not walk like a man. He did not look like a man. He was a travesty of the human. It was a twisted and stunted and nameless piece of life that shambled like a sickly ape, arms loose-hanging, stoop-shouldered, narrow-chested, grotesque and terrible.

He passed by a small railroad station and lay down in the grass under a tree. All afternoon he lay there. Sometimes he dozed, with muscles that twitched in his sleep. When awake, he lay without movement, watching the birds or looking up at the sky through the branches of the tree above him. Once or twice he laughed aloud, but without relevance to anything he had seen or felt.

After twilight had gone, in the first darkness of the night, a freight train rumbled into the station. When the engine was switching cars on the side-track, Johnny crept along the side of the train. He pulled open the side-door of an empty box-car and awkwardly and laboriously climbed in. He closed the door. The engine whistled. Johnny was lying down, and in the darkness he smiled.

Mauki

He weighed one hundred and ten pounds. His hair was kinky and negroid, and he was black. He was peculiarly black. He was neither blue-black nor purple-black, but plum-black. His name was Mauki, and he was the son of a chief. He had three *tambos*. *Tambo* is Melanesian for *taboo*, and is first cousin to that Polynesian word. Mauki's three *tambos* were as follows: first, he must never shake hands with a woman, nor have a woman's hand touch him or nay of his personal belongings; secondly, he must never eat clams or any food from a fire in which clams had been cooked; thirdly, he must never touch a crocodile, nor travel in a canoe that carried any part of a crocodile even if as large as a tooth.

Of a different black were his teeth, which were deep black, or, perhaps better, *lamp*-black. They had been made so in a single night, by his mother, who had compressed about them a powdered mineral which was dug from the landslide back of Port Adams. Port Adams is a salt-water village on Malaita, and Malaita is the most savage island in the Solomons—so savage that no traders nor planters have yet gained a foothold on it; while, from the time of the earliest bêche-de-mer fishers and sandalwood traders down to the latest labor recruiters equipped with automatic rifles and gasolene engines, scores of white adventurers have been passed out by tomahawks and soft-nosed Snider bullets. So Malaita remains to-day, in the twentieth century, the stamping ground of the labor recruiters, who farm its coasts for laborers who engage and contract themselves to toil on the plantations of the neighboring and more civilized islands for a wage of thirty dollars a year. The natives of those neighboring and more civilized islands have themselves become too civilized to work on plantations.

Mauki's ears were pierced, not in one place, nor two places, but in a couple of dozen places. In one of the smaller holes he carried a clay pipe. The larger holes were too large for such use. The bowl of the pipe would have fallen through. In fact, in the largest hole in each ear he habitually wore round wooden plugs that were an even four inches in diameter. Roughly speaking, the circumference of said holes was twelve and one-half inches. Mauki was catholic in his tastes. In the various smaller holes he carried such things as empty rifle cartridges, horseshoe nails, copper screws, pieces of string, braids of sennit, strips of green leaf, and, in the cool of the day, scarlet hibiscus flowers. From which it will be seen that pockets were not necessary to his well-being. Besides, pockets were impossible, for his only wearing apparel consisted of a piece of calico several inches wide. A pocket knife he wore in his hair, the black snapped down on a kinky lock. His most prized possession was the handle of a china cup, which he suspended from a ring of turtle-shell, which, in turn, was passed through the partition-cartilage of his nose.

But in spite of embellishments, Mauki had a nice face. It was really a pretty face, viewed by any standard, and for a Melanesian it was a remarkably good-looking face. It's one fault was its lack of strength. It was softly effeminate, almost girlish. The features were small, regular, and delicate. The chin was weak, and the mouth was weak. There was no strength nor character in the jaws, forehead, and nose. In the eyes only could be caught any hint of the unknown quantities that were so large a part of his make-up and that other persons could not understand. These unknown quantities were pluck, pertinacity, fearlessness, imagination, and cunning; and when they found expression in some consistent and striking action, those about him were astounded.

Mauki's father was chief over the village at Port Adams, and thus, by birth a salt-water man, Mauki was half amphibian. He knew the way of the fishes and oysters, and the reef was an open book to him. Canoes, also, he knew. He learned to swim when he was a year old. At seven years he could hold his breath a full minute and swim straight down to bottom through thirty feet of water. And at seven years he was stolen by the bushmen, who cannot even swim and who are afraid of salt water. Thereafter Mauki saw the sea only from a distance, through rifts in the jungle and from open spaces on the high mountain sides. He became the slave of old Fanfoa, head chief over a score of scattered bush-villages on the range-lips of Malaita, the smoke of which, on calm mornings, is about the only evidence the seafaring white men have of the teeming interior population. For the whites do not penetrate Malaita. They tried it once, in the days when the search was on for gold, but they always left their heads behind to grin from the smoky rafters of the bushmen's huts.

When Mauki was a young man of seventeen, Fanfoa got out of tobacco. He got dreadfully out of tobacco. It was hard times in all his villages. He had been guilty of a mistake. Suo was a harbor so small that a large schooner could not swing at anchor in it. It was surrounded by mangroves that overhung the deep water. It was a trap, and into the trap sailed two white men in a small ketch. They were after recruits, and they possessed much tobacco and trade-goods, to say nothing of three rifles and plenty of ammunition. Now there were no salt-water men living at

Suo, and it was there that the bushmen could come down to the sea. The ketch did a splendid traffic. It signed on twenty recruits the first day. Even old Fanfoa signed on. And that same day the score of new recruits chopped off the two white men's heads, killed the boat's crew, and burned the ketch. Thereafter, and for three months, there was tobacco and trade-goods in plenty and to spare in all the bush-villages. Then came the man-of-war that threw shells for miles into the hills, frightening the people out of their villages and into the deeper bush. Next the man-of-war sent landing parties ashore. The villages were all burned, along with the tobacco and trade-stuff. The cocoanuts and bananas were chopped down, the taro gardens uprooted, and the pigs and chickens killed.

It taught Fanfoa a lesson, but in the meantime he was out of tobacco. Also, his young men were too frightened to sign on with the recruiting vessels. That was why Fanfoa ordered his slave, Mauki, to be carried down and signed on for half a case of tobacco advance, along with knives, axes, calico, and beads, which he would pay for with his toil on the plantations. Mauki was sorely frightened when they brought him on board the schooner. He was a lamb led to the slaughter. White men were ferocious creatures. They had to be, or else they would not make a practice of venturing along the Malaita coast and into all harbors, two on a schooner, when each schooner carried from fifteen to twenty blacks as boat's crew, and often as high as sixty or seventy black recruits. In addition to this, there was always the danger of the shore population, the sudden attack and the cutting off of the schooner and all hands. Truly, white men must be terrible. Besides, they were possessed of such devil-devils—rifles that shot very rapidly many times, things of iron and brass that made the schooners go when there was no wind, and boxes that talked and laughed just as men talked and laughed. Ay, and he had heard of one white man whose particular devil-devil was so powerful that he could take out all his teeth and put them back at will.

Down into the cabin they took Mauki. On deck, the one white man kept guard with two revolvers in his belt. In the cabin the other white man sat with a book before him, in which he inscribed strange marks and lines. He looked at Mauki as though he had been a pig or a fowl, glanced under the hollows of his arms, and wrote in the book. Then he held out the writing stick and Mauki just barely touched it with his hand, in so doing pledging himself to toil for three years on the plantations of the Moongleam Soap Company. It was not explained to him that the will of the ferocious white men would be used to enforce the pledge, and that, behind all, for the same use, was all the power and all the warships of Great Britain.

Other blacks there were on board, from unheard-of far places, and when the white man spoke to them, they tore the long feather from Mauki's hair, cut that same hair short, and wrapped about his waist a lava-lava of bright yellow calico.

After many days on the schooner, and after beholding more land and islands than he had ever dreamed of, he was landed on New Georgia, and put to work in the field clearing jungle and cutting cane grass. For the first time he knew what work was. Even as a slave to Fanfoa he had not worked like this. And he did not like work. It was up at dawn and in at dark, on two meals a day. And the food was tiresome. For weeks at a time they were given nothing but sweet potatoes to eat, and for weeks at a time it would be nothing but rice. He cut out the cocoanut from the shells day after day; and for long days and weeks he fed the fires that smoked the copra, till his eyes got sore and he was set to felling trees. He was a good axe-man, and later he was put in the bridge-building gang. Once, he was punished by being put in the road-building gang. At times he served as boat's crew in the whale-boats, when they brought in copra from distant beaches or when the white men went out to dynamite fish.

Among other things he learned bêche-de-mer English, with which he could talk with all white men, and with all recruits who otherwise, would have talked in a thousand different dialects. Also, he learned certain things about the white men, principally that they kept their word. If they told a boy he was going to receive a stick of tobacco, he got it. If they told a boy they would knock seven bells out of him if he did a certain thing, when he did that thing seven bells invariably were knocked out of him. Mauki did not know what seven bells were, but they occurred in bêche-de-mer, and he imagined them to be the blood and teeth that sometimes accompanied the process of knocking out seven bells. One other thing he learned: no boy was struck or punished unless he did wrong. Even when the white men were drunk, as they were frequently, they never struck unless a rule had been broken.

Mauki did not like the plantation. He hated work, and he was the son of a chief. Furthermore, it was ten years since he had been stolen from Port Adams by Fanfoa, and he was homesick. He was even homesick for the slavery under Fanfoa. So he ran away. He struck back into the bush, with the idea of working southward to the beach and stealing a canoe in which to go home to Port Adams. But the fever got him, and he was captured and brought back more dead than alive.

A second time he ran away, in the company of two Malaita boys. They got down the coast twenty miles, and were hidden in the hut of a Malaita freeman, who dwelt in that village. But in the dead of night two white men came, who were not afraid of all the village people and who knocked seven bells out of the three runaways, tied them like pigs, and tossed them into the whale-boat. But the man in whose house they had hidden—seven times seven bells must have been knocked out of him from the way the hair, skin, and teeth flew, and he was discouraged for the rest of his natural life from harboring runaway laborers.

For a year Mauki toiled on. Then he was made a house-boy, and had good food and easy times, with light work in keeping the house clean and serving the white man with whiskey and beer at all hours of the day and most hours of the night. He liked it, but he liked Port Adams more. He had two years longer to serve, but two years were too long for him in the throes of homesickness. He had grown wiser with his year of service, and, being now a house-boy, he had opportunity. He had the cleaning of the rifles, and he knew where the key to the store-room was hung. He planned the escape, and one night ten Malaita boys and one boy from San Cristoval sneaked from the barracks and dragged one of the whale-boats down to the beach. It was Mauki who supplied the key that opened the padlock on the boat, and it was Mauki who equipped the boat with a dozen Winchesters, an immense amount of ammunition, a case of dynamite with detonators and fuse, and ten cases of tobacco.

The northwest monsoon was blowing, and they fled south in the night-time, hiding by day on detached and un-inhabited islets, or dragging their whale-boat into the bush on the large islands. Thus they gained Guadalcanar, skirted halfway along it, and crossed the Indispensable Straits to Florida Island. It was here that they killed the San Cristo-val boy, saving his head and cooking and eating the rest of him. The Malaita coast was only twenty miles away, but the last night a strong current and baffling winds prevented them from gaining across. Daylight found them still sev-eral miles from their goal. But daylight brought a cutter, in which were two white man, who were not afraid of eleven Malaita men armed with twelve rifles. Mauki and his com-panions were carried back to Tulagi, where lived the great white master of all the white men. And the great white master held a court, after which, one by one, the runaways were tied up and given twenty lashes each, and sentenced to a fine of fifteen dollars. Then they were sent back to New Georgia, where the white men knocked seven bells out of them all around and put them to work. But Mauki, was no longer house-boy. He was put in the road-making gang. The fine of fifteen dollars had been paid by the white men from whom he had run away, and he was told that he would have to work it out, which meant six months' additional toil. Further, his share of the stolen tobacco earned him another year of toil.

Port Adams was now three years and a half away, so he stole a canoe one night, hid on the islets in Manning Straits, passed through the Straits, and began working along the eastern coast of Ysabel, only to be captured, two-thirds of the way along, by the white men on Meringe Lagoon. After a week, he escaped from them and took to the bush. There were no bush natives on Ysabel, only salt-water men, who were all Christians. The white men put up a reward of five hundred sticks of tobacco, and every time Mauki ventured down to the sea to steal a canoe he was chased by the salt-water men. Four months of this passed, when, the reward having been raised to a thousand sticks, he was caught and sent back to New Georgia and the road-building gang. Now a thousand sticks are worth fifty dollars, and Mauki had to pay the reward himself, which required a year and eight months' labor. So Port Adams was now five years away.

His homesickness was greater than ever, and it did not appeal to him to settle down and be good, work out his four years, and go home. The next time, he was caught in the very act of running away. His case was brought before Mr. Haveby, the island manager of the Moongleam Soap Company, who adjudged him an incorrigible. The Company had plantations on the Santa Cruz Islands, hundreds of miles across the sea, and there it sent its Solomon Islands' incorrigibles. And there Mauki was sent, though he never arrived. The schooner stopped at Santa Anna, and in the night Mauki swam ashore, where he stole two rifles and a case of tobacco from the trader and got away in a canoe to Cristoval. Malaita was now to the north, fifty or sixty miles away. But when he attempted the passage, he was caught by a light gale and driven back to Santa Anna, where the trader clapped him in irons and held him against the return of the schooner from Santa Cruz. The two rifles the trader recovered, but the case of tobacco was charged up to Mauki at the rate of another year. The sum of years he now owed the company was six.

On the way back to New Georgia, the schooner dropped anchor in Marau Sound, which lies at the southeastern extremity of Guadalcanar. Mauki swam ashore with handcuffs on his wrists and got away to the bush. The schooner went on, but the Moongleam trader ashore offered a thousand sticks, and to him Mauki was brought by the bushmen with a year and eight months tacked on to his account. Again, and before the schooner called in, he got away, this time in a whale-boat accompanied by a case of the trader's tobacco. But a northwest gale wrecked him upon Ugi, where the Christian natives stole his tobacco and turned him over to the Moongleam trader who resided there. The tobacco the natives stole meant another year for him, and the tale was now eight years and a half.

"We'll send him to Lord Howe," said Mr. Haveby. "Bunster is there, and we'll let them settle it between them. It will be a case, I imagine, of Mauki getting Bunster, or Bunster getting Mauki, and good riddance in either event."

If one leaves Meringe Lagoon, on Ysabel, and steers a course due north, magnetic, at the end of one hundred and fifty miles he will lift the pounded coral beaches of Lord Howe above the sea. Lord Howe is a ring of land some one hundred and fifty miles in circumference, several hundred yards wide at its widest, and towering in places to a height of ten feet above sea-level. Inside this ring of sand is a mighty lagoon studded with coral patches. Lord Howe belongs to the Solomons neither geographically nor ethnologically. It is an atoll, while the Solomons are high islands; and its people and language are Polynesian, while the inhabitants of the Solomons are Melanesian. Lord Howe has been populated by the westward Polynesian drift which continues to this day, big outrigger canoes being washed upon its beaches by the southeast trade. That there has been a slight Melanesian drift in the period of the northwest monsoon, is also evident.

Nobody ever comes to Lord Howe, or Ontong-Java as it is sometimes called. Thomas Cook & Son do not sell tickets to it, and tourists do not dream of its existence. Not even a white missionary has landed on its shore. Its five thousand natives are as peaceable as they are primitive. Yet they were not always peaceable. The *Sailing Directions* speak of them as hostile and treacherous. But the men who compile the *Sailing Directions* have never heard of the change that was worked in the hearts of the inhabitants, who, not many years ago, cut off a big bark and killed all hands with the exception of the second mate. This survivor carried the news to his brothers. The captains of three trading schooners returned with him to Lord Howe. They sailed their vessels right into the lagoon and proceeded to preach the white man's gospel that only white men shall kill white men and that the lesser breeds must keep hands off. The schooners sailed up and down the lagoon, harrying and destroying. There was no escape from the narrow sand-circle, no bush to which to flee. The men were shot down at sight, and there was no avoiding being sighted. The villages were burned, the canoes smashed, the chickens and pigs killed, and the precious cocoanut-trees chopped down. For a month this continued, when the schooners sailed away; but the fear of the white man had been seared into the souls of the islanders and never again were they rash enough to harm one.

Max Bunster was the one white man on Lord Howe, trading in the pay of the ubiquitous Moongleam Soap Company. And the Company billeted him on Lord Howe, because, next to getting rid of him, it was the most out-of-the-way place to be found. That the Company did not get rid of him was due to the difficulty of finding another man to take his place. He was a strapping big German, with something wrong in his brain. Semi-madness would be a charitable statement of his condition. He was a bully and a coward, and a thrice-bigger savage than any savage on the island. Being a coward, his brutality was of the cowardly order. When he first went into the Company's employ, he was stationed on Savo. When a consumptive colonial was sent to take his place, he beat him up with his fists and sent him off a wreck in the schooner that brought him.

Mr. Haveby next selected a young Yorkshire giant to relieve Bunster. The Yorkshire man had a reputation as a bruiser and preferred fighting to eating. But Bunster wouldn't fight. He was a regular little lamb—for ten days, at the end of which time the Yorkshire man was prostrated by a combined attack of dysentery and fever. Then Bunster went for him, among other things getting him down and jumping on him a score or so of times. Afraid of what would happen when his victim recovered, Bunster fled away in a cutter to Guvutu, where he signalized himself by beating up a young Englishman already crippled by a Boer bullet through both hips.

Then it was that Mr. Haveby sent Bunster to Lord Howe, the falling-off place. He celebrated his landing by mopping up half a case of gin and by thrashing the elderly and wheezy mate of the schooner which had brought him. When the schooner departed, he called the kanakas down to the beach and challenged them to throw him in a wrestling bout, promising a case of tobacco to the one who succeeded. Three kanakas he threw, but was promptly thrown by a fourth, who, instead of receiving the tobacco, got a bullet through his lungs.

And so began Bunster's reign on Lord Howe. Three thousand people lived in the principal village; but it was deserted, even in broad day, when he passed through. Men, women, and children fled before him. Even the dogs and pigs got out of the way, while the king was not above hiding under a mat. The two prime ministers lived in terror of Bunster, who never discussed any moot subject, but struck out with his fists instead.

And to Lord Howe came Mauki, to toil for Bunster for eight long years and a half. There was no escaping from Lord Howe. For better or worse, Bunster and he were tied together. Bunster weighed two hundred pounds. Mauki weighed one hundred and ten. Bunster was a degenerate brute. But Mauki was a primitive savage. While both had wills and ways of their own.

Mauki had no idea of the sort of master he was to work for. He had had no warnings, and he had concluded as a matter of course that Bunster would be like other white men, a drinker of much whiskey, a ruler and a lawgiver who always kept his word and who never struck a boy undeserved. Bunster had the advantage. He knew all about Mauki, and gloated over the coming into possession of him. The last cook was suffering from a broken arm and a dislocated shoulder, so Bunster made Mauki cook and general house-boy.

And Mauki soon learned that there were white men and white men. On the very day the schooner departed he was ordered to buy a chicken from Samisee, the native Tongan missionary. But Samisee had sailed across the lagoon and would not be back for three days. Mauki returned with the information. He climbed the steep stairway (the house stood on piles twelve feet above the sand), and entered the living-room to report. The trader demanded the chicken. Mauki opened his mouth to explain the missionary's absence. But Bunster did not care for explanations. He struck out with his fist. The blow caught Mauki on the mouth and lifted him into the air. Clear through the doorway he flew, across the narrow veranda, breaking the top railing, and down to the ground. His lips were a contused, shapeless mass, and his mouth was full of blood and broken teeth.

"That'll teach you that back talk don't go with me," the trader shouted, purple with rage, peering down at him over the broken railing.

Mauki had never met a white man like this, and he resolved to walk small and never offend. He saw the boat-boys knocked about, and one of them put in irons for three days with nothing to eat for the crime of breaking a rowlock while pulling. Then, too, he heard the gossip of the village and learned why Bunster had taken a third wife—by force, as was well known. The first and second wives lay in the graveyard, under the white coral sand, with slabs of coral rock at head and feet. They had died, it was said, from beatings he had given them. The third wife was certainly ill-used, as Mauki could see for himself.

But there was no way by which to avoid offending the white man, who seemed offended with life. When Mauki kept silent, he was struck and called a sullen brute. When he spoke, he was struck for giving back talk. When he was grave, Bunster accused him of plotting and gave him a thrashing in advance; and when he strove to be cheerful and to smile, he was charged with sneering at his lord and master and given a taste of stick. Bunster was a devil. The village would have done for him, had it not remembered the lesson of the three schooners. It might have done for him anyway, if there had been a bush to which to flee. As it was, the murder of the white men, of any white man, would bring a man-of-war that would kill the offenders and chop down the precious cocoanut-trees. Then there were the boat-boys, with minds fully made up to drown him by accident at the first opportunity to capsize the cutter. Only Bunster saw to it that the boat did not capsize.

Mauki was of a different breed, and, escape being impossible while Bunster lived, he was resolved to get the white man. The trouble was that he could never find a chance. Bunster was always on guard. Day and night his revolvers were ready to hand. He permitted nobody to pass behind his back, as Mauki learned after having been knocked down several times Bunster knew that he had more to fear from the good natured, even sweet-faced, Malaita boy than from the entire population of Lord Howe; and it gave added zest to the programme of torment he was carrying out. And Mauki walked small, accepted his punishments, and waited.

All other white men had respected his *tambos*, but not so Bunster. Mauki's weekly allowance of tobacco was two sticks. Bunster passed them to his woman and ordered

Mauki to receive them from her hand. But this could not be, and Mauki went without his tobacco. In the same way he was made to miss many a meal, and to go hungry many a day. He was ordered to make chowder out of the big clams that grew in the lagoon. This he could not do, for clams were *tambo*. Six times in succession he refused to touch the clams, and six times he was knocked senseless. Bunster knew that the boy would die first, but called his refusal mutiny, and would have killed him had there been another cook to take his place.

One of the trader's favorite tricks was to catch Mauki's kinky locks and bat his head against the wall. Another trick was to catch Mauki unawares and thrust the live end of a cigar against his flesh. This Bunster called vaccination, and Mauki was vaccinated a number of times a week. Once, in a rage, Bunster ripped the cup handle from Mauki's nose, tearing the hole clear out of the cartilage.

"Oh, what a mug!" was his comment, when he surveyed the damage he had wrought.

The skin of a shark is like sandpaper, but the skin of a ray fish is like a rasp. In the South Seas the natives use it as a wood file in smoothing down canoes and paddles. Bunster had a mitten made of ray fish skin. The first time he tried it on Mauki, with one sweep of the hand it fetched the skin off his back from neck to armpit. Bunster was delighted. He gave his wife a taste of the mitten, and tried it out thoroughly on the boat-boys. The prime ministers came in for a stroke each, and they had to grin and take it for a joke.

"Laugh, damn you, laugh!" was the cue he gave.

Mauki came in for the largest share of the mitten. Never a day passed without a caress from it. There were times when the loss of so much cuticle kept him awake at night, and often the half-healed surface was raked raw afresh by the facetious Mr. Bunster. Mauki continued his patient wait, secure in the knowledge that sooner or later his time would come. And he knew just what he was going to do, down to the smallest detail, when the time did come.

One morning Bunster got up in a mood for knocking seven bells out of the universe. He began on Mauki, and wound up on Mauki, in the interval knocking down his wife and hammering all the boat-boys. At breakfast he called the coffee slops and threw the scalding contents of the cup into Mauki's face. By ten o'clock Bunster was shivering with ague, and half an hour later he was burning with fever. It was no ordinary attack. It quickly became pernicious, and developed into black-water fever. The days passed, and he grew weaker and weaker, never leaving his bed. Mauki waited and watched, the while his skin grew intact once more. He ordered the boys to beach the cutter, scrub her bottom, and give her a general overhauling. They thought the order emanated from Bunster, and they obeyed. But Bunster at the time was lying unconscious and giving no orders. This was Mauki's chance, but still he waited.

When the worst was past, and Bunster lay convalescent and conscious, but weak as a baby, Mauki packed his few trinkets, including the china cup handle, into his trade box. Then he went over to the village and interviewed the king and his two prime ministers.

"This fella Bunster, him good fella you like too much?" he asked.

They explained in one voice that they liked the trader not at all. The ministers poured forth a recital of all the indignities and wrongs that had been heaped upon them. The king broke down and wept. Mauki interrupted rudely.

"You savve me—me big fella marster my country. You no like 'm this fella white marster. Me no like 'm. Plenty good you put hundred cocoanut, two hundred cocoanut, three hundred cocoanut along cutter. Him finish, you go sleep 'm good fella. Altogether kanaka sleep 'm good fella. Bime by big fella noise along house, you no savve hear 'm that fella noise. You altogether sleep strong fella too much."

In like manner Mauki interviewed the boat-boys. Then he ordered Bunster's wife to return to her family house.

Had she refused, he would have been in a quandary, for his *tambo* would not have permitted him to lay hands on her.

The house deserted, he entered the sleeping-room, where the trader lay in a doze. Mauki first removed the revolvers, then placed the ray fish mitten on his hand. Bunster's first warning was a stroke of the mitten that removed the skin the full length of his nose.

"Good fella, eh?" Mauki grinned, between two strokes, one of which swept the forehead bare and the other of which cleaned off one side of his face. "Laugh, damn you, laugh."

Mauki did his work thoroughly, and the kanakas, hiding in their houses, heard the "big fella noise" that Bunster made and continued to make for an hour or more.

When Mauki was done, he carried the boat compass and all the rifles and ammunition down to the cutter, which he proceeded to ballast with cases of tobacco. It was while engaged in this that a hideous, skinless thing came out of the house and ran screaming down the beach till it fell in the sand and moved and gibbered under the scorching sun. Mauki looked toward it and hesitated. Then he went over and removed the head, which he wrapped in a mat and stowed in the stern-locker of the cutter.

So soundly did the kanakas sleep through that long hot day that they did not see the cutter run out through the passage and head south, close-hauled on the southeast trade. Nor was the cutter ever sighted on that long tack to the shores of Ysabel, and during the tedious head-beat from there to Malaita. He landed at Port Adams with a wealth of rifles and tobacco such as no one man had ever possessed before. But he did not stop there. He had taken a white man's head, and only the bush could shelter him. So back he went to the bush-villages, where he shot old Fanfoa and half a dozen of the chief men, and made himself the chief over all the villages. When his father died, Mauki's brother ruled in Port Adams, and, joined together, salt-water men and bushmen, the resulting combinations was the strongest of the ten score fighting tribes of Malaita.

More than his fear of the British government was Mauki's fear of the all-powerful Moongleam Soap Company; and one day a message came up to him in th bush, reminding him that he owed the Company eight and one-half years of labor. He sent back a favorable answer, and then appeared the inevitable white man, the captain of the schooner, the only white man during Mauki's reign who ventured the bush and came out alive. This man not only came out, but he brought with him seven hundred and fifty dollars in gold sovereigns—the money price of eight years and a half of labor plus the cost price of certain rifles and cases of tobacco.

Mauki no longer weighs one hundred and ten pounds. His stomach is three times its former girth, and he has four wives. He had many other things—rifles and revolvers, the handle of a china cup, and an excellent collection of bush-men's heads. But more precious than the entire collection is another head, perfectly dried and cured, with sandy hair and a yellowish beard, which is kept wrapped in the finest of fibre lava-lavas. When Mauki goes to war with villages beyond his realm, he invariably gets out this head, and, alone in his grass palace, contemplates it long and solemnly. At such times the hush of death falls on the village, and not even a pickaninny dares makes a noise. The head is esteemed the most powerful devil-devil on Malaita, and to the possession of it is ascribed all of Mauki's greatness.

An Odyssey of the North

I

The sleds were singing their eternal lament to the creaking of the harnesses and the tinkling bells of the leaders; but the men and dogs were tired and made no sound. The trail was heavy with new-fallen snow, and they had come far, and the runners, burdened with flint-like quarters of frozen moose, clung tenaciously to the unpacked surface and held back with a stubbornness almost human. Darkness was coming on, but there was no camp to pitch that night. The snow fell gently through the pulseless air, not in flakes, but in tiny frost crystals of delicate design. It was very warm,—barely ten below zero,—and the men did not mind. Meyers and Bettles had raised their earflaps, while Malemute Kid had even taken off his mittens.

The dogs had been fagged out early in the afternoon, but they now began to show new vigor. Among the more astute there was a certain restlessness,—an impatience at the restraint of the traces, an indecisive quickness of movement, a sniffing of snouts and pricking of ears. These became incensed at their more phlegmatic brothers, urging them on with numerous sly nips on their hinder-quarters. Those, thus chidden, also contracted and helped spread the contagion. At last, the leader of the foremost sled uttered a sharp whine of satisfaction, crouching lower in the snow and throwing himself against the collar. The rest followed suit. There was an ingathering of back-bands, a tightening of traces; the sleds leaped forward, and the men clung to the gee-poles, violently accelerating the uplift of their feet that they might escape going under the runners. The weariness of the day fell from them, and they whooped encouragement to the dogs. The animals responded with joyous yelps. They were swinging through the gathering darkness at a rattling gallop.

'Gee! Gee!" the men cried, each in turn, as their sleds abruptly left the main-trail, heeling over on single runners like luggers on the wind.

Then came a hundred yards' dash to the lighted parchment window, which told its own story of the home-cabin, the roaring Yukon stove, and the steaming pots of tea. But the home cabin had been invaded. Three-score huskies chorused defiance, and as many furry forms precipitated themselves upon the dogs which drew the first sled. The door was flung open, and a man, clad in the scarlet tunic of the Northwest Police, waded knee-deep among the furious brutes, calmly and impartially dispensing soothing justice with the butt end of a dog-whip. After that, the men shook hands; and in this wise was Malemute Kid welcomed to his own cabin by a stranger.

Stanley Prince, who should have welcomed him, and who was responsible for the Yukon stove and hot tea aforementioned, was busy with his guests. There were a dozen or so of them, as nondescript a crowd as ever served the Queen in the enforcement of her laws or the delivery of her mails. They were of many breeds, but their common life had formed of them a certain type,—a lean and wiry type, with trail-hardened muscles, and sun-browned faces,

and untroubled souls which gazed frankly forth, clear-eyed
and steady. They drove the dogs of the Queen, wrought
fear in the hearts of her enemies, ate of her meagre fare,
and were happy. They had seen life, and done deeds, and
lived romances; but they did not know it.

And they were very much at home. Two of them were
sprawled upon Malemute Kid's bunk, singing chansons
which their French forbears sang in the days when first
they entered the Northwest-land and mated with its Indian
women. Bettles' bunk had suffered a similar invasion, and
three or four lusty *voyageurs* worked their toes among its
blankets as they listened to the tale of one who had served
on the boat brigade with Wolseley when he fought his way
to Khartoum. And when he tired, a cowboy told of courts
and kings and lords and ladies he had seen when Buffalo
Bill toured the capitals of Europe. In a corner, two half-
breeds, ancient comrades in a lost campaign, mended harnesses and talked of the days when the Northwest flamed
with insurrection and Louis Reil was king.

Rough jests and rougher jokes went up and down, and
great hazards by trail and river were spoken of in the light
of commonplaces, only to be recalled by virtue of some
grain of humor or ludicrous happening. Prince was led
away by these uncrowned heroes who had seen history
made, who regarded the great and the romantic as but the
ordinary and the incidental in the routine of life. He passed
his precious tobacco among them with lavish disregard,
and rusty chains of reminiscence were loosened, and forgotten odysseys resurrected for his especial benefit.

When conversation dropped and the travelers filled the
last pipes and unlashed their tight-rolled sleeping-furs,
Prince fell back upon his comrade for further information.

"Well, you know what the cowboy is," Malemute Kid
answered, beginning to unlace his moccasins; "and it's not
hard to guess the British blood in his bed-partner. As for
the rest, they're all children of the *coureurs du bois*, min-
gled with God knows how many other bloods. The two
turning in by the door are the regulation 'breeds' or *bois*

brules. That lad with the worsted breech scarf—notice his eyebrows and the turn of his jaw—shows a Scotchman wept in his mother's smoky tepee. And that handsome-looking fellow putting the capote under his head is a French half-breed,—you heard him talking; he doesn't like the two Indians turning in next to him. You see, when the 'breeds' rose under Reil the full-bloods kept the peace, and they've not lost much love for one another since."

"But I say, what's that glum-looking fellow by the stove? I'll swear he can't talk English. He hasn't opened his mouth all night."

"You're wrong. He knows English well enough. Did you follow his eyes when he listened? I did. But he's neither kith nor kin to the others. When they talked their own patois you could see he didn't understand. I've been wondering myself what he is. Let's find out."

"Fire a couple of sticks into the stove!" Malemute Kid commanded, raising his voice and looking squarely at the man in question.

He obeyed at once.

"Had discipline knocked into him somewhere," Prince commented in a low tone.

Malemute Kid nodded, took off his socks, and picked his way among the recumbent men to the stove. There he hung his damp footgear among a score or so of mates.

"When do you expect to get to Dawson?" he asked tentatively.

The man studied him a moment before replying. "They say seventy-five mile. So? Maybe two days."

The very slightest accent was perceptible, while there was no awkward hesitancy or groping for words.

"Been in the country before?"

"No."

"Northwest Territory?"

"Yes."

"Born there?"

"No."

"Well, where the devil were you born? You're none of

these." Malemute Kid swept his hand over the dog-drivers, even including the two policemen who had turned into Prince's bunk. "Where did you come from? I've seen faces like yours before, though I can't remember just where."

"I know you," he irrelevantly replied, at once turning the drift of Malemute Kid's questions.

"Where? Ever see me?"

"No; your partner, him priest, Pastilik, long time ago. Him ask me if I see you, Malemute Kid. Him give me grub. I no stop long. You hear him speak 'bout me?"

"Oh! you're the fellow that traded the otter skins for the dogs?"

The man nodded, knocked out his pipe, and signified his disinclination for conversation by rolling up in his furs. Malemute Kid blew out the slush-lamp and crawled under the blankets with Prince.

"Well, what is he?"

"Don't know—turned me off, somehow, and then shut up like a clam. But he's a fellow to whet your curiosity. I've heard of him. All the Coast wondered about him eight years ago. Sort of mysterious, you know. He came down out of the North, in the dead of winter, many a thousand miles from here, skirting Bering Sea and traveling as though the devil were after him. No one ever learned where he came from, but he must have come far. He was badly travel-worn when he got food from the Swedish missionary on Golovin Bay and asked the way south. We heard of this afterward. Then he abandoned the shore-line, heading right across Norton Sound. Terrible weather, snowstorms and high winds, but he pulled through where a thousand other men would have died, missing St. Michael's and making the land at Pastilik. He'd lost all but two dogs, and was nearly gone with starvation.

"He was so anxious to go on that Father Roubeau fitted him out with grub; but he couldn't let him have any dogs, for he was only waiting my arrival to go on a trip himself. Mr. Ulysses knew too much to start on without animals, and fretted around for several days. He had on his sled a bunch of beautifully cured otter skins, sea-otters, you know, worth their weight in gold. There was also at Pastilik an old Shylock of a Russian trader, who had dogs to kill. Well, they didn't dicker very long, but when the Strange One headed south again, it was in the rear of a spanking dog-team. Mr. Shylock, by the way, had the otter skins. I saw them, and they were magnificent. We figured it up and found the dogs brought him at least five hundred apiece. And it wasn't as if the Strange One didn't know the value of sea-otter; he was an Indian of some sort, and what little he talked showed he'd been among white men.

"After the ice passed out of the Sea, word came up from Nunivak Island that he'd gone in there for grub. Then he dropped from sight, and this is the first heard of him in eight years. Now where did he come from? and what was he doing there? and why did he come from there? He's Indian, he's been nobody knows where, and he's had discipline, which is unusual for an Indian. Another mystery of the North for you to solve, Prince."

"Thanks, awfully; but I've got too many on hand as it is," he replied.

Malemute Kid was already breathing heavily; but the young mining engineer gazed straight up through the thick darkness, waiting for the strange orgasm which stirred his blood to die away. And when he did sleep, his brain worked on, and for the nonce he, too, wandered through the white unknown, struggled with the dogs on endless trails, and saw men live, and toil, and die like men.

The next morning, hours before daylight, the dog-drivers and policemen pulled out for Dawson. But the powers that saw to her Majesty's interests, and ruled the destinies of her lesser creatures, gave the mailmen little rest; for a week later they appeared at Stuart River, heavily burdened with letters for Salt Water. However, their dogs had been replaced by fresh ones; but then, they were dogs.

The men had expected some sort of a lay-over in which

to rest up; besides, this Klondike was a new section of the Northland, and they had wished to see a little something of the Golden City where dust flowed like water, and dance halls rang with never ending revelry. But they dried their socks and smoked their evening pipes with much the same gusto as on their former visit, though one or two bold spirits speculated on desertion and the possibility of crossing the unexplored Rockies to the east, and thence, by the Mackenzie Valley, of gaining their old stamping-grounds in the Chippewyan Country. Two or three even decided to return to their homes by that route when their terms of service had expired, and they began to lay plans forthwith, looking forward to the hazardous undertaking in much the same way a city-bred man would to a day's holiday in the woods.

He of the Otter Skins seemed very restless, though he took little interest in the discussion, and at last he drew Malemute Kid to one side and talked for some time in low tones. Prince cast curious eyes in their direction, and the mystery deepened when they put on caps and mittens, and went outside. When they returned, Malemute Kid placed his gold-scales on the table, weighed out the matter of sixty ounces, and transferred them to the Strange One's sack. Then the chief of the dog-drivers joined the conclave, and certain business was transacted with him. The next day the gang went on up river, but He of the Otter Skins took several pounds of grub and turned his steps back toward Dawson.

"Didn't know what to make of it," said Malemute Kid in response to Prince's queries; "but the poor beggar wanted to be quit of the service for some reason or other—at least it seemed a most important one to him, though he wouldn't let on what. You see, it's just like the army; he signed for two years, and the only way to get free was to buy himself out. He couldn't desert and then stay here, and he was just wild to remain in the country. Made up his mind when he got to Dawson, he said; but no one knew him, hadn't a cent, and I was the only one he'd spoken two words with. So he talked it over with the Lieutenant-Governor, and made arrangements in case he could get the money from me—loan, you know. Said he'd pay back in the year, and if I wanted, would put me onto something rich. Never'd seen it, but knew it was rich.

"And talk! why, when he got me outside he was ready to weep. Begged and pleaded; got down in the snow to me till I hauled him out of it. Palavered around like a crazy man. Swore he's worked to this very end for years and years, and couldn't bear to be disappointed now. Asked him what end, but he wouldn't say. Said they might keep him on the other half of the trail and he wouldn't get to Dawson in two years, and then it would be too late. Never saw a man take on so in my life. And when I said I'd let him have it, had to yank him out of the snow again. Told him to consider it in the light of a grub-stake. Then he'd have it? No, sir! Swore he'd give me all he found, make me rich beyond the dreams of avarice, and all such stuff. Now a man who puts his life and time against a grub-stake ordinarily finds it hard enough to turn over half of what he finds. Something behind all this, Prince; just you make a note of it. We'll hear of him if he stays in the country"—

"And if he doesn't?"

"Then my good nature gets a shock, and I'm sixty some odd ounces out."

The cold weather had come on with the long nights, and the sun had begun to play his ancient game of peekaboo along the southern snow-line ere aught was heard of Malemute Kid's grub-stake. And then, one bleak morning in early January, a heavily laden dog-train pulled into his cabin below Stuart River. He of the Otter Skins was there, and with him walked a man such as the gods had almost forgotten how to fashion. Men never talked of luck and pluck and five-hundred-dollar dirt without bringing in the name of Axel Gunderson; nor could tales of nerve or strength or daring pass up and down the camp-fire without the summoning of his presence. And when the conversation flagged, it blazed anew at mention of the woman who shared his fortunes.

As has been noted, in the making of Axel Gunderson the gods had remembered their old-time cunning, and cast him after the manner of men who were born when the world was young. Full seven feet he towered in his picturesque costume which marked a king of Eldorado. His chest, neck, and limbs were those of a giant. To bear his three hundred pounds of bone and muscle, his snowshoes were greater by a generous yard than those of other men. Rough-hewn, with rugged brow and massive jaw and unflinching eyes of palest blue, his face told the tale of one who knew but the law of might. Of the yellow of ripe corn silk, his frost-incrusted hair swept like day across the night, and fell far down his coat of bear-skin. A vague tradition of the sea seemed to cling about him, as he swung down the narrow trail in advance of the dogs; and he brought the butt of his dog-whip against Malemute Kid's door as a Norse sea rover, on southern foray, might thunder for admittance at the castle gate.

Prince bared his womanly arms and kneaded sour-dough bread, casting, as he did so, many a glance at the three guests,—three guests the like of which might never come under a man's roof in a lifetime. The Strange One, whom Malemute Kid had surnamed Ulysses, still fascinated him; but his interest chiefly gravitated between Axel Gunderson and Axel Gunderson's wife. She felt the day's journey, for she had softened in comfortable cabins during the many days since her husband mastered the wealth of frozen pay-streaks, and she was tired. She rested against his great breast like a slender flower against a wall, replying lazily to Malemute Kid's good-natured banter, and stirring Prince's blood strangely with an occasional sweep of her deep, dark eyes. For Prince was a man, and healthy, and had seen few women in many months. And she was older than he, and an Indian besides. But she was different from all native wives he had met: she had traveled,—had been in his country among others, he gathered from the conversation; and she knew most of the things the women of his own race knew, and much more that it was not in the nature of things for them to know. She could make a meal of sun-dried fish or a bed in the snow; yet she teased them with tantalizing details of many-course dinners, and caused strange internal dissensions to arise at the mention of various quondam dishes which they had well-nigh forgotten. She knew the ways of the moose, the bear, and the little blue fox, and of the wild amphibians of the Northern seas; she was skilled in the lore of the woods and the streams, and the tale writ by man and bird and beast upon the delicate snow crust was to her an open book; yet Prince caught the appreciative twinkle in her eye as she read the Rules of the Camp. These rules had been fathered by the Unquenchable Bettles at a time when his blood ran high, and were remarkable for the terse simplicity of their humor. Prince always turned them to the wall before the arrival of ladies; but who could suspect that this native wife—Well, it was too late now.

This, then, was the wife of Axel Gunderson, a woman whose name and fame had traveled with her husband's, hand in hand, through all the Northland. At table, Malemute Kid baited her with the assurance of an old friend, and Prince shook off the shyness of first acquaintance and joined in. But she held her own in the unequal contest, while her husband, slower in wit, ventured naught but applause. And he was very proud of her; his every look and action revealed the magnitude of the place she occupied in his life. He of the Otter Skins ate in silence, forgotten in the merry battle; and long ere the others were done he pushed back from the table and went out among the dogs. Yet all too soon his fellow traders drew on their mittens and *parkas*, and followed him.

There had been no snow for many days, and the sleds slipped along the hard-packed Yukon trail as easily as if it had been glare ice. Ulysses led the first sled; with the sec-

ond came Prince and Axel Gunderson's wife; while Malemute Kid and the yellow-haired giant brought up the third.

"It's only a 'hunch,' Kid," he said; "but I think it's
straight. He's never been there, but he tells a good story,
and shows a map I heard of when I was in the Kootenay
country, years ago. I'd like to have you go along; but he's
a strange one, and swore point-blank to throw it up if any
one was brought in. But when I come back you'll get first
tip, and I'll stake you next to me, and give you a half
share in the town site besides.

"No! no!" he cried, as the other strove to interrupt. "I'm
running this, and before I'm done it'll need two heads. If
it's all right, why it'll be a second Cripple Creek, man; do
you hear?—a second Cripple Creek! It's quartz, you know,
not placer; and if we work it right we'll corral the whole
thing,—millions upon millions. I've heard of the place before, and so have you. We'll build a town—thousands of
workmen—good waterways—steamship lines—big carrying trade—light-draught steamers for head-reaches—
survey a railroad, perhaps—sawmills—electric-light
plant—do our own banking—commercial company—
syndicate—Say! just you hold your hush till I get back!"

The sleds came to a halt where the trail crossed the
mouth of Stuart River. An unbroken sea of frost, its wide
expanse stretched away into the unknown east. The snowshoes were withdrawn from the lashings of the sleds. Axel
Gunderson shook hands and stepped to the fore, his great
webbed shoes sinking a fair half yard into the feathery surface and packing the snow so the dogs should not wallow.
His wife fell in behind the last sled, betraying long practice in the art of handling the awkward footgear. The stillness was broken with cheery farewells; the dogs whined;
and He of the Otter Skins talked with his whip to a recal-
citrant wheeler.

An hour later, the train had taken on the likeness of a
black pencil crawling in a long, straight line across a
mighty sheet of foolscap.

II

One night, many weeks later, Malemute Kid and Prince fell to solving chess problems from the torn page of an ancient magazine. The Kid had just returned from his Bonanza properties, and was resting up preparatory to a long moose hunt. Prince too had been on creek and trail nearly all winter, and had grown hungry for a blissful week of cabin life.

"Interpose the black knight, and force the king. No, that won't do. See, the next move"—

"Why advance the pawn two squares? Bound to take it in transit, and with the bishop out of the way"—

"But hold on! That leaves a hole, and"—

"No; it's protected. Go ahead! You'll see it works."

It was very interesting. Somebody knocked at the door a second time before Malemute Kid said, "Come in." The door swung open. Something staggered in. Prince caught one square look, and sprang to his feet. The horror in his eyes caused Malemute Kid to whirl about; and he too was startled, though he had seen bad things before. The thing tottered blindly toward them. Prince edged away till he reached the nail from which hung his Smith & Wesson.

"My God! what is it?" he whispered to Malemute Kid.

"Don't know. Looks like a case of freezing and no grub," replied the Kid, sliding away in the opposite direction. "Watch out! It may be mad," he warned, coming back from closing the door.

The thing advanced to the table. The bright flame of the slush-lamp caught its eye. It was amused, and gave voice to eldritch cackles which betokened mirth. Then, suddenly, he—for it was a man—swayed back, with a hitch to his skin trousers, and began to sing a chanty, such as men lift when they swing around the capstan circle and the sea snorts in their ears:—

"Yan-kee ship come down de ri-ib-er,
    Pull! my bully boys! Pull!

D'yeh want—to know de captain ru-uns her?
 Pull! my bully boys! Pull!
Jon-a-than Jones ob South Caho-li-in-a,
 Pull! my bully"—

He broke off abruptly, tottered with a wolfish snarl to the meat-shelf, and before they could intercept was tearing with his teeth at a chunk of raw bacon. The struggle was fierce between him and Malemute Kid; but his mad strength left him as suddenly as it had come, and he weakly surrendered the spoil. Between them they got him upon a stool, where he sprawled with half his body across the table. A small dose of whiskey strengthened him, so that he could dip a spoon into the sugar caddy which Malemute Kid placed before him. After his appetite had been somewhat cloyed, Prince, shuddering as he did so, passed him a mug of weak beef tea.

The creature's eyes were alight with a sombre frenzy, which blazed and waned with every mouthful. There was very little skin to the face. The face, for that matter, sunken and emaciated, bore very little likeness to human countenance. Frost after frost had bitten deeply, each depositing its stratum of scab upon the half-healed scar that went before. This dry, hard surface was of a bloody-black color, serrated by grievous cracks wherein the raw red flesh peeped forth. His skin garments were dirty and in tatters, and the fur of one side was singed and burned away, showing where he had lain upon his fire.

Malemute Kid pointed to where the sun-tanned hide had been cut away, strip by strip,—the grim signature of famine.

"Who—are—you?" slowly and distinctly enunciated the Kid.

The man paid no heed.

"Where do you come from?"

"Yan-kee ship come down de ri-ib-er," was the quavering response.

"Don't doubt the beggar came down the river," the Kid

said, shaking him in an endeavor to start a more lucid flow of talk.

But the man shrieked at the contact, clapping a hand to his side in evident pain. He rose slowly to his feet, half leaning on the table.

"She laughed at me—so—with the hate in her eye; and she—would—not—come."

His voice died away, and he was sinking back when Malemute Kid gripped him by the wrist, and shouted, "Who? Who would not come?"

"She, Unga. She laughed, and struck at me, so, and so. And then"—

"Yes?"

"And then"—

"And then what?"

"And then he lay very still, in the snow, a long time. He is—still in—the—snow."

The two men looked at each other helplessly.

"Who is in the snow?"

"She, Unga. She looked at me with the hate in her eye, and then"—

"Yes, yes."

"And then she took the knife, so; and once, twice—she was weak. I traveled very slow. And there is much gold in that place, very much gold."

"Where is Unga?" For all Malemute Kid knew, she might be dying a mile away. He shook the man savagely, repeating again and again, "Where is Unga? Who is Unga?"

"She—is—in—the—snow."

"Go on!" The Kid was pressing his wrist cruelly.

"So—I—would—be—in—the snow—but—I—had—a—debt—to—pay. It—was—heavy—I—had—a—debt—to—pay—a—debt—to—pay—I—had"—The faltering monosyllables ceased, as he fumbled in his pouch and drew forth a buckskin sack. "A—debt—to—pay—five—pounds—of—gold—grub—stake—Mal—e—mute—Kid—

I"—The exhausted head dropped upon the table; nor could Malemute Kid rouse it again.

"It's Ulysses," he said quietly, tossing the bag of dust on the table. "Guess it's all day with Axel Gunderson and the woman. Come on, let's get him between the blankets. He's Indian; he'll pull through, and tell a tale besides."

As they cut his garments from him, near his right breast could be seen two unhealed, hard-lipped knife thrusts.

III

"I will talk of the things which were, in my own way; but you will understand. I will begin at the beginning, and tell of myself and the woman, and, after that, of the man."

He of the Otter Skins drew over to the stove as do men who have been deprived of fire and are afraid the Promethean gift may vanish at any moment. Malemute Kid pricked up the slush-lamp, and placed it so its light might fall upon the face of the narrator. Prince slid his body over the edge of the bunk and joined them.

"I am Naass, a chief, and the son of a chief, born between a sunset and a rising, on the dark seas, in my father's oomiak. All of a night the men toiled at the paddles, and the women cast out the waves which threw in upon us, and we fought with the storm. The salt spray froze upon my mother's breast till her breath passed with the passing of the tide. But I,—I raised my voice with the wind and the storm, and lived.

"We dwelt in Akatan"—

"Where?" asked Malemute Kid.

"Akatan, which is in the Aleutians; Akatan, beyond Chignik, beyond Kardalak, beyond Unimak. As I say, we dwelt in Akatan, which lies in the midst of the sea on the edge of the world. We farmed the salt seas for the fish, the seal, and the otter; and our homes shouldered about one another on the rocky strip between the rim of the forest and the yellow beach where our kayaks lay. We were not many, and the world was very small. There were strange lands to the east,—islands like Akatan; so we thought all the world was islands, and did not mind.

"I was different from my people. In the sands of the beach were the crooked timbers and wave-warped planks of a boat such as my people never built; and I remember on the point of the island which overlooked the ocean three ways there stood a pine tree which never grew there, smooth and straight and tall. It is said the two men came to that spot, turn about, through many days, and watched with the passing of the light. These two men came from out of the sea in the boat which lay in pieces on the beach. And they were white like you, and weak as the little children when the seal have gone away and the hunters come home empty. I know of these things from the old men and the old women, who got them from their fathers and mothers before them. These strange white men did not take kindly to our ways at first, but they grew strong, what of the fish and the oil, and fierce. And they built them each his own house, and took the pick of our women, and in time children came. Thus he was born who was to become the father of my father's father.

"As I said, I was different from my people, for I carried the strong, strange blood of this white man who came out of the sea. It is said we had other laws in the days before these men; but they were fierce and quarrelsome, and fought with our men till there were no more left who dared to fight. Then they made themselves chiefs, and took away our old laws and gave us new ones, insomuch that the man was the son of his father, and not his mother, as our way had been. They also ruled that the son, firstborn, should have all things which were his father's before him, and that the brothers and sisters should shift for themselves. And they gave us other laws. They showed us new ways in the catching of fish and the killing of bear which were thick in the woods; and they taught us to lay by bigger stores for the time of famine. And these things were good.

"But when they had become chiefs, and there were no more men to face their anger, they fought, these strange white men, each with the other. And the one whose blood I carry drove his seal spear the length of an arm through the other's body. Their children took up the fight, and their children's children; and there was great hatred between them, and black doings, even to my time, so that in each family but one lived to pass down the blood of them that went before. Of my blood I was alone; of the other man's there was but a girl, Unga, who lived with her mother. Her father and my father did not come back from the fishing one night; but afterward they washed up to the beach on the big tides, and they held very close to each other.

"The people wondered, because of the hatred between the houses, and the old men shook their heads and said the fight would go on when children were born to her and children to me. They told me this as a boy, till I came to believe, and to look upon Unga as a foe, who was to be the mother of children which were to fight with mine. I thought of these things day by day, and when I grew to a stripling I came to ask why this should be so. And they answered, 'We do not know, but that in such way your fathers did.' And I marveled that those which were to come should fight the battles of those that were gone, and in it I could see no right. But the people said it must be, and I was only a stripling.

"And they said I must hurry, that my blood might be the older and grow strong before hers. This was easy, for I was head man, and the people looked up to me because of the deeds and the laws of my fathers, and the wealth which was mine. Any maiden would come to me, but I found none to my liking. And the old men and the mothers of maidens told me to hurry, for even then were the hunters bidding high to the mother of Unga; and should her children grow strong before mine, mine would surely die.

"Nor did I find a maiden till one night coming back from the fishing. The sunlight was lying, so, low and full in the eyes, the wind free, and the kayaks racing with the white seas. Of a sudden the kayak of Unga came driving past me, and she looked upon me, so, with her black hair flying like a cloud of night and the spray wet on her cheek. As I say, the sunlight was full in the eyes, and I was a stripling; but somehow it was all clear, and I knew it to be the call of kind to kind. As she whipped ahead she looked back within the space of two strokes,—looked as only the woman Unga could look,—and again I knew it as the call of kind. The people shouted as we ripped past the lazy oomiaks and left them far behind. But she was quick at the paddle, and my heart was like the belly of a sail, and I did not gain. The wind freshened, the sea whitened, and, leaping like the seals on the windward breech, we roared down the golden pathway of the sun."

Naass was crouched half out of his stool, in the attitude of one driving a paddle, as he ran the race anew. Somewhere across the stove he beheld the tossing kayak and the flying hair of Unga. The voice of the wind was in his ears, and its salt beat fresh upon his nostrils.

"But she made the shore, and ran up the sand, laughing, to the house of her mother. And a great thought came to me that night,—a thought worthy of him that was chief over all the people of Akatan. So, when the moon was up, I went down to the house of her mother, and looked upon the goods of Yash-Noosh, which were piled by the door,— the goods of Yash-Noosh, a strong hunter who had it in mind to be the father of the children of Unga. Other young men had piled their goods there, and taken them away again; and each young man had made a pile greater than the one before.

"And I laughed to the moon and the stars, and went to my own house where my wealth was stored. And many trips I made, till my pile was greater by the fingers of one hand than the pile of Yash-Noosh. There were fish, dried in the sun and smoked; and forty hides of the hair seal, and half as many of the fur, and each hide was tied at the mouth and big-bellied with oil; and ten skins of bear which I killed in the woods when they came out in the spring. And there were beads and blankets and scarlet cloths, such as I got in trade from the people who lived to the east, and who got them in trade from the people who lived still beyond in the east. And I looked upon the pile of Yash-Noosh and laughed; for I was head man in Akatan, and my wealth was greater than the wealth of all my young men, and my fathers had done deeds, and given laws, and put their names for all time in the mouths of the people.

"So, when the morning came, I went down to the beach, casting out of the corner of my eye at the house of the mother of Unga. My offer yet stood untouched. And the women smiled, and said sly things one to the other. I wondered, for never had such a price been offered; and that night I added more to the pile, and put beside it a kayak of well-tanned skins which never yet had swam in the sea. But in the day it was yet there, open to the laughter of all men. The mother of Unga was crafty, and I grew angry at the shame in which I stood before my people. So that night I added till it became a great pile, and I hauled up my oomiak, which was of the value of twenty kayaks. And in the morning there was no pile.

"Then made I preparation for the wedding, and the people that lived even to the east came for the food of the feast and the *potlach* token. Unga was older than I by the age of four suns in the way we reckoned the years. I was only a stripling; but then I was a chief, and the son of a chief, and it did not matter.

"But a ship shoved her sails above the floor of the ocean, and grew larger with the breath of the wind. From her scuppers she ran clear water, and the men were in haste and worked hard at the pumps. On the bow stood a mighty man, watching the depth of the water and giving commands with a voice of thunder. His eyes were of the pale blue of the deep waters, and his head was maned like that of a sea lion. And his hair was yellow, like the straw of a southern harvest or the manila rope-yarns which sailormen plait.

"Of late years we had seen ships from afar, but this was the first to come to the beach of Akatan. The feast was broken, and the women and children fled to the houses, while we men strung our bows and waited with spears in hand. But when the ship's forefoot smelt the beach the strange men took no notice of us, being busy with their own work. With the falling of the tide they careened the schooner and patched a great hole in her bottom. So the women crept back, and the feast went on.

"When the tide rose, the sea wanderers kedged the schooner to deep water, and then came among us. They bore presents and were friendly; so I made room for them, and out of the largeness of my heart gave them tokens such as I gave all the guests; for it was my wedding day, and I was head man in Akatan. And he with the mane of the sea lion was there, so tall and strong that one looked to see the earth shake with the fall of his feet. He looked much and straight at Unga, with his arms folded, so, and stayed till the sun went away and the stars came out. Then he went down to his ship. After that I took Unga by the hand and led her to my own house. And there was singing and great laughter, and the women said sly things, after the manner of women at such times. But we did not care. Then the people left us alone and went home.

"The last noise had not died away, when the chief of the sea wanderers came in by the door. And he had with him black bottles, from which we drank and made merry. You see, I was only a stripling, and had lived all my days on the edge of the world. So my blood became as fire, and my heart as light as the froth that flies from the surf to the cliff. Unga sat silent among the skins in the corner, her eyes wide, for she seemed to fear. And he with the mane of the sea lion looked upon her straight and long. Then his men came in with bundles of goods, and he piled before me wealth such as was not in all Akatan. There were guns, both large and small, and powder and shot and shell, and bright axes and knives of steel, and cunning tools, and strange things the like of which I had never seen. When he showed me by sign that it was all mine, I thought him a great man to be so free; but, he showed me also that Unga was to go away with him in his ship. Do you understand?—that Unga was to go away with him in his ship. The blood of my fathers flamed hot on the sudden, and I made to drive him through with my spear. But the spirit of the bottles had stolen the life from my arm, and he took me by the neck, so, and knocked my head against the wall of the house. And I was made weak like a newborn child, and my legs would no more stand under me. Unga screamed, and she laid hold of the things of the house with her hands, till they fell all about us as he dragged her to the door. then he took her in his great arms, and when she tore at his yellow hair laughed with a sound like that of the big bull seal in the rut.

"I crawled to the beach and called upon my people; but they were afraid. Only Yash-Noosh was a man, and they struck him on the head with an oar, till he lay with his face in the sand and did not move. And they raised the sails to the sound of their songs, and the ship went away on the wind.

"The people said it was good, for there would be no more war of the bloods in Akatan; but I said never a word, waiting till the time of the full moon, when I put fish and oil in my kayak, and went away to the east. I saw many islands and many people, and I, who had lived on the edge, saw that the world was very large. I talked by signs; but they had not seen a schooner nor a man with the mane of a sea lion, and they pointed always to the east. And I slept in queer places, and ate odd things, and met strange faces. Many laughed, for they thought me light of head; but sometimes old men turned my face to the light and blessed me, and the eyes of the young women grew soft as they asked me of the strange ship, and Unga, and the men of the sea.

"And in this manner, through rough seas and great storms, I came to Unalaska. There were two schooners there, but neither was the one I sought. So I passed on to the east, with the world growing ever larger, and in the Island of Unamok there was no word of the ship, nor in Kadiak, nor in Atognak. And so I came one day to a rocky land, where men dug great holes in the mountain. And there was a schooner, but not my schooner, and men loaded upon it the rocks which they dug. This I thought childish, for all the world was made of rocks; but they gave me food and set me to work. When the schooner was deep in the water, the captain gave me money and told me to go; but I asked which way he went, and he pointed south. I made signs that I would go with him; and he laughed at first, but then, being short of men, took me to help work the ship. So I came to talk after their manner, and to heave on ropes, and to reef the stiff sails in sudden squalls, and to take my turn at the wheel. But it was not strange, for the blood of my fathers was the blood of the men of the sea.

"I had thought it an easy task to find him I sought, once I got among his own people; and when we raised the land one day, and passed between a gateway of the sea to a port, I looked for perhaps as many schooners as there were fingers to my hands. But the ships lay against the wharves for miles, packed like so many little fish; and when I went among them to ask for a man with the mane of a sea lion, they laughed, and answered me in the tongues of many peoples. And I found that they hailed from the uttermost parts of the earth.

"And I went into the city to look upon the face of every man. But they were like the cod when they run thick on the banks, and I could not count them. And the noise smote upon me till I could not hear, and my head was dizzy with much movement. So I went on and on, through the lands which sang in the warm sunshine; where the harvests lay rich on the plains; and where great cities were fat with men that lived like women, with false words in their mouths and their hearts black with the lust of gold. And all the while my people of Akatan hunted and fished, and were happy in the thought that the world was small.

"But the look in the eyes of Unga coming home from the fishing was with me always, and I knew I would find her when the time was met. She walked down quiet lanes in the dusk of the evening, or led me chases across the thick fields wet with the morning dew, and there was a promise in her eyes such as only the woman Unga could give.

"So I wandered through a thousand cities. Some were gentle and gave me food, and others laughed, and still others cursed; but I kept my tongue between my teeth, and went strange ways and saw strange sights. Sometimes, I, who was a chief and the son of a chief, toiled for men,— men rough of speech and hard as iron, who wrung gold from the sweat and sorrow of their fellow men. Yet no word did I get of my quest, till I came back to the sea like a homing seal to the rookeries. But this was at another part, in another country which lay to the north. And there I heard dim tales of the yellow-haired sea wanderer, and I learned that he was a hunter of seals, and that even then he was abroad on the ocean.

"So I shipped on a seal schooner with the lazy Siwashes, and followed his trackless trail to the north where the hunt was then warm. And we were away weary months, and spoke many of the fleet, and heard much of the wild doings of him I sought; but never once did we raise him above the sea. We went north, even to the Pribyloffs, and killed the seals in herds on the beach, and brought their warm bodies aboard till our scuppers ran grease and blood and no man could stand upon the deck. Then we were chased by a ship of slow steam, which fired upon us with great guns. But we put on sail till the sea was over our decks and washed them clean, and lost ourselves in a fog.

"It is said, at this time, while we fled with fear at our hearts, that the yellow-haired sea wanderer put into the Pribyloffs, right to the factory, and while the part of his men held the servants of the company, the rest loaded ten thousand green skins from the salt-houses. I say it is said, but I believe; for in the voyages I made on the coast with never a meeting, the northern seas rang with his wildness and daring, till the three nations which have lands there sought him with their ships. And I heard of Unga, for the captains sang loud in her praise, and she was always with him. She had learned the ways of his people, they said, and was happy. But I knew better,—knew that her heart harked back to her own people by the yellow beach of Akatan.

"So, after a long time, I went back to the port which is by a gateway of the sea, and there I learned that he had gone across the girth of the great ocean to hunt for the seal to the east of the warm land which runs south from the Russian Seas. And I, who was become a sailorman, shipped with men of his own race, and went after him in the hunt of the seal. And there were few ships off that new land; but we hung on the flank of the seal pack and harried it north through all the spring of the year. And when the cows were heavy with pup and crossed the Russian line, our men grumbled and were afraid. For there was much fog, and every day men were lost in the boats. They would not work, so the captain turned the ship back toward the way it came. But I knew the yellow-haired sea wanderer was unafraid, and would hang by the pack, even to the Russian Isles, where few men go. So I took a boat, in the black of night, when the lookout dozed on the fok'slehead, and went alone to the warm, long land. And I journeyed south to meet the men by Yeddo Bay, who are wild and unafraid. And the Yoshiwara girls were small, and bright like steel, and good to look upon; but I could not stop, for I knew that Unga rolled on the tossing floor by the rookeries of the north.

"The men by Yeddo Bay had met from the ends of the earth, and had neither gods nor homes, sailing under the flags of the Japanese. And with them I went to the rich beaches of Copper Island, where our salt-piles became high with skins. And in that silent sea we saw no man till we were ready to come away. Then, one day, the fog lifted on the edge of a heavy wind, and there jammed down upon us a schooner, with close in her wake the cloudy funnels of a Russian man-of-war. We fled away on the beam of the wind, with the schooner jamming still closer and plunging ahead three feet to our two. And upon her poop was the man with the mane of the sea lion, pressing the rails under with the canvas and laughing in his strength of life. And Unga was there,—I knew her on the moment,—but he sent her below when the cannons began to talk across the sea. As I say, with three feet to our two, till we saw the rudder lift green at every jump,—and I swinging on to the wheel and cursing, with my back to the Russian shot. For we knew he had it in mind to run before us, that he might get away while we were caught. And they knocked our masts out of us till we dragged into the wind like a wounded gull; but he went on over the edge of the sky-line,—he and Unga.

"What could we? The fresh hides spoke for themselves. So they took us to a Russian port, and after that to a lone country, where they set us to work in the mines to dig salt. And some died, and—and some did not die."

Naass swept the blanket from his shoulders, disclosing the gnarled and twisted flesh, marked with the unmistakable striations of the knout. Prince hastily covered him, for it was not nice to look upon.

"We were there a weary time; and sometimes men got away to the south, but they always came back. So, when we who hailed from Yeddo Bay rose in the night and took the guns from the guards, we went to the north. And the land was very large, with plains, soggy with water, and great forests. And the cold came, with much snow on the ground, and no man knew the way. Weary months we journeyed through the endless forest,—I do not remember now, for there was little food and often we lay down to die. But at last we came to the cold sea, and but three were left to look upon it. One had shipped from Yeddo as captain, and he knew in his head the lay of the great lands, and of the place where men may cross from one to the other on the ice. And he led us,—I do not know, it was so long—till there were but two. When we came to that place we found five of the strange people which live in that country, and they had dogs and skins, and we were very poor. We fought in the snow till they died, and the captain died, and the dogs and skins were mine. Then I crossed on the ice, which was broken, and once I drifted till a gale from the west put me upon the shore. And after that, Golovin Bay, Pastilik, and the priest. Then south, south, to the warm sunlands where first I wandered.

"But the sea was no longer fruitful, and those who went upon it after the seal went to little profit and great risk. The fleets scattered, and the captains and the men had no word of those I sought. So I turned away from the ocean which never rests, and went among the lands, where the trees, the houses, and the mountains sit always in one place and do not move. I journeyed far, and came to learn many things, even to the way of reading and writing from books. It was well I should do this, for it came upon me that Unga must know these things, and that some day, when the time was met—we—you understand, when the time was met.

"So I drifted, like those little fish which raise a sail to the wind, but cannot steer. But my eyes and my ears were open always, and I went among men who traveled much, for I knew they had but to see those I sought, to remember. At last there came a man, fresh from the mountains, with pieces of rock in which the free gold stood to the size of peas, and he had heard, he had met, he knew them. They were rich, he said, and lived in the place where they drew the gold from the ground.

"It was in a wild country, and very far away; but in time I came to the camp, hidden between the mountains, where men worked night and day, out of the sight of the sun. Yet the time was not come. I listened to the talk of the people. He had gone away,—they had gone away,—to England, it was said, in the matter of bringing men with much money together to form companies. I saw the house they had lived in; more like a palace, such as one sees in the old countries. In the nighttime I crept in through a window that I might see in what manner he treated her. I went from room to room, and in such way thought kings and queens must live, it was all so very good. And they all said he treated her like a queen, and many marveled as to what breed of woman she was; for there was other blood in her veins, and she was different from the women of Akatan, and no one knew her for what she was. Ay, she was a queen; but I was a chief, and the son of a chief, and I had paid for her an untold price of skin and boat and bead.

"But why so many words? I was a sailorman, and knew the way of the ships of the seas. I followed to England, and then to other countries. Sometimes I heard of them by word of mouth, sometimes I read of them in the papers; yet never once could I come by them, for they had much money, and traveled fast, while I was a poor man. Then came trouble upon them and their wealth slipped away, one day, like a curl of smoke. The paper were full of it at the time; but after that nothing was said, and I knew they had gone back where more gold could be got from the ground.

"They had dropped out of the world, being now poor; and so I wandered from camp to camp, even north to the Koo tenay Country, where I picked up the cold scent. They had come and gone, some said this way, and some that, and still others that they had gone to the Country of the Yukon. And I went this way, and I went that, ever journeying from place to place, till it seemed I must grow weary of the world which was so large. But in the Kootenay I traveled a bad trail, and a long trail, with a 'breed' of the Northwest, who saw fit to die when the famine pinched. He had been to the Yukon by an unknown way over the mountains, and when he knew his time was near gave me the map and the secret of a place where he swore by his gods there was much gold.

"After that all the world began to flock into the north. I was a poor man; I sold myself to be a driver of dogs.

The rest you know. I met him and her in Dawson. She did not know me, for I was only a stripling, and her life had been large, so she had no time to remember the one who had paid for her an untold price.

"So? You bought me from my term of service. I went back to bring things about in my own way; for I had waited long, and now that I had my hand upon him was in no hurry. As I say, I had it in mind to do my own way; for I read back in my life, through all I had seen and suffered, and remembered the cold and hunger of the endless forest by the Russian Seas. As you know, I led him into the east,—him and Unga,—into the east where many have gone and few returned. I led them to the spot where the bones and the curses of men lie with the gold which they may not have.

"The way was long and the trail unpacked. Our dogs were many and ate much; nor could our sleds carry till the break of spring. We must come back before the river ran free. So here and there we cached grub, that our sleds might be lightened and there be no chance of famine on the back trip. At the McQuestion there were three men, and near them we built a cache, as also did we at the Mayo, where was a hunting-camp of a dozen Pellys which had crossed the divide from the south. After that, as we went on into the east, we saw no men; only the sleeping river, the moveless forest, and the White Silence of the North. As I say, the way was long and the trail unpacked. Sometimes, in a day's toil, we made no more than eight miles, or ten, and at night we slept like dead men. And never once did they dream that I was Naass, head man of Akatan, the righter of wrongs.

"We now made smaller caches, and in the nighttime it was a small matter to go back on the trail we had broken, and change them in such way that one might deem the wolverines the thieves. Again, there be places where there is a fall to the river, and the water is unruly, and the ice makes above and is eaten away beneath. In such a spot the sled I drove broke through, and the dogs; and to him and

Unga it was ill luck, but no more. And there was much grub on that sled, and the dogs the strongest. But he laughed, for he was strong of life, and gave the dogs that were left little grub till we cut them from the harnesses, one by one, and fed them to their mates. We would go home light, he said, traveling and eating from cache to cache, with neither dogs nor sleds; which was true, for our grub was very short, and the last dog died in the traces the night we came to the gold and the bones and the curses of men.

"To reach that place,—and the map spoke true,—in the heart of the great mountains, we cut ice steps against the wall of a divide. One looked for a valley beyond, but there was no valley; the snow spread away, level as the great harvest plains, and here and there about us mighty mountains shoved their white heads among the stars. And midway on that strange plain which should have been a valley, the earth and the snow fell away, straight down towards the heart of the world. Had we not been sailormen our heads would have swung round with the sight; but we stood on the dizzy edge that we might see a way to get down. And on one side, and one side only, the wall had fallen away till it was like the slope of the decks in a topsail breeze. I do not know why this thing should be so, but it was so. 'It is the mouth of hell,' he said; 'let us go down.' And we went down.

"And on the bottom there was a cabin, built by some man, of logs which he had cast down from above. It was a very old cabin; for men had died there alone at different times, and on pieces of birch bark which were there we read their last words and their curses. One had died of scurvy; another's partner had robbed him of his last grub and powder and stolen away; a third had been mauled by a bald-face grizzly; a fourth had hunted for game and starved,—and so it went, and they had been loath to leave the gold, and had died by the side of it in one way or another. And the worthless gold they had gathered yellowed the floor of the cabin like in a dream.

"But his soul was steady, and his head clear, this man I had led thus far. 'We have nothing to eat,' he said, 'and we will only look upon this gold, and see whence it comes and how much there be. Then we will go away quick, before it gets into our eyes and steals away our judgment. And in this way we may return in the end, with more grub, and possess it all.' So we looked upon the great vein, which cut the wall of the pit as a true vein should; and we measured it, and traced it from above and below, and drove the stakes of the claims and blazed the trees in token of our rights. Then, our knees shaking with lack of food, and a sickness in our bellies, and our hearts chugging close to our mouths, we climbed the mighty wall for the last time and turned our faces to the back trip.

"The last stretch we dragged Unga between us, and we fell often, but in the end we made the cache. And lo, there was no grub. It was well done, for he thought it the wolverines, and damned them and his gods in the one breath. But Unga was brave, and smiled and put her hand in his, till I turned away that I might hold myself. 'We will rest by the fire,' she said, 'till morning, and we will gather strength from our moccasins.' So we cut the tops of our moccasins in strips, and boiled them half of the night, that we might chew them and swallow them. And in the morning we talked of our chance. The next cache was five days' journey; we could not make it. We must find game.

" 'We will go forth and hunt,' he said.

" 'Yes,' said I, 'we will go forth and hunt.'

"And he ruled that Unga stay by the fire and save her strength. As we went forth, he in quest of the moose, and I to the cache I had changed. But I ate little, so they might not see in me much strength. And in the night he fell many times as he drew into camp. And I too made to suffer great weakness, stumbling over my snowshoes as though each step might be my last. And we gathered strength from our moccasins.

"He was a great man. His soul lifted his body to the last; nor did he cry aloud, save for the sake of Unga. On the second day I followed him, that I might not miss the end. And he lay down to rest often. That night he was near gone; but in the morning he swore weakly and went forth again. He was like a drunken man, and I looked many times for him to give up; but his was the strength of the strong, and his soul the soul of a giant, for he lifted his body through all the weary day. And he shot two ptarmigan, but would not eat them. He needed no fire; they meant life; but his thought was for Unga, and he turned toward camp. He no longer walked, but crawled on hand and knee through the snow. I came to him, and read death in his eyes. Even then it was not too late to eat of the ptarmigan. He cast away his rifle, and carried the birds in his mouth like a dog. I walked by his side, upright. And he looked at me during the moments he rested, and wondered that I was so strong. I could see it, though he no longer spoke; and when his lips moved, they moved without sound. As I say, he was a great man, and my heart spoke for softness; but I read back in my life, and remembered the cold and hunger of the endless forest by the Russian Seas. Besides, Unga was mine, and I had paid for her an untold price of skin and boat and bead.

"And in this manner we came through the white forest, with the silence heavy upon us like a damp sea mist. And the ghosts of the past were in the air and all about us; and I saw the yellow beach of Akatan, and the kayaks racing home from the fishing, and the houses on the rim of the forest. And the men who had made themselves chiefs were there, the lawgivers whose blood I bore, and whose blood I had wedded in Unga. Ay, and Yash-Noosh walked with me, the wet sand in his hair, and his war spear, broken as he fell upon it, still in his hand. And I knew the time was met, and saw in the eyes of Unga the promise.

"As I say, we came thus through the forest, till the smell of the camp smoke was in our nostrils. And I bent above him, and tore the ptarmigan from his teeth. He turned on his side and rested, the wonder mounting in his eyes, and the hand which was under slipping slow toward the knife at his hip. But I took it from him, smiling close in his face. Even then he did not understand. So I made to drink from black bottles, and to build high upon the snow a pile of goods, and to live again the things which happened on the night of my marriage. I spoke no word, but he understood. Yet he was unafraid. There was a sneer to his lips, and cold anger, and he gathered new strength with the knowledge. It was not far, but the snow was deep, and he dragged himself very slow. Once, he lay so long, I turned him over and gazed into his eyes. And sometimes he looked forth, and sometimes death. And when I loosed him he struggled on again. In this way we came to the fire. Unga was at his side on the instant. His lips moved, without sound; then he pointed at me, that Unga might understand. And after that he lay in the snow, very still, for a long while. Even now is he there in the snow.

"I said no word till I had cooked the ptarmigan. Then I spoke to her, in her own tongue, which she had not heard in many years. She straightened herself, so, and her eyes were wonder-wide, and she asked who I was, and where I had learned that speech.

"'I am Naass,' I said.

"'You?' she said. 'You?' And she crept close that she might look upon me.

"'Yes,' I answered; 'I am Naass, head man of Akatan, the last of the blood, as you are the last of the blood.'

"And she laughed. By all the things I have seen and the deeds I have done, may I never hear such a laugh again. It put the chill to my soul, sitting there in the White Silence, alone with death and this woman who laughed.

"'Come!' I said, for I thought she wandered. 'Eat of the food and let us be gone. It is a far fetch from here to Akatan.'

"But she shoved her face in his yellow mane, and laughed till it seemed the heavens must fall about our ears. I had thought she would be overjoyed at the sight of me, and eager to go back to the memory of old times; but this seemed a strange form to take.

" 'Come!' I cried, taking her strong by the hand. 'The way is long and dark. Let us hurry!'

" 'Where?' she asked, sitting up, and ceasing from her strange mirth.

" 'To Akatan,' I answered, intent on the light to grow on her face at the thought. But it became like his, with a sneer to the lips, and cold anger.

" 'Yes,' she said; 'we will go, hand in hand, to Akatan, you and I. And we will live in the dirty huts, and eat of the fish and oil, and bring forth a spawn,—a spawn to be proud of all the days of our life. We will forget the world and be happy, very happy. It is good, most good. Come! Let us hurry. Let us go back to Akatan.'

"And she ran her hand through his yellow hair, and smiled in a way which was not good. And there was no promise in her eyes.

"I sat silent, and marveled at the strangeness of woman. I went back to the night when he dragged her from me, and she screamed and tore at his hair,—at his hair which now she played with and would not leave. Then I remembered the price and the long years of waiting; and I gripped her close, and dragged her away as he had done. And she held back, even as on that night, and fought like a she-cat for its whelp. And when the fire was between us and the man, I loosed her, and she sat and listened. And I told her of all that lay between, of all that had happened me on strange seas, of all that I had done in strange lands; of my weary quest, and the hungry years, and the promise which had been mine from the first. Ay, I told all, even to what had passed that day between the man and me, and in the days yet young. And as I spoke I saw the promise grow in her eyes, full and large like the break of dawn. And I read pity there, the tenderness of woman, the love, the heart and the soul of Unga. And I was a stripling again, for the look was the look of Unga as she ran up the beach, laughing, to the home of her mother. The stern unrest was gone, and the hunger, and the weary waiting. The time was met. I felt the call of her breast, and it seemed there I must pillow my head and forget. She opened her arms to me, and I came against her. Then, sudden, the hate flamed in her eye, her hand was at my hip. And once, twice, she passed the knife.

" 'Dog!' she sneered, as she flung me into the snow. 'Swine!' And then she laughed till the silence cracked, and went back to her dead.

"As I say, once she passed the knife, and twice; but she was weak with hunger, and it was not meant that I should die. Yet was I minded to stay in that place, and to close my eyes in the last long sleep with those whose lives had crossed with mine and led my feet on unknown trails. But there lay a debt upon me which would not let me rest.

"And the way was long, the cold bitter, and there was little grub. The Pellys had found no moose, and had robbed my cache. And so had the three white men; but they lay thin and dead in their cabin as I passed. After that I do not remember till I came here, and found food and fire,—much fire."

As he finished, he crouched closely, even jealously, over the stove. For a long while the slush-lamp shadows played tragedies upon the wall.

"But Unga!" cried Prince, the vision still strong upon him.

"Unga? She would not eat of the ptarmigan. She lay with her arms about his neck, her face deep in his yellow hair. I drew the fire close, that she might not feel the frost; but she crept to the other side. And I built a fire there; yet it was little good, for she would not eat. And in this manner they still lie up there in the snow."

"And you?" asked Malemute Kid.

"I do not know; but Akatan is small, and I have little wish to go back and live on the edge of the world. Yet is there small use in life. I can go to Constantine, and he will put irons upon me, and one day they will tie a piece of rope, so, and I will sleep good. Yet—no; I do not know."

"But, Kid," protested Prince, "this is murder!"

"Hush!" commanded Malemute Kid. "There be things

greater than our wisdom, beyond our justice. The right and the wrong of this we cannot say, and it is not for us to judge."

Naass drew yet closer to the fire. There was a great silence, and in each man's eyes many pictures came and went.

A Piece of Steak

With the last morsel of bread Tom King wiped his plate clean of the last paricle of flour gravy and chewed the resulting mouthful in a slow and meditative way. When he arose from the table, he was oppressed by the feeling that he was distinctly hungry. Yet he alone had eaten. The two children in the other room had been sent early to bed in order that in sleep they might forget they had gone supperless. His wife had touched nothing, and had sat silently and watched him with solicitous eyes. She was a thin, worn woman of the working-class, though signs of an earlier prettiness were not wanting in her face. The flour for the gravy she had borrowed from the neighbor across the hall. The last two ha'pennies had gone to buy the bread.

He sat down by the window on a rickety chair that protested under his weight, and quite mechanically he put his pipe in his mouth and dipped into the side pocket of his coat. The absence of any tobacco made him aware of his action, and, with a scowl for his forgetfulness, he put the pipe away. His movements were slow, almost hulking, as though he were burdened by the heavy weight of his muscles. He was a solid-bodied, stolid-looking man, and his appearance did not suffer from being overprepossessing. His rough clothes were old and slouchy. The uppers of his shoes were too weak to carry the heavy resoling that was itself of no recent date. And his cotton shirt, a cheap, two-shilling affair, showed a frayed collar and ineradicable paint stains.

But it was Tom King's face that advertised him unmistakably for what he was. It was the face of a typical prizefighter; of one who had put in long years of service in the squared ring and, by that means, developed and emphasized all the marks of the fighting beast. It was distinctly a lowering countenance, and, that no feature of it might escape notice, it was clean-shaven. The lips were shapeless, and constituted a mouth harsh to excess, that was like a gash in his face. The jaw was aggressive, brutal, heavy. The eyes, slow of movement and heavy-lidded, were almost expressionless under the shaggy, indrawn brows. Sheer animal that he was, the eyes were the most animallike feature about him. They were sleepy, lion-like—the eyes of a fighting animal. The forehead slanted quickly back to the hair, which, clipped close, showed every bump of a villainous-looking head. A nose, twice broken and moulded variously by countless blows, and a cauliflower ear, permanently swollen and distorted to twice its size, completed his adornment, while the beard, fresh-shaven as it was, sprouted in the skin and gave the face a blue-black stain.

All together, it was the face of a man to be afraid of in a dark alley or lonely place. And yet Tom King was not a criminal, nor had he ever done anything criminal. Outside of brawls, common to his walk in life, he had harmed no one. Nor had he ever been known to pick a quarrel. He was a professional, and all the fighting brutishness of him was reserved for his professional appearances. Outside the ring he was slow-going, easy-natured, and, in his younger days, when money was flush, too open-handed for his own good. He bore no grudges and had few enemies. Fighting was a business with him. In the ring he struck to hurt, struck to maim, struck to destroy; but there was no animus in it. It was a plain business proposition. Audiences assembled and paid for the spectacle of men knocking each other out. The winner took the big end of the purse. When Tom King faced the Woolloomoolloo Gouger, twenty years before, he knew that the Gouger's jaw was only four months healed after having been broken in a Newcastle bout. And he had played for that jaw and broken it again in the ninth round, not because he bore the Gouger any ill-will, but because that was the surest way to put the Gouger out and win the big end of the purse. Nor had the Gouger borne him any ill-will for it. It was the game, and both knew the game and played it.

Tom King had never been a talker, and he sat by the window, morosely silent, staring at his hands. The veins stood out on the backs of the hands, large and swollen; and the knuckles, smashed and battered and malformed, testified to the use to which they had been put. He had never heard that a man's life was the life of his arteries, but well he knew the meaning of those big, upstanding veins. His heart had pumped too much blood through them at top pressure. They no longer did the work. He had stretched the elasticity out of them, and with their distention had passed his endurance. He tired easily now. No longer could he do a fast twenty rounds, hammer and tongs, fight, fight, fight, from gong to gong, with fierce rally on top of fierce rally, beaten to the ropes and in turn beating his opponent to the ropes, and rallying fiercest and fastest of all in that last, twentieth round, with the house on its feet and yelling, himself rushing, striking, ducking, raining showers of blows upon showers of blows and receiving showers of blows in return, and all the time the heart faithfully pumping the surging blood through the adequate veins. The veins, swollen at the time, had always shrunk down again, though not quite—each time, imperceptibly at first, remaining just a trifle larger than before. He stared at them and at his battered knuckles, and, for the moment, caught a vision of the youthful excellence of those hands before the first knuckle had been smashed on the head of Benny Jones, otherwise known as the Welsh Terror.

The impression of his hunger came back on him.

"Blimey, but couldn't I go a piece of steak!" he muttered aloud, clenching his huge fists and spitting out a smothered oath.

"I tried both Burke's an' Sawley's," his wife said half apologetically.

"An' they wouldn't?" he demanded.

"Not a ha'penny. Burke said—" She faltered.

"G'wan! Wot'd he say?"

"As how 'e was thinkin' Sandel ud do ye to-night, an' as how yer score was comfortable big as it was."

Tom King grunted, but did not reply. He was busy thinking of the bull terrier he had kept in his younger days to which he had fed steaks without end. Burke would have given him credit for a thousand steaks—then. But times had changed. Tom King was getting old; and old men, fighting before second-rate clubs, couldn't expect to run bills of any size with the tradesmen.

He had got up in the morning with a longing for a piece of steak, and the longing had not abated. He had not had a fair training for this fight. It was a drought year in Australia, times were hard, and even the most irregular work was difficult to find. He had had no sparring partner, and his food had not been of the best nor always sufficient. He had done a few days' navvy work when he could get it, and he had run around the Domain in the early mornings to get his legs in shape. But it was hard, training without a partner and with a wife and two kiddies that must be fed. Credit with the tradesmen had undergone very slight expansion when he was matched with Sandel. The secretary of the Gayety Club had advanced him three pounds—the loser's end of the purse—and beyond that had refused to go. Now and again he had managed to borrow a few shillings from old pals, who would have lent more only that it was a drought year and they were hard put themselves. No—and there was no use in disguising the fact—his training had not been satisfactory. He should have had better food and no worries. Besides, when a man is forty, it is harder to get into condition than when he is twenty.

"What time is it, Lizzie?" he asked.

His wife went across the hall to inquire, and came back. "Quarter before eight."

"They'll be startin' the first bout in a few minutes," he said. "Only a try-out. Then there's a four-round spar 'tween Dealer Wells an' Gridley, an' a ten-round go 'tween Starlight an' some sailor bloke. I don't come on for over an hour."

At the end of another silent ten minutes, he rose to his feet.

"Truth is, Lizzie, I ain't had proper trainin'."

He reached for his hat and started for the door. He did not offer to kiss her—he never did on going out—but on this night she dared to kiss him, throwing her arms around him and compelling him to bend down to her face. She looked quite small against the massive bulk of the man.

"Good luck, Tom," she said. "You gotter do 'im."

"Ay, I gotter do 'im," he repeated. "That's all there is to it. I jus' gotter do 'im."

He laughed with an attempt at heartiness, while she pressed more closely against him. Across her shoulders he looked around the bare room. It was all he had in the world, with the rent overdue, and her and the kiddies. And he was leaving it to go out into the night to get meat for his mate and cubs—not like a modern working-man going to his machine grind, but in the old, primitive, royal, animal way, by fighting for it.

"I gotter do 'im," he repeated, this time a hint of desperation in his voice. "If it's a win, it's thirty quid—an' I can pay all that's owin', with a lump o' money left over. If it's a lose, I get naught—not even a penny for me to ride home on the train. The secretary's give all that's comin' from a loser's end. Good-by, old woman. I'll come straight home if it's a win."

"An' I'll be waitin' up," she called to him along the hall.

It was full two miles to the Gayety, and as he walked along he remembered how in his palmy days—he had once been the heavyweight champion of New South Wales—he would have ridden in a cab to the fight, and how, most likely, some heavy backer would have paid for the cab and ridden with him. There were Tommy Burns, and that Yankee nigger, Jack Johnson—they rode about in motor-cars. And he walked! And, as any man knew, a hard two miles was not the best preliminary to a fight. He was an old un, and the world did not wag well with old uns. He was good for nothing now except navvy work, and his broken nose and swollen ear were against him even in that. He found himself wishing that he had learned a trade. It would have been better in the long run. But no one had told him, and he knew, deep down in his heart, that he would not have listened if they had. It had been so easy. Big money—sharp, glorious fights—periods of rest and loafing in between—a following of eager flatterers, the slaps on the back, the shakes of the hand, the toffs glad to buy him a drink for the privilege of five minutes' talk— and the glory of it, the yelling houses, the whirlwind finish, the referee's "King wins!" and his name in the sporting columns next day.

Those had been times! But he realized now, in his slow, ruminating way, that it was the old uns he had been putting away. He was Youth, rising; and they were Age, sinking. No wonder it had been easy—they with their swollen veins and battered knuckles and weary in the bones of them from the long battles they had already fought. He remembered the time he put out old Stowsher Bill, at Rush-Cutters Bay, in the eighteenth round, and how old Bill had cried afterward in the dressing-room like a baby. Perhaps old Bill's rent had been overdue. Perhaps he'd had at home a missus an' a couple of kiddies. And perhaps Bill, that very day of the fight, had had a hungering for a piece of steak. Bill had fought game and taken incredible punishment. He could see now, after he had gone through the mill himself, that Stowsher Bill had fought for a bigger stake, that night twenty years ago, than had young Tom King, who had fought for glory and easy money. No wonder Stowsher Bill had cried afterward in the dressing-room.

Well, a man had only so many fights in him, to begin with. It was the iron law of the game. One man might have a hundred hard fights in him, another man only twenty; each, according to the make of him and the quality of his fibre, had a definite number, and, when he had fought them, he was done. Yes, he had had more fights in him than most of them, and he had had far more than his share of the hard, gruelling fights—the kind that worked the heart and lungs to bursting, that took the elastic out of the arteries and made hard knots of muscle out of Youth's sleek suppleness, that wore out nerve and stamina and made brain and bones weary from excess of effort and endurance overwrought. Yes, he had done better than all of them. There was none of his old fighting partners left. He was the last of the old guard. He had seen them all finished, and he had had a hand in finishing some of them.

They had tried him out against the old uns, and one after another he had put them away—laughing when, like old Stowsher Bill, they cried in the dressing-room. And now he was an old un, and they tried out the youngsters on him. There was that bloke, Sandel. He had come over from New Zealand with a record behind him. But nobody in Australia knew anything about him, so they put him up against old Tom King. If Sandel made a showing, he would be given better men to fight, with bigger purses to win; so it was to be depended upon that he would put up a fierce battle. He had everything to win by it—money and glory and career; and Tom King was the grizzled old chopping-block that guarded the highway to fame and fortune. And he had nothing to win except thirty quid, to pay to the landlord and the tradesmen. And, as Tom King thus ruminated, there came to his stolid vision the form of Youth, glorious Youth, rising exultant and invincible, supple of muscle and silken of skin, with heart and lungs that had never been tired and torn and that laughed at limitation of effort. Yes, Youth was the Nemesis. It destroyed the old uns and recked not that, in so doing, it destroyed itself. It enlarged its arteries and smashed its knuckles, and was in turn destroyed by Youth. For Youth was ever youthful. It was only Age that grew old.

At Castlereagh Street he turned to the left, and three blocks along came to the Gayety. A crowd of young larrikins hanging outside the door made respectful way for him, and he heard one say to another: "That's 'im! That's Tom King!"

Inside, on the way to his dressing-room, he encountered the secretary, a keen-eyed, shrewd-faced young man, who shook his hand.

"How are you feelin', Tom?" he asked.

"Fit as a fiddle," King answered, though he knew that he lied, and that if he had a quid, he would give it right there for a good piece of steak.

When he emerged from the dressing-room, his seconds behind him, and came down the aisle to the squared ring in the centre of the hall, a burst of greeting and applause went up from the waiting crowd. He acknowledged salutations right and left, though few of the faces did he know. Most of them were the faces of kiddies unborn when he was winning his first laurels in the squared ring. He leaped lightly to the raised platform and ducked through the ropes to his corner, where he sat down on a folding stool. Jack

Ball, the referee, came over and shook his hand. Ball was a broken-down pugilist who for over ten years had not entered the ring as a principal. King was glad that he had him for referee. They were both old uns. If he should rough it with Sandel a bit beyond the rules, he knew Ball could be depended upon to pass it by.

Aspiring young heavyweights, one after another, were climbing into the ring and being presented to the audience by the referee. Also, he issued their challenges for them.

"Young Pronto," Bill announced, "from North Sydney, challenges the winner for fifty pounds side bet."

The audience applauded, and applauded again as Sandel himself sprang through the ropes and sat down in his corner. Tom King looked across the ring at him curiously, for in a few minutes they would be locked together in merciless combat, each trying with all the force of him to knock the other into unconsciousness. But little could he see, for Sandel, like himself, had trousers and sweater on over his ring costume. His face was strongly handsome, crowned with a curly mop of yellow hair, while his thick, muscular neck hinted at bodily magnificence.

Young Pronto went to one corner and then the other, shaking hands with the principals and dropping down out of the ring. The challenges went on. Ever Youth climbed through the ropes—Youth unknown, but insatiable—crying out to mankind that with strength and skill it would match issues with the winner. A few years before, in his own heyday of invincibleness, Tom King would have been amused and bored by these preliminaries. But now he sat fascinated, unable to shake the vision of Youth from his eyes. Always were these youngsters rising up in the boxing game, springing through the ropes and shouting their defiance; and always were the old uns going down before them. They climbed to success over the bodies of the old uns. And ever they came, more and more youngsters— Youth unquenchable and irresistible—and ever they put the old uns away, themselves becoming old uns and travelling the same downward path, while behind them, ever pressing on them, was Youth eternal—the new babies, grown lusty and dragging their elders down, with behind them more babies to the end of time—Youth that must have its will and that will never die.

King glanced over to the press box and nodded to Morgan, of the *Sportsman*, and Corbett, of the *Referee*. Then he held out his hands, while Sid Sullivan and Charley Bates, his seconds, slipped on his gloves and laced them tight, closely watched by one of Sandel's seconds, who first examined critically the tapes on King's knuckles. A second of his own was in Sandel's corner, performing a like office. Sandel's trousers were pulled off, and, as he stood up, his sweater was skinned off over his head. And Tom King, looking, saw Youth incarnate, deep-chested, heavy-thewed, with muscles that slipped and slid like live things under the white satin skin. The whole body was acrawl with life, and Tom King knew that it was a life that had never oozed its freshness out through the aching pores during the long fights wherein Youth paid its toll and departed not quite so young as when it entered.

The two men advanced to meet each other, and, as the gong sounded and the seconds clattered out of the ring with the folding stools, they shook hands and instantly took their fighting attitudes. And instantly, like a mechanism of steel and springs balanced on a hair trigger, Sandel was in and out and in again, landing a left to the eyes, a right to the ribs, ducking a counter, dancing lightly away and dancing menacingly back again. He was swift and clever. It was a dazzling exhibition. The house yelled its approbation. But King was not dazzled. He had fought too many fights and too many youngsters. He knew the blows for what they were—too quick and too deft to be dangerous. Evidently Sandel was going to rush things from the start. It was to be expected. It was the way of Youth, expending its splendor and excellence in wild insurgence and furious onslaught, overwhelming opposition with its own unlimited glory of strength and desire.

Sandel was in and out, here, there, and everywhere, light-footed and eager-hearted, a living wonder of white flesh and stinging muscle that wove itself into a dazzling fabric of attack, slipping and leaping like a flying shuttle from action to action through a thousand actions, all of them centred upon the destruction of Tom King, who stood between him and fortune. And Tom King patiently endured. He knew his business, and he knew Youth now that Youth was no longer his. There was nothing to do till the other lost some of his steam, was his thought, and he grinned to himself as he deliberately ducked so as to receive a heavy blow on the top of his head. It was a wicked thing to do, yet eminently fair according to the rules of the boxing game. A man was supposed to take care of his own knuckles, and if he insisted on hitting an opponent on the top of the head, he did so at his own peril. King could have ducked lower and let the blow whiz harmlessly past, but he remembered his own early fights and how he smashed his first knuckle on the head of the Welsh Terror. He was but playing the game. That duck had accounted for one of Sandel's knuckles. Not that Sandel would mind it now. He would go on, superbly regardless, hitting as hard as ever throughout the fight. But later on, when the long ring battles had begun to tell, he would regret that knuckle and look back and remember how he smashed it on Tom King's head.

The first round was all Sandel's, and he had the house yelling with the rapidity of his whirlwind rushes. He overwhelmed King with avalanches of punches, and King did nothing. He never struck once, contenting himself with covering up, blocking and ducking and clinching to avoid punishment. He occasionally feinted, shook his head when the weight of a punch landed, and moved stolidly about, never leaping or springing or wasting an ounce of strength. Sandel must foam the froth of Youth away before discreet

Age could dare to retaliate. All King's movements were slow and methodical, and his heavy-lidded, slow-moving eyes gave him the appearance of being half asleep or dazed. Yet they were eyes that saw everything, that had been trained to see everything through all his twenty years and odd in the ring. They were eyes that did not blink or waver before an impending blow, but that coolly saw and measured distance.

Seated in his corner for the minute's rest at the end of the round, he lay back with outstretched legs, his arms resting on the right angle of the ropes, his chest and abdomen heaving frankly and deeply as he gulped down the air driven by the towels of his seconds. He listened with closed eyes to the voices of the house, "Why don't yeh fight, Tom?" many were crying. "Yeh ain't afraid of 'im, are yeh?"

"Muscle-bound," he heard a man on a front seat comment. "He can't move quicker. Two to one on Sandel, in quids."

The gong struck and the two men advanced from their corners. Sandel came forward fully three-quarters of the distance, eager to begin again; but King was content to advance the shorter distance. It was in line with his policy of economy. He had not been well trained, and he had not had enough to eat, and every step counted. Besides, he had already walked two miles to the ringside. It was a repetition of the first round, with Sandel attacking like a whirl-wind and with the audience indignantly demanding why King did not fight. Beyond feinting and several slowly delivered and ineffectual blows he did nothing save block and stall and clinch. Sandel wanted to make the pace fast, while King, out of his wisdom, refused to accommodate him. He grinned with a certain wistful pathos in his ring-battered countenance, and went on cherishing his strength with the jealousy of which only Age is capable. Sandel was Youth, and he threw his strength away with the munificent abandon of Youth. To King belonged the ring generalship, the wisdom bred of long, aching fights. He watched with cool eyes and head, moving slowly and waiting for Sandel's froth to foam away. To the majority of the on-lookers it seemed as though King was hopelessly out-classed, and they voiced their opinion in offers of three to one on Sandel. But there were wise ones, a few, who knew King of old time, and who covered what they considered easy money.

The third round began as usual, one-sided, with Sandel doing all the leading and delivering all the punishment. A half-minute had passed when Sandel, overconfident, left an opening. King's eyes and right arm flashed in the same instant. It was his first real blow—a hook, with the twisted arch of the arm to make it rigid, and with all the weight of the half-pivoted body behind it. It was like a sleepy-seeming lion suddenly thrusting out a lightning paw. Sandel, caught on the side of the jaw, was felled like a bullock. The audience gasped and murmured awe-stricken applause. The man was not muscle-bound, after all, and he could drive a blow like a trip-hammer.

Sandel was shaken. He rolled over and attempted to rise, but the sharp yells from his seconds to take the count restrained him. He knelt on one knee, ready to rise, and waited, while the referee stood over him, counting the sec-onds loudly in his ear. At the ninth he rose in fighting at-titude, and Tom King, facing him, knew regret that the blow had not been an inch nearer the point of the jaw. That would have been a knockout, and he could have car-ried the thirty quid home to the missus and the kiddies.

The round continued to the end of its three minutes, Sandel for the first time respectful of his opponent and King slow of movement and sleepy-eyed as ever. As the round neared its close, King, warned of the fact by sight of the seconds crouching outside ready for the spring in through the ropes, worked the fight around to his own cor-ner. And when the gong struck, he sat down immediately on the waiting stool, while Sandel had to walk all the way across the diagonal of the square to his own corner. It was a little thing, but it was the sum of little things that counted. Sandel was compelled to walk that many more steps, to give up that much energy, and to lose a part of the precious minute of rest. At the beginning of every round King loafed slowly out from his corner, forcing his opponent to advance the greater distance. The end of every round found the fight maneuvred by King into his own corner so that he could immediately sit down.

Two more rounds went by, in which King was parsimonious of effort and Sandel prodigal. The latter's attempt to force a fast pace made King uncomfortable, for a fair percentage of the multitudinous blows showered upon him went home. Yet King persisted in his dogged slowness, despite the crying of the young hotheads for him to go in and fight. Again, in the sixth round, Sandel was careless, again Tom King's fearful right flashed out to the jaw, and again Sandel took the nine seconds count.

By the seventh round Sandel's pink of condition was gone, and he settled down to what he knew was to be the hardest fight in his experience. Tom King was an old un, but a better old un than he had ever encountered—an old un who never lost his head, who was remarkably able at defence, whose blows had the impact of a knotted club, and who had a knockout in either hand. Nevertheless, Tom King dared not hit often. He never forgot his battered knuckles, and knew that every hit must count if the knuckles were to last out the fight. As he sat in his corner, glancing across at his opponent, the thought came to him that the sum of his wisdom and Sandel's youth would constitute a world's champion heavyweight. But that was the trouble. Sandel would never become a world champion. He lacked the wisdom, and the only way for him to get it was to buy it with Youth; and when wisdom was his, Youth would have been spent in buying it.

King took every advantage he knew. He never missed an opportunity to clinch, and in effecting most of the clinches his shoulder drove stiffly into the other's ribs. In the philosophy of the ring a shoulder was as good as a punch so far as damage was concerned, and a great deal better so far as concerned expenditure of effort. Also, in the clinches King rested his weight on his opponent, and was loath to let go. This compelled the interference of the referee, who tore them apart, always assisted by Sandel, who had not yet learned to rest. He could not refrain from using those glorious flying arms and writhing muscles of his, and when the other rushed into a clinch, striking shoulder against ribs, and with head resting under Sandel's left arm, Sandel almost invariably swung his right behind his own back and into the projecting face. It was a clever stroke, much admired by the audience, but it was not dangerous, and was, therefore, just that much wasted strength. But Sandel was tireless and unaware of limitations, and King grinned and doggedly endured.

Sandel developed a fierce right to the body, which made it appear that King was taking an enormous amount of punishment, and it was only the old ringsters who appreciated the deft touch of King's left glove to the other's biceps just before the impact of the blow. It was true, the blow landed each time; but each time it was robbed of its power by that touch on the biceps. In the ninth round, three times inside a minute, King's right hooked its twisted arch to the jaw; and three times Sandel's body, heavy as it was, was levelled to the mat. Each time he took the nine seconds allowed him and rose to his feet, shaken and jarred, but still strong. He had lost much of his speed, and he wasted less effort. He was fighting grimly; but he continued to draw upon his chief asset, which was Youth. King's chief asset was experience. As his vitality had dimmed and his vigor abated, he had replaced them with cunning, with wisdom born of the long fights and with a careful shepherding of strength. Not alone had he learned never to make a superfluous movement, but he had learned how to seduce an opponent into throwing his strength away. Again and again, by feint of foot and hand and body he continued to inveigle Sandel into leaping back, ducking, or countering. King rested, but he never permitted Sandel to rest. It was the strategy of Age.

Early in the tenth round King began stopping the other's rushes with straight lefts to the face, and Sandel, grown wary, responded by drawing the left, then by ducking it and delivering his right in a swinging hook to the side of the head. It was too high up to be vitally effective; but when first it landed, King knew the old, familiar descent of the black veil of unconsciousness across his mind. For the instant, or for the slightest fraction of an instant, rather, he ceased. In the one moment he saw his opponent ducking out of his field of vision and the background of white, watching faces; in the next moment he again saw his opponent and the background of faces. It was as if he had slept for a time and just opened his eyes again, and yet the interval of unconsciousness was so microscopically short that there had been no time for him to fall. The audience saw him totter and his knees give, and then saw him recover and tuck his chin deeper into the shelter of his left shoulder.

Several times Sandel repeated the blow, keeping King partially dazed, and then the latter worked out his defence, which was also a counter. Feinting with his left he took a half-step backward, at the same time upper cutting with the whole strength of his right. So accurately was it timed that it landed squarely on Sandel's face in the full, downward sweep of the duck, and Sandel lifted in the air and curled backward, striking the mat on his head and shoulders. Twice King achieved this, then turned loose and hammered his opponent to the ropes. He gave Sandel no chance to rest or to set himself, but smashed blow in upon blow till the house rose to its feet and the air was filled with an unbroken roar of applause. But Sandel's strength and endurance were superb, and he continued to stay on his feet. A knockout seemed certain, and a captain of police, appalled at the dreadful punishment, arose by the ringside to stop the fight. The gong struck for the end of the round and Sandel staggered to his corner, protesting to the captain that he was sound and strong. To prove it, he threw two back air-springs, and the police captain gave in.

Tom King, leaning back in his corner and breathing hard, was disappointed. If the fight had been stopped, the referee, perforce, would have rendered him the decision and the purse would have been his. Unlike Sandel, he was not fighting for glory or career, but for thirty quid. And now Sandel would recuperate in the minute of rest.

Youth will be served—this saying flashed into King's mind, and he remembered the first time he had heard it, the night when he had put away Stowsher Bill. The toff who had bought him a drink after the fight and patted him on the shoulder had used those words. Youth will be served! The toff was right. And on that night in the long ago he had been Youth. To-night Youth sat in the opposite corner. As for himself, he had been fighting for half an hour now, and he was an old man. Had he fought like Sandel, he would not have lasted fifteen minutes. But the point was that he did not recuperate. Those upstanding arteries and that sorely tried heart would not enable him to gather strength in the intervals between the rounds. And he had not had sufficient strength in him to begin with. His legs were heavy under him and beginning to cramp. He should not have walked those two miles to the fight. And there was the steak which he had got up longing for that morning. A great and terrible hatred rose up in him for the butchers who had refused him credit. It was hard for an old man to go into a fight without enough to eat. And a piece of steak was such a little thing, a few pennies at best; yet it meant thirty quid to him.

With the gong that opened the eleventh round, Sandel rushed, making a show of freshness which he did not really possess. King knew it for what it was—a bluff as old as the game itself. He clinched to save himself, then, going free, allowed Sandel to get set. This was what King desired. He feinted with his left, drew the answering duck and swinging upward hook, then made the half-step backward, delivered the upper cut full to the face and crumpled Sandel over to the mat. After that he never let him rest, receiving punishment himself, but inflicting far more, smashing Sandel to the ropes, hooking and driving all manner of blows into him, tearing away from his clinches or punching him out of attempted clinches, and ever when Sandel would have fallen, catching him with one uplifting hand and with the other immediately smashing him into the ropes where he could not fall.

The house by this time had gone mad, and it was his house, nearly every voice yelling: "Go it, Tom!" "Get 'im! Get 'im!" "You've got 'im, Tom! You've got 'im!" It was to be a whirlwind finish, and that was what a ringside audience paid to see.

And Tom King, who for half an hour had conserved his strength, now expended it prodigally in the one great effort he knew he had in him. It was his one chance—now or not at all. His strength was waning fast, and his hope was that before the last of it ebbed out of him he would have beaten his opponent down for the count. And as he continued to strike and force, coolly estimating the weight of his blows and the quality of the damage wrought, he realized how hard a man Sandel was to knock out. Stamina and endurance were his to an extreme degree, and they were the virgin stamina and endurance of Youth. Sandel was certainly a coming man. He had it in him. Only out of such rugged fibre were successful fighters fashioned.

Sandel was reeling and staggering, but Tom King's legs were cramping and his knuckles going back on him. Yet he steeled himself to strike the fierce blows, every one of which brought anguish to his tortured hands. Though now he was receiving practically no punishment, he was weakening as rapidly as the other. His blows went home, but there was no longer the weight behind them, and each blow was the result of a severe effort of will. His legs were like lead, and they dragged visibly under him; while Sandel's backers, cheered by this symptom, began calling encouragement to their man.

King was spurred to a burst of effort. He delivered two blows in succession—a left, a trifle too high, to the solar plexus, and a right cross to the jaw. They were not heavy blows, yet so weak and dazed was Sandel that he went down and lay quivering. The referee stood over him, shouting the count of the fatal seconds in his ear. If before the tenth second was called, he did not rise, the fight was lost. The house stood in hushed silence. King rested on trembling legs. A mortal dizziness was upon him, and before his eyes the sea of faces sagged and swayed, while to his ears, as from a remote distance, came the count of the referee. Yet he looked upon the fight as his. It was impossible that a man so punished could rise.

Only Youth could rise, and Sandel rose. At the fourth second he rolled over on his face and groped blindly for the ropes. By the seventh second he had dragged himself to his knee, where he rested, his head rolling groggily on his shoulders. As the referee cried "Nine!" Sandel stood upright, in proper stalling position, his left arm wrapped about his face, his right wrapped about his stomach. Thus were his vital points guarded, while he lurched forward toward King in the hope of effecting a clinch and gaining more time.

At the instant Sandel arose, King was at him, but the two blows he delivered were muffled on the stalled arms. The next moment Sandel was in the clinch and holding on desperately while the referee strove to drag the two men apart. King helped to force himself free. He knew the rapidity with which Youth recovered, and he knew that Sandel was his if he could prevent that recovery. One stiff punch would do it. Sandel was his, indubitably his. He had outgeneralled him, outfought him, outpointed him. Sandel reeled out of the clinch, balanced on the hair line between defeat or survival. One good blow would topple him over and down and out. And Tom King, in a flash of bitterness, remembered the piece of steak and wished that he had it then behind that necessary punch he must deliver. He nerved himself for the blow, but it was not heavy enough nor swift enough. Sandel swayed, but did not fall, staggering back to the ropes and holding on. King staggered after him, and, with a pang like that of dissolution, delivered another blow. But his body had deserted him. All that was left of him was a fighting intelligence that was dimmed and clouded from exhaustion. The blow that was aimed for the jaw struck no higher than the shoulder. He had willed the blow higher, but the tired muscles had not been able to obey. And, from the impact of the blow, Tom King himself reeled back and nearly fell. Once again he strove. This time his punch missed altogether, and, from absolute weakness, he fell against Sandel and clinched, holding on to him to save himself from sinking to the floor.

King did not attempt to free himself. He had shot his bolt. He was gone. And Youth had been served. Even in the clinch he could feel Sandel growing stronger against him. When the referee thrust them apart, there, before his eyes, he saw Youth recuperate. From instant to instant Sandel grew stronger. His punches, weak and futile at first, became stiff and accurate. Tom King's bleared eyes saw the gloved fist driving at his jaw, and he willed to guard it by interposing his arm. He saw the danger, willed the act; but the arm was too heavy. It seemed burdened with a hundredweight of lead. It would not lift itself, and he strove to lift it with his soul. Then the gloved fist landed home. He experienced a sharp snap that was like an electric spark, and, simultaneously, the veil of blackness enveloped him.

When he opened his eyes again he was in his corner, and he heard the yelling of the audience like the roar of the surf at Bondi Beach. A wet sponge was being pressed against the base of his brain, and Sid Sullivan was blowing cold water in a refreshing spray over his face and chest. His gloves had already been removed, and Sandel, bending over him, was shaking his hand. He bore no ill-will toward the man who had put him out, and he returned the grip with a heartiness that made his battered knuckles protest. Then Sandel stepped to the centre of the ring and the audience hushed its pandemonium to hear him accept young Pronto's challenge and offer to increase the side bet to one hundred pounds. King looked on apathetically while his seconds mopped the streaming water from him, dried his face, and prepared him to leave the ring. He felt hungry. It was not the ordinary, gnawing kind, but a great faintness, a palpitation at the pit of the stomach that communicated itself to all his body. He remembered back into the fight to the moment when he had Sandel swaying and tottering on the hair-line balance of defeat. Ah, that piece of steak would have done it! He had lacked just that for the decisive blow, and he had lost. It was all because of the piece of steak.

His seconds were half-supporting him as they helped him through the ropes. He tore free from them, ducked through the ropes unaided, and leaped heavily to the floor, following on their heels as they forced a passage for him down the crowded centre aisle. Leaving the dressing-room for the street, in the entrance to the hall, some young fellow spoke to him.

"W'y didn't yuh go in an' get 'em when yuh 'ad 'im?" the young fellow asked.

"Aw, go to hell!" said Tom King, and passed down the steps to the sidewalk.

The doors of the public house at the corner were swinging wide, and he saw the lights and the smiling barmaids, heard the many voices discussing the fight and the prosperous chink of money on the bar. Somebody called to him to have a drink. He hesitated perceptibly, then refused and went on his way.

He had not a copper in his pocket, and the two-mile walk home seemed very long. He was certainly getting old. Crossing the Domain, he sat down suddenly on a bench, unnerved by the thought of the missus sitting up for him, waiting to learn the outcome of the fight. That was harder than any knockout, and it seemed almost impossible to face.

He felt weak and sore, and the pain of his smashed knuckles warned him that, even if he could find a job at navvy work, it would be a week before he could grip a pick handle or a shovel. The hunger palpitation at the pit of the stomach was sickening. His wretchedness over-whelmed him, and into his eyes came an unwonted mois-ture. He covered his face with his hands, and, as he cried, he remembered Stowsher Bill and how he had served him that night in the long ago. Poor old Stowsher Bill! He could understand now why Bill had cried in the dressing-room.

The Strength of the Strong

Parables don't lie, but liars will parable.
                                    —Lip-King

Old Long Beard paused in his narrative, licked his greasy fingers, and wiped them on his naked sides where his one piece of ragged bearskin failed to cover him. Crouched around him, on their hams, were three young men, his grandsons, Deer-Runner, Yellow-Head, and Afraid-of-the-Dark. In appearance they were much the same. Skins of wild animals partly covered them. They were lean and meager of build, narrow-hipped and crooked-legged, and at the same time deep-chested, with heavy arms and enormous hands. There was much hair on their chests and shoulders, and on the outsides of their arms and legs. Their heads were matted with uncut hair, long locks of which often strayed before their eyes, beady and black and glittering like the eyes of birds. They were narrow between the eyes and broad between the cheeks, while their lower jaws were projecting and massive.

It was a night of clear starlight, and below them, stretching away remotely, lay range on range of forest-covered hills. In the distance the heavens were red from the glow of a volcano. At their backs yawned the black mouth of a cave, out of which, from time to time, blew draughty gusts of wind. Immediately in front of them blazed a fire. At one side, partly devoured, lay the carcass of a bear, with about it, at a respectable distance, several large dogs, shaggy and wolf-like. Beside each man lay his bow and arrows and a huge club. In the cave-mouth a number of rude spears leaned against the rock.

"So that was how we moved from the cave to the tree," old Long Beard spoke up.

They laughed boisterously, like big children, at recollection of a previous story his words called up. Long Beard laughed, too, the five-inch bodkin of bone, thrust midway through the cartilage of his nose, leaping and dancing and adding to his ferocious appearance. He did not exactly say the words recorded, but he made animal-like sounds with his mouth that meant the same thing.

"And that is the first I remember of the Sea Valley," Long Beard went on. "We were a very foolish crowd. We did not know the secret of strength. For, behold, each family lived by itself, and took care of itself. There were thirty families, but we got not strength from one another. We were in fear of each other all the time. No one ever paid visits. In the top of our tree we built a grass house, and on the platform outside was a pile of rocks, which were for the heads of any that might chance to try to visit us. Also, we had our spears and arrows. We never walked under the trees of the other families, either. My brother did, once, under old Boo-oogh's tree, and he got his head broken and that was the end of him.

"Old Boo-oogh was very strong. It was said he could pull a grown man's head right off. I never heard of him doing it, because no man would give him a chance. Father wouldn't. One day, when father was down on the beach, Boo-oogh took after mother. She couldn't run fast, for the day before she had got her leg clawed by a bear when she was up on the mountain gathering berries. So Boo-oogh caught her and carried her up into his tree. Father never got her back. He was afraid. Old Boo-oogh made faces at him.

"But father did not mind. Strong-Arm was another strong man. He was one of the best fishermen. But one day, climbing after seagull eggs, he had a fall from the cliff. He was never strong after that. He coughed a great deal, and his shoulders drew near to each other. So father took Strong-Arm's wife. When he came around and coughed under our tree, father laughed at him and threw rocks at him. It was our way in those days. We did not know how to add strength together and become strong."

"Would a brother take a brother's wife?" Deer-Runner demanded.

"Yes, if he had gone to lie in another tree by himself."

"But we do not do such things now," Afraid-of-the-Dark objected.

"It is because I have taught your fathers better." Long Beard thrust his hairy paw into the bear meat and drew out a handful of suet, which he sucked with a meditative air. Again he wiped his hands on his naked sides and went on. "What I am telling you happened in the long ago, before we knew any better."

"You must have been fools not to know better," was Deer-Runner's comment, Yellow-Head grunting approval.

"So we were, but we became bigger fools, as you shall see. Still, we did learn better, and this was the way of it. We Fish-Eaters had not learned to add our strength until our strength was the strength of all of us. But the Meat-Eaters, who lived across the divide in the Big Valley, stood together, hunted together, fished together, and fought together. One day they came into our valley. Each family of us got into its own cave and tree. There were only ten Meat-Eaters, but they fought together, and we fought each family by itself."

Long Beard counted long and perplexedly on his fingers.

"There were sixty men of us," was what he managed to say with fingers and lips combined. "And we were very strong, only we did not know it. So we watched the ten men attack Boo-oogh's tree. He made a good fight, but he had no chance. We looked on. When some of the Meat-Eaters tried to climb the tree, Boo-oogh had to show himself in order to drop stones on their heads, whereupon the other Meat-Eaters, who were waiting for that very thing, shot him full of arrows. And that was the end of Boo-oogh.

"Next, the Meat-Eaters got One-Eye and his family in his cave. They built a fire int he mouth and smoked him out, like we smoked out the bear there to-day. Then they went after Six-Fingers, up his tree, and, while they were killing him and his grown son, the rest of us ran away. They caught some of our women, and killed two old men who could not run fast and several children. The women they carried away with them to the Big Valley.

"After that the rest of us crept back, and, somehow, perhaps because we were in fear and felt the need for one another, we talked the thing over. It was our first council—our first real council. And in that council we formed our first tribe. For we had learned the lesson. Of the ten Meat-Eaters, each man had the strength of ten, for the ten had fought as one man. They had added their strength together. But of the thirty families and the sixty men of us, we had had the strength of but one man, for each had fought alone.

"It was a great talk we had, and it was hard talk, for we did not have the words then as now with which to talk. The Bug made some of the words long afterward, and so did others of us make words from time to time. But in the end we agreed to add our strength together and to be as one man when the Meat-Eaters came over the divide to steal our women. And that was the tribe.

"We set two men on the divide, one for the day and one for the night, to watch if the Meat-Eaters came. These were the eyes of the tribe. Then, also, day and night, there were to be ten men awake with their clubs and spears and arrows in their hands, ready to fight. Before, when a man went after fish, or clams, or gull-eggs, he carried his weapons with him, and half the time he was getting food and half the time watching for fear some other man would get him. Now that was all changed. The men went out without their weapons and spent all their time getting food. Likewise, when the women went into the mountains after roots and berries, five of the ten men went with them to guard them. While all the time, day and night, the eyes of the tribe watched from the top of the divide.

"But troubles came. As usual, it was about the women. Men without wives wanted other men's wives, and there was much fighting between men, and now and again one got his head smashed or a spear through his body. While one of the watchers was on top the divide, another man stole his wife, and he came down to fight. Then the other watcher was in fear that someone would take his wife, and he came down likewise. Also, there was trouble among the ten men who carried always their weapons, and they fought five against five, till some ran away down the coast and the others ran after them.

"So it was that the tribe was left without eyes or guards. We had not the strength of sixty. We had no strength at all. So we held a council and made our first laws. I was but a cub at the time, but I remember. We said that, in order to be strong, we must not fight one another, and we made a law that when a man killed another him would the tribe kill. We made another law that whoso stole another man's wife him would the tribe kill. We said that whatever man had too great strength, and by that strength hurt his brothers in the tribe, him would we kill that his strength might hurt no more. For, if we let his strength hurt, the brothers would become afraid and the tribe would fall apart, and we would be as weak as when the Meat-Eaters first came upon us and killed Boo-oogh.

"Knuckle-Bone was a strong man, a very strong man, and he knew not law. He knew only his own strength, and in the fullness thereof he went forth and took the wife of Three-Clams. Three-Clams tried to fight, but Knuckle-Bone clubbed out his brains. Yet had Knuckle-Bone forgotten that all the men of us had added our strength to keep the law among us, and him we killed, at the foot of his tree, and hung his body on a branch as a warning that the law was stronger than any man. For we were the law, all of us, and no man was greater than the law.

"Then there were other troubles, for know, O Deer-Runner, and Yellow-Head, and Afraid-of-the-Dark, that it is not easy to make a tribe. There were many things, little things, that it was a great trouble to call all the men together to have a council about. We were having councils morning, noon, and night, and in the middle of the night. We could find little time to go out and get food, what of the councils, for there was always some little thing to be settled, such as naming two new watchers to take the place of the old one on the hill, or naming how much food should fall to the share of the men who kept their weapons always in their hands and got no food for themselves.

"We stood in need of a chief man to do these things, who would be the voice of the council, and who would account to the council for the things he did. So we named Fith-Fith the chief man. He was a strong man, too, and very cunning, and when he was angry he made noises just like that, *fith-fith*, like a wildcat.

"The ten men who guarded the tribe were set to work making a wall of stones across the narrow part of the valley. The women and large children helped, as did other men, until the wall was strong. After that, all the families came down out of their caves and trees and built grass houses behind the shelter of the wall. These houses were large and much better than the caves and trees, and everybody had a better time of it because the men had added their strength together and become a tribe. Because of that wall and the guards and the watchers, there was more time to hunt and fish and pick roots and berries; there was more food, and better food, and no one went hungry. And Three-Legs, so named because his legs had been smashed when a boy and who walked with a stick—Three-Legs got the seed of the wild corn and planted it in the ground in the valley near his house. Also, he tried planting fat roots and other things he found in the mountain valleys.

"Because of the safety in the Sea Valley, which was because of the wall and the watchers and the guards, and because there was food in plenty for all without having to fight for it, many families came in from the coast valleys on both sides and from the high back mountains where they had lived more like wild animals than men. And it was not long before the Sea Valley filled up, and in it were countless families. But, before this happened, the land, which had been free to all and belonged to all, was divided up. Three-Legs began it when he planted corn. But most of us did not care about the land. We thought the marking of the boundaries with fences of stone was a foolishness. We had plenty to eat, and what more did we want? I remember that my father and I built stone fences for Three-Legs and were given corn in return.

"So only a few got all the land, and Three-Legs got most of it. Also, others that had taken land gave it to the few that held on, being paid in return with corn and fat roots, and bearskins, and fishes which the farmers got from the fishermen in exchange for corn. And, the first thing we knew, all the land was gone.

"It was about this time that Fith-Fith died and Dog-Tooth, his son, was made chief. He demanded to be made chief anyway, because his father had been chief before him. Also, he looked upon himself as a greater chief than his father. He was a good chief at first, and worked hard, so that the council had less and less to do. Then arose a new voice in the Sea Valley. It was Twisted-Lip. We had never thought much of him, until he began to talk with the spirits of the dead. Later we called him Big-Fat, because he ate over-much, and did no work, and grew round and large. One day big-Fat told us that the secrets of the dead were his, and that he was the voice of God. He became great friends with Dog-Tooth, who commanded that we build Big-Fat a grass house. And Big-Fat put taboos all around this house and kept God inside.

"More and more Dog-Tooth became greater than the council, and when the council grumbled and said it would name a new chief, Big-Fat spoke with the voice of God and said no. Also, Three-Legs and the others who held the land stood behind Dog-Tooth. Moreover, the strongest man in the council was Sea-Lion, and him the land-owners gave land to secretly, along with many bearskins and baskets of corn. So Sea-Lion said that Big-Fat's voice was truly the voice of God and must be obeyed. And soon afterward Sea-Lion was named the voice of Dog-Tooth and did most of his talking for him.

"Then there was Little-Belly, a little man, so thin in the middle that he looked as if he had never had enough to eat. Inside the mouth of the river, after the sand-bar had combed the strength of the breakers, he built a big fish-trap. No man had ever seen or dreamed a fish-trap before. He worked weeks on it, with his son and his wife, while the rest of us laughed at their labors. But, when it was done, the first day he caught more fish in it than could the whole tribe in a week, whereat there was great rejoicing. There was only one other place in the river for a fish-trap, but, when my father and I and a dozen other men started to make a very large trap, the guards came from the big grass-house we had built for Dog-Tooth. And the guards poked us with their spears and told us begone, because Little-Belly was going to build a trap there himself on the word of Sea-Lion, who was the voice of Dog-Tooth.

"There was much grumbling, and my father called a

council. But, when he rose to speak, him the Sea-Lion thrust through the throat with a spear and he died. And Dog-Tooth and Little-Belly, and Three-Legs and all that held land said it was good. And Big-Fat said it was the will of God. And after that all men were afraid to stand up in the council, and there was no more council.

"Another man, Pig-Jaw, began to keep goats. He had heard about it as among the Meat-Eaters, and it was not long before he had many flocks. Other men, who had no land and no fish-traps, and who else would have gone hungry, were glad to work for Pig-Jaw, caring for his goats, guarding them from wild dogs and tigers, and driving them to the feeding pastures in the mountains. In return, Pig-Jaw gave them goat-meat to eat and goat-skins to wear, and sometimes they traded the goat-meat for fish and corn and fat roots.

"It was this time that money came to be. Sea-Lion was the man who first though of it, and he talked it over with Dog-Tooth and Big-Fat. You see, these three were the ones that got a share of everything in the Sea Valley. One basket out of every three of corn was theirs, one fish out of every three, one goat out of every three. In return, they fed the guards and the watchers, and kept the rest for themselves. Sometimes, when a big haul of fish was made, they did not know what to do with all their share. So Sea-Lion set the women to making money out of shell—little round pieces, with a hole in each one, and all made smooth and fine. These were strung on strings, and the strings were called money.

"Each string was of the value of thirty fish, or forty fish, but the women, who made a string a day, were given two fish each. The fish came out of the shares of Dog-Tooth, Big-Fat, and Sea-Lion, which they three did not eat. So all the money belonged to them. Then they told Three-Legs and the land owners that they would take their share of corn and roots in money, Little-Belly that they would take their share of fish in money, the Pig-Jaw that they would take their share of goats and cheese in money. Thus, a man who had nothing, worked for one who had, and was paid in money. With this money he bought corn, and fish, and meat, and cheese. And Three-Legs and all owners of things paid Dog-Tooth and Sea-Lion and Big-Fat their share in money. And they paid the guards and watchers in money, and the guards and watchers bought their food with the money. And, because money was cheap, Dog-Tooth made many more men into guards. And, because money was cheap to make, a number of men began to make money out of shell themselves. But the guards stuck spears in them and shot them full of arrows, because they were trying to break up the tribe. It was bad to break up the tribe, for then the Meat-Eaters would come over the divide and kill them all.

"Big-Fat was the voice of God, but he took Broken-Rib and made him into a priest, so that he became the voice of Big-Fat and did most of his talking for him. And both had other men to be servants to them. So, also, did Little-Belly and Three-Legs and Pig-Jaw have other men to lie in the sun about their grass houses and carry messages for them and give commands. And more and more were men taken away from work, so that those that were left worked harder than ever before. It seemed that men desired to do no work and strove to seek out other ways whereby men should work for them. Crooked-Eyes found such a way. He made the first fire-brew out of corn. And thereafter he worked no more, for he talked secretly with Dog-Tooth and Big-Fat and the other masters, and it was agreed that he should be the only one to make fire-brew. But Crooked-Eyes did no work himself. Men made the brew for him, and he paid them in money. Then he sold the fire-brew for money, and all men bought. And many strings of money did he give Dog-Tooth and Sea-Lion and all of them.

"Big-Fat and Broken-rib stood by Dog-Tooth when he took his second wife, and his third wife. They said Dog-Tooth was different from other men and second only to

God that Big-Fat kept in his taboo house, and Dog-Tooth said so, too, and wanted to know who were they to grumble about how many wives he took. Dog-Tooth had a big canoe made, and many more men he took from work, who did nothing and lay in the sun, save only when Dog-Tooth went in the canoe, when they paddled for him. And he made Tiger-Face head man over all the guards, so that Tiger-Face became his right arm, and when he did not like a man Tiger-Face killed that man for him. And Tiger-Face, also, made another man to be his right arm, and to give commands, and to kill for him.

"But this was the strange thing: as the days went by we who were left worked harder and harder, and yet did we get less and less to eat."

"But what of the goats and the corn and the fat roots and the fish-trap," spoke up Afraid-of-the-Dark, "what of all this? Was there not more food to be gained by man's work?"

"It is so," Long-Beard agreed. "Three men on the fish-trap got more fish than the whole tribe before there was a fish-trap. But have I not said we were fools? The more food we were able to get, the less food did we have to eat."

"But was it not plain that the many men who did not work ate it all up?" Yellow-Head demanded.

Long-Beard nodded his head sadly. "Dog-Tooth's dogs were stuffed with meat, and the men who lay in the sun and did no work were rolling in fat, and, at the same time, there were little children crying themselves to sleep with hunger biting them with every wail."

Deer-Runner was spurred by the recital of famine to tear out a chunk of bear-meat and broil it on a stick over the coals. This he devoured with smacking lips, while Long-Beard went on:

"When we grumbled Big-Fat arose, and with the voice of God said that God had chosen the wise men to own the land and the goats and the fish-trap and the fire-brew, and that without these wise men we would all be animals, as in the days when we lived in trees.

"And there arose one who became a singer of songs for the king. Him they called the Bug, because he was small and ungainly of face and limb and excelled not in work or deed. He loved the fattest marrow bones, the choicest fish, the milk warm from the goats, the first corn that was ripe, and the snug place by the fire. And thus, becoming singer of songs to the king, he found a way to do nothing and be fat. And when the people grumbled more and more, and some threw stones at the king's grass house, the Bug sang a song of how good it was to be a Fish-Eater. In his song he told that the Fish-Eaters were the chosen of God and the finest men God had made. He sang of the Meat-Eaters as pigs and crows, and sang how fine and good it was for the Fish-Eaters to fight and die doing God's work, which was the killing of Meat-Eaters. The words of his song were like fire in us, and we clamored to be led against the Meat-Eaters. And we forgot that we were hungry, and why we had grumbled, and were glad to be led by Tiger-Face over the divide, where we killed many Meat-Eaters and were content.

"But things were no better in the Sea Valley. The only way to get food was to work for Three-Legs or Little-Belly or Pig-Jaw; for there was no land that a man might plant with corn for himself. And often there were more men than Three-Legs and the others had work for. So these men went hungry, and so did their wives and children and their old mothers. Tiger-Face said they could become guards if they wanted to, and many of them did, and thereafter they did no work except to poke spears in the men who did work and who grumbled at feeding so many idlers.

"And when we grumbled, ever the Bug sang new songs. He said that Three-Legs and Pig-Jaw and the rest were strong men, and that that was why they had so much. He said that we should be glad to have strong men with us, else would we perish of our own worthlessness and the Meat-Eaters. Therefore, we should be glad to let such strong men have all they could lay hands on. And Big-Fat and Pig-Jaw and Tiger-Face and all the rest said it was true.

" 'All right,' said Long-Fang, 'then will I, too, be a strong man.' And he got himself corn and began to make fire-brew and sell it for strings of money. And, when Crooked-Eyes complained, Long-Fang said that he was himself a strong man, and that if Crooked-Eyes made any more noise he would bash his brains out for him. Whereat Crooked-Eyes was afraid and went and talked with Three-Legs and Pig-Jaw. And all three went and talked to Dog-Tooth. And Dog-Tooth spoke to Sea-Lion, and Sea-Lion sent a runner with a message to Tiger-Face. And Tiger-Face sent his guards, who burned Long-Fang's house along with the fire-brew he had made. Also, they killed him and all his family. And Big-Fat said it was good, and the Bug sang another song about how good it was to observe the law, and what a fine land the Sea Valley was, and how every man who loved the Sea Valley should go forth and kill the bad Meat-Eaters. And again his song was as fire to us, and we forgot to grumble.

"It was very strange. When Little-Belly caught too many fish, so that it took a great many to sell for a little money, he threw many of the fish back into the sea, so that more money would be paid for what was left. And Three-Legs often let many large fields lie idle so as to get more money for his corn. And the women, making so much money out of shell that much money was needed to buy with, Dog-Tooth stopped the making of money. And the women had no work, so they took the places of the men. I worked on the fish-trap, getting a string of money every five days. But my sister now did my work, getting a string of money for every ten days. The women worked cheaper and there was less food, and Tiger-Face said for us to become guards. Only I could not become a guard because I

was lame of one leg and Tier-Face would not have me.
And there were many like me. We were broken men and
only fit to beg for work or to take care of the babies while
the women worked."

Yellow-Head, too, was made hungry by the recital and
broiled a piece of bear-meat on the coals.

"But why didn't you rise up, all of you, and kill Three-
Legs and Pig-Jaw and Big-Fat and the rest and get enough
to eat?" Afraid-of-the-Dark demanded.

"Because we could not understand," Long-Beard answered. "There was too much to think about, and, also,
there were the guards sticking spears into us, and Big-Fat
talking about God, and the Bug singing new songs. And
when any man did think right, and said so, Tiger-Face and
the guards got him, and he was tied out to the rocks at low
tide so that the rising waters drowned him.

"It was a strange thing—the money. It was like the
Bug's songs. It seemed all right, but it wasn't, and we
were slow to understand. Dog-Tooth began to gather the
money in. He put it in a big pile, in a grass house, with
guards to watch it day and night. And the more money he
piled in the house the dearer money became, so that a man
worked a longer time for a string of money than before.
Then, too, there was always talk of war with the Meat-
Eaters, and Dog-Tooth and Tiger-Face filed many houses
with corn, and dried fish, and smoked goat-meat, and
cheese. And with the food piled there in mountains the
people had not enough to eat. But what did it matter?
Whenever the people grumbled too loudly the Bug sang a
new song, and Big-Fat said it was God's word that we
should kill Meat-Eaters, and Tiger-Face led us over the divide to kill and be killed. I was not good enough to be a
guard and lie fat in the sun, but, when we made war,
Tiger-Face was glad to take me along. And when we had
eaten all the food stored in the houses we stopped fighting
and went back to work to pile up more food."

"Then were you all crazy," commented Deer-Runner.

"Then were we indeed all crazy," Long-Beard agreed.

"It was strange, all of it. There was Split-Nose. He said everything was wrong. He said it was true that we grew strong by adding our strength together. And he said that, when we first formed the tribe, it was right that then men whose strength hurt the tribe should be shorn of their strength—men who bashed their brothers' heads and stole their brother's wives. And now, he said the tribe was not getting stronger, but was getting weaker, because there were men with another kind of strength that were hurting the tribe—men who had the strength of the land, like Three-Legs; who had the strength of the fish-trap, like Little-Belly; who had the strength of all the goat meat, like Pig-Jaw. The thing to do, Split-Nose said, was to shear these men of their evil strength; to make them go to work, all of them, and to let no man eat who did not work.

"And the Bug sang another song about men like Split-Nose, who wanted to go back and live in trees.

"Yet Split-Nose said no; that he did not want to go back, but ahead; that they grew strong only as they added their strength together; and that, if the Fish-Eaters would add their strength to the Meat-Eaters, there would be no more fighting and no more watchers and no more guards, and that, with all men working, there would be so much food that each man would have to work not more than two hours a day.

"Then the Bug sang again, and he sang that Split-Nose was lazy, and he sang also the 'Song of the Bees.' It was a strange song, and those who listened were made mad, as from the drinking of strong fire-brew. The song was of a swarm of bees, and of a robber wasp who had come in to live with the bees and who was stealing all their honey. The wasp was lazy and told them there was no need to work; also, he told them to make friends with the bears, who were not honey-stealers but only very good friends. And the Bug sang in crooked words, so that those who listened knew that the swarm was the Sea Valley tribe, that the bears were the Meat-Eaters, and that the lazy wasp was Split-Nose. And, when the Bug sang that the bees listened to the wasp till the swarm was near to perishing, the people growled and snarled, and when the Bug sang that at last the good bees arose and stung the wasp to death, the people picked up stones from the ground and stoned Split-Nose to death till there was naught to be seen of him but the heap of stones they had flung on top of him. And there were many poor people who worked long and hard and had not enough to eat that helped throw the stones on Split-Nose.

"And, after the death of Split-Nose, there was but one other man that dared rise up and speak his mind, and that man was Hair-Face. 'Where is the strength of the strong?' he asked. 'We are the strong, all of us, and we are stronger than Dog-Tooth and Tiger-Face and Three-Legs and Pig-Jaw and all the rest who do nothing and eat much and weaken us by the hurt of their strength which is bad strength. Men who are slaves are not strong. If the man who first found the virtue and use of fire had used his strength we would have been his slaves, as we are the slaves to-day of Little-Belly, who found the virtue and use of the fish-trap; and of the men who found the virtue and use of the land, and the goats, and the fire-brew. Before, we lived in trees, my brothers, and no man was safe. But we fight no more with one another. We have added our strength together. Then let us fight no more with the Meat-Eaters. Let us add our strength and their strength together. Then will we be indeed strong. And then we will go out together, the Fish-Eaters and the Meat-Eaters, and we will kill the tigers and the lions and the wolves and the wild dogs, and we will pasture our goats on all the hillsides and plant our corn and fat roots in all the high mountain valleys. In that day we will be so strong that all the wild animals will flee before us and perish. And nothing will withstand us, for the strength of each man will be the strength of all men in the world.'

"So said Hair-Face, and they killed him, because, they said, he was a wild man and wanted to go back and live in a tree. It was very strange. Whenever a man arose and wanted to go forward all those that stood still said he went backward and should be killed. And the poor people helped stone him, and were fools. We were all fools, except those who were fat and did no work. The fools were called wise, and the wise were stoned. Men who worked did not get enough to eat, and the men who did not work ate too much.

"And the tribe went on losing strength. The children were weak and sickly. And, because we ate not enough, strange sicknesses came among us and we died like flies. And then the Meat-Eaters came upon us. We had followed Tiger-Face too often over the divide and killed them. And now they came to repay in blood. We were too weak and sick to man the big wall. And they killed us, all of us, except some of the women, which they took away with them. The Bug and I escaped, and I hid in the wildest places, and became a hunter of meat and went hungry no more. I stole a wife from the Meat-Eaters, and went to live in the caves of the high mountains where they could not find me. And we had three sons, and each son stole a wife from the Meat-Eaters. And the rest you know, for are you not the sons of my sons?"

"But the Bug?" queried Deer-Runner. "What became of him?"

"He went to live with the Meat-Eaters and to be a singer of songs to the king. He is an old man now, but he sings the same old songs; and, when a man rises up to go forward, he sings that that man is walking backward to live in a tree."

Long Beard dipped into the bear-carcass and sucked with toothless gums at a fist of suet.

"Some day," he said, wiping his hands on his sides, "all the fools with be dead and then all live men will go forward. The strength of the strong will be theirs, and they will add their strength together, so that, of all the men in the world, not one will fight with another. There will be no guards nor watchers on the walls. And all the hunting animals will be killed, and, as Hair-Face said, all the hillsides will be pastured with goats and all the high mountain valleys will be planted with corn and fat roots. And all men will be brothers, and no man will lie idle in the sun and be fed by his fellows. And all that will come to pass in the time when the fools are dead, and when there will be no more singers to stand still and sing the 'Song of the Bees.' Bees are not men."

The Red One

There it was! The abrupt liberation of sound, as he timed it with his watch, Bassett likened to the trump of an archangel. Walls of cities, he meditated, might well fall down before so vast and compelling a summons. For the thousandth time vainly he tried to analyze the tone-quality of that enormous peal that dominated the land far into the strongholds of the surrounding tribes. The mountain gorge which was its source rang to the rising tide of it until it brimmed over and flooded earth and sky and air. With the wantonness of a sick man's fancy, he likened it to the mighty cry of some Titan of the Elder World vexed with misery or wrath. Higher and higher it arose, challenging and demanding in such profounds of volume that it seemed intended for ears beyond the narrow confines of the solar system. There was in it, too, the clamor of protest in that there were no ears to hear and comprehend its utterance.

—Such the sick man's fancy. Still he strove to analyze the sound. Sonorous as thunder was it, mellow as a golden bell, thin and sweet as a thrummed taut cord of silver—no; it was none of these, nor a blend of these. There were no words nor semblances in his vocabulary and experience with which to describe the totality of that sound.

Time passed. Minutes merged into quarters of hours, and quarters of hours into half hours, and still the sound persisted, ever changing from its initial vocal impulse yet never receiving fresh impulse—fading, dimming, dying as enormously as it had sprung into being. It became a confusion of troubled mutterings and babblings and colossal whisperings. Slowly it withdrew, sob by sob, into whatever great bosom had birthed it, until it whimpered deadly whispers of wrath and as equally seductive whispers of delight, striving still to be heard, to convey some cosmic secret, some understanding of infinite import and value. It dwindled to a ghost of sound that had lost its menace and promise, and became a thing that pulsed on in the sick man's consciousness for minutes after it had ceased. When he could hear it no longer, Bassett glanced at his watch. An hour had elapsed ere that archangel's trump had subsided into tonal nothingness.

Was this, then, *his* dark tower?—Bassett pondered, remembering his Browning and gazing at his skeleton-like and fever-wasted hands. And the fancy made him smile—of Childe Roland bearing a slug-horn to his lips with an arm as feeble as his was. Was it months, or years, he asked himself, since he first heard that mysterious call on the beach at Ringmanu? To save himself he could not tell. The long sickness had been most long. In conscious count of time he knew of months, many of them; but he had no way of estimating the long intervals of delirium and stupor. And how fared Captain Bateman of the blackbirder *Nari*? he wondered; and had Captain Bateman's drunken mate died of delirium tremens yet?

From which vain speculations, Bassett turned idly to review all that had occurred since that day on the beach of Ringmanu when he first heard the sound and plunged into the jungle after it. Sagawa had protested. He could see him yet, his queer little monkeyish face eloquent with fear, his back burdened with specimen cases, in his hands Bassett's butterfly net and naturalist's shotgun, as he quavered in Beche de mer English: "Me fella too much fright along bush. Bad fella boy too much stop'm along bush."

Bassett smiled sadly at the recollection. The little New Hanover boy had been frightened, but had proved faithful, following him without hesitancy into the bush in the quest after the source of the wonderful sound. No fire-hollowed tree-trunk, that, throbbing war through the jungle depths, had been Bassett's conclusion. Erroneous had been his next conclusion, namely, that the source or cause could not be more distant than an hour's walk and that he would easily be back by mid-afternoon to be picked up by the *Nari's* whaleboat.

"That big fella noise no good, all the same devil-devil," Sagawa had adjudged. And Sagawa had been right. Had he not had his head hacked off within the day? Bassett shuddered. Without doubt Sagawa had been eaten as well by the bad fella boys too much that stopped along the bush. He could see him, as he had last seen him, stripped of the shotgun and all the naturalist's gear of his master, lying on the narrow trail where he had been decapitated barely the moment before. Yes, within a minute the thing had happened. Within a minute, looking back, Bassett had seen him trudging patiently along under his burdens. Then Bassett's own trouble had come upon him. He looked at the cruelly healed stumps of the first and second fingers of his left hand, then rubbed them softly into the indentation in the back of his skull. Quick as had been the flash of the long-handled tomahawk, he had been quick enough to duck away his head and partially to deflect the stroke with his up-flung hand. Two fingers and a nasty scalp-wound had been the price he paid for his life. With one barrel of his ten-gauge shotgun he had blown the life out of the bushman who had so nearly got him; with the other barrel he had peppered the bushmen bending over Sagawa, and had the pleasure of knowing that the major portion of the charge had gone into the one who leaped away with Sagawa's head. Everything had occurred in a flash. Only himself, the slain bushman, and what remained of Sagawa, were in the narrow, wild-pig run of a path. From the dark jungle on either side came no rustle of movement or sound of life. And he had suffered distinct and dreadful shock. For the first time in his life he had killed a human being, and he knew nausea as he contemplated the mess of his handiwork.

Then had begun the chase. He retreated up the pig-run before his hunters, who were between him and the beach. How many there were, he could not guess. There might have been one, or a hundred, for aught he saw of them. That some of them took to the trees and traveled along through the jungle roof he was certain; but at the most he never glimpsed more than an occasional flitting of shadows. No bow-strings twanged that he could hear; but every little while, whence discharged he knew not, tiny arrows whispered past him or struck tree-boles and fluttered to the ground beside him. They were bone-tipped and feather-shafted, and the feathers, torn from the breasts of hummingbirds, iridesced like jewels.

Once—and now, after the long lapse of time, he chuckled gleefully at the recollection—he had detected a shadow above him that came to instant rest as he turned his gaze upward. He could make out nothing, but, deciding to chance it, had fired at it a heavy charge of number five shot. Squalling like an infuriated cat, the shadow crashed down through tree-ferns and orchids and thudded upon the earth at his feet, and, still squalling its rage and pain, had sunk its human teeth into the ankle of his stout tramping boot. He, on the other hand, was not idle, and with his free foot had done what reduced the squalling to silence. So inured to savagery had Bassett since become, that he chuckled again with the glee of the recollection.

What a night had followed! Small wonder that he had accumulated such a virulence and variety of fevers, he thought, as he recalled that sleepless night of torment, when the throb of his wounds was as nothing compared with the myriad stings of the mosquitoes. There had been no escaping them, and he had not dared to light a fire. They had literally pumped his body full of poison, so that, with the coming of day, eyes swollen almost shut, he had stumbled blindly on, not caring much when his head should be hacked off and his carcass started on the way of Sagawa's to the cooking fire. Twenty-four hours had made a wreck of him—of mind as well as body. He had scarcely retained his wits at all, so maddened was he by the tremendous inoculation of poison he had received. Several times he fired his shotgun with effect into the shadows that dogged him. Stinging day insects and gnats added to his torment, while his bloody wounds attracted hosts of loathsome flies that clung sluggishly to his flesh and had to be brushed off and crushed off.

Once, in that day, he heard again the wonderful sound, seemingly more distant, but rising imperiously above the nearer war-drums in the bush. Right there was where he had made his mistake. Thinking that he had passed beyond it and that, therefore, it was between him and the beach of Ringmanu, he had worked back toward it when in reality he was penetrating deeper and deeper into the mysterious heart of the unexplored island. That night, crawling in among the twisted roots of a banyan tree, he had slept from exhaustion while the mosquitoes had had their will of him.

Followed days and nights that were vague as nightmares in his memory. One clear vision he remembered was of suddenly finding himself in the midst of a bush village and watching the old men and children fleeing into the jungle. All had fled but one. From close at hand and above him, a whimpering as of some animal in pain and terror had startled him. And looking up he had seen her—a girl, or young woman, rather, suspended by one arm in the cooking sun. Perhaps for days she had so hung. Her swollen, protruding tongue spoke as much. Still alive, she gazed at him with eyes of terror. Past help, he decided, as he noted the swellings of her legs which advertised that the joints had been crushed and the great bones broken. He resolved to shoot her, and there the vision terminated. He could not remember whether he had nor not, any more than could he remember how he chanced to be in that village or how he succeeded in getting away from it.

Many pictures, unrelated, came and went in Bassett's mind as he reviewed that period of his terrible wanderings. He remembered invading another village of a dozen houses and driving all before him with his shotgun save for one old man, too feeble to flee, who spat at him and whined and snarled as he dug open a ground-oven and from amid the hot stones dragged forth a roasted pig that steamed its essence deliciously through its green-leaf wrappings. It was at this place that a wantonness of savagery had seized upon him. Having feasted, ready to depart with a hind quarter of the pig in his hand, he deliberately fired the grass thatch of a house with his burning glass.

But seared deepest of all in Bassett's brain, was the dank and noisome jungle. It actually stank with evil, and it was always twilight. Rarely did a shaft of sunlight penetrate its matted roof a hundred feet overhead. And beneath that roof was an aërial ooze of vegetation, a monstrous, parasitic dripping of decadent life-forms that rooted in death and lived on death. And through all this he drifted, ever pursued by the flitting shadows of the anthropophagi, themselves ghosts of evil that dared not face him in battle but that knew, soon or late, that they would feed on him. Bassett remembered that at the time, in lucid moments, he had likened himself to a wounded bull pursued by plains' coyotes too cowardly to battle with him for the meat of him, yet certain of the inevitable end of him when they would be full gorged. As the bull's horns and stamping hoofs kept off the coyotes, so his shotgun kept off these Solomon Islanders, these twilight shades of bushmen of the island of Guadalcanal.

Came the day of the grass lands. Abruptly, as if cloven

by the sword of God in the hand of God, the jungle terminated. The edge of it, perpendicular and as black as the infamy of it, was a hundred feet up and down. And, beginning at the edge of it, grew the grass—sweet, soft, tender, pasture grass that would have delighted the eyes and beasts of any husbandman and that extended, on and on, for leagues and leagues of velvet verdure, to the backbone of the great island, the towering mountain range flung up by some ancient earth-cataclysm, serrated and gullied but not yet erased by the erosive tropic rains. But the grass! He had crawled into it a dozen yards, buried his face in it, smelled it, and broken down in a fit of involuntary weeping.

And, while he wept, the wonderful sound had pealed forth—if by *peal*, he had often thought since, an adequate description could be given of the enunciation of so vast a sound so melting sweet. Sweet it was as no sound ever heard. Vast it was, of so mighty a resonance that it might have proceeded from some brazen-throated monster. And yet it called to him across that leagues-wide savannah, and was like a benediction to his long-suffering, pain-wracked spirit.

He remembered how he lay there in the grass, wet-cheeked but no longer sobbing, listening to the sound and wondering that he had been able to hear it on the beach of Ringmanu. Some freak of air pressures and air currents, he reflected, had made it possible for the sound to carry so far. Such conditions might not happen again in a thousand days or ten thousand days; but the one day it had happened had been the day he landed from the *Nari* for several hours' collecting. Especially had he been in quest of the famed jungle butterfly, a foot across from wing-tip to wing-tip, as velvet-dusky of lack of color as was the gloom of the roof, of such lofty arboreal habits that it resorted only to the jungle roof and could be brought down only by a dose of shot. It was for this purpose that Sagawa had carried the twenty-gauge shotgun.

Two days and nights he had spent crawling across that

belt of grass land. He had suffered much, but pursuit had ceased at the jungle-edge. And he would have died of thirst had not a heavy thunderstorm revived him on the second day.

And then had come Balatta. In the first shade, where the savannah yielded to the dense mountain jungle, he had collapsed to die. At first she had squealed with delight at sight of his helplessness, and was for beating his brain out with a stout forest branch. Perhaps it was his very utter helplessness that had made her refrain. At any rate, she had refrained, for he opened his eyes again under the impending blow, and saw her studying him intently. What especially struck her about him were his blue eyes and white skin. Coolly she had squatted on her hams, spat on his arm, and with her finger-tips scrubbed away the dirt of days and nights of muck and jungle that sullied the pristine whiteness of his skin.

And everything about her had struck him especially, although there was nothing conventional about her at all. He laughed weakly at the recollection, for she had been as innocent of garb as Eve before the fig-leaf adventure. Squat and lean at the same time, asymmetrically limbed, string-muscled as if with lengths of cordage, dirt-caked from infancy save for casual showers, she was as unbeautiful a prototype of woman as he, with a scientist's eye, had ever gazed upon. Her breasts advertised at the one time her maturity and youth; and, if by nothing else, her sex was advertised by the one article of finery with which she was adorned, namely a pig's tail, thrust through a hole in her left ear-lobe. So lately had the tail been severed, that its raw end still oozed blood that dried upon her shoulder like so much candle-droppings. And her face! A twisted and wizened complex of apish features, perforated by upturned, sky-open, Mongolian nostrils, by a mouth that sagged from a huge upper lip and faded precipitately into a retreating chin, and by peering querulous eyes that blinked as blink the eyes of denizens of monkey-cages.

Not even the water she brought him in a forest-leaf, and

the ancient and half-putrid chunk of roast pig, could redeem in the slightest the grotesque hideousness of her. When he had eaten weakly for a space, he closed his eyes in order not to see her, although again and again she poked them open to peer at the blue of them. Then had come the sound. Nearer, much nearer, he knew it to be; and he knew equally well, despite the weary way he had come, that it was still many hours distant. The effect of it on her had been startling. She cringed under it, with averted face, moaning and chattering with fear. But after it had lived its full life of an hour, he closed his eyes and fell asleep with Balatta brushing the flies from him.

When he awoke it was night, and she was gone. But he was aware of renewed strength, and, by then too thoroughly inoculated by the mosquito poison to suffer further inflammation, he closed his eyes and slept an unbroken stretch till sun-up. A little later Balatta had returned, bringing with her a half dozen women who, unbeautiful as they were, were patently not so unbeautiful as she. She evidenced by her conduct that she considered him her find, her property, and the pride she took in showing him off would have been ludicrous had his situation not been so desperate.

Later, after what had been to him a terrible journey of miles, when he collapsed in front of the devil-devil house in the shadow of the breadfruit tree, she had shown very lively ideas on the matter of retaining possession of him. Ngurn, whom Bassett was to know afterward as the devil-devil doctor, priest, or medicine man of the village, had wanted his head. Others of the grinning and chattering monkey-men, all as stark of clothes and bestial of appearance as Balatta, had wanted his body for the roasting oven. At that time he had not understood their language, if by *language* might be dignified the uncouth sounds they made to represent ideas. But Bassett had thoroughly understood the matter of debate, especially when the men pressed and prodded and felt of the flesh of him as if he were so much commodity in a butcher's stall.

Balatta had been losing the debate rapidly, when the accident happened. One of the men, curiously examining Bassett's shotgun, managed to cock and pull a trigger. The recoil of the butt into the pit of the man's stomach had not been the most sanguinary result, for the charge of shot, at a distance of a yard, had blown the head of one of the debaters into nothingness.

Even Balatta joined the others in flight, and, ere they returned, his senses already reeling from the oncoming fever-attack, Bassett had regained possession of the gun. Whereupon, although his teeth chattered with the ague and his swimming eyes could scarcely see, he held onto his fading consciousness until he could intimidate the bushmen with the simple magics of compass, watch, burning glass, and matches. At the last, with due emphasis of solemnity and awfulness, he had killed a young pig with his shotgun and promptly fainted.

Bassett flexed his arm-muscles in quest of what possible strength might reside in such weakness, and dragged himself slowly and totteringly to his feet. He was shockingly emaciated; yet, during the various convalescences of the many months of his long sickness, he had never regained quite the same degree of strength as this time. What he feared was another relapse such as he had already frequently experienced. Without drugs, without even quinine, he had managed so far to live through a combination of the most pernicious and most malignant of malarial and black-water fevers. But could he continue to endure? Such was his everlasting query. For, like the genuine scientist he was, he would not be content to die until he had solved the secret of the sound.

Supported by a staff, he staggered the few steps to the devil-devil house where death and Ngurn reigned in gloom. Almost as infamously dark and evil-stinking as the jungle was the devil-devil house—in Bassett's opinion. Yet therein was usually to be found his favorite crony and gossip, Ngurn, always willing for a yarn or a discussion, the while he sat in the ashes of death and in a slow smoke shrewdly revolved curing human heads suspended from the rafters. For, through the months' interval of consciousness of his long sickness, Bassett had mastered the psychological simplicities and lingual difficulties of the language of the tribe of Ngurn and Balatta, and Gngngn—the latter the addle-headed young chief who was ruled by Ngurn, and who, whispered intrigue had it, was the son of Ngurn.

"Will the Red One speak to-day?" Bassett asked, by this time so accustomed to the old man's gruesome occupation as to take even an interest in the progress of the smoke-curing.

With the eye of an expert Ngurn examined the particular head he was at work upon.

"It will be ten days before I can say 'finish,'" he said. "Never has any man fixed heads like these."

Bassett smiled inwardly at the old fellow's reluctance to talk with him of the Red One. It had always been so. Never, by any chance, had Ngurn or any other member of the weird tribe divulged the slightest hint of any physical characteristic of the Red One. Physical the Red One must be, to emit the wonderful sound, and though it was called the Red One, Bassett could not be sure that red represented the color of it. Red enough were the deeds and powers of it, from what abstract clews he had gleaned. Not alone, had Ngurn informed him, was the Red One more bestial powerful than the neighbor tribal gods, ever a-thirst for the red blood of living human sacrifices, but the neighbor gods themselves were sacrificed and tormented before him. He was the god of a dozen allied villages similar to this one, which was the central and commanding village of the federation. By virtue of the Red One many alien villages had been devastated and even wiped out, the prisoners sacrificed to the Red One. This was true to-day, and it extended back into old history carried down by word of mouth through the generations. When he, Ngurn, had been a young man, the tribes beyond the grass lands had made a war raid. In the counter raid, Ngurn and his fighting folk had made many prisoners. Of children alone over five score living had been bled white before the Red One, and many, many more men and women.

The Thunderer, was another of Ngurn's names for the mysterious deity. Also at times was he called The Loud Shouter, The God-Voiced, The Bird-Throated, The One with the Throat Sweet as the Throat of the Honey-Bird, The Sun Singer, and The Star-Born.

Why The Star Born? In vain Bassett interrogated Ngurn. According to that old devil-devil doctor, the Red One had always been, just where he was at present, forever singing and thundering his will over men. But Ngurn's father, wrapped in decaying grass-matting and hanging even then over their heads among the smoky rafters of the devil-devil house, had held otherwise. That departed wise one had believed that the Red One came from out of the starry night, else why—so his argument had run—had the old and forgotten ones passed his name down as the Star-Born? Bassett could not but recognize something cogent in such argument. But Ngurn affirmed the long years of his long life, wherein he had gazed upon many starry nights, yet never had he found a star on grass land or in jungle depth—and he had looked for them. True, he had beheld shooting stars (this in reply to Bassett's contention); but likewise had he beheld the phosphorescence of fungoid growths and rotten meat and fireflies on dark nights, and the flames of wood-fires and of blazing candle-nuts; yet what were flame and blaze and glow when they had flamed, and blazed and glowed? Answer: memories, memories only, of things which had ceased to be, like memories of matings accomplished, of feasts forgotten, of desires that were the ghosts of desires, flaring, flaming, burning, yet unrealized in achievement of easement and satisfaction. Where was the appetite of yesterday? the roasted flesh of the wild pig the hunter's arrow failed to slay? the maid, unwed and dead, ere the young man knew her?

A memory was not a star, was Ngurn's contention. How

could a memory be a star? Further, after all his long life he still observed the starry night-sky unaltered. Never had he noted the absence of a single star from its accustomed place. Besides, stars were fire, and the Red One was not fire—which last involuntary betrayal told Bassett nothing.

"Will the Red One speak to-morrow?" he queried.

Ngurn shrugged his shoulders as who should say.

"And the day after?—and the day after that?" Bassett persisted.

"I would like to have the curing of your head," Ngurn changed the subject. "It is different from any other head. No devil-devil has a head like it. Besides, I would cure it well. I would take months and months. The moons would come and the moons would go, and the smoke would be very slow, and I should myself gather the materials for the curing smoke. The skin would not wrinkle. It would be as smooth as your skin now."

He stood up, and from the dim rafters grimed with the smoking of countless heads, where day was no more than a gloom, took down a matting-wrapped parcel and began to open it.

"It is a head like yours," he said, "but it is poorly cured."

Bassett had pricked up his ears at the suggestion that it was a white man's head; for he had long since come to accept that these jungle-dwellers, in the midmost center of the great island, had never had intercourse with white men. Certainly he had found them without the almost universal Beche de mer English of the west South Pacific. Nor had they knowledge of tobacco, nor of gunpowder. Their few precious knives, made from lengths of hoop-iron, and their few and more precious tomahawks, made from cheap trade hatchets, he had surmised they had captured in war from the bushmen of the jungle beyond the grass lands, and that they, in turn, had similarly gained them from the salt water men who fringed the coral beaches of the shore and had contact with the occasional white men.

"The folk in the out beyond do not know how to cure

heads," old Ngurn explained, as he drew forth from the filthy matting and placed in Bassett's hands an indubitable white man's head.

Ancient it was beyond question; white it was as the blond hair attested. He could have sworn it once belonged to an Englishman, and to an Englishman of long before by token of the heavy gold circlets still threaded in the withered ear-lobes.

"Now your head . . ." the devil-devil doctor began on his favorite topic.

"I'll tell you what," Bassett interrupted, struck by a new idea. "When I die I'll let you have my head to cure, if, first, you take me to look upon the Red One."

"I will have your head anyway when you are dead," Ngurn rejected the proposition. He added, with the brutal frankness of the savage: "Besides, you have not long to live. You are almost a dead man now. You will grow less strong. In not many months I shall have you here turning and turning in the smoke. It is pleasant, through the long afternoons, to turn the head of one you have known as well as I know you. And I shall talk to you and tell you the many secrets you want to know. Which will not matter, for you will be dead."

"Ngurn," Bassett threatened in sudden anger. "You know the Baby Thunder in the Iron that is mine." (This was in reference to his all-potent and all-awful shotgun.) "I can kill you any time, and then you will not get my head."

"Just the same, will Gngngn, or some one else of my folk get it," Ngurn complacently assured him. "And just the same will it turn and turn here in the devil-devil house in the smoke. The quicker you slay me with your Baby Thunder, the quicker will your head turn in the smoke."

And Bassett knew he was beaten in the discussion.

What was the Red One?—Bassett asked himself a thousand times in the succeeding week, while he seemed to grow stronger. What was the source of the wonderful sound? What was this Sun Singer, this Star-Born One, this mysterious deity, as bestial-conducted as the black and kinky-headed and monkey-like human beasts who worshiped it, and whose silver-sweet, bull-mouthed singing and commanding he had heard at the taboo distance for so long?

Ngurn had he failed to bribe with the inevitable curing of his head when he was dead. Gngngn, imbecile and chief that he was, was too imbecilic, too much under the sway of Ngurn, to be considered. Remained Balatta, who, from the time she found him and poked his blue eyes open to recrudescence of her grotesque, female hideousness, had continued his adorer. Woman she was, and he had long known that the only way to win from her treason to her tribe was through the woman's heart of her.

Bassett was a fastidious man. He had never recovered from the initial horror caused by Balatta's female awfulness. Back in England, even at best, the charm of woman, to him, had never been robust. Yet now, resolutely, as only a man can do who is capable of martyring himself for the cause of science, he proceeded to violate all the fineness and delicacy of his nature by making love to the unthinkably disgusting bushwoman.

He shuddered, but with averted face hid his grimaces and swallowed his gorge as he put his arm around her dirt-crusted shoulders and felt the contact of her rancid-oily and kinky hair with his neck and chin. But he nearly screamed when she succumbed to that caress so at the very first of the courtship and mowed and gibbered and squealed little, queer, pig-like gurgly noises of delight. It was too much. And the next he did in the singular courtship was to take her down to the stream and give her a vigorous scrubbing.

From then on he devoted himself to her like a true swain as frequently and for as long at a time as his will could override his repugnance. But marriage, which she ardently suggested, with due observance of tribal custom, he balked at. Fortunately, taboo rule was strong in the tribe. Thus, Ngurn could never touch bone, or flesh, or hide of crocodile. This had been ordained at his birth. Gngngn was denied ever the touch of woman. Such pollution, did it chance to occur, could be purged only by the death of the offending female. It had happened once, since Bassett's arrival, when a girl of nine, running in play, stumbled and fell against the sacred chief. And the girl-child was seen no more. In whispers, Balatta told Bassett that she had been three days and nights in dying before the Red One. As for Balatta, the breadfruit was taboo to her. For which Bassett was thankful. The taboo might have been water.

For himself, he fabricated a special taboo. Only could he marry, he explained, when the Southern Cross rode highest in the sky. Knowing his astronomy, he thus gained a reprieve of nearly nine months; and he was confident that within that time he would either be dead or escaped to the coast with full knowledge of the Red One and of the source of the Red One's wonderful voice. At first he had fancied the Red One to be some colossal statue, like Memnon, rendered vocal under certain temperature conditions of sunlight. But when, after a war raid, a batch of prisoners was brought in and the sacrifice made at night, in the midst of rain, when the sun could play no part, the Red One had been more vocal than usual, Bassett discarded that hypothesis.

In company with Balatta, sometimes with men and parties of women, the freedom of the jungle was his for three quadrants of the compass. But the fourth quadrant, which contained the Red One's abiding place, was taboo. He made more thorough love to Balatta—also saw to it that she scrubbed herself more frequently. Eternal female she was, capable of any treason for the sake of love. And, though the sight of her was provocative of nausea and the contact of her provocative of despair, although he could not escape her awfulness in his dream-haunted nightmares of her, he nevertheless was aware of the cosmic verity of sex that animated her and that made her own life of less value than the happiness of her lover with whom she hoped to mate. Juliet or Balatta? Where was the intrinsic difference? The soft and tender product of ultra-civilization, or her bestial prototype of a hundred thousand years before her?—there was no difference.

Bassett was a scientist first, a humanist afterward. In the jungle-heart of Guadalcanal he put the affair to the test, as in the laboratory he would have put to the test any chemical reaction. He increased his feigned ardor for the bushwoman, at the same time increasing the imperiousness of his will of desire over her to be led to look upon the Red One face to face. It was the old story, he recognized, that the woman must pay, and it occurred when the two of them, one day, were catching the unclassified and unnamed little black fish, an inch long, half-eel and half-scaled, rotund with salmon-golden roe, that frequented the fresh water and that were esteemed, raw and whole, fresh or putrid, a perfect delicacy. Prone in the muck of the decaying jungle-floor, Balatta threw herself, clutching his ankles with her hands, kissing his feet and making slubbery noises that chilled his backbone up and down again. She begged him to kill her rather than exact this ultimate love-payment. She told him of the penalty of breaking the taboo of the Red One—a week of torture, living, the details of which she yammered out from her face in the mire until he realized that he was yet a tyro in knowledge of the frightfulness the human was capable of wreaking on the human.

Yet did Bassett insist on having his man's will satisfied, at the woman's risk, that he might solve the mystery of the Red One's singing, though she should die long and horribly and screaming. And Balatta, being mere woman, yielded. She led him into the forbidden quadrant. An abrupt mountain, shouldering in from the north to meet a similar intrusion from the south, tormented the stream in which they had fished into a deep and gloomy gorge. After a mile along the gorge, the way plunged sharply upward until they crossed a saddle of raw limestone which attracted his geologist's eye. Still climbing, although he paused often from sheer physical weakness, they scaled

forest-clad heights until they emerged on a naked mesa or
tableland. Bassett recognized the stuff of its composition
as black volcanic sand, and knew that a pocket magnet
could have captured a full load of the sharply angular
grains he trod upon.

And then, holding Balatta by the hand and leading her
onward, he came to it—a tremendous pit, obviously artificial, in the heart of the plateau. Old history, the South Seas
Sailing Directions, scores of remembered data and conno-
tations swift and furious, surged through his brain. It was
Mendana who had discovered the islands and named them
Solomon's, believing that he had found that monarch's fa-
bled mines. They had laughed at the old navigator's child-
like credulity; and yet here stood himself, Bassett, on the
rim of an excavation for all the world like the diamond
pits of South Africa.

But no diamond this that he gazed down upon. Rather
was it a pearl, with the depth of iridescence of a pearl; but
of a size all pearls of earth and time welded into one,
could not have totaled; and of a color undreamed of any
pearl, or of anything else, for that matter, for it was the
color of the Red One. And the Red One himself Bassett
knew it to be on the instant. A perfect sphere, fully two
hundred feet in diameter, the top of it was a hundred feet
below the level of the rim. He likened the color quality of
it to lacquer. Indeed, he took it to be some sort of lacquer,
applied by man, but a lacquer too marvelously clever to
have been manufactured by the bush-folk. Brighter than
bright cherry-red, its richness of color was as if it were red
builded upon red. It glowed and iridesced in the sunlight
as if gleaming up from underlay under underlay of red.

In vain Balatta strove to dissuade him from descending.
She threw herself in the dirt; but, when he continued down
the trail that spiraled the pit-wall, she followed, cringing
and whimpering her terror. That the red sphere had been
dug out as a precious thing, was patent. Considering the
paucity of members of the federated twelve villages and
their primitive tools and methods, Bassett knew that the

toil of a myriad generations could scarcely have made that enormous excavation.

He found the pit bottom carpeted with human bones, among which, battered and defaced, lay village gods of wood and stone. Some, covered with obscene totemic figures and designs, were carved from solid tree trunks forty or fifty feet in length. He noted the absence of the shark and turtle gods, so common among the shore villages, and was amazed at the constant recurrence of the helmet motive. What did these jungle savages of the dark heart of Guadalcanal know of helmets? Had Mendana's men-at-arms worn helmets and penetrated here centuries before? And if not, then whence had the bush-folk caught the motive?

Advancing over the litter of gods and bones, Balatta whimpering at his heels, Bassett entered the shadow of the Red One and passed on under its gigantic overhang until he touched it with his finger-tips. No lacquer that. Nor was the surface smooth as it should have been in the case of lacquer. On the contrary, it was corrugated and pitted, with here and there patches that showed signs of heat and fusing. Also, the substance of it was metal, though unlike any metal or combination of metals he had ever known. As for the color itself, he decided it to be no application. It was the intrinsic color of the metal itself.

He moved his finger-tips, which up to that had merely rested, along the surface, and felt the whole gigantic sphere quicken and live and respond. It was incredible! So light a touch on so vast a mass! Yet did it quiver under the finger-tip caress in rhythmic vibrations that became whisperings and rustlings and mutterings of sound—but of sound so different; so elusive thin that it was shimmeringly sibilant; so mellow that it was maddening sweet, piping like an elfin horn, which last was just what Bassett decided would be like a peal from some bell of the gods reaching earthward from across space.

He looked to Balatta with swift questioning; but the

voice of the Red One he had evoked had flung her face-downward and moaning among the bones. He returned to contemplation of the prodigy. Hollow it was, and of no metal known on earth, was his conclusion. It was right-named by the ones of old-time as the Star-Born. Only from the stars could it have come, and no thing of chance was it. It was a creation of artifice and mind. Such perfection of form, such hollowness that it certainly possessed, could not be the result of mere fortuitousness. A child of intelligences, remote and unguessable, working corporally in metals, it indubitably was. He stared at it in amaze, his brain a racing wild-fire of hypotheses to account for this far-journeyer who had adventured the night of space, threaded the stars, and now rose before him and above him, exhumed by patient anthropophagi, pitted and lacquered by its fiery bath in two atmospheres.

But was the color a lacquer of heat upon some familiar metal? Or was it an intrinsic quality of the metal itself? He thrust in the blade-point of his pocket-knife to test the constitution of the stuff. Instantly the entire sphere burst into a mighty whispering, sharp with protest, almost twanging goldenly if a whisper could possibly be considered to twang, rising higher, sinking deeper, the two extremes of the registry of sound threatening to complete the circle and coalesce into the bull-mouthed thundering he had so often heard beyond the taboo distance.

Forgetful of safety, of his own life itself, entranced by the wonder of the unthinkable and unguessable thing, he raised his knife to strike heavily from a long stroke, but was prevented by Balatta. She upreared on her own knees in an agony of terror, clasping his knees and supplicating him to desist. In the intensity of her desire to impress him, she put her forearm between her teeth and sank them to the bone.

He scarcely observed her act, although he yielded automatically to his gentler instincts and withheld the knife-hack. To him, human life had dwarfed to microscopic

proportions before this colossal portent of higher life form
within the distances of the sidereal universe. As had she
been a dog, he kicked the ugly little bushwoman to her
feet and compelled her to start with him on an encircle-
ment of the base. Part way around, he encountered horrors.
Even, among the others, did he recognize the sun-shriveled
remnant of the nine-years girl who had accidentally broken
Chief Gngngn's personality taboo. And, among what was
left of these that had passed, he encountered what was left
of one who had not yet passed. Truly had the bush-folk
named themselves into the name of the Red One, seeing in
him their own image which they strove to placate and
please with such red offerings.

Farther around, always treading the bones and images of
humans and gods that constituted the floor of this ancient
charnel house of sacrifice, he came upon the device by
which the Red One was made to send his call singing
thunderingly across the jungle-belts and grass-lands to the
far beach of Ringmanu. Simple and primitive was it as
was the Red One's consummate artifice. A great king-post,
half a hundred feet in length, seasoned by centuries of su-
perstitious care, carven into dynasties of gods, each super-
imposed, each helmeted, each seated in the open mouth of
a crocodile, was slung by ropes, twisted of climbing vegetable parasites, from the apex of a tripod of three great
forest trunks, themselves carved into grinning and grotesque adumbrations of man's modern concepts of art and
god. From the striker king-post, were suspended ropes of
climbers to which men could apply their strength and direction. Like a battering ram, this king-post could be
driven end-onward against the mighty, red-iridescent
sphere.

Here was where Ngurn officiated and functioned reli-
giously for himself and the twelve tribes under him.
Bassett laughed aloud, almost with madness, at the thought
of this wonderful messenger, winged with intelligence
across space, to fall into a bushman stronghold and be

worshiped by ape-like, mean-eating and head-hunting savages. It was as if God's Word had fallen into the muck mire of the abyss underlying the bottom of hell; as if Jehovah's Commandments had been presented on carved stone to the monkeys of the monkey cage at the Zoo; as if the Sermon on the Mount had been preached in a roaring bedlam of lunatics.

The slow weeks passed. The nights, by election, Bassett spent on the ashen floor of the devil-devil house, beneath the ever-swinging, slow-curing heads. His reason for this was that it was taboo to the lesser sex of woman, and, therefore, a refuge for him from Balatta, who grew more persecutingly and perilously loverly as the Southern Cross rode higher in the sky and marked the imminence of her nuptials. His days Bassett spent in a hammock swung under the shade of the great breadfruit tree before the devil-devil house. There were breaks in this program, when, in the comas of his devastating fever-attacks, he lay for days and nights in the house of heads. Ever he struggled to combat the fever, to live, to continue to live, to grow strong and stronger against the day when he would be strong enough to dare the grass-lands and the belted jungle beyond, and win to the beach, and to some labor-recruiting, black-birding ketch or schooner, and on to civilization and the men of civilization, to whom he could give news of the message from other words that lay, darkly worshiped by beast-men, in the black heart of Guadalcanal's mid-most center.

On other nights, lying late under the breadfruit tree, Bassett spent long hours watching the slow setting of the western stars beyond the black wall of jungle where it had been thrust back by the clearing for the village. Possessed of more than a cursory knowledge of astronomy, he took a sick man's pleasure in speculating as to the dwellers on the unseen worlds of those incredibly remote suns, to haunt whose houses of light, life came forth, a shy visitant, from the rayless crypts of matter. He could no more apprehend limits to time than bounds to space. No subversive radium speculations had shaken his steady scientific faith in the conservation of energy and the indestructibility of matter. Always and forever must there have been stars. And surely, in that cosmic ferment, all must be comparatively alike, comparatively of the same substance, or substances, save for the freaks of the ferment. All must obey, or compose, the same laws that ran without infraction through the entire experience of man. Therefore, he argued and agreed, must worlds and life be appanages to all the suns as they were appanges to the particular sun of his own solar system.

Even as he lay here, under the breadfruit tree, an intelligence that stared across the starry gulfs, so must all the universe be exposed to the ceaseless scrutiny of innumerable eyes, like his, though grantedly different, with behind them, by the same token, intelligences that questioned and sought the meaning and the construction of the whole. So reasoning, he felt his soul go forth in kinship with that august company, that multitude whose gaze was forever upon the arras of infinity.

Who were they, what were they, those far distant and superior ones who had bridged the sky with their gigantic, red-iridescent, heaven-singing message? Surely, and long since, had they, too, trod the path on which man had so recently, by the calendar of the cosmos, set his feet. And to be able to send such a message across the pit of space, surely they had reached those heights to which man, in tears and travail and bloody sweat, in darkness and confusion of many counsels, was so slowly struggling. And what were they on their heights? Had they won Brotherhood? Or had they learned that the law of love imposed the penalty of weakness and decay? Was strife, life? Was the rule of all the universe the pitiless rule of natural selection? And, and most immediately and poignantly, were their far conclusions, their long-won wisdoms, shut even then in the huge, metallic heart of the Red One, waiting for the first earth-man to read? Of one thing he was certain: No drop of red dew shaken from the lion-mane of some sun in torment, was the sounding sphere. It was of design, not chance, and it contained the speech and wisdom of the stars.

What engines and elements and mastered forces, what lore and mysteries and destiny-controls, might be there! Undoubtedly, since so much could be inclosed in so little a thing as the foundation stone of public building, this enormous sphere should contain vast histories, profounds of research achieved beyond man's wildest guesses, laws and formulæ that, easily mastered, would make man's life on earth, individual and collective, spring up from its present mire to inconceivable heights of purity and power. It was Time's greatest gift to blindfold, insatiable, and sky-aspiring man. And to him, Bassett, had been vouchsafed the lordly fortune to be the first to receive this message from man's interstellar kin!

No white man, much less no outland man of the other bush-tribes, had gazed upon the Red One and lived. Such the law expounded by Ngurn to Bassett. There was such a thing as blood brotherhood, Bassett, in return, had often argued in the past. But Ngurn had stated solemnly no. Even the blood brotherhood was outside the favor of the Red One. Only a man born within the tribe could look upon the Red One and live. But now, his guilty secret known only to Balatta, whose fear of immolation before the Red One fast-sealed her lips, the situation was different. What he had to do was to recover from the abominable fevers that weakened him and gain to civilization. Then would he lead an expedition back, and, although the entire population of Guadalcanal be destroyed, extract from the heart of the Red One the message of the world from other worlds.

But Bassett's relapses grew more frequent, his brief convalescences less and less vigorous, his periods of coma longer, until he came to know, beyond the last promptings of the optimism inherent in so tremendous a constitution as his own, that he would never live to cross the grass lands, perforate the perilous coast jungle, and reach the sea. He faded as the Southern Cross rose higher in the sky, till even Balatta knew that he would be dead ere the nuptial date determined by his taboo. Ngurn made pilgrimage personally and gathered the smoke materials for the curing of Bassett's head, and to him made proud announcement and exhibition of the artistic perfectness of his intention when Bassett should be dead. As for himself, Bassett was not shocked. Too long and too deeply had life ebbed down in him to bite him with fear of its impending extinction. He continued to persist, alternating periods of unconsciousness with periods of semi-consciousness, dreamy and unreal, in which he idly wondered whether he had ever truly beheld the Red One or whether it was a nightmare fancy of delirium.

Came the day when all mists and cobwebs dissolved, when he found his brain clear as a bell, and took just appraisement of his body's weakness. Neither hand nor foot could he lift. So little control of his body did he have, that he was scarcely aware of possessing one. Lightly indeed his flesh sat upon his soul, and his soul, in its briefness of clarity, knew by its very clarity, that the black of cessation was near. He knew the end was close; knew that in all truth he had with his eyes beheld the Red One, the messenger between the worlds; knew that he would never live to carry that message to the world—that message, for aught to the contrary, which might already have waited man's hearing in the heart of Guadalcanal for ten thousand years. And Bassett stirred with resolve, calling Ngurn to him, out under the shade of the breadfruit tree, and with the old devil-devil doctor discussing the terms and arrangements of his last life effort, his final adventure in the quick of the flesh.

"I know the law, O Ngurn," he concluded the matter.

"Whoso is not of the folk may not look upon the Red One and live. I shall not live anyway. Your young men shall carry me before the face of the Red One, and I shall look upon him, and hear his voice, and thereupon die, under your hand, O Ngurn. Thus will the three things be satisfied: the law, my desire, and your quicker possession of my head for which all your preparations wait."

To which Ngurn consented, adding:

"It is better so. A sick man who cannot get well is foolish to live on for so little a while. Also, is it better for the living that he should go. You have been much in the way of late. Not but what it was good for me to talk to such a wise one. But for moons of days we have held little talk. Instead, you have taken up room in the house of heads, making noises like a dying pig, or talking much and loudly in your own language which I do not understand. This has been a confusion to me, for I like to think on the great things of the light and dark as I turn the heads in the smoke. Your much noise has thus been a disturbance to the long-learning and hatching of the final wisdom that will be mine before I die. As for you, upon whom the dark has already brooded, it is well that you die now. And I promise you, in the long days to come when I turn your head in the smoke, no man of the tribe shall come in to disturb us. And I will tell you many secrets, for I am an old man and very wise, and I shall be adding wisdom to wisdom as I turn your head in the smoke."

So a litter was made, and, borne on the shoulders of half a dozen of the men, Bassett departed on the last little adventure that was to cap the total adventure, for him, of living. With a body of which he was scarcely aware, for even the pain had been exhausted out of it, and with a bright clear brain that accommodated him to a quiet ecstasy of sheer lucidity of thought, he lay back on the lurching litter and watched the fading of the passing world, beholding for the last time the breadfruit tree before the devil-devil house, the dim day beneath the matted jungle roof, the gloomy gorge between the shouldering mountains, the saddle of raw limestone, and the mesa of black, volcanic sand.

Down the spiral path of the pit they bore him, encircling the sheening, glowing Red One that seemed ever imminent to iridesce from the color and light into sweet singing and thunder. And over bones and logs of immolated men and gods they bore him, past the horrors of other immolated ones that yet lived, to the three-king-post tripod and the huge king-post striker.

Here Bassett, helped by Ngurn and Balatta, weakly sat up, swaying weakly from the hips, and with clear, unfaltering, all-seeing eyes gazed upon the Red One.

"Once, O Ngurn," he said, not taking his eyes from the sheening, vibrating surface whereon and wherein all the shades of cherry-red played unceasingly, ever a-quiver to change into sound, to become silken rustlings, silvery whisperings, golden thrummings of cords, velvet pipings of elfland, mellow-distances of thunderings.

"I wait," Ngurn prompted after a long pause, the long-handled tomahawk unassumingly ready in his hand.

"Once, O Ngurn," Bassett repeated, "let the Red One speak so that I may see it speak as well as hear it. Then strike, thus, when I raise my hand; for, when I raise my hand, I shall drop my head forward and make place for the stroke at the base of my neck. But, O Ngurn, I, who am about to pass out of the light of day forever, would like to pass with the wonder-voice of the Red One singing greatly in my ears."

"And I promise you that never will a head be so well cured as yours," Ngurn assured him, at the same time signaling the tribesmen to man the propelling ropes suspended from the king-post striker. "Your head shall be my greatest piece of work in the curing of heads."

Bassett smiled quietly to the old one's conceit, as the great carved log, drawn back through two-score feet of space, was released. The next moment he was lost in ecstasy at the abrupt and thunderous liberation of sound. But such thunder! Mellow it was with preciousness of all sounding metals. Archangels spoke in it; it was magnificently beautiful before all other sounds; it was invested with the intelligence of supermen of planets of other suns; it was the voice of God, seducing and commanding to be heard. And—the everlasting miracle of that interstellar metal! Bassett, with his own eyes, saw color and colors transform into sound till the whole visible surface of the vast sphere was a-crawl and titillant and vaporous with what he could not tell was color or was sound. In that moment the interstices of matter were his, and the interfusings and intermating transfusing of matter and force.

Time passed. At the last Bassett was brought back from his ecstasy by an impatient movement of Ngurn. He had quite forgotten the old devil-devil one. A quick flash of fancy brought a husky chuckle into Bassett's throat. His shotgun lay beside him in the litter. All he had to do, muzzle to head, was press the trigger and blow his head into nothingness.

But why cheat him? was Bassett's next thought. Head-hunting, cannibal beast of a human that was as much ape as human, nevertheless Old Ngurn had, according to his lights, played squarer than square. Ngurn was in himself a fore-runner of ethics and contract, of consideration, and gentleness in man. No, Bassett decided; it would be a ghastly pity and an act of dishonor to cheat the old fellow at the last. His head was Ngurn's, and Ngurn's head to cure it would be.

And Bassett, raising his hand in signal, bending forward his head as agreed so as to expose cleanly the articulation to his taut spinal cord, forgot Balatta, who was merely a woman, a woman merely and only and undesired. He knew, without seeing, when the razor-edged hatchet rose in the air behind him. And for that instant, ere the end, there fell upon Bassett the shadow of the Unknown, a sense of impending marvel of the rending of walls before the imaginable. Almost, when he knew the blow had started and just ere the edge of steel bit the flesh and nerves, it seemed that he gazed upon the serene face of the Medusa, Truth—And, simultaneous with the bite of the steel on the onrush of the dark, in a flashing instant of fancy, he saw the vision of his head turning slowly, always turning, in the devil-devil house beside the breadfruit tree.

The Wit of Porportuk

El-Soo had been a Mission girl. Her mother had died when she was very small, and Sister Alberta had plucked El-Soo as a brand from the burning, one summer day, and carried her away to the Holy Cross Mission and dedicated her to God. El-Soo was a full-blooded Indian, yet she exceeded all the half-breed and quarter-breed girls. Never had the good sisters dealt with a girl so adaptable and at the same time so spirited.

El-Soo was quick, and deft, and intelligent; but above all she was fire, the living flame of life, a blaze of personality that was compounded of will, sweetness, and daring. Her father was a chief, and his blood ran in her veins. Obedience, on the part of El-Soo, was a matter of terms and arrangement. She had a passion for equity, and perhaps it was because of this that she excelled in mathematics.

But she excelled in other things. She learned to read and write English as no girl had ever learned in the Mission. She led the girls in singing, and into song she carried her sense of equity. She was an artist, and the fire of her flowed toward creation. Had she from birth enjoyed a more favorable environment, she would have made literature or music.

Instead, she was El-Soo, daughter of Klakee-Nah, a chief, and she lived in the Holy Cross Mission where were no artists, but only pure-souled Sisters who were interested in cleanliness and righteousness and the welfare of the spirit in the land of immortality that lay beyond the skies.

The years passed. She was eight years old when she entered the Mission; she was sixteen, and the Sisters were corresponding with their superiors in the Order concerning the sending of El-Soo to the United States to complete her education, when a man of her own tribe arrived at Holy Cross and had talk with her. El-Soo was somewhat appalled by him. He was dirty. He was a Caliban-like creature, primitively ugly, with a mop of hair that had never been combed. He looked at her disapprovingly and refused to sit down.

"Thy brother is dead," he said, shortly.

El-Soo was not particularly shocked. She remembered little of her brother. "Thy father is an old man, and alone," the messenger went on. "His house is large and empty, and he would hear thy voice and look upon thee."

Him she remembered—Klakee-Nah, the head-man of the village, the friend of the missionaries and the traders, a large man thewed like a giant, with kindly eyes and masterful ways, and striding with a consciousness of crude royalty in his carriage.

"Tell him that I will come," was El-Soo's answer.

Much to the despair of the Sisters, the brand plucked from the burning went back to the burning. All pleading with El-Soo was vain. There was much argument, expostulation, and weeping. Sister Alberta even revealed to her the project of sending her to the United States. El-Soo stared wide-eyed into the golden vista thus opened up to her, and shook her head. In her eyes persisted another vista. It was the mighty curve of the Yukon at Tana-naw

Station, with the St. George Mission on one side, and the trading post on the other, and midway between the Indian village and a certain large log house where lived an old man tended upon by slaves.

All dwellers on the Yukon bank for twice a thousand miles knew the large log house, the old man and the tending slaves; and well did the Sisters know the house, its unending revelry, its feasting and its fun. So there was weeping at Holy Cross when El-Soo departed.

There was a great cleaning up in the large house when El-Soo arrived. Klakee-Nah, himself masterful, protested at this masterful conduct of his young daughter; but in the end, dreaming barbarically of magnificence, he went forth and borrowed a thousand dollars from old Porportuk, than whom there was no richer Indian on the Yukon. Also, Klakee-Nah ran up a heavy bill at the trading post. El-Soo re-created the large house. She invested it with new splendor, while Klakee-Nah maintained its ancient traditions of hospitality and revelry.

All this was unusual for a Yukon Indian, but Klakee-Nah was an unusual Indian. Not alone did he like to render inordinate hospitality, but, what of being a chief and acquiring much money, he was able to do it. In the primitive trading days he had been a power over his people, and he had dealt profitably with the white trading companies. Later on, with Porportuk, he had made a gold-strike on the Koyokuk River. Klakee-Nah was by training and nature an aristocrat. Porportuk was bourgeois, and Porportuk bought him out of the gold-mine. Porportuk was content to plod and accumulate. Klakee-Nah went back to his large house and proceeded to spend. Porportuk was known as the richest Indian in Alaska. Klakee-Nah was known as the whitest. Porportuk was a money-lender and a usurer. Klakee-Nah was an anachronism—a medival ruin, a fighter and a feaster, happy with wine and song.

El-Soo adapted herself to the large house and its ways as readily as she had adapted herself to Holy Cross Mission and its ways. She did not try to reform her father and direct his footsteps toward God. It is true, she reproved him when he drank overmuch and profoundly, but that was for the sake of his health and the direction of his footsteps on solid earth.

The latchstring to the large house was always out. What with the coming and the going, it was never still. The rafters of the great living-room shook with the roar of wassail and of song. At table sat men from all the world and chiefs from distant tribes—Englishmen and Colonials, lean Yankee traders and rotund officials of the great companies, cowboys from the Western ranges, sailors from the sea, hunters and dog-mushers of a score of nationalities.

El-Soo drew breath in a cosmopolitan atmosphere. She could speak English as well as she could her native tongue, and she sang English songs and ballads. The passing Indian ceremonials she knew, and the perishing traditions. The tribal dress of the daughter of a chief she knew how to wear upon occasion. But for the most part she dressed as white women dress. Not for nothing was her needlework at the Mission and her innate artistry. She carried her clothes like a white woman, and she made clothes that could be so carried.

In her way she was as unusual as her father, and the position she occupied was as unique as his. She was the one Indian woman who was the social equal with the several white women at Tana-naw Station. She was the one Indian woman to whom white men honorably made proposals of marriage. And she was the one Indian woman whom no white man ever insulted.

For El-Soo was beautiful—not as white women are beautiful, not as Indian women are beautiful. It was the flame of her, that did not depend upon feature, that was her beauty. So far as mere line and feature went, she was the classic Indian type. The black hair and the fine bronze were hers, and the black eyes, brilliant and bold, keen as sword-light, proud; and hers the delicate eagle nose with the thin, quivering nostrils, the high cheek-bones that were not broad apart, and the thin lips that were not too thin.

But over all and through all poured the flame of her—the unanalyzable something that was fire and that was the soul of her, that lay mellow-warm or blazed in her eyes, that sprayed the cheeks of her, that distended the nostrils, that curled the lip, or, when the lip was in repose, that was still there in the lip, the lip palpitant with its presence.

And El-Soo had wit—rarely sharp to hurt, yet quick to search out forgivable weakness. The laughter of her mind played like lambent flame over all about her, and from all about her arose answering laughter. Yet she was never the centre of things. This she would not permit. The large house, and all of which it was significant, was her father's; and through it, to the last, moved his heroic figure—host, master of the revels, and giver of the law. It is true, as the strength oozed from him, that she caught up responsibilities from his failing hands. But in appearance he still ruled, dozing oft-times at the board, a bacchanalian ruin, yet in all seeming the ruler of the feast.

And through the large house moved the figure of Porportuk, ominous, with shaking head, coldly disapproving, paying for it all. Not that he really paid, for he compounded interest in weird ways, and year by year absorbed the properties of Klakee-Nah. Porportuk once took it upon himself to chide El-Soo upon the wasteful way of life in the large house—it was when he had about absorbed the last of Klakee-Nah's wealth—but he never ventured so to chide again. El-Soo, like her father, was an aristocrat, as disdainful of money as he, and with an equal sense of honor as finely strung.

Porportuk continued grudgingly to advance money, and ever the money flowed in golden foam away. Upon one thing El-Soo was resolved—her father should die as he had lived. There should be for him no passing from high to low, no diminution of the revels, no lessening of the lavish hospitality. When there was famine, as of old, the Indians came groaning to the large house and went away content. When there was famine and no money, money was borrowed from Porportuk, and the Indians still went away content. El-Soo might well have repeated, after the aristocrats of another time and place, that after her came the deluge. In her case the deluge was old Porportuk. With every advance of money, he looked upon her with a more possessive eye, and felt bourgeoning within him ancient fires.

But El-Soo had no eyes for him. Nor had she eyes for the white men who wanted to marry her at the Mission with ring and priest and book. For at Tana-naw Station was a young man, Akoon, of her own blood, and tribe, and village. He was strong and beautiful in her eyes, a great hunter, and, in that he had wandered far and much, very poor; he had been to all the unknown wastes and places; he had journeyed to Sitka and to the United States; he had crossed the continent to Hudson Bay and back again, and as seal-hunter on a ship he had sailed to Siberia and for Japan.

When he returned from the gold-strike in Klondike he came, as was his wont, to the large house to make report to old Klakee-Nah of all the world that he had seen; and there he first saw El-Soo, three years back from the Mission. Thereat, Akoon wandered no more. He refused a wage of twenty dollars a day as pilot on the big steamboats. He hunted some and fished some, but never far from Tana-naw Station, and he was at the large house often and long. And El-Soo measured him against many men and found him good. He sang songs to her, and was ardent and glowed until all Tana-naw Station knew he loved her. And Porportuk but grinned and advanced more money for the upkeep of the large house.

Then came the death table of Klakee-Nah. He sat at feast, with death in his throat, that he could not drown with wine. And laughter and joke and song went around, and Akoon told a story that made the rafters echo. There were no tears or sighs at that table. It was no more than fit that Klakee-Nah should die as he had lived, and none knew this better than El-Soo, with her artist sympathy. The old roystering crowd was there, and, as of old, three frost-bitten sailors were there, fresh from the long traverse from the Arctic, survivors of a ship's company of seventy-four. At Klakee-Nah's back were four old men, all that were left him of the slaves of his youth. With rheumy eyes they saw to his needs, with palsied hands filling his glass or striking him on the back between the shoulders when death stirred and he coughed and gasped.

It was a wild night, and as the hours passed and the fun laughed and roared along, death stirred more restlessly in Klakee-Nah's throat. Then it was that he sent for Porportuk. And Porportuk came in from the outside frost to look with disapproving eyes upon the meat and wine on the table for which he had paid. But as he looked down the length of flushed faces to the far end and saw the face of El-Soo, the light in his eyes flared up, and for a moment the disapproval vanished.

Place was made for him at Klakee-Nah's side, and a glass placed before him. Klakee-Nah, with his own hands, filled the glass with fervent spirits. "Drink!" he cried. "Is it not good?"

And Porportuk's eyes watered as he nodded his head and smacked his lips.

"When, in your own house, have you had such drink?" Klakee-Nah demanded.

"I will not deny that the drink is good to this old throat of mine," Porportuk made answer, and hesitated for the speech to complete the thought.

"But it costs overmuch," Klakee-Nah roared, completing it for him.

Porportuk winced at the laughter that went down the table. His eyes burned malevolently. "We were boys together, of the same age," he said. "In your throat is death. I am still alive and strong."

An ominous murmur arose from the company. Klakee-Nah coughed and strangled, and the old slaves smote him between the shoulders. He emerged gasping, and waved his hand to still the threatening rumble.

"You have grudged the very fire in your house because the wood cost overmuch!" he cried. "You have grudged life. To live cost overmuch, and you have refused to pay the price. Your life has been like a cabin where the fire is out and there are no blankets on the floor." He signalled to a slave to fill his glass, which he held aloft. "But I have lived. And I have been warm with life as you have never been warm. It is true, you shall live long. But the longest nights are the cold nights when a man shivers and lies awake. My nights have been short, but I have slept warm."

He drained the glass. The shaking hand of a slave failed to catch it as it crashed to the floor. Klakee-Nah sank back, panting, watching the upturned glasses at the lips of the drinkers, his own lips slightly smiling to the applause. At a sign, two slaves attempted to help him sit upright again. But they were weak, his frame was mighty, and the four old men tottered and shook as they helped him forward.

"But manner of life is neither here nor there," he went on. "We have our business, Porportuk, you and I, to-night. Debts are mischances, and I am in mischance with you. What of my debt, and how great is it?"

Porportuk searched in his pouch and brought forth a memorandum. He sipped at his glass and began. "There is the note of August, 1889, for three hundred dollars. The interest has never been paid. And the note of the next year for five hundred dollars. This note was included in the note of two months later for a thousand dollars. Then there is the note—"

"Never mind the many notes!" Klakee-Nah cried out impatiently. "They make my head go around and all the things inside my head. The whole! The round whole! How much is it?"

Porportuk referred to his memorandum. "Fifteen thousand nine hundred and sixty-seven dollars and seventy-five cents," he read with careful precision.

"Make it sixteen thousand, make it sixteen thousand," Klakee-Nah said grandly. "Odd numbers were ever a worry. And now—and it is for this that I have sent for you—make me out a new note for sixteen thousand, which I shall sign. I have no thought of the interest. Make it as large as you will, and make it payable in the next world, when I shall meet you by the fire of the Great Father of all Indians. Then the note will be paid. This I promise you. It is the word of Klakee-Nah."

Porportuk looked perplexed, and loudly the laughter arose and shook the room. Klakee-Nah raised his hands. "Nay," he cried. "It is not a joke. I but speak in fairness. It was for this I sent for you, Porportuk. Make out the note."

"I have no dealings with the next world," Porportuk made answer slowly.

"Have you no thought to meet me before the Great Father!" Klakee-Nah demanded. Then he added, "I shall surely be there."

"I have no dealings with the next world," Porportuk repeated sourly.

The dying man regarded him with frank amazement.

"I know naught of the next world," Porportuk explained. "I do business in this world."

Klakee-Nah's face cleared. "This comes of sleeping cold of nights," he laughed. He pondered for a space, then said, "It is in this world that you must be paid. There remains to me this house. Take it, and burn the debt in the candle there."

"It is an old house and not worth the money," Porportuk made answer.

"There are my mines on the Twisted Salmon."

"They have never paid to work," was the reply.

"There is my share in the steamer *Koyokuk*. I am half owner."

"She is at the bottom of the Yukon."

Klakee-Nah started. "True, I forgot. It was last spring when the ice went out." He mused for a time, while the glasses remained untasted, and all the company waited upon his utterance.

"Then it would seem I owe you a sum of money which I cannot pay . . . in this world?" Porportuk nodded and glanced down the table.

"Then it would seem that you, Porportuk, are a poor business man," Klakee-Nah said slyly. And boldly Porportuk made answer, "No; there is security yet untouched."

"What!" cried Klakee-Nah. "Have I still property? Name it, and it is yours, and the debt is no more."

"There it is." Porportuk pointed at El-Soo.

Klakee-Nah could not understand. He peered down the table, brushed his eyes, and peered again.

"Your daughter, El-Soo—her will I take and the debt be no more. I will burn the debt there in the candle."

Klakee-Nah's great chest began to heave. "Ho! ho!—a joke—Ho! ho! ho!" he laughed Homerically. "And with your cold bed and daughters old enough to be the mother of El-Soo! Ho! ho! ho!" He began to cough and strangle, and the old slaves smote him on the back. "Ho! ho!" he began again, and went off into another paroxysm.

Porportuk waited patiently, sipping from his glass and studying the double row of faces down the board. "It is no joke," he said finally. "My speech is well meant."

Klakee-Nah sobered and looked at him, then reached for his glass, but could not touch it. A slave passed it to him, and glass and liquor he flung into the face of Porportuk.

"Turn him out!" Klakee-Nah thundered to the waiting table that strained like a pack of hounds in leash. "And roll him in the snow!"

As the mad riot swept past him and out of doors, he signalled to the slaves, and the four tottering old men supported him on his feet as he met the returning revellers, upright, glass in hand, pledging them a toast to the short night when a man sleeps warm.

It did not take long to settle the estate of Klakee-Nah. Tommy, the little Englishman, clerk at the trading post, was called in by El-Soo to help. There was nothing but debts, notes overdue, mortgaged properties, and properties mortgaged but worthless. Notes and mortgages were held by Porportuk. Tommy called him a robber many times as he pondered the compounding of the interest.

"Is it a debt, Tommy?" El-Soo asked.

"It is a robbery," Tommy answered.

"Nevertheless, it is a debt," she persisted.

The winter wore away, and the early spring, and still the claims of Porportuk remained unpaid. He saw El-Soo often and explained to her at length, as he had explained to her father, the way the debt could be cancelled. Also, he brought with him old medicine-men, who elaborated to her the everlasting damnation of her father if the debt were not paid. One day, after such an elaboration, El-Soo made final announcement to Porportuk.

"I shall tell you two things," she said. "First, I shall not be your wife. Will you remember that? Second, you shall be paid the last cent of the sixteen thousand dollars—"

"Fifteen thousand nine hundred and sixty-seven dollars and seventy-five cents," Porportuk corrected.

"My father said sixteen thousand," was her reply. "You shall be paid."

"How?"

"I know not how, but I shall find out how. Now go, and bother me no more. If you do"—she hesitated to find fitting penalty—"if you do, I shall have you rolled in the snow again as soon as the first snow flies."

This was still in the early spring, and a little later El-Soo surprised the country. Word went up and down the Yukon from Chilcoot to the Delta, and was carried from camp to camp to the farthermost camps, that in June, when the first salmon ran, El-Soo, daughter of Klakee-Nah, would sell herself at public auction to satisfy the claims of Porportuk. Vain were the attempts to dissuade her. The missionary at St. George wrestled with her, but she replied:—

"Only the debts to God are settled in the next world. The debts of men are of this world, and in this world are they settled."

Akoon wrestled with her, but she replied: "I do love thee, Akoon; but honor is greater than love, and who am I that I should blacken my father?" Sister Alberta journeyed all the way up from Holy Cross on the first steamer, and to no better end.

"My father wanders in the thick and endless forests," said El-Soo. "And there will he wander, with the lost souls crying, till the debt be paid. Then, and not until then, may he go on to the house of the Great Father."

"And you believe this?" Sister Alberta asked.

"I do not know," El-Soo made answer. "It was my father's belief."

Sister Alberta shrugged her shoulders incredulously.

"Who knows but that the things we believe come true?" El-Soo went on. "Why not? The next world to you may be heaven and harps . . . because you have believed heaven and harps; to my father the next world may be a large house where he will sit always at table feasting with God."

"And you?" Sister Alberta asked. "What is your next world?"

El-Soo hesitated but for a moment. "I should like a little of both," she said. "I should like to see your face as well as the face of my father."

The day of the auction came. Tana-naw Station was populous. As was their custom, the tribes had gathered to await the salmon-run, and in the meantime spent the time in dancing and frolicking, trading and gossiping. Then there was the ordinary sprinkling of white adventurers, traders, and prospectors, and, in addition, a large number of white men who had come because of curiosity or interest in the affair.

It had been a backward spring, and the salmon were late in running. This delay but keyed up the interest. Then, on the day of the auction, the situation was made tense by Akoon. He arose and made public and solemn announcement that whosoever bought El-Soo would forthwith and immediately die. He flourished the Winchester in his hand to indicate the manner of the taking-off. El-Soo was angered threat; but he refused to speak with her, and went to the trading post to lay in extra ammunition.

The first salmon was caught at ten o'clock in the evening, and at midnight the auction began. It took place on top of the high bank alongside the Yukon. The sun was due north just below the horizon, and the sky was lurid red. A great crowd gathered about the table and the two chairs that stood near the edge of the bank. To the fore were many white men and several chiefs. And most prominently to the fore, rifle in hand, stood Akoon. Tommy, at El-Soo's request, served as auctioneer, but she made the opening speech and described the goods about to be sold. She was in native costume, in the dress of a chief's daughter, splendid and barbaric, and she stood on a chair, that she might be seen to advantage.

"Who will buy a wife?" she asked. "Look at me. I am twenty years old and a maid. I will be a good wife to the man who buys me. If he is a white man, I shall dress in the fashion of white women; if he is an Indian, I shall dress as"—she hesitated a moment—"a squaw. I can make my own clothes, and sew, and wash, and mend. I was taught for eight years to do these things at Holy Cross Mission. I can read and write English, and I know how to play the organ. Also I can do arithmetic and some algebra—a little. I shall be sold to the highest bidder, and to him I will make out a bill of sale of myself. I forgot to say that I can sing very well, and that I have never been sick in my life. I weigh one hundred and thirty-two pounds; my father is dead and I have no relatives. Who wants me?"

She looked over the crowd with flaming audacity and stepped down. At Tommy's request she stood upon the chair again, while he mounted the second chair and started the bidding.

Surrounding El-Soo stood the four old slaves of her father. They were age-twisted and palsied, faithful to their meat, a generation out of the past that watched unmoved the antics of younger life. In the front of the crowd were several Eldorado and Bonanza kings from the Upper Yukon, and beside them, on crutches, swollen with scurvy, were two broken prospectors. From the midst of the crowd, thrust out by its own vividness, appeared the face of a wild-eyed squaw from the remote regions of the Upper Tana-naw; a strayed Sitkan from the coast stood side by side with a Stick from Lake Le Barge, and, beyond, a half-dozen French-Canadian voyageurs, grouped by themselves. From afar came the faint cries of myriads of wild-fowl on the nesting-grounds. Swallows were skimming up overhead from the placid surface of the Yukon, and robins were singing. The oblique rays of the hidden sun shot through the smoke, high-dissipated from forest fires a thousand miles away, and turned the heavens to sombre red, while the earth shone red in the reflected glow. This red glow shone in the faces of all, and made everything seem unearthly and unreal.

The bidding began slowly. The Sitkan, who was a stranger in the land and who had arrived only half an hour before, offered one hundred dollars in a confident voice, and was surprised when Akoon turned threateningly upon him with the rifle. The bidding dragged. An Indian from the Tozikakat, a pilot, bid one hundred and fifty, and after some time a gambler, who had been ordered out of the Upper Country, raised the bid to two hundred. El-Soo was saddened; her pride was hurt; but the only effect was that she flamed more audaciously upon the crowd.

There was a disturbance among the onlookers as Porportuk forced his way to the front. "Five hundred dollars!" he bid in a loud voice, then looked about him proudly to note the effect.

He was minded to use his great wealth as a bludgeon with which to stun all competition at the start. But one of the voyageurs, looking on El-Soo with sparkling eyes, raised the bid a hundred.

"Seven hundred!" Porportuk returned promptly.

And with equal promptness came the "Eight hundred," of the voyageur.

Then Porportuk swung his club again. "Twelve hundred!" he shouted.

With a look of poignant disappointment, the voyageur succumbed. There was no further bidding. Tommy worked hard, but could not elicit a bid.

El-Soo spoke to Porportuk. "It were good, Porportuk, for you to weigh well your bid. Have you forgotten the thing I told you—that I would never marry you!"

"It is a public auction," he retorted. "I shall buy you with a bill of sale. I have offered twelve hundred dollars. You come cheap."

"Too damned cheap!" Tommy cried. "What if I am auctioneer? That does not prevent me from bidding. I'll make it thirteen hundred."

"Fourteen hundred," from Porportuk.

"I'll buy you in to be my—my sister," Tommy whispered to El-Soo, then called aloud, "Fifteen hundred!"

At two thousand, one of the Eldorado kings took a hand, and Tommy dropped out.

A third time Porportuk swung the club of his wealth, making a clean raise of five hundred dollars. But the Eldorado king's pride was touched. No man could club him. And he swung back another five hundred.

El-Soo stood at three thousand. Porportuk made it thirty-five hundred, and gasped when the Eldorado king raised it a thousand dollars. Porportuk again raised it five hundred, and again gasped when the king raised a thousand more.

Porportuk became angry. His pride was touched; his strength was challenged, and with him strength took the form of wealth. He would not be ashamed for weakness before the world. El-Soo became incidental. The savings and scrimpings from the cold nights of all his years were ripe to be squandered. El-Soo stood at six thousand. He made it seven thousand. And then, in thousand-dollar bids, as fast as they could be uttered, her price went up. At fourteen thousand the two men stopped for breath.

Then the unexpected happened. A still heavier club was swung. In the pause that ensued, the gambler, who had scented a speculation and formed a syndicate with several of his fellows, bid sixteen thousand dollars.

"Seventeen thousand," Porportuk said weakly.

"Eighteen thousand," said the king.

Porportuk gathered his strength. "Twenty thousand."

The syndicate dropped out. The Eldorado king raised a thousand, and Porportuk raised back; and as they did, Akoon turned from one to the other, half menacingly, half curiously, as though to see what manner of man it was that he would have to kill. When the king prepared to make his next bid, Akoon having pressed closer, the king first loosed the revolver at his hip, then said:—

"Twenty-three thousand."

"Twenty-four thousand," said Porportuk. He grinned viciously, for the certitude of his bidding had at last shaken the king. The latter moved over close to El-Soo. He studied her carefully, for a long while.

"And five hundred," he said at last.

"Twenty-five thousand," came Porportuk's raise.

The king looked for a long space, and shook his head. He looked again, and said reluctantly, "And five hundred."

"Twenty-six thousand," Porportuk snapped.

The king shook his head and refused to meet Tommy's pleading eye. In the meantime Akoon had edged close to Porportuk. El-Soo's quick eye noted this, and, while Tommy wrestled with the Eldorado king for another bid, she bent, and spoke in a low voice in the ear of a slave. And while Tommy's "Going—going—going—" dominated the air, the slave went up to Akoon and spoke in a low voice in his ear. Akoon made no sign that he had heard, though El-Soo watched him anxiously.

"Gone!" Tommy's voice rang out. "To Porportuk, for twenty-six thousand dollars."

Porportuk glanced uneasily at Akoon. All eyes were centred upon Akoon, but he did nothing.

"Let the scales be brought," said El-Soo.

"I shall make payment at my house," said Porportuk.

"Let the scales be brought," El-Soo repeated. "Payment shall be made here where all can see."

So the gold-scales were brought from the trading post, while Porportuk went away and came back with a man at his heels, on whose shoulders was a weight of gold-dust in moose-hide sacks. Also, at Porportuk's back, walked another man with a rifle, who had eyes only for Akoon.

"Here are the notes and mortgages," said Porportuk, "for fifteen thousand nine hundred and sixty-seven dollars and seventy-five cents."

El-Soo received them into her hands and said to Tommy, "Let them be reckoned as sixteen thousand."

"There remains ten thousand dollars to be paid in gold," Tommy said.

Porportuk nodded, and untied the mouths of the sacks. El-Soo, standing at the edge of the bank, tore the papers to shreds and sent them fluttering out over the Yukon. The weighing began, but halted.

"Of course, at seventeen dollars," Porportuk had said to Tommy, as he adjusted the scales.

"At sixteen dollars," El-Soo said sharply.

"It is the custom of all the land to reckon gold at seventeen dollars for each ounce," Porportuk replied. "And this is a business transaction."

El-Soo laughed. "It is a new custom," she said. "It began this spring. Last year, and the years before, it was sixteen dollars an ounce. When my father's debt was made, it was sixteen dollars. When he spent at the store the money he got from you, for one ounce he was given sixteen dollars' worth of flour, not seventeen. Wherefore, shall you pay for me at sixteen, and not at seventeen." Porportuk grunted and allowed the weighing to proceed.

"Weigh it in three piles, Tommy," she said. "A thousand dollars here, three thousand here, and here six thousand."

It was slow work, and, while the weighing went on, Akoon was closely watched by all.

"He but waits till the money is paid," one said; and the word went around and was accepted, and they waited for what Akoon should do when the money was paid. And Porportuk's man with the rifle waited and watched Akoon.

The weighing was finished, and the gold-dust lay on the table in three dark-yellow heaps. "There is a debt of my father to the Company for three thousand dollars," said El-Soo. "Take it, Tommy, for the Company. And here are four old men, Tommy. You know them. And here is one thousand dollars. Take it, and see that the old men are never hungry and never without tobacco."

Tommy scooped the gold into separate sacks. Six thousand dollars remained on the table. El-Soo thrust the scoop into the heap, and with a sudden turn whirled the contents out and down to the Yukon in a golden shower. Porportuk seized her wrist as she thrust the scoop a second time into the heap.

"It is mine," she said calmly. Porportuk released his grip, but he gritted his teeth and scowled darkly as she continued to scoop the gold into the river till none was left.

The crowd had eyes for naught but Akoon, and the rifle of Porportuk's man lay across the hollow of his arm, the muzzle directed at Akoon a yard away, the man's thumb on the hammer. But Akoon did nothing.

"Make out the bill of sale," Porportuk said grimly.

And Tommy made out the bill of sale, wherein all right and title in the woman El-Soo was vested in the man

Porportuk. El-Soo signed the document, and Porportuk folded it and put it away in his pouch. Suddenly his eyes flashed, and in sudden speech he addressed El-Soo.

"But it was not your father's debt," he said. "What I paid was the price for you. Your sale is business of to-day and not of last year and the years before. The ounces paid for you will buy at the post to-day seventeen dollars of flour, and not sixteen. I have lost a dollar on each ounce. I have lost six hundred and twenty-five dollars."

El-Soo thought for a moment, and saw the error she had made. She smiled, and then she laughed.

"You are right," she laughed. "I made a mistake. But it is too late. You have paid, and the gold is gone. You did not think quick. It is your loss. Your wit is slow these days, Porportuk. You are getting old."

He did not answer. He glanced uneasily at Akoon, and was reassured. His lips tightened, and a hint of cruelty came into his face. "Come," he said, "we will go to my house."

"Do you remember the two things I told you in the spring?" El-Soo asked, making no movement to accompany him.

"My head would be full with the things women say, did I heed them," he answered.

"I told you that you would be paid," El-Soo went on carefully. "And I told you that I would never be your wife."

"But that was before the bill of sale." Porportuk crackled the paper between his fingers inside the pouch. "I have bought you before all the world. You belong to me. You will not deny that you belong to me."

"I belong to you," El-Soo said steadily.

"I own you."

"You own me."

Porportuk's voice rose slightly and triumphantly. "As a dog, I own you."

"As a dog you own me," El-Soo continued calmly. "But, Porportuk, you forget the thing I told you. Had any other man bought me, I should have been that man's wife. I should have been a good wife to that man. Such was my will. But my will with you was that I should never be your wife. Wherefore, I am your dog."

Porportuk knew that he played with fire, and he resolved to play firmly. "Then I speak to you, not as El-Soo, but as a dog," he said; "and I tell you to come with me." He half reached to grip her arm, but with a gesture she held him back.

"Not so fast, Porportuk. You buy a dog. The dog runs away. It is your loss. I am your dog. What if I run away?"

"As the owner of the dog, I shall beat you—"

"When you catch me?"

"When I catch you."

"Then catch me."

He reached swiftly for her, but she eluded him. She laughed as she circled around the table. "Catch her!" Porportuk commanded the Indian with the rifle, who stood near to her. But as the Indian stretched forth his arm to her, the Eldorado king felled him with a fist blow under the ear. The rifle clattered to the ground. Then was Akoon's chance. His eyes glittered, but he did nothing.

Porportuk was an old man, but his cold nights retained for him his activity. He did not circle the table. He came across suddenly, over the top of the table. El-Soo was taken off her guard. She sprang back with a sharp cry of alarm, and Porportuk would have caught her had it not been for Tommy. Tommy's leg went out. Porportuk tripped and pitched forward on the ground. El-Soo got her start.

"Then catch me," she laughed over her shoulder, as she fled away.

She ran lightly and easily, but Porportuk ran swiftly and savagely. He outran her. In his youth he had been swiftest of all the young men. But El-Soo dodged in a willowy, elusive way. Being in native dress, her feet were not cluttered with skirts, and her pliant body curved a flight that defied the gripping fingers of Porportuk.

With laughter and tumult, the great crowd scattered out

to see the chase. It led through the Indian encampment;
and ever dodging, circling, and reversing, El-Soo and Porportuk appeared and disappeared among the tents. El-Soo
seemed to balance herself against the air with her arms,
now one side, now on the other, and sometimes her body,
too, leaned out upon the air far from the perpendicular as
she achieved her sharpest curves. And Porportuk, always a
leap behind, or a leap this side or that, like a lean hound
strained after her.

They crossed the open ground beyond the encampment
and disappeared in the forest. Tana-naw Station waited
their reappearance, and long and vainly it waited.

In the meantime Akoon ate and slept, and lingered
much at the steamboat landing, deaf to the rising resent-
ment of Tana-naw Station in that he did nothing. Twenty-
four hours later Porportuk returned. He was tired and
savage. He spoke to no one but Akoon, and with him tried
to pick a quarrel. But Akoon shrugged his shoulders and
walked away. Porportuk did not waste time. He outfitted
half a dozen of the young men, selecting the best trackers
and travellers, and at their head plunged into the forest.

Next day the steamer *Seattle*, bound up river, pulled in
to the shore and wooded up. When the lines were cast off
and she churned out from the bank, Akoon was on board
in the pilot-house. Not many hours afterward, when it was
his turn at the wheel, he saw a small birch-bark canoe put
off from the shore. There was only one person in it. He
studied it carefully, put the wheel over, and slowed down.

The captain entered the pilot-house. "What's the matter?" he demanded. "The water's good."

Akoon grunted. He saw a larger canoe leaving the bank,
and in it were a number of persons. As the *Seattle* lost
headway, he put the wheel over some more.

The captain fumed. "It's only a squaw," he protested.

Akoon did not grunt. He was all eyes for the squaw and
the pursuing canoe. In the latter six paddles were flashing,
while the squaw paddled slowly.

"You'll be aground," the captain protested, seizing the wheel.

But Akoon countered his strength on the wheel and looked him in the eyes. The captain slowly released the spokes.

"Queer beggar," he sniffed to himself.

Akoon held the *Seattle* on the edge of the shoal water and waited till he saw the squaw's fingers clutch the forward rail. Then he signalled for full speed ahead and ground the wheel over. The large canoe was very near, but the gap between it and the steamer was widening.

The squaw laughed and leaned over the rail. "Then catch me, Porportuk!" she cried.

Akoon left the steamer at Fort Yukon. He outfitted a small poling-boat and went up the Porcupine River. And with him went El-Soo. It was a weary journey, and the way led across the backbone of the world; but Akoon had travelled it before. When they came to the head-waters of the Porcupine, they left the boat and went on foot across the Rocky Mountains.

Akoon greatly liked to walk behind El-Soo and watch the movement of her. There was a music in it that he loved. And especially he loved the well-rounded calves in their sheaths of soft-tanned leather, the slim ankles, and the small moccasined feet that were tireless through the longest days.

"You are light as air," he said, looking up at her. "It is no labor for you to walk. You almost float, so lightly do your feet rise and fall. You are like a deer, El-Soo; you are like a deer, and your eyes are like deer's eyes, sometimes when you look at me, or when you hear a quick sound and wonder if it be danger that stirs. Your eyes are like a deer's eyes now as you look at me."

And El-Soo, luminous and melting, bent and kissed Akoon.

"When we reach the Mackenzie, we will not delay," Akoon said later. "We will go south before the winter catches us. We will go to the sunlands where there is no snow. But we will return. I have seen much of the world, and there is no land like Alaska, no sun like our sun, and the snow is good after the long summer."

"And you will learn to read," said El-Soo.

And Akoon said, "I will surely learn to read."

But there was delay when they reached the Mackenzie. They fell in with a band of Mackenzie Indians and, hunting, Akoon was shot by accident. The rifle was in the hands of a youth. The bullet broke Akoon's right arm and, ranging farther, broke two of his ribs. Akoon knew rough surgery, while El-Soo had learned some refinements at Holy Cross. The bones were finally set, and Akoon lay by the fire for them to knit. Also, he lay by the fire so that the smoke would keep the mosquitoes away.

Then it was that Porportuk, with his six young men, arrived. Akoon groaned in his helplessness and made appeal to the Mackenzies. But Porportuk made demand, and the Mackenzies were perplexed. Porportuk was for seizing upon El-Soo, but this they would not permit. Judgment must be given, and, as it was an affair of man and woman, the council of the old men was called—this that warm judgment might not be given by the young men, who were warm of heart.

The old men sat in a circle about the smudge-fire. Their faces were lean and wrinkled, and they gasped and panted for air. The smoke was not good for them. Occasionally they struck with withered hands at the mosquitoes that braved the smoke. After such exertion they coughed hollowly and painfully. Some spat blood, and one of them sat a bit apart with head bowed forward, and bled slowly and continuously at the mouth; the coughing sickness had gripped them. They were as dead men; their time was short. It was a judgment of the dead.

"And I paid for her a heavy price," Porportuk concluded his complaint. "Such a price you have never seen. Sell all that is yours—sell your spears and arrows and rifles, sell your skins and furs, sell your tents and boats and dogs, sell everything, and you will not have maybe a thousand dollars. Yet did I pay for the woman, El-Soo, twenty-six times the price of all your spears and arrows and rifles, your skins and furs, your tents and boats and dogs. It was a heavy price."

The old men nodded gravely, though their weazened eyeslits widened with wonder that any woman should be worth such a price. The one that bled at the mouth wiped his lips. "Is it true talk?" he asked each of Porportuk's six young men. And each answered that it was true.

"Is it true talk?" he asked El-Soo, and she answered, "It is true."

"But Porportuk has not told that he is an old man," Akoon said, "and that he has daughters older than El-Soo."

"It is true, Porportuk is an old man," said El-Soo.

"It is for Porportuk to measure the strength of his age," said he who bled at the mouth. "We be old men. Behold! Age is never so old as youth would measure it."

And the circle of old men champed their gums, and nodded approvingly, and coughed.

"I told him that I would never be his wife," said El-Soo.

"Yet you took from him twenty-six times all that we possess?" asked a one-eyed old man.

El-Soo was silent.

"It is true?" And his one eye burned and bored into her like a fiery gimlet.

"It is true," she said.

"But I will run away again," she broke out passionately, a moment later. "Always will I run away."

"That is for Porportuk to consider," said another of the old men. "It is for us to consider the judgment."

"What price did you pay for her?" was demanded of Akoon.

"No price did I pay for her," he answered. "She was above price. I did not measure her in gold-dust, nor in dogs, and tents, and furs."

The old men debated among themselves and mumbled in undertones. "These old men are ice," Akoon said in English. "I will not listen to their judgment, Porportuk. If you take El-Soo, I will surely kill you."

The old men ceased and regarded him suspiciously. "We do not know the speech you make," one said.

"He but said that he would kill me," Porportuk volunteered. "So it were well to take from him his rifle, and to have some of your young men sit by him, that he may not do me hurt. He is a young man ,and what are broken bones to youth!"

Akoon, lying helpless, had rifle and knife taken from him, and to either side of his shoulders sat young men of the Mackenzies. The one-eyed old man arose and stood upright. "We marvel at the price paid for one mere woman," he began; "but the wisdom of the price is no concern of ours. We are here to give judgment, and judgment we give. We have no doubt. It is known to all that Porportuk paid a heavy price for the woman El-Soo. Wherefore does the woman El-Soo belong to Porportuk and none other." He sat down heavily, and coughed. The old men nodded and coughed.

"I will kill you," Akoon cried in English.

Porportuk smiled and stood up. "You have given true judgment," he said to the council, "and my young men will give to you much tobacco. Now let the woman be brought to me."

Akoon gritted his teeth. The young men took El-Soo by the arms. She did not resist, and was led, her face a sullen flame, to Porportuk.

"Sit there at my feet till I have made my talk," he commanded. He paused a moment. "It is true," he said, "I am an old man. Yet can I understand the ways of youth. The fire has not all gone out of me. Yet am I no longer young, nor am I minded to run these old legs of mine through all the years that remain to me. El-Soo can run fast and well. She is a deer. This I know, for I have seen and run after her. It is not good that a wife should run so fast. I paid for her a heavy price, yet does she run away from me. Akoon paid no price at all, yet does she run to him.

"When I came among you people of the Mackenzie, I was of one mind. As I listened in the council and thought of the swift legs of El-Soo, I was of many minds. Now am I of one mind again, but it is a different mind from the one I brought to the council. Let me tell you my mind. When a dog runs once away from a master, it will run away again. No matter how many times it is brought back, each time it will run away again. When we have such dogs, we sell them. El-Soo is like a dog that runs away. I will sell her. Is there any man of the council that will buy?"

The old men coughed and remained silent.

"Akoon would buy," Porportuk went on, "but he has no money. Wherefore I will give El-Soo to him, as he said, without price. Even now will I give her to him."

Reaching down, he took El-Soo by the hand and led her across the space to where Akoon lay on his back.

"She has a bad habit, Akoon," he said, seating her at Akoon's feet. "As she has run away from me in the past, in the days to come she may run away from you. But there is no need to fear that she will ever run away, Akoon. I shall see to that. Never will she run away from you—this the word of Porportuk. She has great wit. I know, for often has it bitten into me. Yet am I minded myself to give my wit play for once. And by my wit will I secure her to you, Akoon."

Stooping, Porportuk crossed El-Soo's feet, so that the instep of one lay over that of the other; and then, before his purpose could be divined, he discharged his rifle through the two ankles. As Akoon struggled to rise against the weight of the young men, there was heard the crunch of the broken bone rebroken.

"It is just," said the old men, one to another.

El-Soo made no sound. She sat and looked at her shattered ankles, on which she would never walk again.

"My legs are strong, El-Soo," Akoon said. "But never will they bear me away from you."

El-Soo looked at him, and for the first time in all the time he had known her, Akoon saw tears in her eyes.

"Your eyes are like deer's eyes, El-Soo," he said.

"Is it just?" Porportuk asked, and grinned from the edge of the smoke as he prepared to depart.

"It is just," the old men said. And they sat on in the silence.

The God of His Fathers

I

On every hand stretched the forest primeval,—the home of noisy comedy and silent tragedy. Here the struggle for survival continued to wage with all its ancient brutality. Briton and Russian were still to overlap in the Land of the Rainbow's End—and this was the very heart of it—nor had Yankee gold yet purchased its vast domain. The wolf-pack still clung to the flank of the cariboo-herd, singling out the weak and the big with calf, and pulling them down as remorselessly as were it a thousand, thousand generations into the past. The sparse aborigines still acknowledged the rule of their chiefs and medicine men, drove out bad spirits, burned their witches, fought their neighbors, and ate their enemies with a relish which spoke well of their bellies. But it was at the moment when the stone age was drawing to a close. Already, over unknown trails and chartless wildernesses, were the harbingers of the steel arriving,—fair-faced, blue-eyed, indomitable men, incarnations of the unrest of their race. By accident or design, single-handed and in twos and threes, they came from no one knew whither, and fought, or died, or passed on, no one knew whence. The priests raged against them, the chiefs called forth their fighting men, and stone clashed with steel; but to little purpose. Like water seeping from some mighty reservoir, they trickled through the dark forests and mountain passes, threading the highways in bark canoes, or with their moccasined feet breaking trail for the wolf-dogs. They came of a great breed, and their mothers were many; but the fur-clad denizens of the Northland had this yet to learn. So many an unsung wanderer fought his last and died under the cold fire of the aurora, as did his brothers in burning sands and reeking jungles, and as they shall continue to do till in the fulness of time the destiny of their race be achieved.

It was near twelve. Along the northern horizon a rosy glow, fading to the west and deepening to the east, marked the unseen dip of the midnight sun. The gloaming and the dawn were so commingled that there was no night,— simply a wedding of day with day, scarcely perceptible blending of two circles of the sun. A kildee timidly chirped good-night; the full, rich throat of a robin proclaimed good-morrow. From an island on the breast of the Yukon a colony of wild fowl voiced its interminable wrongs, while a loon laughed mockingly back across a still stretch of river.

In the foreground, against the bank of a lazy eddy, birch-bark canoes were lined two and three deep. Ivory-bladed spears, bone-barbed arrows, buckskin-thonged bows, and simple basket-woven traps bespoke the fact that in the muddy current of the river the salmon-run was on. In the background, from the tangle of skin tents and drying frames, rose the voices of the fisher folk. Bucks skylarked with bucks or flirted with the maidens, while the older squaws, shut out from this by virtue of having fulfilled the end of their existence in reproduction, gossiped as they braided rope from the green roots of trailing vines. At their feet their naked progeny played and squabbled, or rolled in the muck with the tawny wolf-dogs.

To one side of the encampment, and conspicuously apart from it, stood a second camp of two tents. But it was a white man's camp. If nothing else, the choice of position at least bore convincing evidence of this. In case of offence, it commanded the Indian quarters a hundred yards away; of defence, a rise to the ground and the cleared intervening space; and last, of defeat, the swift slope of a score of yards to the canoes below. From one of the tents came the petulant cry of a sick child and the crooning song of a mother. In the open, over the smouldering embers of a fire, two men held talk.

"Eh? I love the church like a good son. *Bien!* So great a love that my days have been spent in fleeing away from her, and my nights in dreaming dreams of reckoning. Look you!" the half-breed's voice rose to an angry snarl. "I am Red River born. My father was white—as white as you. But you are Yankee, and he was British bred, and a gentleman's son. And my mother was the daughter of a chief, and I was a man. Ay, and one had to look the second time to see what manner of blood ran in my veins; for I lived with the whites, and was one of them, and my father's heart beat in me. It happened there was a maiden—white—who looked on me with kind eyes. Her father had much land and many horses; also he was a big man among his people, and his blood was the blood of the French. He said the girl knew not her own mind, and talked overmuch with her, and became wroth that such things should be.

"But she knew her mind, for we came quick before the priest. And quicker had come her father, with lying words, false promises, I know not what; so that the priest stiffened his neck and would not make us that we might live one with the other. As at the beginning it was the church which would not bless my birth, so now it was the church which refused me marriage and put the blood of men upon my hands. *Bien!* Thus have I cause to love the church. So I struck the priest on his woman's mouth, and we took swift horses, the girl and I, to Fort Pierre, where was a minister of good heart. But hot on our trail was her father, and brothers, and other men he had gathered to him. And we fought, our horses on the run, till I emptied three saddles and the rest drew off and went on to Fort Pierre. Then we took east, the girl and I, to the hills and forests, and we lived one with the other, and we were not married,—the work of the good church which I love like a son.

"But mark you, for this is the strangeness of woman, the way of which no man may understand. One of the saddles I emptied was that of her father's, and the hoofs of those who came behind him had pounded him into the earth. This we saw, the girl and I, and this I had forgot had she not remembered. And in the quiet of the evening, after the day's hunt were done, it came between us, and in the silence of the night when we lay beneath the stars and should have been one. It was there always. She never spoke, but it sat by our fire and held us ever apart. She tried to put it aside, but at such times it would rise up till I could read it in the look of her eyes, in the very in-take of her breath.

"So in the end she bore me a child, a woman-child, and died. Then I went among my mother's people, that it might nurse at a warm breast and live. But my hands were wet with the blood of men, look you, because of the church, wet with the blood of men. And the Riders of the North came for me, but my mother's brother, who was then chief in his own right, hid me and gave me horses and food. And we went away, my woman-child and I, even to the Hudson Bay Country, where white men were few and the questions they asked not many. And I worked for the company as a hunter, as a guide, as a driver of dogs, till my woman-child was become a woman, tall, and slender, and fair to the eye.

"You know the winter, long and lonely, breeding evil thoughts and bad deeds. The Chief Factor was a hard man, and bold. And he was not such that a woman would delight in looking upon. But he cast eyes upon my woman-child who was become a woman. Mother of God! he sent me away on a long trip with the dogs, that he might—you understand, he was a hard man and without heart. She was most white, and her soul was white, and a good woman, and—well, she died.

"It was bitter cold the night of my return, and I had been away months, and the dogs were limping sore when I came to the fort. The Indians and breeds looked on me in silence, and I felt the fear of I knew not what, but I said nothing till the dogs were fed and I had eaten as a man with work before him should. Then I spoke up, demanding the word, and they shrank from me, afraid of my anger and what I should do; but the story came out, the pitiful story, word for word and act for act, and they marvelled that I should be so quiet.

"When they had done I went to the Factor's house, calmer than now in the telling of it. He had been afraid and called upon the breeds to help him; but they were not pleased with the deed, and had left him to lie on the bed he had made. So he had fled to the house of the priest. Thither I followed. But when I was come to that place, the priest stood in my way, and spoke soft words, and said a man in anger should go neither to the right nor left, but straight to God. I asked by the right of a father's wrath that he give me past, but he said only over his body, and besought with me to pray. Look you, it was the church, always the church; for I passed over his body and sent the Factor to meet my woman-child before his god, which is a bad god, and the god of the white men.

"Then was there hue and cry, for word was sent to the station below, and I came away. Through the Land of the Great Slave, down the Valley of the Mackenzie to the never-opening ice, over the White Rockies, past the Great Curve of the Yukon, even to this place did I come. And from that day to this, yours is the first face of my father's people I have looked upon. May it be the last! These people, which are my people, are a simple folk, and I have been raised to honor among them. My word is their law, and their priests but do my bidding, else would I not suffer them. When I speak for them I speak for myself. We ask to be let alone. We do not want your kind. If we permit you to sit by our fires, after you will come your church, your priests, and your gods. And know this, for each white man who comes to my village, him will I make deny his god. You are the first, and I give you grace. So it were well you go, and go quickly."

"I am not responsible for my brother," the second man spoke up, filling his pipe in a meditative manner. Hay Stockard was at times as thoughtful of speech as he was wanton of action; but only at times.

"But I know your breed," responded the other. "Your brothers are many, and it is you and yours who break the trail for them to follow. In time they shall come to possess the land, but not in my time. Already, have I heard, are they on the head-reaches of the Great River, and far away below are the Russians."

Hay Stockard lifted his head with a quick start. This was startling geographical information. The Hudson Bay post at Fort Yukon had other notions concerning the course of the river, believing it to flow into the Arctic.

"Then the Yukon empties into Bering Sea?" he asked.

"I do not know, but below there are Russians, many Russians. Which is neither here nor there. You may go on and see for yourself; you may go back to your brothers; but up the Koyukuk you shall not go while the priests and fighting men do my bidding. Thus do I command, I, Baptiste the Red, whose word is law and who am head man over this people."

"And should I not go down to the Russians, or back to my brothers?"

"Then shall you go swift-footed before your god, which is a bad god, and the god of the white men."

The red sun shot up above the northern skyline, dripping and bloody. Baptiste the Red came to his feet, nodded curtly, and went back to his camp amid the crimson shadows and the singing of the robins.

Hay Stockard finished his pipe by the fire, picturing in smoke and coal the unknown upper reaches of the Koyukuk, the strange stream which ended here its arctic travels and merged its waters with the muddy Yukon flood. Somewhere up there, if the dying words of a shipwrecked sailorman who had made the fearful overland journey were to be believed, and if the vial of golden grains in his pouch attested to anything,—somewhere up there, in that home of winter, stood the Treasure House of the North. And as keeper of the gate, Baptiste the Red, English half-breed and renegade, barred the way.

"Bah!" He kicked the embers apart and rose to his full height, arms lazily outstretched, facing the flushing north with careless soul.

II

Hay Stockard swore, harshly, in the rugged monosyllables of his mother tongue. His wife lifted her gaze from the pots and pans, and followed his in a keen scrutiny of the river. She was a woman of the Teslin Country, wise in the ways of her husband's vernacular when it grew intensive. From the slipping of a snowshoe thong to the forefront of sudden death, she could gauge occasion by the pitch and volume of his blasphemy. So she knew the present occasion merited attention. A long canoe, with paddles flashing back the rays of the westering sun, was crossing the current from above the urging in for the eddy. Hay Stockard watched it intently. Three men rose and dipped, rose and dipped, in rhythmical precision; but a red bandanna, wrapped about the head of one, caught and held his eye.

"Bill!" he called. "Oh, Bill!"

A shambling, loose-jointed giant rolled out of one of the tents, yawning and rubbing the sleep from his eyes. Then he sighted the strange canoe and was wide awake on the instant.

"By the jumping Methuselah! That damned sky-pilot!"

Hay Stockard nodded his head bitterly, half-reached for his rifle, then shrugged his shoulders.

"Pot-shot him," Bill suggested, "and settle the thing out of hand. He'll spoil us sure if we don't." But the other declined this drastic measure and turned away, at the same time bidding the woman return to her work, and calling Bill back from the bank. The two Indians in the canoe moored it on the edge of the eddy, while its white occupant, conspicuous by his gorgeous head-gear, came up the bank.

"Like Paul of Tarsus, I give you greeting. Peace be unto you and grace before the Lord."

His advances were met sullenly, and without speech.

"To you, Hay Stockard, blasphemer and Philistine, greeting. In your heart is the lust of Mammon, in your mind cunning devils, in your tent this woman whom you live with in adultery; yet of these divers sins, even here in the wilderness, I, Sturges Owen, apostle to the Lord, bid you to repent and cast from you your iniquities."

"Save your cant! Save your cant!" Hay Stockard broke in testily. "You'll need all you've got, and more, for Red Baptiste over yonder."

He waved his hand toward the Indian camp, where the half-breed was looking steadily across, striving to make out the new-comers. Sturges Owen, disseminator of light and apostle to the Lord, stepped to the edge of the steep and commanded his men to bring up the camp outfit. Stockard followed him.

"Look here," he demanded, plucking the missionary by the shoulder and twirling him about. "Do you value your hide?"

"My life is in the Lord's keeping, and I do but work in His vineyard," he replied solemnly.

"Oh, stow that! Are you looking for a job of martyrship?"

"If He so wills."

"Well, you'll find it right here, but I'm going to give you some advice first. Take it or leave it. If you stop here, you'll be cut off in the midst of your labors. And not you alone, but your men, Bill, my wife—"

"Who is a daughter of Belial and hearkeneth not to the true Gospel."

"And myself. Not only do you bring trouble upon yourself, but upon us. I was frozen in with you last winter, as you will well recollect, and I know you for a good man and a fool. If you think it your duty to strive with the heathen, well and good; but do exercise some wit in the way you go about it. This man, Red Baptiste, is no Indian. He comes of our common stock, is as bull-necked as I ever dared be, and as wild a fanatic the one way as you are the other. When you two come together, hell'll be to pay, and I don't care to be mixed up in it. Understand? So take my advice and go away. If you go down-stream, you'll fall in with the Russians. There's bound to be Greek priests among them, and they'll see you safe through to Bering Sea,—that's where the Yukon empties,—and from there it won't be hard to get back to civilization. Take my word for it and get out of here as fast as God'll let you."

"He who carries the Lord in his heart and the Gospel in his hand hath no fear of the machinations of man or devil," the missionary answered stoutly. "I will see this man and wrestle with him. One backslider returned to the fold is a greater victory than a thousand heathen. He who is strong for evil can be as mighty for good, witness Saul when he journeyed up to Damascus to bring Christian captives to Jerusalem. And the voice of the Saviour came to him, crying, 'Saul, Saul, why persecutest thou me?' And therewith Paul arrayed himself on the side of the Lord, and thereafter was most mighty in the saving of souls. And even as thou, Paul of Tarsus, even so do I work in the vineyard of the Lord, bearing trials and tribulations, scoffs and sneers, stripes and punishments, for His dear sake."

"Bring up the little bag with the tea and a kettle of water," he called the next instant to his boatmen; "not forgetting the haunch of cariboo and the mixing-pan."

When his men, converts by his own hand, had gained the bank, the trio fell to their knees, hands and backs burdened with camp equipage, and offered up thanks for their passage through the wilderness and their safe arrival. Hay Stockard looked upon the function with sneering disapproval, the romance and solemnity of it lost to his matter-of-fact soul. Baptiste the Red, still gazing across, recognized the familiar postures, and remembered the girl who had shared his star-roofed couch in the hill and forests, and the woman-child who lay somewhere by bleak Hudson's Bay.

III

"Confound it, Baptiste, couldn't think of it. Not for a moment. Grant that this man is a fool and of small use in the nature of things, but still, you know, I can't give him up."

Hay Stockard paused, striving to put into speech the rude ethics of his heart.

"He's worried me, Baptiste, in the past and now, and caused me all manner of troubles; but can't you see, he's my own breed—white—and—and—why, I couldn't buy my life with his, not if he was a nigger."

"So be it," Baptiste the Red made answer. "I have given you grace and choice. I shall come presently, with my priests and fighting men, and either shall I kill you, or you deny your god. Give up the priest to my pleasure, and you shall depart in peace. Otherwise your trail ends here. My people are against you to the babies. Even now have the children stolen away your canoes." He pointed down to the river. Naked boys had slipped down the water from the point above, cast loose the canoes, and by then had worked them into the current. When they had drifted out of rifle-shot they clambered over the sides and paddled ashore.

"Give me the priest, and you may have them back again. Come! Speak your mind, but without haste."

Stockard shook his head. His glance dropped to the woman of the Teslin Country with his boy at her breast, and he would have wavered had he not lifted his eyes to the men before him.

"I am not afraid," Sturges Owen spoke up. "The Lord bears me in his right hand, and alone am I ready to go into the camp of the unbeliever. It is not too late. Faith may move mountains. Even in the eleventh hour may I win his soul to the true righteousness."

"Trip the beggar up and make him fast," Bill whispered hoarsely in the ear of his leader, while the missionary kept the floor and wrestled with the heathen. "Make him hostage, and bore him if they get ugly."

"No," Stockard answered. "I gave him my word that he could speak with us unmolested. Rules of warfare, Bill; rules of warfare. He's been on the square, given us warning, and all that, and—why, damn it, man, I can't break my word!"

"He'll keep his, never fear."

"Don't doubt it, but I won't let a half-breed outdo me in fair dealing. Why not do what he wants,—give him the missionary and be done with it?"

"N-no," Bill hesitated doubtfully.

"Shoe pinches, eh?"

Bill flushed a little and dropped the discussion. Baptiste the Red was still waiting the final decision. Stockard went up to him.

"It's this way, Baptiste. I came to your village minded to go up the Koyukuk. I intended no wrong. My heart was clean of evil. It is still clean. Along comes this priest, as you call him. I didn't bring him here. He'd have come whether I was here or not. But now that he is here, being of my people, I've got to stand by him. And I'm going to. Further, it will be no child's play. When you have done, your village will be silent and empty, your people wasted as after a famine. True, we will be gone; likewise the pick of your fighting men—"

"But those who remain shall be in peace, nor shall the word of strange gods and the tongues of strange priests be buzzing in their ears."

Both men shrugged their shoulders and turned away, the half-breed going back to his own camp. The missionary called his two men to him, and they fell into prayer. Stockard and Bill attacked the few standing pines with their axes, felling them into convenient breastworks. The child had fallen asleep, so the woman placed it on a heap of furs and lent a hand in fortifying the camp. Three sides were thus defended, the steep declivity at the rear precluding attack from that direction. When these arrangements had been completed, the two men stalked into the open, clearing away, here and there, the scattered underbrush. From the opposing camp came the booming of war-drums and the voices of the priests stirring the people to anger.

"Worst of it is they'll come in rushes," Bill complained as they walked back with shouldered axes.

"And wait till midnight, when the light gets dim for shooting."

"Can't start the ball a-rolling too early, then." Bill exchanged the axe for a rifle, and took a careful rest. One of the medicine-men, towering above his tribesmen, stood out distinctly. Bill drew a bead on him.

"All ready?" he asked.

Stockard opened the ammunition box, placed the woman where she could reload in safety, and gave the word. The medicine-man dropped. For a moment there was silence, then a wild howl went up and a flight of bone arrows fell short.

"I'd like to take a look at the beggar," Bill remarked, throwing a fresh shell into place. "I'll swear I drilled him clean between the eyes."

"Didn't work." Stockard shook his head gloomily. Baptiste had evidently quelled the more warlike of his followers, and instead of precipitating an attack in the bright light of day, the shot had caused a hasty exodus, the Indians drawing out the village beyond the zone of fire.

In the full tide of his proselyting fervor, borne along by the hand of God, Sturges Owen would have ventured alone into the camp of the unbeliever, equally prepared for miracle or martyrdom; but in the waiting which ensued, the fever of conviction died away gradually, as the natural man asserted itself. Physical fear replaced spiritual hope; the love of life, the love of God. It was no new experience. He could feel his weakness coming on, and knew it of old time. He had struggled against it and been overcome by it before.

He remembered when the other men had driven their paddles like mad in the van of a roaring ice-flood, how, at the critical moment, in a panic of worldly terror, he had dropped his paddle and besought wildly with his God for pity. And there were other times. The recollection was not pleasant. It brought shame to him that his spirit should be so weak and his flesh so strong. But the love of life! the love of life! He could not strip it from him. Because of it had his dim ancestors perpetuated their line; because of it was he destined to perpetuate his. His courage, if courage it might be called, was bred of fanaticism. The courage of Stockard and Bill was the adherence to deep-rooted ideals. Not that the love of life was less, but the love of race tradition more; not that they were unafraid to die, but that they were brave enough not to live at the price of shame.

The missionary rose, for the moment swayed by the mood of sacrifice. He half crawled over the barricade to proceed to the other camp, but sank back, a trembling mass, wailing: "As the spirit moves! As the spirit moves! Who am I that I should set aside the judgments of God? Before the foundations of the world were all things written in the book of life. Worm that I am, shall I erase the page or any portion thereof? As God wills, so shall the spirit move!"

Bill reached over, plucked him to his feet, and shook him, fiercely, silently. Then he dropped the bundle of quivering nerves and turned his attention to the two converts. But they showed little fright and a cheerful alacrity in preparing for the coming passage at arms.

Stockard, who had been talking in undertones with the Teslin woman, now turned to the missionary.

"Fetch him over here," he commanded of Bill.

"Now," he ordered, when Sturges Owen had been duly deposited before him, "make us man and wife, and be lively about it." Then he added apologetically to Bill: "No telling how it's to end, so I just thought I'd get my affairs straightened up."

The woman obeyed the behest of her white lord. To her the ceremony was meaningless. By her lights she was his wife, and had been from the day they first foregathered. The converts served as witnesses. Bill stood over the missionary, prompting him when he stumbled. Stockard put the responses in the woman's mouth, and when the time came, for want of better, ringed her finger with thumb and forefinger of his own.

"Kiss the bride!" Bill thundered, and Sturges Owen was too weak to disobey.

"Now baptize the child!"

"Neat and tidy," Bill commented.

"Gathering the proper outfit for a new trail," the father explained, taking the boy from the mother's arms. "I was grub-staked, once, into the Cascades, and had everything in the kit except salt. Never shall forget it. And if the woman and the kid cross the divide to-night they might as well be prepared for pot-luck. A long shot, Bill, between ourselves, but nothing lost if it misses."

A cup of water served the purpose, and the child was laid away in a secure corner of the barricade. The men built the fire, and the evening meal was cooked.

The sun hurried round to the north, sinking closer to the horizon. The heavens in that quarter grew red and bloody. The shadows lengthened, the light dimmed, and in the sombre recesses of the forest life slowly died away. Even the wild fowl in the river softened their raucous chatter and feigned the nightly farce of going to bed. Only the tribesmen increased their clamor, war-drums booming and voices raised in savage folk songs. But as the sun dipped they ceased their tumult. The rounded hush of midnight was complete. Stockard rose to his knees and peered over the logs. Once the child wailed in pain and disconcerted him. The mother bent over it, but it slept again. The silence was interminable, profound. Then, of a sudden, the robins burst into full-throated song. The night had passed.

A flood of dark figures boiled across the open. Arrows whistled and bow-thongs sang. The shrill-tongued rifles answered back. A spear, and a mighty cast, transfixed the Teslin woman as she hovered above the child. A spent arrow, diving between the logs, lodged in the missionary's arm.

There was no stopping the rush. The middle distance was cumbered with bodies, but the rest surged on, breaking against and over the barricade like an ocean wave. Sturges Owen fled to the tent, while the men were swept from their feet, buried beneath the human tide. Hay Stockard alone regained the surface, flinging the tribesmen aside like yelping curs. He had managed to seize an axe. A dark hand grasped the child by a naked foot, and drew it from beneath its mother. At arm's length its puny body circled through the air, dashing to death against the logs. Stockard clove the man to the chin and fell to clearing space. The ring of savage faces closed in, raining upon him spear-thrusts and bone-barbed arrows. The sun shot up, and they swayed back and forth in the crimson shadows. Twice, with his axe blocked by too deep a blow, they rushed him; but each time he flung them clear. They fell underfoot and he trampled dead and dying, the way slippery with blood. And still the day brightened and the robins sang. Then they drew back from him in awe, and he leaned breathless upon his axe.

"Blood of my soul!" cried Baptiste the Red. "But thou art a man. Deny thy god, and thou shalt yet live."

Stockard swore his refusal, feebly but with grace.

"Behold! A woman!" Sturges Owen had been brought before the half-breed.

Beyond a scratch on the arm, he was uninjured, but his eyes roved about him in an ecstasy of fear. The heroic figure of the blasphemer, bristling with wounds and arrows, leaning defiantly upon his axe, indifferent, indomitable, superb, caught his wavering vision. And he felt a great envy of the man who could go down serenely to the dark gates of death. Surely Christ, and not he, Sturges Owen, had been moulded in such manner. And why not he? He felt dimly the curse of ancestry, the feebleness of spirit which had come down to him out of the past, and he felt an anger at the creative force, symbolize it as he would, which had formed him, its servant, so weakly. For even a stronger man, this anger and the stress of circumstance were sufficient to breed apostasy, and for Sturges Owen it was inevitable. In the fear of man's anger he would dare the wrath of God. He had been raised up to serve the Lord only that he might be cast down. He had been given faith without the strength of faith; he had been given spirit without the power of spirit. It was unjust.

"Where now is thy god?" the half-breed demanded.

"I do not know." He stood straight and rigid, like a child repeating a catechism.

"Hast thou then a god at all?"

"I had."

"And now?"

"No."

Hay Stockard swept the blood from his eye and laughed. The missionary looked at him curiously, as in a dream. A feeling of infinite distance came over him, as though of a great remove. In that which had transpired, and which was to transpire, he had no part. He was a spectator—at a distance, yes, at a distance. The words of Baptiste came to him faintly:—

"Very good. See that this man go free, and that no harm befall him. Let him depart in peace. Give him a canoe and food. Set his face toward the Russians, that he may tell their priests of Baptiste the Red, in whose country there is no god."

They led him to the edge of the steep, where they paused to witness the final tragedy. The half-breed turned to Hay Stockard.

"There is no god," he prompted.

The man laughed in reply. One of the young men poised a war-spear for the cast.

"Hast thou a god?"

"Ay, the God of my fathers."

He shifted the axe for a better grip. Baptiste the Red gave the sign, and the spear hurtled full against his breast. Sturges Owen saw the ivory head stand out beyond his back, saw the man sway, laughing, and snap the shaft short as he fell upon it. Then he went down to the river, that he might carry to the Russians the message of Baptiste the Red, in whose country there was no god.

In a Far Country

When a man journeys into a far country, he must be prepared to forget many of the things he has learned, and to acquire such customs as are inherent with existence in the new land; he must abandon the old ideals and the old gods, and oftentimes he must reverse the very codes by which his conduct has hitherto been shaped. To those who have the protean faculty of adaptability, the novelty of such change may even be a source of pleasure; but to those who happen to be hardened to the ruts in which they were created, the pressure of the altered environment is unbearable, and they chafe in body and in spirit under the new restrictions which they do not understand. This chafing is bound to act and react, producing divers evils and leading to various misfortunes. It were better for the man who cannot fit himself to the new groove to return to his own country; if he delay too long, he will surely die.

The man who turns his back upon the comforts of an elder civilization, to face the savage youth, the primordial simplicity of the North, may estimate success at an inverse ratio to the quantity and quality of his hopelessly fixed habits. He will soon discover, if he be a fit candidate, that the material habits are the less important. The exchange of such things as a dainty menu for rough fare, of the stiff leather shoe for the soft, shapeless moccasin, of the feather bed for a couch in the snow, is after all a very easy matter. But his pinch will come in learning properly to shape his mind's attitude toward all things, and especially toward his fellow man. For the courtesies of ordinary life, he must substitute unselfishness, forbearance, and tolerance. Thus, and thus only, can he gain that pearl of great price,—true comradeship. He must not say "Thank you;" he must mean it without opening his mouth, and prove it by responding in kind. In short, he must substitute the deed for the word, the spirit for the letter.

When the world rang with the tale of Arctic gold, and the lure of the North gripped the heartstrings of men, Carter Weatherbee threw up his snug clerkship, turned the half of his savings over to his wife, and with the remainder bought an outfit. There was no romance in his nature,—the bondage of commerce had crushed all that; he was simply tired of the ceaseless grind, and wished to risk great hazards in view of corresponding returns. Like many another fool, disdaining the old trails used by the Northland pioneers for a score of years, he hurried to Edmonton in the spring of the year; and there, unluckily for his soul's welfare, he allied himself with a party of men.

There was nothing unusual about this party, except its plans. Even its goal, like that of all other parties, was the Klondike. But the route it had mapped out to attain that goal took away the breath of the hardiest native, born and bred to the vicissitudes of the Northwest. Even Jacques Baptiste, born of a Chippewa woman and a renegade *voyageur* (having raised his first whimpers in a deerskin lodge north of the sixty-fifth parallel, and had the same hushed by blissful sucks of raw tallow), was surprised. Though he sold his services to them and agreed to travel even to the never-opening ice, he shook his head ominously whenever his advice was asked.

Percy Cuthfert's evil star must have been in the ascendant, for he, too, joined this company of argonauts. He was an ordinary man, with a bank account as deep as his culture, which is saying a good deal. He had no reason to embark on such a venture,—no reason in the world, save that he suffered from an abnormal development of sentimentality. He mistook this for the true spirit of romance and adventure. Many another man has done the like, and made as fatal a mistake.

The first break-up of spring found the party following the ice-run of Elk River. It was an imposing fleet, for the outfit was large, and they were accompanied by a disreputable contingent of half-breed *voyageurs* with their women and children. Day in and day out, they labored with the bateaux and canoes, fought mosquitoes and other kindred pests, or sweated and swore at the portages. Severe toil like this lays a man naked to the very roots of his soul, and ere Lake Athabasca was lost in the south, each member of the party had hoisted his true colors.

The two shirks and chronic grumblers were Carter Weatherbee and Percy Cuthfert. The whole party complained less of its aches and pains than did either of them. Not once did they volunteer for the thousand and one petty duties of the camp. A bucket of water to be brought, an extra armful of wood to be chopped, the dishes to be washed and wiped, a search to be made through the outfit for some suddenly indispensable article,—and these two effete scions of civilization discovered sprains or blisters requiring instant attention. They were the first to turn in at night, with a score of tasks yet undone; the last to turn out in the morning, when the start should be in readiness before the breakfast was begun. They were the first to fall to at meal-time, the last to have a hand in the cooking; the first to dive for a slim delicacy, the last to discover they had added to their own another man's share. If they toiled at the oars, they slyly cut the water at each stroke and allowed the boat's momentum to float up the blade. They thought nobody noticed; but their comrades swore under their breaths and grew to hate them, while Jacques Baptiste sneered openly and damned them from morning till night. But Jacques Baptiste was no gentleman.

At the Great Slave, Hudson Bay dogs were purchased, and the fleet sank to the guards with its added burden of dried fish and pemmican. Then canoe and bateau answered to the swift current of the Mackenzie, and they plunged into the Great Barren Ground. Every likely-looking "feeder" was prospected, but the elusive "pay-dirt" danced ever to the north. At the Great Bear, overcome by the common dread of the Unknown Lands, their *voyageurs* began to desert, and Fort of Good Hope saw the last and bravest bending to the tow-lines as they bucked the current down which they had so treacherously glided. Jacques Baptiste alone remained. Had he not sworn to travel even to the never opening ice?

The lying charts, compiled in main from hearsay, were now constantly consulted. And they felt the need of hurry, for the sun had already passed its northern solstice and was leading the winter south again. Skirting the shores of the bay, where the Mackenzie disembogues into the Arctic Ocean, they entered the mouth of the Little Peel River. Then began the arduous upstream toil, and the two Incapables fared worse then ever. Tow-line and pole, paddle and tump-line, rapids and portages,—such tortures served to give the one a deep disgust for great hazards, and printed for the other a fiery text on the true romance of adventure. One day they waxed mutinous, and being vilely cursed by Jacques Baptiste, turned, as worms sometimes will. But the half-breed thrashed the twain, and sent them, bruised and bleeding, about their work. It was the first time either had been man-handled.

Abandoning their river craft at the head-waters of the Little Peel, they consumed the rest of the summer in the great portage over the Mackenzie watershed to the West Rat. This little stream fed the Porcupine, which in turn joined the Yukon where that mighty highway of the North countermarches on the Arctic Circle. But they had lost in the race with winter, and one day they tied their rafts to the thick eddy-ice and hurried their goods ashore. That night the river jammed and broke several times; the following morning it had fallen asleep for good.

"We can't be more 'n four hundred miles from the Yukon," concluded Sloper, multiplying his thumb nails by the scale of the map. The council, in which the two Incapables had whined to excellent disadvantage, was drawing to a close.

"Hudson Bay Post, long time ago. No use um now." Jacques Baptiste's father had made the trip for the Fur Company in the old days, incidentally marking the trail with a couple of frozen toes.

"Sufferin' cracky!" cried another of the party. "No whites?"

"Nary white," Sloper sententiously affirmed; "but it's only five hundred more up the Yukon to Dawson. Call it a rough thousand from here."

Weatherbee and Cuthfert groaned in chorus.

"How long'll that take, Baptiste?"

The half-breed figured for a moment. "Workum like hell, no man play out, ten—twenty—forty—fifty days. Um babies come" (designating the Incapables), "no can tell. Mebbe when hell freeze over; mebbe not then."

The manufacture of snowshoes and moccasins ceased. Somebody called the name of an absent member, who came out of an ancient cabin at the edge of the camp-fire and joined them. The cabin was one of the many mysteries which lurk in the vast recesses of the north. Built when and by whom, no man could tell. Two graves in the open, piled high with stones, perhaps contained the secret of those early wanderers. But whose hand had piled the stones?

The moment had come. Jacques Baptiste paused in the fitting of a harness and pinned the struggling dog in the snow. The cook made mute protest for delay, threw a handful of bacon into a noisy pot of beans, then came to attention. Sloper rose to his feet. His body was a ludicrous contrast to the healthy physiques of the Incapables. Yellow and weak, fleeing from a South American fever-hole, he had not broken his flight across the zones, and was still able to toil with men. His weight was probably ninety pounds, with the heavy hunting-knife thrown in, and his grizzled hair told of a prime which had ceased to be. The fresh young muscles of either Weatherbee or Cuthfert were equal to ten times the endeavor of his; yet he could walk them into the earth in a day's journey. And all this day he had whipped his stronger comrades into venturing a thousand miles of the stiffest hardship man can conceive. He was the incarnation of the unrest of his race, and the old Teutonic stubbornness, dashed with the quick grasp and action of the Yankee, held the flesh in the bondage of the spirit.

"All those in favor of going on with the dogs as soon as the ice sets, say ay."

"Ay!" rang out eight voices,—voices destined to string a trail of oaths along many a hundred miles of pain.

"Contrary minded?"

"No!" For the first time the Incapables were united without some compromise of personal interests.

"And what are you going to do about it?" Weatherbee added belligerently.

"Majority rule! Majority rule!" clamored the rest of the party.

"I know the expedition is liable to fall through if you don't come," Sloper replied sweetly; "but I guess, if we try real hard, we can manage to do without you. What do you say, boys?"

The sentiment was cheered to the echo.

"But I say, you know," Cuthfert ventured apprehensively; "what's a chap like me to do?"

"Ain't you coming with us?"

"No-o."

"Then do as you damn well please. We won't have nothing to say."

"Kind o' calkilate yuh might settle it with that canoodlin' pardner of yourn," suggested a heavy-going Westerner from the Dakotas, at the same time pointing out Weatherbee. "He'll be shore to ask yuh what yur a-goin' to do when it comes to cookin' an' gatherin' the wood."

"Then we'll consider it all arranged," concluded Sloper. "We'll pull out to-morrow, if we camp within five miles,—just to get everything in running order and remember if we've forgotten anything."

The sleds groaned by on their steel-shod runners, and the dogs strained low in the harnesses in which they were born to die. Jacques Baptiste paused by the side of Sloper to get a last glimpse of the cabin. The smoke curled up pathetically from the Yukon stove-pipe. The two Incapables were watching them from the doorway.

Sloper laid his hand on the other's shoulder.

"Jacques Baptiste, did you ever hear of the Kilkenny cats?"

The half-breed shook his head.

"Well, my friend and good comrade, the Kilkenny cats fought till neither hide, nor hair, nor yowl, was left. You understand?—till nothing was left. Very good. Now, these two men don't like work. They won't work. We know that. They'll be all alone in that cabin all winter,—a mighty long, dark winter. Kilkenny cats,—well?"

The Frenchman in Baptiste shrugged his shoulders, but the Indian in him was silent. Nevertheless, it was an eloquent shrug, pregnant with prophecy.

Things prospered in the little cabin at first. The rough badinage of their comrades had made Weatherbee and Cuthfert conscious of the mutual responsibility which had devolved upon them; besides, there was not so much work after all for two healthy men. And the removal of the cruel whip-hand, or in other words the bulldozing half-breed, had brought with it a joyous reaction. At first, each strove to outdo the other, and they performed petty tasks with an unction which would have opened the eyes of their comrades who were now wearing out bodies and souls on the Long Trail.

All care was banished. The forest, which shouldered in upon them from three sides, was in inexhaustible woodyard. A few yards from their door slept the Porcupine, and a hole through its winter robe formed a bubbling spring of water, crystal clear and painfully cold. But they soon grew to find fault with even that. The hole would persist in freezing up, and thus gave them many a miserable hour of ice-chopping. The unknown builders of the cabin had extended the side-logs so as to support a cache at the rear. In this was stored the bulk of the party's provisions. Food there was, without stint, for three times the men who were fated to live upon it. But the most of it was the kind which built up brawn and sinew, but did not tickle the palate. True, there was sugar in plenty for two ordinary men; but these two were little else than children. They early discovered the virtues of hot water judiciously saturated with sugar, and they prodigally swam their flapjacks and soaked their crusts in the rich, white syrup. Then coffee and tea, and especially the dried fruits, made disastrous inroads upon it. The first words they had were over the sugar question. And it is a really serious thing when two men, wholly dependent upon each other for company, begin to quarrel.

Weatherbee loved to discourse blatantly on politics, while Cuthfert, who had been prone to clip his coupons and let the commonwealth jog on as best it might, either ignored the subject or delivered himself of startling epigrams. But the clerk was too obtuse to appreciate the clever shaping of thought, and this waste of ammunition irritated Cuthfert. He had been used to blinding people by his brilliancy, and it worked him quite a hardship, this loss of an audience. He felt personally aggrieved and unconsciously held his mutton-head companion responsible for it.

Save existence, they had nothing in common,—came in touch on no single point. Weatherbee was a clerk who had known naught but clerking all his life; Cuthfert was a master of arts, a dabbler in oils, and had written not a little. The one was a lower-class man who considered himself a gentleman, and the other was a gentleman who knew himself to be such. From this it may be remarked that a man can be a gentleman without possessing the first instinct of true comradeship. The clerk was as sensuous as the other was æsthetic, and his love adventures, told at great length and chiefly coined from his imagination, affected the supersensitive master of arts in the same way as so many whiffs of sewer gas. He deemed the clerk a filthy, uncultured brute, whose place was in the muck with the swine, and told him so; and he was reciprocally informed that he was a milk-and-water sissy and a cad. Weatherbee could not have defined "cad" for his life; but it satisfied its purpose, which after all seems the main point in life.

Weatherbee flatted every third note and sang such songs as "The Boston Burglar" and "The Handsome Cabin Boy," for hours at a time, while Cuthfert wept with rage, till he could stand it no longer and fled into the outer cold. But there was no escape. The intense frost could not be endured for long at a time, and the little cabin crowded them—beds, stove, table, and all—into a space of ten by twelve. The very presence of either became a personal affront to the other, and they lapsed into sullen silences which increased in length and strength as the days went by. Occasionally, the flash of an eye or the curl of a lip got the better of them, though they strove to wholly ignore each other during these mute periods. And a great wonder sprang up in the breast of each, as to how God had come to create the other.

With little to do, time became an intolerable burden to them. This naturally made them still lazier. They sank into a physical lethargy which there was no escaping, and which made them rebel at the performance of the smallest chore. One morning when it was his turn to cook the common breakfast, Weatherbee rolled out of his blankets, and to the snoring of his companion, lighted first the slush-lamp and then the fire. The kettles were frozen hard, and there was no water in the cabin with which to wash. But he did not mind that. Waiting for it to thaw, he sliced the bacon and plunged into the hateful task of bread-making. Cuthfert had been slyly watching through his half-closed lids. Consequently there was a scene, in which they fervently blessed each other, and agreed, thenceforth, that each do his own cooking. A week later, Cuthfert neglected his morning ablutions, but none the less complacently ate the meal which he had cooked. Weatherbee grinned. After that the foolish custom of washing passed out of their lives.

As the sugar-pile and other little luxuries dwindled, they began to be afraid they were not getting their proper shares, and in order that they might not be robbed, they fell to gorging themselves. The luxuries suffered in this gluttonous contest, as did also the men. In the absence of fresh vegetables and exercise, their blood became impoverished, and a loathsome, purplish rash crept over their bodies. Yet they refused to heed the warning. Next, their muscles and joints began to swell, the flesh turning black, while their mouths, gums, and lips took on the color of rich cream. Instead of being drawn together by their misery, each gloated over the other's symptoms as the scurvy took its course.

They lost all regard for personal appearance, and for that matter, common decency. The cabin became a pigpen, and never once were the beds made or fresh pine boughs laid underneath. Yet they could not keep to their blankets, as they would have wished: for the frost was inexorable, and the fire box consumed much fuel. The hair of their heads and faces grew long and shaggy, while their garments would have disgusted a ragpicker. But they did not care. They were sick, and there was no one to see; besides, it was very painful to move about.

To all this was added a new trouble,—the Fear of the North. This Fear was the joint child of the Great Cold and the Great Silence, and was born in the darkness of December, when the sun dipped below the southern horizon for good. It affected them according to their natures. Weatherbee fell prey to the grosser superstitions, and did his best to resurrect the spirits which slept in the forgotten graves. It was a fascinating thing, and in his dreams they came to him from out of the cold, and snuggled into his blankets, and told him of their toils and troubles ere they died. He shrank away from the clammy contact as they drew closer and twined their frozen limbs about him, and when they whispered in his ear of things to come, the cabin rang with his frightened shrieks. Cuthfert did not understand,—for they no longer spoke,—and when thus awakened he invariably grabbed for his revolver. Then he would sit up in bed, shivering nervously, with the weapon trained on the unconscious dreamer. Cuthfert deemed the man going mad, and so came to fear for his life.

His own malady assumed a less concrete form. The mysterious artisan who had laid the cabin, log by log, had pegged a wind-vane to the ridge-pole. Cuthfert noticed it always pointed south, and one day, irritated by its steadfastness of purpose, he turned it toward the east. He watched eagerly, but never a breath came by to disturb it. Then he turned the vane to the north, swearing never again to touch it till the wind did blow. But the air frightened him with its unearthly calm, and he often rose in the middle of the night to see if the vane had veered,—ten degrees would have satisfied him. But no, it poised above him as unchangeable as fate. His imagination ran riot, till it became to him a fetich. Sometimes he followed the path it pointed across the dismal dominions, and allowed his soul to become saturated with the Fear. He dwelt upon the unseen and the unknown till the burden of eternity appeared to be crushing him. Everything in the Northland had that crushing effect,—the absence of life and motion; the darkness; the infinite peace of the brooding land; the ghastly silence, which made the echo of each heart-beat a sacrilege; the solemn forest which seemed to guard an awful, inexpressible something, which neither word nor thought could compass.

The world he had so recently left, with its busy nations and great enterprises, seemed very far away. Recollections occasionally obtruded,—recollections of marts and galleries and crowded thoroughfares, of evening dress and social functions, of good men and dear women he had known, —but they were dim memories of a life he had lived long centuries agone, on some other planet. This phantasm was the Reality. Standing beneath the wind-vane, his eyes fixed on the polar skies, he could not bring himself to realize that the Southland really existed, that at that very moment it was a-roar with life and action. There was no Southland, no men being born of women, no giving and taking in marriage. Beyond his bleak sky-line there stretched vast solitudes, and beyond these still vaster solitudes. There were no lands of sunshine, heavy with the perfume of flowers. Such things were only old dreams of paradise. The sunlands of the West and the spicelands of the East, the smiling Arcadias and blissful Islands of the Blest,—ha! ha! His laughter split the void and shocked him with its unwonted sound. There was no sun. This was the Universe, dead and cold and dark, and he its only citizen. Weatherbee? At such moments Weatherbee did not count. He was a Caliban, a monstrous phantom, fettered to him for untold ages, the penalty of some forgotten crime.

He lived with Death among the dead, emasculated by the sense of his own insignificance, crushed by the passive mastery of the slumbering ages. The magnitude of all things appalled him. Everything partook of the superlative save himself,—the perfect cessation of wind and motion, the immensity of the snow-covered wilderness, the height of the sky and the depth of the silence. That wind-vane,—if it would only move. If a thunderbolt would fall, or the forest flare up in flame. The rolling up of the heavens as a scroll, the crash of Doom—anything, anything! But no, nothing moved; the Silence crowded in, and the Fear of the North laid icy fingers on his heart.

Once, like another Crusoe, by the edge of the river he came upon a track,—the faint tracery of a snowshoe rabbit on the delicate snow-crust. It was a revelation. There was life in the Northland. He would follow it, look upon it, gloat over it. He forgot his swollen muscles, plunging through the deep snow in an ecstasy of anticipation. The forest swallowed him up, and the brief midday twilight vanished; but he pursued his quest till exhausted nature asserted itself and laid him helpless in the snow. There he groaned and cursed his folly, and knew the track to be the fancy of his brain; and late that night he dragged himself into the cabin on hands and knees, his cheeks frozen and a strange numbness about his feet. Weatherbee grinned malevolently, but made no offer to help him. He thrust needles into his toes and thawed them out by the stove. A week later mortification set in.

But the clerk had his own troubles. The dead men came out of their graves more frequently now, and rarely left him, waking or sleeping. He grew to wait and dread their coming, never passing the twin cairns without a shudder. One night they came to him in his sleep and led him forth to an appointed task. Frightened into inarticulate horror, he awoke between the heaps of stones and fled wildly to the cabin. But he had lain there for some time, for his feet and cheeks were also frozen.

Sometimes he became frantic at their insistent presence, and danced about the cabin, cutting the empty air with an axe, and smashing everything within reach. During these ghostly encounters, Cuthfert huddled into his blankets and followed the madman about with a cocked revolver, ready to shoot him if he came too near. But, recovering from one of these spells, the clerk noticed the weapon trained upon him. His suspicions were aroused, and thenceforth he, too, lived in fear of his life. They watched each other closely after that, and faced about in startled fright whenever either passed behind the other's back. This apprehensiveness became a mania which controlled them even in their sleep. Through mutual fear they tacitly let the slush-lamp burn all night, and saw to a plentiful supply of bacon-grease before retiring. The slightest movement on the part of one was sufficient to arouse the other, and many a still watch their gazes countered as they shook beneath their blankets with fingers on the trigger-guards.

What with the Fear of the North, the mental strain, and the ravages of the disease, they lost all semblance of humanity, taking on the appearance of wild beasts, hunted and desperate. Their cheeks and noses, as an aftermath of the freezing, had turned black. Their frozen toes had begun to drop away at the first and second joints. Every movement brought pain, but the fire box was insatiable, wringing a ransom of torture from their miserable bodies. Day in, day out, it demanded its food,—a veritable pound of flesh,—and they dragged themselves into the forest to chop wood on their knees. Once, crawling thus in search of dry sticks, unknown to each other they entered a thicket from opposite sides. Suddenly, without warning, two peering death's-heads confronted each other. Suffering had so transformed them that recognition was impossible. They sprang to their feet, shrieking with terror, and dashed away on their mangled stumps; and falling at the cabin door, they clawed and scratched like demons till they discovered their mistake.

Occasionally they lapsed normal, and during one of these sane intervals, the chief bone of contention, the sugar, had been divided equally between them. They guarded their separate sacks, stored up in the cache, with jealous eyes; for there were but a few cupfuls left, and they were totally devoid of faith in each other. But one day Cuthfert made a mistake. Hardly able to move, sick with pain, with his head swimming and eyes blinded, he crept into the cache, sugar canister in hand, and mistook Weatherbee's sack for his own.

January had been born but a few days when this occurred. The sun had some time since passed its lowest southern declination, and at meridian now threw flaunting streaks of yellow light upon the northern sky. On the day following his mistake with the sugar-bag, Cuthfert found himself feeling better, both in body and in spirit. As noontime drew near and the day brightened, he dragged himself outside to feast on the evanescent glow, which was to him an earnest of the sun's future intentions. Weatherbee was also feeling somewhat better, and crawled out beside him. They propped themselves in the snow beneath the moveless wind-vane, and waited.

The stillness of death was about them. In other climes, when nature falls into such moods, there is a subdued air of expectancy, a waiting for some small voice to take up the broken strain. Not so in the North. The two men had lived seeming æons in this ghostly peace. They could remember no song of the past; they could conjure no song of the future. This unearthly calm had always been,—the tranquil silence of eternity.

Their eyes were fixed upon the north. Unseen, behind their backs, behind the towering mountains to the south, the sun swept toward the zénith of another sky than theirs. Sole spectators of the mighty canvas, they watched the false dawn slowly grow. A faint flame began to glow and smoulder. It deepened in intensity, ringing the changes of reddish-yellow, purple, and saffron. So bright did it become that Cuthfert thought the sun must surely be behind it,—a miracle, the sun rising in the north! Suddenly, without warning and without fading, the canvas was swept clean. There was no color in the sky. The light had gone out of the day. They caught their breaths in half-sobs. But lo! the air was a-glint with particles of scintillating frost, and there, to the north, the wind-vane lay in vague outline on the snow. A shadow! A shadow! It was exactly midday. They jerked their heads hurriedly to the south. A golden rim peeped over the mountain's snowy shoulder, smiled upon them an instant, then dipped from sight again.

There were tears in their eyes as they sought each other. A strange softening came over them. They felt irresistibly drawn toward each other. The sun was coming back again. It would be with them to-morrow, and the next day, and the next. And it would stay longer every visit, and a time would come when it would ride their heaven day and night, never once dropping below the sky-line. There would be no night. The ice-locked winter would be broken; the winds would blow and the forests answer; the land would bathe in the blessed sunshine, and life renew. Hand in hand, they would quit this horrid dream and journey back to the Southland. They lurched blindly forward, and their hands met,—their poor maimed hands, swollen and distorted beneath their mittens.

But the promise was destined to remain unfulfilled. The Northland is the Northland, and men work out their souls by strange rules, which other men, who have not journeyed into far countries, cannot come to understand.

An hour later, Cuthfert put a pan of bread into the oven, and fell to speculating on what the surgeons could do with his feet when he got back. Home did not seem so very far away now. Weatherbee was rummaging in the cache. Of a sudden, he raised a whirlwind of blasphemy, which in turn ceased with startling abruptness. The other man had robbed his sugar-sack. Still, things might have happened differently, had not the two dead men come out from under the stones and hushed the hot words in his throat. They led him quite gently from the cache, which he forgot to close. That consummation was reached; that something they had whispered to him in his dreams was about to happen. They guided him gently, very gently, to the woodpile, where they put the axe in his hands. Then they helped him shove open the cabin door, and he felt sure they shut it after him,—at least he heard it slam and the latch fall sharply into place. And he knew they were waiting just without, waiting from him to do his task.

"Carter! I say, Carter!"

Percy Cuthfert was frightened at the look on the clerk's face, and he made haste to put the table between them.

Carter Weatherbee followed, without haste and without enthusiasm. There was neither pity nor passion in his face, but rather the patient, stolid look of one who has certain work to do and goes about it methodically.

"I say, what's the matter?"

The clerk dodged back, cutting off his retreat to the door, but never opening his mouth.

"I say, Carter, I say; let's talk. There's a good chap."

The master of arts was thinking rapidly, now, shaping a skillful flank movement on the bed where his Smith & Wesson lay. Keeping his eyes on the madman, he rolled backward on the bunk, at the same time clutching the pistol.

"Carter!"

The powder flashed full in Weatherbee's face, but he swung his weapon and leaped forward. The axe bit deeply at the base of the spine, and Percy Cuthfert felt all consciousness of his lower limbs leave him. Then the clerk fell heavily upon him, clutching him by the throat with feeble fingers. The sharp bite of the axe had caused Cuthfert to drop the pistol, and as his lungs panted for release, he fumbled aimlessly for it among the blankets. Then he remembered. He slid a hand up the clerk's belt to the sheath-knife; and they drew very close to each other in that last clinch.

Percy Cuthfert felt his strength leave him. The lower portion of his body was useless. The inert weight of Weatherbee crushed him,—crushed him and pinned him there like a bear under a trap. The cabin became filled with a familiar odor, and he knew the bread to be burning. Yet what did it matter? He would never need it. And there were all of six cupfuls of sugar in the cache,—if he had foreseen this he would not have been so saving the last several days. Would the wind-vane ever move? It might even be veering now. Why not? Had he not seen the sun to-day? He would go and see. No; it was impossible to move. He had not thought the clerk so heavy a man.

How quickly the cabin cooled! The fire must be out. The cold was forcing in. It must be below zero already, and the ice creeping up the inside of the door. He could not see it, but his past experience enabled him to gauge its progress by the cabin's temperature. The lower hinge must be white ere now. Would the tale of this ever reach the world? How would his friends take it? They would read it over their coffee, most likely, and talk it over at the clubs. He could see them very clearly. "Poor Old Cuthfert," they murmured; "not such a bad sort of a chap, after all." He smiled at their eulogies, and passed on in search of a Turkish bath. It was the same old crowd upon the streets. Strange, they did not notice his moosehide moccasins and tattered German socks! He would take a cab. And after the bath a shave would not be bad. No; he would eat first. Steak, and potatoes, and green things,—how fresh it all was! And what was that? Squares of honey, streaming liquid amber! But why did they bring so much? Ha! ha! he could never eat it all. Shine! Why certainly. He put his foot on the box. The bootblack looked curiously up at him, and he remembered his moosehide moccasins and went away hastily.

Hark! The wind-vane must be surely spinning. No; a mere singing in his ears. That was all,—a mere singing. The ice must have passed the latch by now. More likely the upper hinge was covered. Between the moss-chinked roof-poles, little points of frost began to appear. How slowly they grew! No; not so slowly. There was a new one, and there another. Two—three—four; they were coming too fast to count. There were two growing together. And there, a third had joined them. Why, there were no more spots. They had run together and formed a sheet.

Well, he would have company. If Gabriel ever broke the silence of the North, they would stand together, hand in hand, before the great White Throne. And God would judge them, God would judge them!

Then Percy Cuthfert closed his eyes and dropped off to sleep.

To the Man on Trail

D ump it in."

"But I say, Kid, isn't that going it a little too strong? Whiskey and alcohol's bad enough; but when it comes to brandy and pepper-sauce and"—

"Dump it in. Who's making this punch, anyway?" And Malemute Kid smiled benignantly through the clouds of steam. "By the time you've been in this country as long as I have, my son, and lived on rabbit-tracks and salmon-belly, you'll learn that Christmas comes only once per annum. And a Christmas without punch is sinking a hole to bedrock with nary a pay-streak."

"Stack up on that fer a high cyard," approved Big Jim Belden, who had come down from his claim on Mazy May to spend Christmas, and who, as every one knew, had been living the two months past on straight moose-meat. "Hain't fergot the *hooch* we-uns made on the Tanana, hev yeh?"

"Well, I guess yes. Boys, it would have done your

hearts good to see that whole tribe fighting drunk—and all because of a glorious ferment of sugar and sour dough. That was before your time," Malemute Kid said as he turned to Stanley Prince, a young mining expert who had been in two years. "No white women in the country then, and Mason wanted to get married. Ruth's father was chief of the Tananas, and objected, like the rest of the tribe. Stiff? Why, I used my last pound of sugar; finest work in that line I ever did in my life. You should have seen the chase, down the river and across the portage."

"But the squaw?" asked Louis Savoy, the tall French-Canadian, becoming interested; for he had heard of this wild deed, when at Forty Mile the preceding winter.

Then Malemute Kid, who was a born raconteur, told the unvarnished tale of the Northland Lochinvar. More than one rough adventurer of the North felt his heart-strings draw closer, and experienced vague yearnings for the sunnier pastures of the Southland, where life promised something more than a barren struggle with cold and death.

"We struck the Yukon just behind the first ice-run," he concluded, "and the tribe only a quarter of an hour behind. But that saved us; for the second run broke the jam above and shut them out. When they finally got into Nuklukyeto, the whole Post was ready for them. And as to the foregathering, ask Father Roubeau here: he performed the ceremony."

The Jesuit took the pipe from his lips, but could only express his gratification with patriarchal smiles, while Protestant and Catholic vigorously applauded.

"By gar!" ejaculated Louis Savoy, who seemed overcome by the romance of it. "La petite squaw; mon Mason brav. By gar!"

Then, as the first tin cups of punch went round, Bettles the Unquenchable sprang to his feet and struck up his favorite drinking song:—

"There's Henry Ward Beecher
And Sunday-school teachers,
    All drink of the sassafras root;
But you bet all the same,
If it had its right name,
    It's the juice of the forbidden fruit."

"Oh the juice of the forbidden fruit,"

roared out the Bacchanalian chorus,—

"Oh the juice of the forbidden fruit;
    But you bet all the same,
    If it had its right name,
It's the juice of the forbidden fruit."

Malemute Kid's frightful concoction did its work; the men of the camps and trails unbent in its genial glow, and jest and song and tales of past adventure went round the board. Aliens from a dozen lands, they toasted each and all. It was the Englishman, Prince, who pledged "Uncle Sam, the precocious infant of the New World;" the Yankee, Bettles, who drank to "The Queen, God bless her;" and together, Savoy and Meyers, the German trader, clanged their cups to Alsace and Lorraine.

Then Malemute Kid arose, cup in hand, and glanced at the greased-paper window, where the frost stood full three inches thick. "A health to the man on trail this night; may his grub hold out; may his dogs keep their legs; may his matches never miss fire."

Crack! Crack!—they heard the familiar music of the dog-whip, the whining howl of the Malemutes, and the crunch of a sled as it drew up to the cabin. Conversation languished while they waited the issue.

"An old-timer; cares for his dogs and then himself," whispered Malemute Kid to Prince, as they listened to the snapping jaws and the wolfish snarls and yelps of pain which proclaimed to their practiced ears that the stranger was beating back their dogs while he fed his own.

Then came the expected knock, sharp and confident, and the stranger entered. Dazzled by the light, he hesitated a moment at the door, giving to all a chance for scrutiny. He was a striking personage, and a most picturesque one, in his Arctic dress of wool and fur. Standing six foot two or three, with proportionate breadth of shoulders and depth of chest, his smooth-shaven face nipped by the cold to a gleaming pink, his long lashes and eyebrows white with ice, and the ear and neck flaps of his great wolfskin cap loosely raised, he seemed, of a verity, the Frost King, just stepped in out of the night. Clasped outside his mackinaw jacket, a beaded belt held two large Colt's revolvers and a hunting-knife, while he carried, in addition to the inevitable dogwhip, a smokeless rifle of the largest bore and latest pattern. As he came forward, for all his step was firm and elastic, they could see that fatigue bore heavily upon him.

An awkward silence had fallen, but his hearty "What cheer, my lads?" put them quickly at ease, and the next instant Malemute Kid and he had gripped hands. Though they had never met, each had heard of the other, and the recognition was mutual. A sweeping introduction and a mug of punch were forced upon him before he could explain his errand.

"How long since that basket-sled, with three men and eight dogs, passed?" he asked.

"An even two days ahead. Are you after them?"

"Yes; my team. Run them off under my very nose, the cusses. I've gained two days on them already,—pick them up on the next run."

"Reckon they'll show spunk?" asked Belden, in order to keep up the conversation, for Malemute Kid already had the coffee-pot on and was busily frying bacon and moose-meat.

The stranger significantly tapped his revolvers.

"When'd yeh leave Dawson?"

"Twelve o'clock."

"Last night?"—as a matter of course.

"To-day."

A murmur of surprise passed round the circle. And well it might; for it was just midnight, and seventy-five miles of rough river trail was not to be sneered at for a twelve hours' run.

The talk soon became impersonal, however, harking back to the trails of childhood. As the young stranger ate of the rude fare, Malemute Kid attentively studied his face. Nor was he long in deciding that it was fair, honest, and open, and that he liked it. Still youthful, the lines had been firmly traced by toil and hardship. Though genial in conversation, and mild when at rest, the blue eyes gave promise of the hard steel-glitter which comes when called into action, especially against odds. The heavy jaw and square-cut chin demonstrated rugged pertinacity and indomitability. Nor, though the attributes of the lion were there, was there wanting the certain softness, the hint of womanliness, which bespoke the emotional nature.

"So thet's how me an' the ol' woman got spliced," said Belden, concluding the exciting tale of his courtship. " 'Here we be, dad,' sez she. 'An' may yeh be damned,' sez he to her, an' then to me, 'Jim, yeh—yeh git outen them good duds o' yourn; I want a right peart slice o' thet forty acre ploughed 'fore dinner.' An' then he turns on her an' sez, 'An' yeh, Sal; yeh sail inter them dishes.' An' then he sort o' sniffled an' kissed her. An' I was thet happy,—but he seen me an' roars out, 'Yeh, Jim!' An' yeh bet I dusted fer the barn."

"Any kids waiting for you back in the States?" asked the stranger.

"Nope; Sal died 'fore any come. Thet's why I'm here." Belden abstractedly began to light his pipe, which had failed to go out, and then brightened up with, "How 'bout yerself, stranger,—married man?"

For reply, he opened his watch, slipped it from the

thong which served for a chain, and passed it over. Belden pricked up the slush-lamp, surveyed the inside of the case critically, and swearing admiringly to himself, handed it over to Louis Savoy. With numerous "By gars!" he finally surrendered it to Prince, and they noticed that his hands trembled and his eyes took on a peculiar softness. And so it passed from horny hand to horny hand—the pasted photograph of a woman, the clinging kind that such men fancy, with a babe at the breast. Those who had not yet seen the wonder were keen with curiosity; those who had, became silent and retrospective. They could face the pinch of famine, the grip of scurvy, or the quick death by field or flood; but the pictured semblance of a stranger woman and child made women and children of them all.

"Never have seen the youngster yet,—he's a boy, she says, and two years old," said the stranger as he received the treasure back. A lingering moment he gazed upon it, then snapped the case and turned away, but not quick enough to hide the restrained rush of tears.

Malemute Kid led him to a bunk and bade him turn in.

"Call me at four, sharp. Don't fail me," were his last words, and a moment later he was breathing in the heaviness of exhausted sleep.

"By Jove! he's a plucky chap," commented Prince. "Three hours' sleep after seventy-five miles with the dogs, and then the trail again. Who is he, Kid?"

"Jack Westondale. Been in going on three years, with nothing but the name of working like a horse, and any amount of bad luck to his credit. I never knew him, but Sitka Charley told me about him."

"It seems hard that a man with a sweet young wife like his should be putting in his years in this God-forsaken hole, where every year counts two on the outside."

"The trouble with him is clean grit and stubbornness. He's cleaned up twice with a stake, but lost it both times."

Here the conversation was broken off by an uproar from

Bettles, for the effect had begun to wear away. And soon the bleak years of monotonous grub and deadening toil were being forgotten in rough merriment. Malemute Kid alone seemed unable to lose himself, and cast many an anxious look at his watch. Once he put on his mittens and beaver-skin cap, and leaving the cabin, fell to rummaging about in the cache.

Nor could he wait the hour designated; for he was fifteen minutes ahead of time in rousing his guest. The young giant had stiffened badly, and brisk rubbing was necessary to bring him to his feet. He tottered painfully out of the cabin, to find his dogs harnessed and everything ready for the start. The company wished him good luck and a short chase, while Father Roubeau, hurriedly blessing him, led the stampede for the cabin; and small wonder, for it is not good to face seventy-four degrees below zero with naked ears and hands.

Malemute Kid saw him to the main trail, and there, gripping his hand heartily, gave him advice.

"You'll find a hundred pounds of salmon-eggs on the sled," he said. "The dogs will go as far on that as with one hundred and fifty of fish, and you can't get dog-food at Pelly, as you probably expected." The stranger started, and his eyes flashed, but he did not interrupt. "You can't get an ounce of food for dog or man till you reach Five Fingers, and that's a stiff two hundred miles. Watch out for open water on the Thirty Mile River, and be sure you take the big cut-off above Le Barge."

"How did you know it? Surely the news can't be ahead of me already?"

"I don't know it; and what's more, I don't want to know it. But you never owned that team you're chasing. Sitka Charley sold it to them last spring. But he sized you up to me as square once, and I believe him. I've seen your face; I like it. And I've seen—why, damn you, hit the high places for salt water and that wife of yours, and"—Here the Kid unmittened and jerked out his sack.

"No; I don't need it," and the tears froze on his

cheeks as he convulsively gripped Malemute Kid's hand.

"Then don't spare the dogs; cut them out of the traces as fast as they drop; buy them, and think they're cheap at ten dollars a pound. You can get them at Five Fingers, Little Salmon, and the Hootalinqua. And watch our for wet feet," was his parting advice. "Keep a-traveling up to twenty-five, but if it gets below that, build a fire and change your socks."

Fifteen minutes had barely elapsed when the jungle of bells announced new arrivals. The door opened, and a mounted policeman of the Northwest Territory entered, followed by two half-breed dog-drivers. Like Westondale, they were heavily armed and showed signs of fatigue. The half-breeds had been born to the trail, and bore it easily; but the young policeman was badly exhausted. Still, the dogged obstinacy of his race held him to the pace he had set, and would hold him till he dropped in his tracks.

"When did Westondale pull out?" he asked. "He stopped here, didn't he?" This was supererogatory, for the tracks told their own tale too well.

Malemute Kid had caught Belden's eye, and he, scenting the wind, replied evasively, "A right peart while back."

"Come, my man; speak up," the policeman admonished.

"Yeh seem to want him right smart. Hez he ben gittin' cantankerous down Dawson way?"

"Held up Harry McFarland's for forty thousand; exchanged it at the P. C. store for a check on Seattle; and who's to stop the cashing of it if we don't overtake him? When did he pull out?"

Every eye suppressed its excitement, for Malemute Kid had given the cue, and the young officer encountered wooden faces on every hand.

Striding over to Prince, he put the question to him.

Though it hurt him, gazing into the frank, earnest face of his fellow countryman, he replied inconsequentially on the state of the trail.

Then he espied Father Roubeau, who could not lie. "A quarter of an hour ago; the priest answered; "but he had four hours' rest for himself and dogs."

"Fifteen minutes' start, and he's fresh! My God!" The poor fellow staggered back, half fainting from exhaustion and disappointment, murmuring something about the run from Dawson in ten hours and the dogs being played out.

Malemute Kid forced a mug of punch upon him; then he turned for the door, ordering the dog-drivers to follow. But the warmth and promise of rest were too tempting, and they objected strenuously. The Kid was conversant with their French patois, and followed it anxiously.

They swore that the dogs were gone up; that Siwash and Babette would have to be shot before the first mile was covered; that the rest were almost as bad; and that it would be better for all hands to rest up.

"Lend me five dogs?" he asked, turning to Malemute Kid.

But the Kid shook his head.

"I'll sign a check on Captain Constantine for five thousand,—here's my papers,—I'm authorized to draw at my own discretion."

Again the silent refusal.

"Then I'll requisition them in the name of the Queen."

Smiling incredulously, the Kid glanced at his well-stocked arsenal, and the Englishman, realizing his impotency, turned for the door. But the dog-drivers still objecting, he whirled upon them fiercely, calling them women and curs. The swart face of the older half-breed blushed angrily, as the drew himself up and promised in good, round terms that he would travel his leader off his legs, and would then be delighted to plant him in the snow.

The young officer—and it required his whole will—walked steadily to the door, exhibiting a freshness he did not possess. But hey all knew and appreciated his proud effort; nor could he veil the twinges of agony that shot across his face. Covered with frost, the dogs were curled up in the snow, and it was almost impossible to get them to their feet. The poor brutes whined under the stinging lash, for the dog-drivers were angry and cruel; nor till Babette, the leader, was cut from the traces, could they break out the sled and get under way.

"A dirty scoundrel and a liar!" "By gar! him no good!" "A thief!" "Worse than an Indian!" It was evident that they were angry—first, at the way they had been deceived; and second, at the outraged ethics of the Northland, where honesty, above all, was man's prime jewel. "An' we gave the cuss a hand, after knowin' what he'd did." All eyes were turned accusingly upon Malemute Kid, who rose from the corner where he had been making Babette comfortable, and silently emptied the bowl for a final round of punch.

"It's a cold night, boys,—a bitter cold night," was the irrelevant commencement of his defense. "You've all traveled trail, and know what that stands for. Don't jump a dog when he's down. You've only heard one side. A whiter man than Jack Westondale never ate from the same pot nor stretched blanket with you or me. Last fall he gave his whole clean-up, forty thousand, to Joe Castrell, to buy in on Dominion. To-day he'd be a millionaire. But while he stayed behind at Circle City, taking care of his partner with the scurvy, what does Castrell do? Goes into McFarland's, jumps the limit, and drops the whole sack. Found him dead in the snow the next day. And poor Jack laying his plans to go out this winter to his wife and the boy he's never seen. You'll notice he took exactly what his partner lost,—forty thousand. Well, he's gone out; and what are you going to do about it?"

The Kid glanced round the circle of his judges, noted the softening of their faces, then raised his mug aloft. "So a health to the man on trail this night; may his grub hold out; may his dogs keep their legs; may his matches never miss fire. God prosper him; good luck go with him; and"—

"Confusion to the Mounted Police!" cried Bettles, to the crash of the empty cups.

The White Silence

Carmen won't last a couple of days." Mason spat out a chunk of ice and surveyed the poor animal ruefully, then put her foot in his mouth and proceeded to bite out the ice which clustered cruelly between the toes.

"I never saw a dog with a highfalutin' name that ever was worth a rap," he said, as he concluded his task and shoved her aside. "They just fade away and die under the responsibility. Did ye ever see one go wrong with a sensible name like Cassiar, Siwash, or Husky? No, sir! Take a look at Shookum here, he's"—

Snap! The lean brute flashed up, the white teeth just missing Mason's throat.

"Ye will, will ye?" A shrewd clout behind the ear with the butt of the dogwhip stretched the animal in the snow, quivering softly, a yellow slaver dripping from his fangs.

"As I was saying, just look at Shookum, here—he's got the spirit. Bet ye he eats Carmen before the week's out."

"I'll bank another proposition against that," replied Malemute Kid, reversing the frozen bread placed before the fire to thaw. "We'll eat Shookum before the trip is over. What d' ye say, Ruth?"

The Indian woman settled the coffee with a piece of ice, glanced form Malemute Kid to her husband, then at the dogs, but vouchsafed no reply. It was such a palpable truism that none was necessary. Two hundred miles of unbroken trail in prospect, with a scant six days' grub for themselves and none for the dogs, could admit no other alternative. The two men and the woman grouped about the fire and began their meagre meal. The dogs lay in their harnesses, for it was a midday halt, and watched each mouthful enviously.

"No more lunches after to-day," said Malemute Kid. "And we've got to keep a close eye on the dogs,—they're getting vicious. They'd just as soon pull a fellow down as not, if they get a chance."

"And I was president of an Epworth once, and taught in the Sunday school." Having irrelevantly delivered himself of this, Mason fell into a dreamy contemplation of his steaming moccasins, but was aroused by Ruth filling his cup. "Thank God, we've got slathers of tea! I've seen it growing, down in Tennessee. What wouldn't I give for a hot corn pone just now! Never mind, Ruth; you won't starve much longer, nor wear moccasins either."

The woman threw off her gloom at this, and in her eyes welled up a great love for her white lord,—the first white man she had ever seen,—the first man whom she had known to treat a woman as something better than a mere animal or beast of burden.

"Yes, Ruth," continued her husband, having recourse to the macaronic jargon in which it was alone possible for them to understand each other; "wait till we clean up and pull for the Outside. We'll take the White Man's canoe and go to the Salt Water. Yes, bad water, rough water,—great mountains dance up and down all the time. And so big, so far, so far away,—you travel ten sleep, twenty sleep, forty sleep" (he graphically enumerated the days on his fingers), "all the time water, bad water. Then you come to great village, plenty people, just the same mosquitoes next summer. Wigwams oh, so high,—ten, twenty pines. Hi-yu skookum!"

He paused impotently, cast an appealing glance at Malemute Kid, then laboriously placed the twenty pines, end on end, by sign language. Malemute Kid smiled with cheery cynicism; but Ruth's eyes were wide with wonder, and with pleasure; for she half believed he was joking, and such condescension pleased her poor woman's heart.

"And then you step into a—a box, and pouf! up you go." He tossed his empty cup in the air by way of illustration, and as he deftly caught it, cried: "And biff! down you come. Oh, great medicine-men! You go Fort Yukon, I go Arctic City,—twenty-five sleep,—big string, all the time,—I catch him string,—I say, 'Hello, Ruth! How are ye?'—and you say, 'Is that my good husband?'—and I say 'Yes,'—and you say, 'No can bake good bread, no more soda,'—then I say, 'Look in cache, under flour; good-by.' You look and catch plenty soda. All the time you Fort Yukon, me Arctic City. Hi-yu medicine-man!"

Ruth smiled so ingenuously at the fairy story, that both men burst into laughter. A row among the dogs cut short the wonders of the Outside, and by the time the snarling combatants were separated, she had lashed the sleds and all was ready for the trail.

"Mush! Baldy! Hi! Mush on!" Mason worked his whip smartly, and as the dogs whined low in the traces, broke out the sled with the gee-pole. Ruth followed with the second team, leaving Malemute Kid, who had helped her start, to bring up the rear. Strong man, brute that he was, capable of felling an ox at a blow, he could not bear to beat the poor animals, but humored them as a dog-driver rarely does,—nay, almost wept with them in their misery.

"Come, mush on there, you poor sore-footed brutes!" he murmured, after several ineffectual attempts to start the load. But his patience was at last rewarded, and though whimpering with pain, they hastened to join their fellows.

No more conversation; the toil of the trail will not permit such extravagance. And of all deadening labors, that of the Northland trail is the worst. Happy is the man who can weather a day's travel at the price of silence, and that on a beaten track.

And of all heart-breaking labors, that of breaking trail is the worst. At every step the great webbed shoe sinks till the snow is level with the knee. Then up, straight up, the deviation of a fraction of an inch being a certain precursor of disaster, the snowshoe must be lifted till the surface is cleared; then forward, down, and the other foot is raised perpendicularly for the matter of half a yard. He who tries this for the first time, if haply he avoids bringing his shoes in dangerous propinquity and measures not his length on the treacherous footing, will give up exhausted at the end of a hundred yards; he who can keep out of the way of the dogs for a whole day may well crawl into his sleeping-bag with a clear conscience and a pride which passeth all understanding; and he who travels twenty sleeps on the Long Trail is a man whom the gods may envy.

The afternoon wore on, and with the awe, born of the White Silence, the voiceless travelers bent to their work. Nature has many tricks wherewith she convinces man of his finity,—the ceaseless flow of the tides, the fury of the storm, the shock of the earthquake, the long roll of heaven's artillery,—but the most tremendous, the most stupefying of all, is the passive phase of the White Silence. All movement ceases, the sky clears, the heavens are as brass; the slightest whisper seems sacrilege, and man becomes timid, affrighted at the sound of his own voice. Sole speck of life journeying across the ghostly wastes of a dead world, he trembles at his audacity, realizes that his is a maggot's life, nothing more. Strange thoughts arise unsummoned, and the mystery of all things strives for utterance. And the fear of death, of God, of the universe, comes over him,—the hope of the Resurrection and the Life, the yearning for immortality, the vain striving of the imprisoned essence,—it is then, if ever, man walks alone with God.

So wore the day away. The river took a great bend, and Mason headed his team for the cut-off across the narrow neck of land. But the dogs balked at the high bank. Again and again, though Ruth and Malemute Kid were shoving on the sled, they slipped back. Then came the concerted effort. The miserable creatures, weak from hunger, exerted their last strength. Up—up—the sled poised on the top of the bank; but the leader swung the string of dogs behind him to the right, fouling Mason's snowshoes. The result was grievous. Mason was whipped off his feet; one of the dogs fell in the traces; and the sled toppled back, dragging everything to the bottom again.

Slash! the whip fell among the dogs savagely, especially upon the one which had fallen.

"Don't, Mason," entreated Malemute Kid; "the poor devil's on its last legs. Wait and we'll put my team on."

Mason deliberately withheld the whip till the last word had fallen, then out flashed the long lash, completely curling about the offending creature's body. Carmen—for it was Carmen—cowered in the snow, cried piteously, then rolled over on her side.

It was a tragic moment, a pitiful incident of the trail,—a dying dog, two comrades in anger. Ruth glanced solicitously from man to man. But Malemute Kid restrained himself, though there was a world of reproach in his eyes, and bending over the dog, cut the traces. No word was spoken. The teams were double-spanned and the difficulty overcome; the sleds were under way again, the dying dog dragging herself along in the rear. As long as an animal can travel, it is not shot, and this last chance is accorded it;—the crawling into camp, if it can, in the hope of a moose being killed.

Already penitent for his angry action, but too stubborn to make amends, Mason toiled on at the head of the cavalcade, little dreaming that danger hovered in the air. The timber clustered thick in the sheltered bottom, and through this they threaded their way. Fifty feet or more from the trail towered a lofty pine. For generations it had stood there, and for generations destiny had had this one end in view,—perhaps the same had been decreed of Mason.

He stooped to fasten the loosened thong of his moccasin. The sleds came to a halt and the dogs lay down in the snow without a whimper. The stillness was weird; not a breath rustled the frost-encrusted forest; the cold and silence of outer space had chilled the heart and smote the trembling lips of nature. A sigh pulsed through the air,—they did not seem to actually hear it, but rather felt it, like the premonition of movement in a motionless void. Then the great tree, burdened with its weight of years and snow, played its last part in the tragedy of life. He heard the warning crash and attempted to spring up, but almost erect, caught the blow squarely on the shoulder.

The sudden danger, the quick death,—how often had Malemute Kid faced it! The pine needles were still quivering as he gave his commands and sprang into action. Nor did the Indian girl faint or raise her voice in idle wailing, as might many of her white sisters. At his order, she threw her weight on the end of a quickly extemporized handspike, easing the pressure and listening to her husband's groans, while Malemute Kid attacked the tree with his axe. The steel rang merrily as it bit into the frozen trunk, each stroke being accompanied by a forced, audible respiration, the "Huh!" "Huh!" of the woodsman.

At last the Kid laid the pitiable thing that was once a man in the snow. But worse than his comrade's pain was the dumb anguish in the woman's face, the blended look of hopeful, hopeless query. Little was said; those of the Northland are early taught the futility of words and the inestimable value of deeds. With the temperature at sixty-five below zero, a man cannot lie many minutes in the snow and live. So the sled-lashings were cut, and the sufferer, rolled in furs, laid on a couch of boughs. Before him roared a fire, built of the very wood which wrought the mishap. Behind and partially over him was stretched the primitive fly,—a piece of canvas, which caught the radiating heat and threw it back and down upon him,—a trick which men may know who study physics at the fount.

And men who have shared their bed with death know when the call is sounded. Mason was terribly crushed. The most cursory examination revealed it. His right arm, leg, and back, were broken; his limbs were paralyzed from the hips; and the likelihood of internal injuries was large. An occasional moan was his only sign of life.

No hope; nothing to be done. The pitiless night crept slowly by,—Ruth's portion, the despairing stoicism of her race, and Malemute Kid adding new lines to his face of bronze. In fact, Mason suffered least of all, for he spent his time in Eastern Tennessee, in the Great Smoky Mountains, living over the scenes of his childhood. And most pathetic was the melody of his long-forgotten Southern vernacular, as he raved of swimming-holes and coon-hunts and watermelon raids. It was as Greek to Ruth, but the Kid understood and felt,—felt as only one can feel who has been shut out for years from all that civilization means.

Morning brought consciousness to the stricken man, and Malemute Kid bent closer to catch his whispers.

"You remember when we foregathered on the Tanana, four years come next ice-run? I didn't care so much for her then. It was more like she was pretty, and there was a smack of excitement about it, I think. But d'ye know, I've come to think a heap of her. She's been a good wife to me, always at my shoulder in the pinch. And when it comes to trading, you know there isn't her equal. D'ye recollect the time she shot the Moosehorn Rapids to pull you and me off that rock, the bullets whipping the water like hailstones?—and the time of the famine at Nuklukyeto?—or when she raced the ice-run to bring the news? Yes, she's been a good wife to me, better 'n that other one. Didn't know I'd been there? Never told you, eh? Well, I tried it once, down in the States. That's why I'm here. Been raised together, too. I came away to give her a chance for divorce. She got it.

"But that's got nothing to do with Ruth. I had thought of cleaning up and pulling for the Outside next year,—her and I,—but it's too late. Don't send her back to her people, Kid. It's beastly hard for a woman to go back. Think of it!—nearly four years on our bacon and beans and flour and dried fruit, and then to go back to her fish and cariboo. It's not good for her to have tried our ways, to come to know they're better 'n her people's, and then return to them. Take care of her, Kid,—why don't you,—but no, you always fought shy of them,—and you never told me why you came to this country. Be kind to her, and send her back to the States as soon as you can. But fix it so as she can come back,—liable to get homesick, you know.

"And the youngster—it's drawn us closer, Kid. I only hope it is a boy. Think of it!—flesh of my flesh, Kid. He mustn't stop in this country. And if it's a girl, why she can't. Sell my furs; they'll fetch at least five thousand, and I've got as much more with the company. And handle my interests with yours. I think that bench claim will show up. See that he gets a good schooling; and Kid, above all, don't let him come back. This country was not made for white men.

"I'm a gone man, Kid. Three or four sleeps at the best. You've got to go on. You must go on! Remember, it's my wife, it's my boy,—O God! I hope it's a boy! You can't stay by me,—and I charge you, a dying man, to pull on."

"Give me three days," pleaded Malemute Kid. "You may change for the better; something may turn up."

"No."

"Just three days."

"You must pull on."

"Two days."

"It's my wife and my boy, Kid. You would not ask it."

"One day."

"No, no! I charge"—

"Only one day. We can shave it through on the grub, and I might knock over a moose."

"No,—all right; one day, but not a minute more. And

Kid, don't—don't leave me to face it alone. Just a shot, one pull on the trigger. You understand. Think of it! Flesh of my flesh, and I'll never live to see him!

"Send Ruth here. I want to say good-by and tell her that she must think of the boy and not wait till I'm dead. She might refuse to go with you if I didn't. Good-by, old man; good-by.

"Kid! I say—a—sink a hole above the pup, next to the slide. I panned out forty cents on my shovel there.

"And Kid!" he stooped lower to catch the last faint words, the dying man's surrender of his pride. "I'm sorry—for—you know—Carmen."

Leaving the girl crying softly over her man, Malemute Kid slipped into his *parka* and snowshoes, tucked his rifle under his arm, and crept away into the forest. He was no tyro in the stern sorrows of the Northland, but never had he faced so stiff a problem as this. In the abstract, it was a plain, mathematical proposition,—three possible lives as against one doomed one. But now he hesitated. For five years, shoulder to shoulder, on the rivers and trails, in the camps and mines, facing death by field and flood and famine, had they knitted the bonds of their comradeship. So close was the tie, that he had often been conscious of a vague jealousy of Ruth, from the first time she had come between. And now it must be severed by his own hand.

Though he prayed for a moose, just one moose, all game seemed to have deserted the land, and nightfall found the exhausted man crawling into camp, light-handed, heavy-hearted. An uproar from the dogs and shrill cries from Ruth hastened him.

Bursting into the camp, he saw the girl in the midst of the snarling pack, laying about her with an axe. The dogs had broken the iron rule of their masters and were rushing the grub. He joined the issue with his rifle reversed, and the hoary game of natural selection was played out with all the ruthlessness of its primeval environment. Rifle and axe went up and down, hit or missed with monotonous regularity; lithe bodies flashed, with wild eyes and dripping fangs; and man and beast fought for supremacy to the bitterest conclusion. Then the beaten brutes crept to the edge of the firelight, licking their wounds, voicing their misery to the stars.

The whole stock of dried salmon had been devoured, and perhaps five pounds of flour remained to tide them over two hundred miles of wilderness. Ruth returned to her husband, while Malemute Kid cut up the warm body of one of the dogs, the skull of which had been crushed by the axe. Every portion was carefully put away, save the hide and offal, which were cast to his fellows of the moment before.

Morning brought fresh trouble. The animals were turning on each other. Carmen, who still clung to her slender thread of life, was downed by the pack. The lash fell among them unheeded. They cringed and cried under the blows, but refused to scatter till the last wretched bit had disappeared,—bones, hide, hair, everything.

Malemute Kid went about his work, listening to Mason, who was back in Tennessee, delivering tangled discourses and wild exhortations to his brethren of other days.

Taking advantage of neighboring pines, he worked rapidly, and Ruth watched him make a cache similar to those sometimes used by hunters to preserve their meat from the wolverines and dogs. One after the other, he bent the tops of two small pines toward each other and nearly to the ground, making them fast with thongs of moosehide. Then he beat the dogs into submission and harnessed them to two of the sleds, loading the same with everything but the furs which enveloped Mason. These he wrapped and lashed tightly about him, fastening either end of the robes to the bent pines. A single stroke of his hunting-knife would release them and send the body high in the air.

Ruth had received her husband's last wishes and made no struggle. Poor girl, she had learned the lesson of obedience well. From a child, she had bowed, and seen all women bow, to the lords of creation, and it did not seem in the nature of things for woman to resist. The Kid permitted her one outburst of grief, as she kissed her husband,—her own people had no such custom,—then led her to the foremost sled and helped her into her snow-shoes. Blindly, instinctively, she took the gee-pole and whip, and "mushed" the dogs out on the trail. Then he returned to Mason, who had fallen into a coma; and long after she was out of sight, crouched by the fire, waiting, hoping, praying for his comrade to die.

It is not pleasant to be alone with painful thoughts in the White Silence. The silence of gloom is merciful, shrouding one as with protection and breathing a thousand intangible sympathies; but the bright White Silence, clear and cold, under steely skies, is pitiless.

An hour passed,—two hours,—but the man would not die. At high noon, the sun, without raising its rim above the southern horizon, threw a suggestion of fire athwart the heavens, then quickly drew it back. Malemute Kid roused and dragged himself to his comrade's side. He cast one glance about him. The White Silence seemed to sneer, and a great fear came upon him. There was a sharp report; Mason swung into his aerial sepulchre; and Malemute Kid lashed the dogs into a wild gallop as he fled across the snow.

The League of the Old Men

At the Barracks a man was being tried for his life. He was an old man, a native from the Whitefish River, which empties into the Yukon below Lake Le Barge. All Dawson was wrought up over the affair, and likewise the Yukon-dwellers for a thousand miles up and down. It has been the custom of the land-robbing and sea-robbing Anglo-Saxon to give the law to conquered peoples, and oftimes this law is harsh. But in the case of Imber the law for once seemed inadequate and weak. In the mathematical nature of things, equity did not reside in the punishment to be accorded him. The punishment was a foregone conclusion, there could be not doubt of that; and though it was capital, Imber had but one life, while the tale against him was one of scores.

In fact, the blood of so many was upon his hands that the killings attributed to him did not permit of precise enumeration. Smoking a pipe by the trailside or lounging around the stove, men made rough estimates of the numbers that had perished at his hand. They had been whites,

all of them, these poor murdered people, and they had
been slain singly, in pairs, and in parties. And so purpose-
less and wanton had been these killings, that they had long
been a mystery to the mounted police, even in the time of
the captains, and later, when the creeks realized, and a
governor came from the Dominion to make the land pay
for its prosperity.

But more mysterious still was the coming of Imber
to Dawson to give himself up. It was in the late spring,
when the Yukon was growling and writhing under its ice,
that the old Indian climbed painfully up the bank from
the river trail and stood blinking on the main street. Men
who had witnessed his advent, noted that he was weak
and tottery, and that he staggered over to a heap of cabin-
logs and sat down. He sat there a full day, staring straight
before him at the unceasing tide of white men that flooded
past. Many a head jerked curiously to the side to meet
his stare, and more than one remark was dropped anent
the old Siwash with so strange a look upon his face. No
end of men remembered afterward that they had been
struck by his extraordinary figure, and forever afterward
prided themselves upon their swift discernment of the unusual.

But it remained for Dickensen, Little Dickensen, to be
the hero of the occasion. Little Dickensen had come into
the land with great dreams and a pocketful of cash; but
with the cash the dreams vanished, and to earn his passage
back to the States he had accepted a clerical position with
the brokerage firm of Holbrook and Mason. Across the
street from the office of Holbrook and Mason was the
heap of cabin-logs upon which Imber sat. Dickensen
looked out of the window at him before he went to lunch;
and when he came back from lunch he looked out of the
window, and the old Siwash was still there.

Dickensen continued to look out of the window, and he,
too, forever afterward prided himself upon his swiftness of
discernment. He was a romantic little chap, and he likened
the immobile old heathen to the genius of the Siwash race,

gazing calm-eyed upon the hosts of the invading Saxon. The hours swept along, but Imber did not vary his posture, did not by a hair's-breadth move a muscle; and Dickensen remembered the man who once sat upright on a sled in the main street where men passed to and fro. They thought the man was resting, but later, when they touched him, they found him stiff and cold, frozen to death in the midst of the busy street. To undouble him, that he might fit into a coffin, they had been forced to lug him to a fire and thaw him out a bit. Dickensen shivered at the recollection.

Later on, Dickensen went out on the sidewalk to smoke a cigar and cool off; and a little later Emily Travis happened along. Emily Travis was dainty and delicate and rare, and whether in London or Klondike she gowned herself as befitted the daughter of a millionaire mining engineer. Little Dickensen deposited his cigar on an outside window ledge where he could find it again, and lifted his hat.

They chatted for ten minutes or so, when Emily Travis, glancing past Dickensen's shoulder, gave a startled little scream, Dickensen turned about to see, and was startled, too. Imber had crossed the street and was standing there, a gaunt and hungry-looking shadow, his gaze riveted upon the girl.

"What do you want?" Little Dickensen demanded, tremulously plucky.

Imber grunted and stalked up to Emily Travis. He looked her over, keenly and carefully, every square inch of her. Especially did he appear interested in her silky brown hair, and in the color of her cheek, faintly sprayed and soft, like the downy bloom of a butterfly wing. He walked around her, surveying her with the calculating eye of a man who studies the lines upon which a horse or a boat is builded. In the course of his circuit the pink shell of her ear came between his eye and the westering sun, and he stopped to contemplate its rosy transparency. Then he returned to her face and looked long and intently into her blue eyes. He grunted and laid a hand on her arm midway between the shoulder and elbow. With his other hand he lifted her forearm and doubled it back. Disgust and wonder showed in his face, and he dropped her arm with a contemptuous grunt. Then he muttered a few guttural syllables, turned his back upon her, and addressed himself to Dickensen.

Dickensen could not understand his speech, and Emily Travis laughed. Imber turned from one to the other, frowning, but both shook their heads. He was about to go away, when she called out:

"Oh, Jimmy! Come here!"

Jimmy came from the other side of the street. He was a big, hulking Indian clad in approved white-man style, with an Eldorado king's sombrero on his head. He talked with Imber, haltingly, with throaty spasms. Jimmy was a Sitkan, possessed of no more than a passing knowledge of the interior dialects.

"Him Whitefish man," he said to Emily Travis. "Me savve um talk no very much. Him want to look see chief white man."

"The Governor," suggested Dickensen.

Jimmy talked some more with the Whitefish man, and his face went grave and puzzled.

"I t'ink um want Cap'n Alexander," he explained. "Him say um kill white man, white woman, white boy, plenty kill um white people. Him want to die."

"Insane, I guess," said Dickensen.

"What you call dat?" queried Jimmy.

Dickensen thrust a finger figuratively inside his head and imparted a rotary motion thereto.

"Mebbe so, mebbe so," said Jimmy, returning to Imber, who still demanded the chief man of the white men.

A mounted policeman (unmounted for Klondike service) joined the group and heard Imber's wish repeated. He was a stalwart young fellow, broad-shouldered, deep-chested, legs cleanly built and stretched wide apart, and tall though Imber was, he towered above him by half a head. His eyes were cool, and gray, and steady, and he carried himself with the peculiar confidence of power that is bred of blood and tradition. His splendid masculinity was emphasized by his excessive boyishness,—he was a mere lad,—and his smooth cheek promised a blush as willingly as the cheek of a maid.

Imber was drawn to him at once. The fire leaped into his eyes at sight of a sabre slash that scarred his cheek. He ran a withered hand down the young fellow's leg and caressed the swelling thew. He smote the broad chest with his knuckles, and pressed and prodded the thick muscle-pads that covered the shoulders like a cuirass. The group had been added to by curious passers-by—husky miners, mountaineers, and frontiersmen, sons of the long-legged and broad-shouldered generations. Imber glanced from one to another then he spoke aloud in the Whitefish tongue.

"What did he say?" asked Dickensen.

"Him say um all the same one man, dat p'liceman," Jimmy interpreted.

Little Dickensen was little, and what of Miss Travis, he felt sorry for having asked the question.

The policeman was sorry for him and stepped into the breath. "I fancy there may be something in his story. I'll take him up to the captain for examination. Tell him to come along with me, Jimmy."

Jimmy indulged in more throaty spasms, and Imber grunted and looked satisfied.

"But ask him what he said, Jimmy, and what he meant when he took hold of my arm."

So spoke Emily Travis, and Jimmy put the question and received the answer.

"Him say you no afraid," said Jimmy.

Emily Travis looked pleased.

"Him say you no *skookum*, no strong, all the same very soft like little baby. Him break you, in um two hands, to little pieces. Him t'ink much funny, very strange, how you can be mother of men so big, so strong, like dat p'liceman.

Emily Travis kept her eyes up and unfaltering, but her cheeks were sprayed with scarlet. Little Dickensen blushed

and was quite embarrassed. The policeman's face blazed
with his boy's blood.

"Come along, you," he said gruffly, setting his shoulder
to the crowd and forcing a way.

Thus it was that Imber found his way to the Barracks,
where he made full and voluntary confession, and from the
precincts of which he never emerged.

Imber looked very tired. The fatigue of hopelessness
and age was in his face. His shoulders drooped depress-
ingly, and his eyes were lack-lustre. His mop of hair
should have been white, but sun and weatherbeat had
burned and bitten it so that it hung limp and lifeless and
colorless. He took no interest in what went on around him.
The courtroom was jammed with the men of the creeks
and trails, and there was an ominous note in the rumble
and grumble of their low-pitched voices, which came to
his ears like the growl of the sea from deep caverns.

He sat close by a window, and his apathetic eyes rested
now and again on the dreary scene without. The sky was
overcast, and a gray drizzle was falling. It was flood-time
on the Yukon. The ice was gone, and the river was up in
the town. Back and forth on the main street, in canoes and
poling-boats, passed the people that never rested. Often he
saw these boats turn aside from the street and enter the
flooded square that marked the Barracks' parade-ground.
Sometimes they disappeared beneath him, and he heard
them jar against the house-logs and their occupants scram-
ble in through the window. After that came the slush of
water against men's legs as they waded across the lower
room and mounted the stairs. Then they appeared in the
doorway, with doffed hats and dripping sea-boots, and
added themselves to the waiting crowd.

And while they centered their looks on him, and in grim
anticipation enjoyed the penalty he was to pay, Imber
looked at them, and mused on their ways, and on their
Law that never slept, but went on unceasing in good times
and bad, in flood and famine, through trouble and terror

and death, and which would go on unceasing, it seemed to him, to the end of time.

A man rapped sharply on a table, and the conversation droned away into silence. Imber looked at the man. He seemed one in authority, yet Imber divined the square-browed man who sat by a desk farther back to be the one chief over them all and over the man who had rapped. Another man by the same table uprose and began to read aloud from many fine sheets of paper. At the top of each sheet he cleared his throat, at the bottom moistened his fingers. Imber did not understand his speech, but the others did, and he knew that it made them angry. Sometimes it made them very angry, and once a man cursed him, in single syllables, stinging and tense, till a man at the table rapped him to silence.

For an interminable period the man read. His monotonous, sing-song utterance lured Imber to dreaming, and he was dreaming deeply when the man ceased. A voice spoke to him in his own Whitefish tongue, and he roused up, without surprise, to look upon the face of his sister's son, a young man who had wandered away years agone to make his dwelling with the whites.

"Thou dost not remember me," he said by way of greeting.

"Nay," Imber answered. "Thou art Howkan who went away. Thy mother be dead."

"She was an old woman," said Howkan.

But Imber did not hear, and Howkan, with hand upon his shoulder, roused him again.

"I shall speak to thee what the man has spoken, which is the tale of the troubles thou hast done and which thou hast told, O fool, to the Captain Alexander. And thou shalt understand say if it be true talk or talk not true. It is so commanded."

Howkan had fallen among the mission folk and been taught by them to read and write. In his hands he held the many fine sheets from which the man had read aloud, and which had been taken down by a clerk when Imber first made confession, through the mouth of Jimmy, to Captain Alexander. Howkan began to read. Imber listened for a space, when a wonderment rose up in his face and he broke in abruptly.

"That be my talk, Howkan. Yet from thy lips it comes when thy ears have not heard.

Howkan smirked with self-appreciation. His hair was parted in the middle. "Nay, from the paper it comes, O Imber. Never have my ears heard. From the paper it comes, through my eyes, into my head, and out of my mouth to thee. Thus it comes."

"Thus it comes? It be there in the paper?" Imber's voice sank in whisperful awe as he crackled the sheets 'twixt thumb and finger and stared at the charactery scrawled thereon. "It be a great medicine, Howkan, and thou art a worker of wonders."

"It be nothing, it be nothing," the young man responded carelessly and pridefully. He read at hazard from the document: *In that year, before the break of the ice, came an old man, and a boy who was lame of one foot. These also did I kill, and the old man made much noise—*"

"It be true," Imber interrupted breathlessly. "He made much noise and would not die for a long time. But how dost thou know, Howkan? The chief man of the white men told thee, mayhap? No one beheld me, and him alone have I told."

Howkan shook his head with impatience. "Have I not told thee it be there in the paper, O fool?"

Imber stared hard at the ink-scrawled surface. "As the hunter looks upon the snow and says, Here but yesterday there passed a rabbit; and here by the willow scrub it stood and listened; and heard, and was afraid; and here it turned upon its trail; and here it went with great swiftness, leaping wide; and here, with greater swiftness and wider leapings, came a lynx; and here, where the claws cut deep into the snow, the lynx made a very great leap; and here it struck, with the rabbit under and rolling belly up; and here leads off the trail of the lynx alone, and there is no more rabbit,—as the hunger looks upon the markings of the snow and says thus and so and here, dost thou, too, look upon the paper and say thus and so and here be the things old Imber hath done?"

"Even so," said Howkan. "And now do thou listen, and keep they woman's tongue between thy teeth till thou art called upon for speech."

Thereafter, and for a long time, Howkan read to him the confession, and Imber remained musing and silent. At the end, he said:

"It be my talk, and true talk, but I am grown old, Howkan, and forgotten things come back to me which were well for the head man there to know. First, there was the man who came over the Ice Mountains, with cunning traps made of iron, who sought the beaver of the Whitefish. Him I slew. And there were three men seeking gold on the Whitefish long ago. Them also I slew, and left them to the wolverines. And at the Five Fingers there was a man with a raft and much meat."

At the moments when Imber paused to remember, Howkan translated and a clerk reduced to writing. The courtroom listened stolidly to each unadorned little tragedy, till Imber told of a red-haired man whose eyes were crossed and whom he had killed with a remarkably long shot.

"Hell," said a man in the forefront of the onlookers. He said it soulfully and sorrowfully. He was red-haired. "Hell," he repeated. "That was my brother Bill." And at regular intervals throughout the session, his solemn "Hell" was heard in the courtroom; nor did his comrades check him, nor did the man at the table rap him to order.

Imber's head drooped once more, and his eyes went dull, as though a film rose up and covered them from the world. And he dreamed as only age can dream upon the colossal futility of youth.

Later, Howkan roused him again, saying: "Stand up, O Imber. It be commanded that thou tellest why you did these troubles, and slew these people, and at the end journeyed here seeking the Law."

Imber rose feebly to his feet and swayed back and forth. He began to speak in a low and faintly rumbling voice, but Howkan interrupted him.

"This old man, he is damn crazy," he said in English to the square-browed man. "His talk is foolish and like that of a child."

"We will hear his talk which is like that of a child," said the square-browed man. "And we will hear it, word for word, as he speaks it. Do you understand?"

Howkan understood, and Imber's eyes flashed, for he had witnessed the play between his sister's son and the man in authority. And then began the story, the epic of a bronze patriot which might well itself be wrought into bronze for the generations unborn. The crowd fell strangely silent, and the square-browed judge leaned head on hand and pondered his soul and the soul of his race. Only was heard the deep tones of Imber, rhythmically alternating with the shrill voice of the interpreter, and now and again, like the bell of the Lord, the wondering and meditative "Hell" of the red-haired man.

"I am Imber of the Whitefish people." So ran the interpretation of Howkan, whose inherent barbarism gripped hold of him, and who lost his mission culture and veneered civilization as he caught the savage ring and rhythm of old Imber's tale. "My father was Otsbaok, a strong man. The land was warm with sunshine and gladness when I was a boy. The people did not hunger after strange things, nor hearken to new voices, and the ways of their fathers were their ways. The women found favor in the eyes of the young men, and the young men looked upon them with content. Babes hung at the breasts of the women, and they were heavy-hipped with increase of the tribe. Men were men in those days. In peace and plenty, and in war and famine, they were men.

"At that time there was more fish in the water than now, and more meat in the forest. Our dogs were wolves, warm with thick hides and hard to the frost and storm. And as with our dogs so with us, for we were likewise hard to the frost and storm. And when the Pellys came into our land we slew them and were slain. For we were men, we Whitefish, and our fathers and our fathers' fathers had fought against the Pellys and determined the bounds of the land.

"As I say, with our dogs, so with us. And one day came the first white man. He dragged himself, so, on hand and knee, in the snow. And his skin was stretched tight, and his bones were sharp beneath. Never was such a man, we thought, and we wondered of what strange tribe he was, and of its land. And he was weak, most weak, like a little child, so that we gave him a place by the fire, and warm furs to lie upon, and we gave him food as little children are given food.

"And with him with a dog, large as three of our dogs, and very weak. The hair of this dog was short, and not warm, and the tail was frozen so that the end fell off. And this strange dog we fed, and bedded by the fire, and fought from it our dogs, which else would have killed him. And what of the moose meat and the sun-dried salmon, the man and dog took strength to themselves; and what of the strength they became big and unafraid. And the man spoke loud words and laughed at the old men and young men, and looked boldly upon the maidens. And the dog fought with our dogs, and for all of his short hair and softness slew three of them in one day.

"When we asked the man concerning his people, he said, 'I have many brothers,' and laughed in a way that was not good. And when he was in his full strength he went away, and with him went Noda, daughter to the chief. First, after that, was one of our bitches brought to pup. And never was there such a breed of dogs,—big-headed, thick-jawed, and short-haired, and helpless. Well do I remember my father, Otsbaok, a strong man. His face was black with anger at such helplessness, and he took a stone, so, and so, and there was no more helplessness. And two summers after that came Noda back to us with a man-child in the hollow of her arm.

"And that was the beginning. Came a second white man, with short-haired dogs, which he left behind him when he went. And with him went six of our strongest dogs, for which, in trade, he had given Koo-So-Tee, my mother's brother, a wonderful pistol that fired with great swiftness six times. And Koo-So-Tee was very big, what of the pistol, and laughed at our bows and arrows. 'Woman's things,' he called them, and went forth against the bald-face grizzly, with the pistol in his hand. Now it be known that it is not good to hunt the bald-face with a pistol, but how were we to know? and how was Koo-So-Tee to know? So he went against the bald-face, very brave, and fired the pistol with great swiftness six times; and the bald-face but grunted and broke in his breast like it were an egg, and like honey from a bee's nest dripped the brains of Koo-So-Tee upon the ground. He was a good hunter, and there was no one to bring meat to his squaw and children. And we were bitter, and we said, 'That which for the white men is well, is for us not well.' And this be true. There be many white men and fat, but their ways have made us few and lean.

"Came the third white man, with great wealth of all manner of wonderful foods and things. And twenty of our strongest dogs he took from us in trade. Also, what of presents and great promises, ten of our young hunters did he take with him on a journey which fared no man knew where. It is said they died in the snow of the Ice Mountains where man has never been, or in the Hills of Silence which are beyond the edge of the earth. Be that as it may, dogs and young hunters were seen never again by the Whitefish people.

"And more white men came with the years, and ever, with pay and presents, they led the young men away with them. And sometimes the young men came back with strange tales of dangers and toils in the lands beyond the Pellys, and sometimes they did not come back. And we said: 'If they be unafraid of life, these white men, it is because they have many lives; but we be few by the Whitefish, and the young men shall go away no more.' But the young men did go away; and the young women went also; and we were very wroth.

"It be true, we ate flour, and salt pork, and drank tea which was a great delight; only, when we could not get tea, it was very bad and we became short of speech and quick of anger. So we grew to hunger for the things the white men brought in trade. Trade! trade! all the time was it trade! One winter we sold our meat for clocks that would not go, and watches with broken guts, and files worn smooth, and pistols without cartridges and worthless. And then came famine, and we were without meat, and two score died ere the break of spring.

" 'Now are we grown weak,' we said; 'and the Pellys will fall upon us, and our bounds be overthrown.' But as it fared with us, so had it fared with the Pellys, and they were too weak to come against us.

"My father, Otsbaok, a strong man, was now old and very wise. And he spoke to the chief, saying: 'Behold, our dogs be worthless. No longer are they thick-furred and strong, and they die in the frost and harness. Let us go into the village and kill them, saving only the wolf ones, and these let us tie out in the night that they may mate with the wild wolves of the forest. Thus shall we have dogs warm and strong again.'

"And his word was harkened to, and we Whitefish became known for our dogs, which were the best in the land. But known we were not for ourselves. The best of our young men and women had gone away with the white men to wander on trail and river to far places. And the young women came back old and broken, as Noda had come, or they came not at all. And the young men came back to sit by our fires for a time, full of ill speech and rough ways, drinking evil drinks and gambling through long nights and days, with a great unrest always in their hearts, till the call of the white men came to them and they went away again to the unknown places. And they were without honor and respect, jeering the old-time customs and laughing in the faces of chief and shamans.

"As I say, we were become a weak breed, we Whitefish. We sold our warm skins and furs for tobacco and whiskey and thin cotton things that left us shivering in the cold. And the coughing sickness came upon us, and men and women coughed and sweated through the long nights, and the hunters on trail spat blood upon the snow. And now one, and now another, bled swiftly from the mouth and died. And the women bore few children, and those they bore were weak and given to sickness. And other sicknesses came to us from the white men, the like of which we had never known and could not understand. Smallpox, likewise measles, have I heard these sicknesses named, and we died of them as die the salmon in the still eddies when in the fall their eggs are spawned and there is no longer need for them to live.

"And yet, and here be the strangeness of it, the white men come as the breath of death; all their ways lead to death, their nostrils are filled with it; and yet they do not die. Theirs the whiskey, and tobacco, and short-haired dogs; theirs the many sicknesses, the smallpox and measles, the coughing and mouth-bleeding; theirs the white skin, and softness to the frost and storm; and theirs the pistols that shoot six times very swift and are worthless. And yet they grow fat on their many ills, and prosper, and lay a heavy hand over all the world and tread mightily upon its peoples. And their women, too, are soft as little babes, most breakable and never broken, the mothers of men. And out of all this softness, and sickness, and weakness, come strength, and power, and authority. They be gods, or devils, as the case may be. I do not know. What do I know, I, old Imber of the Whitefish? Only do I know that they are past understanding, these white men, far-wanderers and fighters over the earth that they be.

"As I say, the meat in the forest became less and less. It be true, the white man's gun is most excellent and kills a long way off; but of what worth the gun, when there is no meat to kill? When I was a boy on the Whitefish there was moose on every hill, and each year came the caribou uncountable. But now the hunter may take the trail ten days and not one moose gladden his eyes, while the caribou uncountable come no more at all. Small worth the gun, I say, killing a long way off, when there be nothing to kill.

"And I, Imber, pondered upon these things, watching the while the Whitefish, and the Pellys, and all the tribes of the land, perishing as perished the meat of the forest. Long I pondered. I talked with the shamans and the old men who were wise. I went apart that the sounds of the village might not disturb me, and I ate no meat so that my belly should not press upon me and make me slow of eye and ear. I sat long and sleepless in the forest, wide-eyed for the sign, my ears patient and keen for the word that was to come. And I wandered alone in the blackness of night to the river bank, where was wind-moaning and sobbing of water, and where I sought wisdom from the ghosts of old shamans in the trees and dead and gone.

"And in the end, as in a vision, came to me the short-haired and detestable dogs, and the way seemed plain. By the wisdom of Otsbaok, my father and a strong man, had the blood of our own wolf-dogs been kept clean, wherefore had they remained warm of hide and strong in the harness. So I returned to my village and made oration to the men. 'This be a tribe, these white men,' I said. 'A very large tribe, and doubtless there is no longer meat in their land, and they are come among us to make a new land for themselves. But they weaken us, and we die. They are a very hungry folk. Already has our meat gone from us, and it were well, if we would live, that we deal by them as we have dealt by their dogs.'

"And further oration I made, counseling fight. And the men of the Whitefish listened, and some said one thing, and some another, and some spoke of other and worthless things, and no man made brave talk of deeds and war. But while the young men were weak as water and afraid, I watched that the old men sat silent, and that in their eyes fires came and went. And later, when the village slept and no one knew, I drew the old men away into the forest and made more talk. And now we were agreed, and we remembered the good young days, and the free land, and the times of plenty, and the gladness and sunshine; and we called ourselves brothers, and swore great secrecy, and a mighty oath to cleanse the land of the evil breed that had come upon it. It be plain we were fools, but how were we to know, we old men of the Whitefish?

"And to hearten the others, I did the first deed. I kept guard upon the Yukon till the first canoe came down. In it were two white men, and when I stood upright upon the bank and raised my hand they changed their course and drove in to me. And as the man in the bow lifted his head, so, that he might know wherefore I wanted him, my arrow sang through the air straight to his throat, and he knew. The second man, who held paddle in the stern, had his rifle half to his shoulder when the first of my three spearcasts smote him.

" 'These be the first,' I said, when the old men had gathered to me. 'Later we will bind together all the old man of all the tribes, and after that the young men who remain strong, and the work will become easy.'

"And then the two dead white men we cast into the river. And of the canoe, which was a very good canoe, we made a fire, and a fire, also, of the things within the canoe. But first we looked at the things, and they were pouches of leather which we cut open with our knives. And inside these pouches were many papers, like that from which thou has read, O Howkan, with markings on them which we marvelled at and could not understand. Now, I am become wise, and I know them for the speech of men as thou hast told me."

A whisper and buzz went around the courtroom when Howkan finished interpreting the affair of the canoe, and one man's voice spoke up: "That was the lost '91 mail,

Peter James and Delaney bringing it in and last spoken at Le Barge by Matthews going out." The clerk scratched steadily away, and another paragraph was added to the history of the North.

"There be little more," Imber went on slowly. "It be there on the paper, the things we did. We were old men, and we did not understand. Even I, Imber, do not now understand. Secretly we slew, and continued to slay, for with our years we were crafty and we had learned the swiftness of going without haste. When white men came among us with black looks and rough words, and took away six of the young men with irons binding them helpless, we knew we must slay wider and farther. And one by one we old men departed up river and down to the unknown lands. It was a brave thing. Old we were, and unafraid, but the fear of far places is a terrible fear to men who are old.

"So we slew, without haste and craftily. On the Chilcoot and in the Delta we slew, from the passes to the sea, wherever the white men camped or broke their trails. It be true, they died, but it was without worth. Ever did they come over the mountains, ever did they grow and grow, while we, being old, became less and less. I remember, by the Caribou Crossing, the camp of a white man. He was a very little white man, and three of the old men came upon him in his sleep. And the next day I came upon the four of them. The white man alone still breathed, and there was breath in him to curse me once and well before he died.

"And so it went, now one old man, and now another. Sometimes the word reached us long after of how they died, and sometimes it did not reach us. And the old men of the other tribes were weak and afraid, and would not join with us. As I say, one by one, till I alone was left. I am Imber, of the Whitefish people. My father was Otsbaok, a strong man. There are no Whitefish now. Of the old men I am the last. The young men and young women are gone away, some to live with the Pellys, some with the Salmons, and more with the white men. I am very old, and very tired, and it being vain fighting the Law, as thou sayest, Howkan, I am come seeking the Law."

"O Imber, thou art indeed a fool," said Howkan.

But Imber was dreaming. The square-browed judge likewise dreamed, and all his race rose up before him in a mighty phantasmagoria—his steel-shod, mail-clad race, the lawgiver and world-maker among the families of men. He saw it dawn red-flickering across the dark forests and sullen seas; he saw it blaze, bloody and red, to full and triumphant noon; and down the shaded slope he saw the blood-red sands dropping into night. And through it all he observed the Law, pitiless and potent, ever unswerving and ever ordaining, greater than the motes of men who fulfilled it or were crushed by it, even as it was greater than he, his heart speaking for softness.

The Wisdom of the Trail

S itka Charley had achieved the impossible. Other Indians might have known as much of the wisdom of the trail as did he; but he alone knew the white man's wisdom, the honor of the trail, and the law. But these things had not come to him in a day. The aboriginal mind is slow to generalize, and many facts, repeated often, are required to compass an understanding. Sitka Charley, from boyhood, had been thrown continually with white men, and as a man he had elected to cast his fortunes with them, expatriating himself, once and for all, from his own people. Even then, respecting, almost venerating their power, and pondering over it, he had yet to divine its secret essence—the honor and the law. And it was only by the cumulative evidence of years that he had finally come to understand. Being an alien, when he did know he knew it better than the white man himself; being an Indian, he had achieved the impossible.

And of these things had been bred a certain contempt for his own people,—a contempt which he had made it a

custom to conceal, but which now burst forth in a polyglot
whirlwind of curses upon the heads of Kah-Chucte and
Gowhee. They cringed before him like a brace of snarling
wolf-dogs, too cowardly to spring, too wolfish to cover
their fangs. They were not handsome creatures. Neither
was Sitka Charley. All three were frightful-looking. There
was no flesh to their faces; their cheek bones were massed
with hideous scabs which had cracked and frozen alter-
nately under the intense frost; while their eyes burned lu-
ridly with the light which is born of desperation and
hunger. Men so situated, beyond the pale of the honor and
the law, are not to be trusted. Sitka Charley knew this;
and this was why he had forced them to abandon their rifles with the rest of the camp outfit ten days before. His
rifle and Captain Eppingwell's were the only ones that remained.

"Come, get a fire started," he commanded, drawing out
the precious match box with its attendant strips of dry
birch bark.

The two Indians fell sullenly to the task of gathering
dead branches and underwood. They were weak, and
paused often, catching themselves, in the act of stooping,
with giddy motions, or staggering to the centre of operations with their knees shaking like castanets. After each
trip they rested for a moment, as though sick and deadly
weary. At times their eyes took on the patient stoicism of
dumb suffering; and again the ego seemed almost bursting
forth with its wild cry, "I, I, I want to exist!"—the dominant note of the whole living universe.

A light breath of air blew from the south, nipping the
exposed portions of their bodies and driving the frost, in
needles of fire, through fur and flesh to the bones. So,
when the fire had grown lusty and thawed a damp circle
in the snow about it, Sitka Charley forced his reluctant
comrades to lend a hand in pitching a fly. It was a primitive affair,—merely a blanket, stretched parallel with the
fire and to windward of it, at an angle of perhaps forty-
five degrees. This shut out the chill wind, and threw the

heat backward and down upon those who were to huddle in its shelter. Then a layer of green spruce boughs was spread, that their bodies might not come in contact with the snow. When this task was completed, Kah-Chucte and Gowhee proceeded to take care of their feet. Their ice-bound moccasins were sadly worn by much travel, and the sharp ice of the river jams had cut them to rags. Their Si-wash socks were similarly conditioned, and when these had been thawed and removed, the dead-white tips of the toes, in the various stages of mortification, told their simple tale of the trail.

Leaving the two to the drying of their foot-gear, Sitka Charley turned back over the course he had come. He, too, had a mighty longing to sit by the fire and tend his complaining flesh, but the honor and the law forbade. He toiled painfully over the frozen field, each step a protest, every muscle in revolt. Several times, where the open water between the jams had recently crusted, he was forced to miserably accelerate his movements as the fragile footing swayed and threatened beneath him. In such places death was quick and easy; but it was not his desire to endure no more.

His deepening anxiety vanished as two Indians dragged into view round a bend in the river. They staggered and panted like men under heavy burdens; yet the packs on their backs were a matter of but few pounds. He questioned them eagerly, and their replies seemed to relieve him. He hurried on. Next came two white men, supporting between them a woman. They also behaved as though drunken, and their limbs shook with weakness. But the woman leaned lightly upon them, choosing to carry herself forward with her own strength. At sight of her, a flash of joy cast its fleeting light across Sitka Charley's face. He cherished a very great regard for Mrs. Eppingwell. He had seen many white women, but this was the first to travel the trail with him. When Captain Eppingwell proposed the hazardous undertaking and made him an offer for his services, he had shaken his head gravely; for it was an unknown journey through the dismal vastnesses of the Northland, and he knew it to be of the kind that try to the uttermost the souls of men. But when he learned that the Captain's wife was to accompany them, he had refused flatly to have anything further to do with it. Had it been a woman of his own race he would have harbored no objections; but these women of the Southland—no, no, they were too soft, too tender, for such enterprises.

Sitka Charley did not know this kind of woman. Five minutes before, he did not even dream of taking charge of the expedition; but when she came to him with her wonderful smile and her straight clean English, and talked to the point, without pleading or persuading, he had incontinently yielded. Had there been a softness and appeal to mercy in the eyes, a tremble to the voice, a taking advantage of sex, he would have stiffened to steel; instead her clear-searching eyes and clear-ringing voice, her utter frankness and tacit assumption of equality, had robbed him of his reason. He felt, then, that this was a new breed of woman; and ere they had been trail-mates for many days, he knew why the sons of such women mastered the land and the sea, and why the sons of his own womankind could not prevail against them. *Tender and soft!* Day after day he watched her, muscle-weary, exhausted, indomitable, and the words beat in upon him in a perennial refrain. *Tender and soft!* He knew her feet had been born to easy paths and sunny lands, strangers to the moccasined pain of the North, unkissed by the chill lips of the frost, and he watched and marveled at them twinkling ever through the weary day.

She had always a smile and a word of cheer, from which not even the meanest packer was excluded. As the way grew darker she seemed to stiffen and gather greater strength, and when Kah-Chucte and Gowhee, who had bragged that they knew every landmark of the way as a child did the skin-bales of the tepee, acknowledged that they knew not where they were, it was she who raised a forgiving voice amid the curses of the men. She had sung to them that night, till they felt the weariness fall from them and were ready to face the future with fresh hope. And when the food failed and each scant stint was measured jealously, she it was who rebelled against the machinations of her husband and Sitka Charley, and demanded and received a share neither greater nor less than that of the others.

Sitka Charley was proud to know this woman. A new richness, a greater breadth, had come into his life with her presence. Hitherto he had been his own mentor, had turned to right or left at no man's beck; he had moulded himself according to his own dictates, nourished his manhood regardless of all save his own opinion. For the first time he had felt a call from without for the best that was in him. Just a glance of appreciation from the clear-searching eyes, a word of thanks from the clear-ringing voice, just a slight wreathing of the lips in the wonderful smile, and he walked with the gods for hours to come. It was a new stimulant to his manhood; for the first time he thrilled with a conscious pride in his wisdom of the trail; and between the twain they ever lifted the sinking hearts of their comrades.

The faces of the two men and the woman brightened as they saw him, for after all he was the staff they leaned upon. But Sitka Charley, rigid as was his wont, concealing pain and pleasure impartially beneath an iron exterior, asked them the welfare of the rest, told the distance to the fire, and continued on the back-trip. Next he met a single Indian, unburdened, limping, lips compressed, and eyes set with the pain of a foot in which the quick fought a losing battle with the dead. All possible care had been taken of him, but in the last extremity the weak and unfortunate must perish, and Sitka Charley deemed his days to be few. The man could not keep up for long, so he gave him rough cheering words. After that came two more Indians, to whom he had allotted the task of helping along Joe, the third white man of the party. They had deserted him. Sitka

Charley saw at a glance the lurking spring in their bodies, and knew they had at last cast off his mastery. So he was not taken unawares when he ordered them back in quest of their abandoned charge, and saw the gleam of the hunting-knives that they drew from the sheaths. A pitiful spectacle, three weak men lifting their puny strength in the face of the mighty vastness; but the two recoiled under the fierce rifle-blows of the one, and returned like beaten dogs to the leash. Two hours later, with Joe reeling between them and Sitka Charley bringing up the rear, they came to the fire, where the remainder of the expedition crouched in the shelter of the fly.

"A few words, my comrades, before we sleep," Sitka Charley said, after they had devoured their slim rations of unleavened bread. He was speaking to the Indians, in their own tongue, having already given the import to the whites. "A few words, my comrades, for your own good, that ye may yet perchance live. I shall give you the law; on his own head be the death of him that breaks it. We have passed the Hills of Silence, and we now travel the head-reaches of the Stuart. It may be one sleep, it may be several, it may be many sleeps, but in time we shall come among the Men of the Yukon, who have much grub. It were well that we look to the law. To-day, Kah-Chucte and Gowhee, whom I commanded to break trail, forgot they were men, and like frightened children ran away. True, they forgot; so let us forget. But hereafter let them remember. If it should happen they do not"——He touched his rifle carelessly, grimly. "To-morrow they shall carry the flour and see that the white man Joe lies not down by the trail. The cups of flour are counted; should so much as an ounce be wanting at nightfall—Do ye understand? To-day there were others that forgot. Moose-Head and Three-Salmon left the white man Joe to lie in the snow. Let them forget no more. With the light of day shall they go forth and break trail. Ye have heard the law. Look well, lest ye break it."

* * *

Sitka Charley found it beyond him to keep the line close up. From Moose-Head, and Three-Salmon, who broke trail in advance, to Kah-Chucte, Gowhee, and Joe, it straggled out over a mile. Each staggered, fell or rested, as he saw fit. The line of march was a progression through a chain of irregular halts. Each drew upon the last remnant of his strength and stumbled onward till it was expended, but in some miraculous way there was always another last remnant. Each time a man fell, it was with the firm belief that he would rise no more; yet he did rise, and again, and again. The flesh yielded, the will conquered; but each triumph was a tragedy. The Indian with the frozen foot, no longer erect, crawled forward on hand and knee. He rarely rested, for he knew the penalty exacted by the frost. Even Mrs. Eppingwell's lips were at last set in a stony smile, and her eyes, seeing, saw not. Often, she stopped, pressing a mittened hand to her heart, gasping and dizzy.

Joe, the white man, had passed beyond the stage of suffering. He no longer begged to be let alone, prayed to die; but was soothed and content under the anodyne of delirium. Kah-Chucte and Gowhee dragged him on roughly, venting upon him many a savage glance or blow. To them it was the acme of injustice. Their hearts were bitter with hate, heavy with fear. Why should they cumber their strength with his weakness? To do so, meant death; not to do so—and they remembered the law of Sitka Charley, and the rifle.

Joe fell with greater frequency as the daylight waned, and so hard was he to raise that they dropped farther and farther behind. Sometimes all three pitched into the snow, so weak had the Indians become. Yet on their backs was life, and strength, and warmth. Within the flour-sacks were all the potentialities of existence. They could not but think of this, and it was not strange, that which came to pass. They had fallen by the side of a great timber-jam where a thousand cords of firewood waited the match. Near by was an air hole through the ice. Kah-Chucte looked on the wood and the water, as did Gowhee; then they looked on each other. Never a word was spoken. Gowhee struck a fire; Kah-Chucte filled a tin cup with water and heated it; Joe babbled of things in another land, in a tongue they did not understand. They mixed flour with the warm water till it was a thin paste, and of this they drank many cups. They did not offer any to Joe; but he did not mind. He did not mind anything, not even his moccasins, which scorched and smoked among the coals.

A crystal mist of snow fell about them, softly, caressingly, wrapping them in clinging robes of white. And their feet would have yet trod many trails had not destiny brushed the clouds aside and cleared the air. Nay, ten minutes' delay would have been salvation. Sitka Charley, looking back, saw the pillared smoke of their fire, and guessed. And he looked ahead at those who were faithful, and at Mrs. Eppingwell.

"So, my good comrades, ye have again forgotten that you were men? Good. Very good. There will be fewer bellies to feed."

Sitka Charley retied the flour as he spoke, strapping the pack to the one on his own back. He kicked Joe till the pain broke through the poor devil's bliss and brought him doddering to his feet. Then he shoved him out upon the trail and started him on his way. The two Indians attempted to slip off.

"Hold, Gowhee! And thou, too, Kah-Chucte! Hath the flour given such strength to thy legs that they may outrun the swift-winged lead? Think not to cheat the law. Be men for the last time, and be content that ye die full-stomached. Come, step up, back to the timber, shoulder to shoulder. Come!"

The two men obeyed, quietly, without fear; for it is the future which presses upon the man, not the present.

"Thou, Gowhee, hast a wife and children and a deerskin lodge in the Chippewyan. What is thy will in the matter?"

"Give thou her of the goods which are mine by the word

of the Captain—the blankets, the beads, the tobacco, the box which makes strange sounds after the manner of the white men. Say that I did die on the trail, but say not how."

"And thou, Kah-Chucte, who hast nor wife nor child?"

"Mine is a sister, the wife of the Factor at Koshim. He beats her, and she is not happy. Give thou her the goods which are mine by the contract, and tell her it were well she go back to her own people. Shouldst thou meet the man, and be so minded, it were a good deed that he should die. He beats her, and she is afraid."

"Are ye content to die by the law?"

"We are."

"Then good-by, my good comrades. May ye sit by the well-filled pot, in warm lodges, ere the day is done."

As he spoke, he raised his rifle, and many echoes broke the silence. Hardly had they died away, when other rifles spoke in the distance. Sitka Charley started. There had been more than one shot, yet there was but one other rifle in the party. He gave a fleeting glance at the men who lay so quietly, smiled viciously at the wisdom of the trail, and hurried on to meet the Men of the Yukon.

Bâtard

Bâtard was a devil. This was recognized throughout the Northland. "Hell's Spawn" he was called by many men, but his master, Black Leclère, chose for him the shameful name "Bâtard." Now Black Leclère was also a devil, and the twain were well matched. There is a saying that when two devils come together, hell is to pay. This is to be expected, and this certainly was to be expected when Bâtard and Black Leclère came together. The first time they met, Bâtard was a part-grown puppy, lean and hungry, with bitter eyes; and they met with snap and snarl, and wicked looks, for Leclère's upper lip had a wolfish way of lifting and showing the white, cruel teeth. And it lifted then, and his eyes glinted viciously, as he reached for Bâtard and dragged him out of the squirming litter. It was certain that they divined each other, for on the instant Bâtard had buried his puppy fangs in Leclère's hand, and Leclère, thumb and finger, was coolly choking his young life out of him.

"*Sacredam,*" the Frenchman said softly, flirting the quick

blood from his bitten hand and gazing down on the little puppy choking and gasping in the snow.

Leclère turned to John Hamlin, storekeeper of the Sixty Mile Post. "Dat fo' w'at Ah lak heem. 'Ow moch, eh, you, *M'sieu'*? 'Ow moch? Ah buy heem, now; Ah buy heem queek."

And because he hated him with an exceeding bitter hate, Leclère bought Bâtard and gave him his shameful name. And for five years the twain adventured across the Northland, from St. Michael's and the Yukon delta to the head-reaches of the Pelly and even so far as the Peace River, Athabasca, and the Great Slave. And they acquired a reputation for uncompromising wickedness, the like of which never before attached itself to man and dog.

Bâtard did not know his father,—hence his name,—but, as John Hamlin knew, his father was a great gray timber wolf. But the mother of Bâtard, as he dimly remembered her, was snarling, bickering, obscene, husky, full-fronted and heavy-chested, with a malign eye, a cat-like grip on life, and a genius for trickery and evil. There was neither faith nor trust in her. Her treachery alone could be relied upon, and her wild-wood amours attested her general depravity. Much of evil and much of strength were there in these, Bâtard's progenitors, and, bone and flesh of their bone and flesh, he had inherited it all. And then came Black Leclère, to lay his heavy hand on the bit of pulsating puppy life, to press and prod and mould till it became a big bristling beast, acute in knavery, overspilling with hate, sinister, malignant, diabolical. With a proper master Bâtard might have made an ordinary, fairly efficient sled-dog. He never got the chance; Leclère but confirmed him in his congenital inquity.

The history of Bâtard and Leclère is a history of war—of five cruel, relentless years, of which their first meeting is fit summary. To begin with, it was Leclère's fault, for he hated with understanding and intelligence, while the long-legged, ungainly puppy hated only blindly, instinctively, without reason or method. At first there were no refinements of cruelty (these were to come later), but simple beatings and crude brutalities. In one of these Bâtard had an ear injured. He never regained control of the riven muscles, and ever after the ear drooped limply down to keep keen the memory of his tormentor. And he never forgot.

He puppyhood was a period of foolish rebellion. He was always worsted, but he fought back because it was his nature to fight back. and he was unconquerable. Yelping shrilly from the pain of lash and club, he none the less contrived always to throw in the defiant snarl, the bitter vindictive menace of his soul which fetched without fail more blows and beatings. But his was his mother's tenacious grip on life. Nothing could kill him. He flourished under misfortune, grew fat with famine, and out of his terrible struggle for life developed a preternatural intelligence. His were the stealth and cunning of the husky, his mother, and the fierceness and valor of the wolf, his father.

Possibly it was because of his father that he never wailed. His puppy yelps passed with his lanky legs, so that he became grim and taciturn, quick to strike, slow to warn. He answered curse with snarl, and blow with snap, grinning the while his implacable hatred; but never again, under the extremest agony, did Leclère bring from him the cry of fear nor of pain. This unconquerableness but fanned Leclère's wrath and stirred him to greater deviltries.

Did Leclère give Bâtard half a fish and to his mates whole ones, Bâtard went forth to rob other dogs of their fish. Also he robbed cachés and expressed himself in a thousand rogueries, till he became a terror to all dogs and masters of dogs. Did Leclère beat Bâtard and fondle Babette,—Babette who was not half the worker he was— why, Bâtard threw her down in the snow and broke her hind leg in his heavy jaws, so that Leclère was forced to shoot her. Likewise, in bloody battles, Bâtard mastered all his team-mates, set them the law of trail and forage, and made them live to the law he set.

In five years he heard but one kind word, received but

one soft stroke of a hand, and then he did not know what manner of things they were. He leaped like the untamed thing he was, and his jaws were together in a flash. It was the missionary at Sunrise, a newcomer in the country, who spoke the kind word and gave the soft stroke of the hand. And for six months after, he wrote no letters home to the States, and the surgeon at McQuestion travelled two hundred miles on the ice to save him from blood-poisoning.

Men and dogs looked askance at Bâtard when he drifted into their camps and posts. The men greeted him with feet threateningly lifted for the kick, the dogs with bristling manes and bared fangs. Once a man did kick Bâtard, and Bâtard, with quick wolf snap, closed his jaws like a steel trap on the man's calf and crunched down to the bone. Whereat the man was determined to have his life, only Black Leclère, with ominous eyes and naked hunting-knife, stepped in between. The killing of Bâtard—ah, *sacredam*, *that* was a pleasure Leclère reserved for himself. Some day it would happen, or else—bah! who was to know? Anyway, the problem would be solved.

For they had become problems to each other. The very breath each drew was a challenge and a menace to the other. Their hate bound them together as love could never bind. Leclère was bent on the coming of the day when Bâtard should wilt in spirit and cringe and whimper at his feet. And Bâtard—Leclère knew what was in Bâtard's mind, and more than once had read it in Bâtard's eyes. And so clearly had he read, that when Bâtard was at his back, he made it a point to glance often over his shoulder.

Men marvelled when Leclère refused large money for the dog. "Some day you'll kill him and be out his price," said John Hamlin once, when Bâtard lay panting in the snow where Leclère had kicked him, and no one knew whether his ribs were broken, and no one dared look to see.

"Dat," said Leclère, dryly, "dat is my biz'ness, *M'sieu'*."

And the man marvelled that Bâtard did not run away. They did not understand. But Leclère understood. He was a man who lived much in the open, beyond the sound of human tongue, and he had learned the voices of wind and storm, the sigh of night, the whisper of dawn, the clash of day. In a dim way he could hear the green things growing, the running of the sap, the bursting of the bud. And he knew the subtle speech of the things that moved, of the rabbit in the snare, the moody raven beating the air with hollow wing, the bald-face shuffling under the moon, the wolf like a gray shadow gliding betwixt the twilight and the dark. And to him Bâtard spoke clear and direct. Full well he understood why Bâtard did not run away, and he looked more often over his shoulder.

When in anger, Bâtard was not nice to look upon, and more than once had he leapt for Leclère's throat, to be stretched quivering and senseless in the snow, by the butt of the ever ready dogwhip. And so Bâtard learned to bide his time. When he reached his full strength and prime of youth, he thought the time had come. He was broad-chested, powerfully muscled, of far more than ordinary size, and his neck from head to shoulders was a mass of bristling hair—to all appearances a full-blooded wolf. Leclère was lying asleep in his furs when Bâtard deemed the time to be ripe. He crept upon him stealthily, head low to earth and lone ear laid back, with a feline softness of tread. Bâtard breathed gently, very gently, and not till he was close at hand did he raise his head. He paused for a moment, and looked at the bronzed bull throat, naked and knotty, and swelling to a deep and steady pulse. The slaver dripped down his fangs and slid off his tongue at the sight, and in that moment he remembered his drooping ear, his uncounted blows and prodigious wrongs, and without a sound sprang on the sleeping man.

Leclère awoke to the pang of the fangs in his throat, and, perfect animal that he was, he awoke clear-headed and with full comprehension. He closed on Bâtard's wind-pipe with both his hands, and rolled out of his furs to get his weight uppermost. But the thousands of Bâtard's an-cestors had clung at the throats of unnumbered moose and caribou and dragged them down, and the wisdom of those ancestors was his. When Leclère's weight came on top of him, he drove his hind legs upward and in, and clawed down chest and abdomen, ripping and tearing through skin and muscle. And when he felt the man's body wince above him and lift, he worried and shook at the man's throat. His team-mates closed around in a snarling circle, and Bâtard, with failing breath and fading sense, knew that their jaws were hungry for him. But that did not matter—it was the man, the man above him, and he ripped and clawed, and shook and worried, to the last ounce of his strength. But Leclère choked him with both his hands, till Bâtard's chest heaved and writhed for the air denied, and his eyes glazed and set, and his jaws slowly loosened, and his tongue protruded black and swollen.

"Eh? *Bon*, you devil!" Leclère gurgled, mouth and throat clogged with his own blood, as he shoved the dizzy dog from him.

And then Leclère cursed the other dogs off as they fell upon Bâtard. They drew back into a wider circle, squatting alertly on their haunches and licking their chops, the hair on every neck bristling and erect.

Bâtard recovered quickly, and at sound of Leclère's voice, tottered to his feet and swayed weakly back and forth.

"A-h-ah! You beeg devil!" Leclère spluttered. "Ah fix you; Ah fix you plentee, by *Gar*!"

Bâtard, the air biting into his exhausted lungs like wine, flashed full into the man's face, his jaws missing and coming together with a metallic clip. They rolled over and over on the snow, Leclère striking madly with his fists. Then they separated, face to face, and circled back and forth before each other. Leclère could have drawn his knife. His rifle was at his feet. But the beast in him was up and raging. He would do the thing with his hands—and his teeth. Bâtard sprang in, but Leclère knocked him over with a blow of the fist, fell upon him, and buried his teeth to the bone in the dog's shoulder.

It was a primordial setting and a primordial scene, such as might have been in the savage youth of the world. An open space in a dark forest, a ring of grinning wolf-dogs, and in the centre two beasts, locked in combat, snapping and snarling, raging madly about, panting, sobbing, cursing, straining, wild with passion, in a fury of murder, ripping and tearing and clawing in elemental brutishness.

But Leclère caught Bâtard behind the ear, with a blow from his fist, knocking him over, and, for the instant, stunning him. Then Leclère leaped upon him with his feet, and sprang up and down, striving to grind him into the earth. Both Bâtard's hind legs were broken ere Leclère ceased that he might catch breath.

"A-a-ah! A-a-ah!" he screamed, incapable of speech, shaking his fist, through sheer impotence of throat and larynx.

But Bâtard was indomitable. He lay there in a helpless welter, his lip feebly lifting and writhing to the snarl he had not the strength to utter, Leclère kicked him, and the tired jaws closed on the ankle, but could not break the skin.

Then Leclère picked up the whip and proceeded almost to cut him to pieces, at each stroke of the lash crying: "Dis taim Ah break you! Eh? By *Gar*! Ah break you!"

In the end, exhausted, fainting from loss of blood, he crumpled up and fell by his victim, and when the wolf-dogs closed in to take their vengeance, with his last consciousness dragged his body on top of Bâtard to shield him from their fangs.

This occurred not far from Sunrise, and the missionary, opening the door to Leclère a few hours later, was surprised to note the absence of Bâtard from the team. Nor did his surprise lessen when Leclère threw back the robes from the sled, gathered Bâtard into his arms, and staggered across the threshold. It happened that the surgeon of MacQuestion, who was something of a gadabout, was up on a gossip, and between them they proceeded to repair Leclère.

"*Merci, non,*" said he. "Do you fix firs' de dog. To die? *Non.* Eet is not good, Becos' heem Ah mus' yet break. Dat fo' w'at he mus' not die."

The surgeon called it a marvel, the missionary a miracle, that Leclère pulled through at all; and so weakened was he, that in the spring the fever got him, and he went on his back again. Bâtard had been in even worse plight, but his grip on life prevailed, and the bones of his hind legs knit, and his organs righted themselves, during the several weeks he lay strapped to the floor. And by the time Leclère, finally convalescent, sallow and shaky, took the sun by the cabin door, Bâtard had reasserted his supremacy among his kind, and brought not only his own teammates but the missionary's dogs into subjection.

He moved never a muscle, nor twitched a hair, when, for the first time, Leclère tottered out on the missionary's arm, and sank down slowly and with infinite caution on the three-legged stool.

"Bon!" he said. "*Bon!* De good sun!" And he stretched out his wasted hands and washed them in the warmth.

Then his gaze fell on the dog, and the old light blazed back in his eyes. He touched the missionary lightly on the arm. "*Mon père*, dat is one beeg devil, dat Bâtard. You will bring me one pistol, so, dat Ah drink de sun in peace."

And thenceforth for many days he sat in the sun before the cabin door. He never dozed, and the pistol lay always across his knees. Bâtard had a way, the first thing each day, of looking for the weapon in its wonted place. At sight of it he would lift his lip faintly in token that he understood, and Leclère would lift his own lip in an answering grin. One day the missionary took note of the trick.

"Bless me!" he said. "I really believe the brute comprehends."

Leclère laughed softly. "Look you, *mon père.* Dat w'at Ah now spik, to dat does he lissen."

As if in confirmation, Bâtard just perceptibly wriggled his lone ear up to catch the sound.

"Ah say 'keel.' "

Bâtard growled deep down in his throat, the hair bristled along his neck, and every muscle went tense and expectant.

'Ah lift de gun, so, like dat." And suiting action to word, he sighted the pistol at Bâtard.

Bâtard, with a single leap, sideways, landed around the corner of the cabin out of sight.

"Bless me!" he repeated at intervals.

Leclère grinned proudly.

"But why does he not run away?"

The Frenchman's shoulders went up in the racial shrug that means all things from total ignorance to infinite understanding.

"Then why do you not kill him?"

Again the shoulders went up.

"Mon père," he said after a pause, "de taim is not yet. He is one beeg devil. Some taim Ah break heem, so, an' so, all to leetle bits. Hey? Some taim. *Bon!*"

A day came when Leclère gathered his dogs together and floated down in a bateau to Forty Mile, and on to the Porcupine, where he took a commission from the P. C. Company, and went exploring for the better part of a year. After that he poled up the Koyokuk to deserted Arctic City, and later came drifting back, from camp to camp, along the Yukon. And during the long months Bâtard was well lessoned. He learned many tortures, and, notably, the torture of hunger, the torture of thirst, the torture of fire, and, worst of all, the torture of music.

Like the rest of his kind, he did not enjoy music. It gave him exquisite anguish, racking him nerve by nerve, and ripping apart every fibre of his being. It made him howl, long and wolf-like, as when the wolves bay the stars on frosty nights. He could not help howling. It was his one weakness in the contest with Leclère, and it was his shame. Leclère, on the other hand, passionately loved music—as passionately as he loved strong drink. And when his soul clamored for expression, it usually uttered itself in one or the other of the two ways, and more usually in both ways. And when he had drunk, his brain a-lilt with unsung song and the devil in him aroused and rampant, his soul found its supreme utterance in torturing Bâtard.

"Now we will haf a leetle museek," he would say. "Eh? W'at you t'ink, Bâtard?"

It was only an old and battered harmonica, tenderly treasured and patiently repaired; but it was the best that money could buy, and out of its silver reeds he drew weird vagrant airs that men had never heard before. Then Bâtard, dumb of throat, with teeth tight clenched, would back away, inch by inch, to the farthest cabin corner. And Leclère, playing, playing, a stout club tucked under his arm, followed the animal up, inch by inch, step by step, till there was no further retreat.

At first Bâtard would crowd himself into the smallest possible space, grovelling close to the floor; but as the music came nearer and nearer, he was forced to uprear, his back jammed into the logs, his fore legs fanning the air as though to beat off the rippling waves of sound. He still kept his teeth together, but severe muscular contractions attacked his body, strange twitchings and jerkings, till he was all a-quiver and writhing in silent torment. As he lost control, his jaws spasmodically wrenched apart, and deep throaty vibrations issued forth, too low in the register of sound for human ear to catch. And then, nostrils distended, eyes dilated, hair bristling in helpless rage, arose the long wolf howl. It came with a slurring rush upward, swelling to a great heart-breaking burst of sound, and dying away in sadly cadenced woe—then the next rush upward, octave upon octave; the bursting heart; and the infinite sorrow and misery, fainting, fading, falling, and dying slowly away.

It was fit for hell. And Leclère, with fiendish ken, seemed to divine each particular nerve and heartstring, and with long wails and tremblings and sobbing minors to make it yield up its last shred of grief. It was frightful, and for twenty-four hours after, Bâtard was nervous and unstrung, starting at common sounds, tripping over his own shadow, but, withal, vicious and masterful with his teammates. Nor did he show signs of a breaking spirit. Rather did he grow more grim and taciturn, biding his time with an inscrutable patience that began to puzzle and weigh upon Leclère. The dog would lie in the firelight, motionless, for hours, gazing straight before him at Leclère, and hating him with his bitter eyes.

Often the man felt that he had bucked against the very essence of life—the unconquerable essence that swept the hawk down out of the sky like a feathered thunderbolt, that drove the great gray goose across the zones, that hurled the spawning salmon through two thousand miles of boiling Yukon flood. At such times he felt impelled to express his own unconquerable essence; and with strong drink, wild music, and Bâtard, he indulged in vast orgies, wherein he pitted his puny strength in the face of things, and challenged all that was, and had been, and was yet to be.

"Dere is somet'ing dere," he affirmed, when the rhythmed vagaries of his mind touched the secret chords of Bâtard's being and brought forth the long lugubrious howl. "Ah pool eet out wid bot' my han's, so, an' so. Ha! Ha! Eet is fonee! Eet is ver' fonee! De priest chant, de womans pray, de mans swear, de leetle bird go *peep-peep*, Bâtard, heem go *yow-yow*—an' eet is all de ver' same t'ing. Ha! Ha!"

Father Gautier, a worthy priest, once reproved him with instances of concrete perdition. He never reproved him again.

"Eet may be so, *mon père*," he made answer. "An' Ah t'ink Ah go troo hell a-snappin', lak de hemlock troo de fire. Eh, *mon père*?"

But all bad things come to an end as well as good, and so with Black Leclère. On the summer low water, in a poling boat, he left McDougall for Sunrise. He left McDougall in company with Timothy Brown, and arrived at Sunrise by himself. Further, it was known that they had quarrelled just previous to pulling out; for the *Lizzie*, a wheezy ten-ton sternwheeler, twenty-four hours behind, beat Leclère in by three days. And when he did get in, it was with a clean-drilled bullet-hole through his shoulder-muscle, and a tale of ambush and murder.

A strike had been made at Sunrise, and things had changed considerably. With the infusion of several hundred gold-seekers, a deal of whiskey, and half a dozen equipped gamblers, the missionary had seen the page of his years of labor with the Indians wiped clean. When the squaws became preoccupied with cooking beans and keeping the fire going for the wifeless miners, and the bucks with swapping their warm furs for black bottles and broken timepieces, he took to his bed, said "bless me" several times, and departed to his final accounting in a rough-hewn, oblong box. Whereupon the gamblers moved their roulette and faro tables into the mission house, and the click of chips and clink of glasses went up from dawn till dark and to dawn again.

Now Timothy Brown was well beloved among these adventurers of the north. The one thing against him was his quick temper and ready fist,—a little thing, for which his kind heart and forgiving hand more than atoned. On the other hand, there was nothing to atone for Black Leclère. He was "black," as more than one remembered deed bore witness, while he was as well hated as the other was beloved. So the men of Sunrise put an antiseptic dressing on his shoulder and haled him before Judge Lynch.

It was a simple affair. He had quarrelled with Timothy Brown at McDougall. With Timothy Brown he had left McDougall. Without Timothy Brown he had arrived at Sunrise. Considered in the light of his evilness, the unanimous conclusion was that he had killed Timothy Brown. On the other hand, Leclère acknowledged their facts, but challenged their conclusion, and gave his own explanation. Twenty miles out of Sunrise he and Timothy Brown were poling the boat along the rocky shore. From that shore two rifle-shots rang out. Timothy Brown pitched out of the boat and went down bubbling red, and that was the last of Timothy Brown. He, Leclère, pitched into the bottom of the boat with a stinging shoulder. He lay very quiet, peeping at the shore. After a time two Indians stuck up their heads and came out to the water's edge, carrying between them a birch-bark canoe. As they launched it, Leclère let fly. He potted one, who went over the side after the manner of Timothy Brown. The other dropped into the bottom of the canoe, and then canoe and poling boat went down the stream in a drifting battle. After that they hung up on a split current, and the canoe passed on one side of an island, the poling boat on the other. That was the last of the canoe, and he came on into Sunrise. Yes, from the way the Indian in the canoe jumped, he was sure he had potted him. That was all.

This explanation was not deemed adequate. They gave him ten hours' grace while the *Lizzie* steamed down to investigate. Ten hours later she came wheezing back to Sunrise. There had been nothing to investigate. No evidence had been found to back up his statements. They told him to make his will, for he possessed a fifty-thousand-dollar Sunrise claim, and they were a law-abiding as well as a law-giving breed.

Leclère shrugged his shoulders. "Bot one t'ing," he said; "a leetle, w'at you call, favor—a leetle favor, dat is eet. I gif my feefty t'ousan' dollair to de church. I gif my husky dog, Bâtard, to de devil. De leetle favor? Firs' you hang heem, an' den you hang me. Eet is good, eh?"

Good it was, they agreed, that Hell's Spawn should break trail for his master across the last divide, and the court was adjourned down to the river bank, where a big spruce tree stood by itself. Slackwater Charley put a hangman's knot in the end of a hauling-line, and the noose was slipped over Leclère's head and pulled tight around his neck. His hands were tied behind his back, and he was assisted to the top of a cracker box. Then the running end of the line was passed over an overhanging branch, drawn taut, and made fast. To kick the box out from under would leave him dancing on the air.

"Now for the dog," said Webster Shaw, sometime mining engineer. "You'll have to rope him, Slackwater."

Leclère grinned. Slackwater took a chew of tobacco, rove a running noose, and proceeded leisurely to coil a few turns in his hand. He paused once or twice to brush particularly offensive mosquitoes from off his face. Everybody was brushing mosquitoes, except Leclère, about whose head a small cloud was visible. Even Bâtard, lying full-stretched on the ground, with his fore paws rubbed the pests away from eyes and mouth.

But while Slackwater waited for Bâtard to lift his head, a faint call came down the quiet air, and a man was seen waving his arms and running across the flat from Sunrise. It was the storekeeper.

"C-call 'er off, boys," he panted, as he came in among them.

"Little Sandy and Bernadotte's jes' got in," he explained with returning breath. "Landed down below an' come up by the short cut. Got the Beaver with 'm. Picked 'm up in his canoe, stuck in a back channel, with a couple of bullet holes in 'm. Other buck was Klok-Kutz, the one that knocked spots out of his squaw and dusted."

"Eh? W'at Ah say? Eh?" Leclère cried exultantly. "Dat de one fo' sure! Ah know. Ah spik true."

"The thing to do is teach these damned Siwashes a little manners," spoke Webster Shaw. "They're getting fat and sassy, and we'll have to bring them down a peg. Round in all the bucks and string up the Beaver for an object lesson. That's the programme. Come on and let's see what he's got to say for himself."

"Heh, M'sieu'!" Leclère called, as the crowd began to

melt away through the twilight in the direction of Sunrise. "Ah lak ver' moch to see de fon."

"Oh, we'll turn you loose when we come back," Webster Shaw shouted over his shoulder. "In the meantime meditate on your sins and the way of providence. It will do you good, so be grateful."

As is the way with men who are accustomed to great hazards, whose nerves are healthy and trained to patience, so it was with Leclère, who settled himself to the long wait—which is to say that he reconciled his mind to it. There was no settling of the body, for the taut rope forced him to stand rigidly erect. The least relaxation of the leg muscles pressed the rough-fibred noose into his neck, while the upright position caused him much pain in his wounded shoulder. He projected his under lip and expelled his breath upward along his face to blow the mosquitoes away from his eyes. But the situation had its compensation. To be snatched from the maw of death was well worth a little bodily suffering, only it was unfortunate that he should miss the hanging of the Beaver.

And so he mused, till his eyes chanced to fall upon Bâtard, head between fore paws and stretched on the ground asleep. And then Leclère ceased to muse. He studied the animal closely, striving to sense if the sleep were real or feigned. Bâtard's sides were heaving regularly, but Leclère felt that the breath came and went a shade too quickly; also he felt that there was a vigilance or alertness to every hair that belied unshackling sleep. He would have given his Sunrise claim to be assured that the dog was not awake, and once, when one of his joints cracked, he looked quickly and guiltily at Bâtard to see if he roused. He did not rouse then, but a few minutes later he got up slowly and lazily, stretched, and looked carefully about him.

"*Sacredam,*" said Leclère, under his breath.

Assured that no one was in sight or hearing, Bâtard sat

down, curled is upper lip almost into a smile, looked up at Leclère, and licked his chops.

"Ah see my feenish," the man said, and laughed sardonically aloud.

Bâtard came nearer, the useless ear wabbling, the good ear cocked forward with devilish comprehension. He thrust his head on one side quizzically, and advanced with mincing, playful steps. He rubbed his body gently against the box till it shook and shook again. Leclère teetered carefully to maintain his equilibrium.

"Bâtard," he said calmly, "look out. Ah keel you."

Bâtard snarled at the word, and shook the box with greater force. Then he upreared, and with his fore paws threw his weight against it higher up. Leclère kicked out with one foot, but the rope bit into his neck and checked so abruptly as nearly to overbalance him.

"Hi, ya! *Chook! Mush-on!*" he screamed.

Bâtard retreated, for twenty feet or so, with a fiendish levity in his bearing that Leclère could not mistake. He remembered the dog often breaking the scum of ice on the water hole, by lifting up and throwing his weight upon it; and, remembering, he understood what he now had in mind. Bâtard faced about and paused. He showed his white teeth in a grin, which Leclère answered; and then hurled his body through the air, in full charge, straight for the box.

Fifteen minutes later, Slackwater Charley and Webster Shaw, returning, caught a glimpse of a ghostly pendulum swinging back and forth in the dim light. As they hurriedly drew in closer, they made out the man's inert body, and a live thing that clung to it, and shook and worried, and gave to it the swaying motion.

"Hi, ya! *Chook!* you Spawn of Hell," yelled Webster Shaw.

But Bâtard glared at him, and snarled threateningly, without loosing his jaws.

Slackwater Charley got out his revolver, but his hand was shaking, as with a chill, and he fumbled.

"Here, you take it," he said, passing the weapon over.

Webster Shaw laughed shortly, drew a sight between the gleaming eyes, and pressed the trigger. Bâtard's body twitched with the shock, threshed the ground spasmodically for a moment, and went suddenly limp. But his teeth still held fast locked.

Afterword

Good news. There's a lot more where this came from. Jack London wrote roughly fifty books (though some critics of course would say he roughly wrote fifty books). He produced a huge number of short stories, most of which are available in collections. There's a wonderful sense of bountiful satisfaction that comes when a person develops a fondness for a prolific writer. Few things bring a reader more joy than the sight of a lengthy span of bookshelf filled by a favorite author.

It's always interesting to try to reconstruct the man himself from his stories. Obviously, London knew a bit about surviving, or succumbing, in the frozen north. He was familiar with factory work. The dehumanization he describes in "The Apostate" is as poignant as a chapter from Dickens. He understood boxing, both as a sport and as a voracious system that extracted too high a price from those who sought a living in the ring. He valued the individual over the institution. And he valued integrity. Men took their punishment without complaint.

He also wrote well and convincingly of that one event no writer can describe from personal experience—death. Whether sudden from a flashing blade or bullet, or slow by way of ice or disease, the deaths he described have the power to haunt us. Perhaps he sensed the flickering of his own flame, which brings us to another path in the game of literary speculation. Given that writing skills don't grow dim with middle age but often blossom at that time and in the decades beyond, we must wonder what Jack London would have produced had he lived past the age of forty. What might he have produced had he lived to see the end of World War I or the beginning of the depression?

But all of this, the analysis, the forewords and afterwords, and all the delving and the what-ifs, wouldn't matter in the least if Jack London didn't, first and foremost, write great stuff. And that's what he did. Lucky for us.

—David Lubar

About the Author

It begins with star-crossed lovers. In 1874, Flora Wellman enters a brief relationship with traveling astrologer William Henry Chaney. By 1876, when her son John is born, Chaney has moved on. Eight months later, Flora marries John London. To avoid confusion, the boy is called Jack. Here, the picture grows both bright and muddy: bright because of the colorful life London leads; muddy because much of what we know about his early years comes from his own writing, and thus must be taken with at least a slight pinch of sea salt.

As a youth, he worked a variety of jobs to help out his family. He later referred to himself as "a boy in years and a man amongst men." While laboring to sell newspapers on the street, sweating in a cannery, and setting pins at a bowling alley, London also developed a lifelong habit. He became a voracious reader, devouring both popular fiction and such heavyweight tomes as *Anna Karenina*. When he was ten, the family moved to Oakland, where the boy haunted the public library. At the age of fifteen he bought a boat, and earned the title "Prince of the Oyster Pirates" by raiding private oyster beds and stealing nets and ropes from other boats. Within a year, he was caught by the Fish Patrol. London must have had a bit of charm about him—

perhaps a glib tongue inherited from his father—because he ended up working for the patrol. Soon after that, he joined a sealing schooner for a trip to Japan.

The sealing trip provided London with the material for an article that won first prize in a newspaper contest. The realization that he could earn, with pen and paper, far more in a few hours than he could make through many days of labor in a cannery or other sweat shop, inspired London to aim for a literary career. He returned to school, quickly finished high school, then attended The University of California at Berkeley for one semester. By this time, he'd started to develop his lifelong fascination with, and vacillation between, the socialist philosophies of Marx and the superman rhetoric of Nietzsche. Given his capitalistic goals and his compassion for the many aborigines he encountered in his travels, he wasn't well suited for either philosophy.

In 1897, London sought his fortune in the Klondike gold rush. This adventure brought him an opportunity for the riches he so passionately desired, not in gold, but in a wealth of experiences. The deadly cold of the frozen north, combined with the romantic array of men and animals who chased the dream of shining fortunes, provided a perfect canvas for London's writing skills.

And those skills proved to be great. Soon after returning to California, London started selling short stories to newspapers and magazines. His first collection, *The Son of the Wolf*, was published in 1900. Other collections and a novel rapidly followed. Then, in 1903, London secured his place forever in the hearts of readers with *The Call of the Wild*. Wild it was—a wild success. Soon, there wasn't a reader in the civilized world who didn't know Jack. London became the richest writer of his time. Or he would have, if he hadn't developed a habit of spending more than he earned. He spent $100,000 on a house that burned to the ground before he could occupy it. He spent another large sum on a schooner that he sailed to Hawaii and Polynesia.

This experience gave him more story material, but it also weakened him.

London died in 1916, a victim of kidney failure at the age of forty. Since his death, it has been popular to view him as a hard-drinking rogue, but recent scholarship disputes this image of a drunken writer. Many readers know him only through his Klondike tales, or possibly through movie interpretations of his books; his legacy is far richer. His novels delve not just into snow and ice, but into social issues, class struggles, and the plight of the working man. His interests went beyond women and alcohol to agriculture, ecology, and animal husbandry. He spoke up for the oppressed and cared for the outcast.

Fortunately, he did much of that speaking with pen and paper. In the brief time he had, Jack London left the world a rich legacy.

—David Lubar

Available from Tor Classics

THE ADVENTURES OF SHERLOCK HOLMES
Sir Arthur Conan Doyle
0-812-50424-0 • $2.99 ($3.50 CAN)

MOBY DICK
Herman Melville
0-812-54307-6 • $3.99 ($4.99 CAN)

THE RED BADGE OF COURAGE
Stephen Crane
0-812-50479-8 • $2.99 ($3.99 CAN)

ANNE OF GREEN GABLES
L. M. Montgomery
0-812-55152-4 • $2.99 ($3.99 CAN)

THE SCARLET LETTER
Nathaniel Hawthorne
0-812-50483-6 • $2.99 ($3.99 CAN)

THE PICKWICK PAPERS
Charles Dickens
0-812-56719-6 • $5.99 ($7.99 CAN)

Available from Tor Classics

TOR®

THE LEGEND OF SLEEPY HOLLOW
Washington Irving
0-812-50475-5 • $2.99 ($3.99 CAN)

THE ADVENTURES OF TOM SAWYER
Mark Twain
0-812-50420-8 • $2.99 ($3.99 CAN)

WHITE FANG
Jack London
0-812-50512-3 • $2.99 ($3.99 CAN)

A CHRISTMAS CAROL
Charles Dickens
0-812-50434-8 • $2.99 ($3.99 CAN)

AGE OF INNOCENCE
Edith Wharton
0-812-56710-2 • $4.99 ($6.50 CAN)

PERSUASION
Jane Austen
0-812-56588-6 • $2.99 ($3.99 CAN)

Available from Tor Classics

TOR®

RIP VAN WINKLE AND OTHER SELECTED STORIES
Washington Irving
0-812-52332-6 • $2.99 ($3.99 CAN)

THE CALL OF THE WILD
Jack London
0-812-50432-1 • $2.99 ($3.99 CAN)

DAVID COPPERFIELD
Charles Dickens
0-812-54404-8 • $4.99 ($6.50 CAN)

THE ADVENTURES OF HUCKLEBERRY FINN
Mark Twain
0-812-50422-4 • $2.99 ($3.99 CAN)

BLACK ARROW
Robert Louis Stevenson
0-812-56562-2 • $3.99 ($4.99 CAN)

THE MAN IN THE IRON MASK
Alexandre Dumas
0-812-56499-5 • $4.99 ($6.50 CAN)

Call toll-free 1-800-288-2131 to use your major credit card or clip and
send this form below to order by mail.

Send to: Publishers Book and Audio Mailing Service
          PO Box 120159, Staten Island, NY 10312-0004

☐ 523326 Rip Van Winkle . . . . $2.99/$3.99   ☐ 504224 Huckleberry Finn . . . . $2.99/$3.99
☐ 504321 The Call of the Wild . . . . $2.99/$3.99   ☐ 565622 Black Arrow . . . . $3.99/$4.99
☐ 544048 David Copperfield . . . . $4.99/$6.50   ☐ 564995 The Man in the Iron Mask . . $4.99/$6.50

Please send me the following books checked above. I am enclosing $_____ . (Please add $1.50 for the first book,
and 50¢ for each additional book to cover postage and handling. Send check or money order only—no CODs).

Name _____

Address _____ City _____ State _____ Zip_____

Available from Tor Classics

TOR®

GREAT EXPECTATIONS
Charles Dickens
0-812-56311-5 • $3.99 ($4.99 CAN)

REBECCA OF SUNNYBROOK FARM
Kate Douglas Wiggin
0-812-56590-8 • $2.99 ($3.99 CAN)

TANGLEWOOD TALES
Nathaniel Hawthorne
0-812-56515-0 • $2.99 ($3.99 CAN)

SPOON RIVER ANTHOLOGY
Edgar Lee Masters
0-812-53904-4 • $4.99 ($6.50 CAN)

MOLL FLANDERS
Daniel Defoe
0-812-56701-3 • $3.99 ($4.99 CAN)

ALICE'S ADVENTURES IN WONDERLAND
Lewis Carroll
0-812-50418-6 • $2.99 ($3.99 CAN)